Shadows
— in the —
Pantry

ROGEL CUIZON

Copyright © 2018 Rogel Cuizon
All rights reserved
First Edition

PAGE PUBLISHING, INC.
New York, NY

First originally published by Page Publishing, Inc. 2018

ISBN 978-1-64214-980-7 (Paperback)
ISBN 978-1-64214-981-4 (Digital)

Printed in the United States of America

Characters

Monica Almadin Douglas (nickname Moni)
Arthur John Douglas—Monica's husband
Monalai Douglas—Monica's daughter
Arthur Shepard Douglas—Moni's son
Simeon Almadin—Monica's father
Maximina Almadin—Monica's mother
Avelino—Moni's brother
Nemesio—Moni's younger brother
Kent Clark Bonedoto—Dr. Solam's adopted son
Darren Bonedoto—Kent's cousin
Dahnow Bonedoto—Kent's cousin
Ernesto Pulos—Monica's friend in Leyte
Indong Rotilles—Moni's uncle
Delena Rotilles—Indong's wife
Pina Rotilles—Indong's daughter
Dorothees Rotilles—Indong's daughter
Susu Yan—personnel manager at the store
Manuel Manguerra—Dorothee's husband
Armando Guzma—Monica's friend in Cebu
Mrs. Esther Romualdo—first employer of Monica (the employer who brought her abroad)
Senora Ramona Romualdo—the elderly mother of Esther
Mrs. Erminda Romualdo Onaje—daughter of Ramona
Raul Onaje—Erminda's husband
Na Pansang—cook at the Romualdo home
Emma—deaf-mute adopted daughter of the Romualdo family

Ting—errand boy/chauffeur of the Romualdo family
Anselmo—errand boy/chauffeur of the Romualdo family
Anding—Anselmo's wife
Alisha—friend of Monica at the beauty parlor
Gloria Greene, RN—Monica's friend
Opal Ross—first attendant to Mr. Onaje
Jorge Pines—male attendant to Mr. Onaje
Mr. Harvey Sloam
Dr. Robert Schick—internist visiting Mr. Sloam
Dr. Kenneth Shuman—student intern visiting Mr. Sloam
Miss Geraldine Keriyas—relief nurse of Mr. Sloan
Mrs. Carol Ann Hutler—boss of Miss Keriyas
George Dumas—driver/chauffeur/errand person of Mr. Sloam
Mary Lindhurst—Mr. Sloam's secretary
Hilda Sansaris—Mr. Sloam's cook
Mr. James Jamieson—the immigration officer
Dr. Solam Bonedoto—visiting doctor at the nursery
Dr. Moises Bonedoto—surgeon/husband of Solam
Juliana Castas—friend of Dr. Moises Bonedoto
Clara—Ting's daughter
Na Goria—owner of rented room/restaurant
Pilar—friend of Monica at Na Goria's home
Tanciang—hired restaurant helper at Na Goria's canteen
Mr. Kim Lim Sun—Susu Yan's husband
Bortong—bodyguard of Mr. Kim and Mr. Lasco
Harriet—Moni's friend
Mother Superior Philomena
Sister Estela—the young nun
Sonia Akil, RN—nurse at Cebu Hospital

Chapter One

It was a beautiful day, but Monalai did not notice the day. Her sleep was her foremost concern. She was startled from deep sleep Monalai hurriedly got up to answer a call from her mother. It was a call for her to work. It was only 2:00 PM. She was still sleepy, being that she had just come home at 5:00 AM. The call from her mom was rather urgent. She grabbed her robe hanging on a hook by the door. The extension phone on the wall outside her room has just been installed for her convenience. Despite their lack of means, her parents had managed to do this for her. The call was from her boss, Michael Petrocelli, asking her to work at 6:00 PM. She gave it a thought before saying yes because she wanted to go out that night. She just came home from a 12-hour shift as a parking attendant. The call was too early. The job was only three hours, and she figured she still would have the time to go out. Besides, she needed the money, and the area she was going would potentially be a good one tip-wise as they knew it. She would work with her favorite people. So she resumed her sleep and told her mother of the plan. She would wear that same uniform again, which was black pants paired with a short-sleeved white cotton blouse draped over the only chair in her room. She rearranged her uniform, hoping to dewrinkle it, and thought of ironing it before she left for work. It was a trip to the Hamptons, a distance from home. The Hamptons was the residence of mostly the rich, which was located on the eastern end of Long Island, New York.

The trip to the Hamptons from Hempstead was not as difficult as she expected. The directions were precise; otherwise, she would never have found the place. The narrow dirt road was lined with dry bushes, and the half mile seemed longer than she had expected. Monalai was watchful, thinking that she might have taken a wrong turn, being that there were driveways of houses not visible from the road, and that she had gotten lost on that huge property.

She was a few minutes late. The road opened into a wide iron gate, and a large well-lit mansion stood proudly in front of her. It was built on a few acres of land and stood with such elegance a few yards from the ocean. It was breathtaking. Monalai looked at it from outside the gate. The driveway circled around a lush of green grass with colorful flowers meticulously arranged at the center. She imagined how grandiose it must be to live inside the magnificent mansion. She recognized one of the cars parked outside the gate. It was owned by Don P. She parked her Oldsmobile next to it. She then walked in and said hello to her colleagues of the night. Andrew G and Don P. had already set up a table inside the Iron Gate with tickets and accompanying keys. Some cars were already parked. Andrew was a tall and husky man, who despite his weight and presumed inability to run was good at his job. He had an impeccable memory and remembered where a particular car had been parked without looking at the ticket. Don P. was a well-built handsome young man who would run if necessary to get the work done. He was very funny. Monalai loved to work with these two guys. They shared food, and the tips they'd get were always distributed fairly. Two cars on the circular driveway were already parked, so the guys started early. She was enjoying the spectacular view, but more guests arrived, and she ran to do her share of work.

Two black-jacketed young men guarded the mansion on each side of the wide doors. They opened the doors for the guests as they walked up the steps and approached the main door. Judging from the number of cars, there were not too many. Andrew and Don were about to take a break. When a Jaguar pulled up, Monalai volunteered to park it. Both men were young, obviously wealthy. They were polite, and one of them was Asian-looking, and the other arguably looked Caucasian. They nodded at her with a smile and a thank-you. Monalai was recognized despite her status.

The evening had quieted down, and it seemed that all the expected guests had arrived. Monalai was curious, wondering what the inside of the house would look like, so safely tucked away behind the green grass that looked like a newly vacuumed rug. So Monalai went up to the guards and asked if she was allowed to go to the back of the house to enjoy the view. The guards looked at each other. It was obvious that they did not trust her. She was about to turn around. What had she been thinking? She was a lowly parking attendant who was curious and might cause some danger to the owner. But much to her surprise, they consented with a watchful eye. The back of the mansion dropped down into a large swimming pool. Down below was the beach. It was a beautiful sight. The walk back to her post made her think of how some people lived their lives. Monalai was wondering what they talked about. Money? Did they compete about who had more? Did they try to outdo each other with exotic destinations and daring adventures? Did the rich enjoy life as much as common folks assumed they did? On the surface, the rich seemed happy. They never had to struggle to earn a living. Monalai envied them.

The number of keys and corresponding tickets signified that she would be able to leave a little early. There were only fifteen cars that night. It did not even fill the circular driveway. They had spaced the cars in such a way that driving them out of the space would only require one maneuver. They were all luxury cars—Mercedes, Jaguars and BMWs. In her experience, all guests left at the same time, and the parking attendants' work would only take half an hour or so, but that half hour might entail constant running and maneuvering of cars so the guests would not have to wait that long.

She figured the drive home would be quick, but she was worried that it might be past midnight when she got home. While the guests were enjoying themselves inside this magnificent home, the parking attendants had nothing to do. In some ways, Monalai envied them. Andrew brought some folding chairs for them to sit while they waited for the guests to leave. Andrew was most thoughtful and did most of the planning when they had work to do.

"Guys, you want food? I'll pick up some sandwiches? Yes? Probably a roast beef sandwich for each?"

He ran off, and Don P and Monalai were left to wait. She felt sleepy, so she asked if she could rest in her car. Monalai drove an old Oldsmobile that her father had bought from an old woman who could no longer drive because her eyesight was failing. It had been fifteen years old when they bought it, with low mileage, and she had already put a few years and many miles on it as a parking attendant and going to school. But it had never failed her. The exterior was faded blue, and the interior was black leather. The old woman had not abused the car while she had driven it. There were no rips or tears on the seats. All in all, it served her purpose, and she was happy with it. Her father took care of it, and she paid for the rest of the necessary upkeep.

She must have dozed off, for when Andrew came back with her snack, he had to wake her. The snack was delicious, and the size of the sandwich was just enough to satisfy her. She would have to use the restroom before the guests started to leave. Would a lowly parking attendant be allowed to use the washroom? She would soon learn. Much to her amazement, she was ushered into the home without any questions. The interior of the house was so enormous—furnished and adorned with pastel colors so perfectly coordinated that it was clearly a professional job. All the guests were at the back room, but nevertheless, she tiptoed in. The washroom was large enough to fit four people. The décor was magnificent. Everything was coordinated with pale yellow drapes, and the wallpaper was of pale peach yellow with prints of delicate fine flowers of varied colors. Even the paper towels folded neatly by the sink coordinated with the motif of the room. She was afraid her dirty sneakers would spoil the clean, beautiful room. She wiped clean the floors she stepped on. After using it, she carefully looked at each item, appreciating their practical beauty. Afraid to overstay her welcome, she hurried back to her station. As anticipated, the guests left in groups. She was grateful that she knew how to drive most of the cars, and she did not have to ask Don or Andrew to do it for her. There were times when she could not find where the ignition was or the ignition would not go on because the car shift was not pushed all the way to drive. Tonight she was proud of herself.

It was almost midnight, and she was ready to leave. She was tired, and the drive to Hempstead would take two hours. But no matter how far it was, the Hamptons assignment was always a sought-for job because it was presumed that the rich tipped more. This was true that night as well. One guest had even given her a fifty-dollar bill. They pooled the tips and divided them. Andrew would get a bigger share because he was the manager, but he was always fair. There were only two cars left, and Monalai was allowed to leave. The dirt road was dark, and it was scary. While she was driving toward the main road, she thought she should have waited for the guys, but she was halfway to the exit, and she continued slowly. The road she had taken coming in looked different, although one did not really remember everything while searching for the place. She eased off the gas, slowing down, and then the corner seemed familiar. Route West 25 has cleared off from traffic, she thought. The city folks had already left the Hamptons for the night. She was very sleepy, and she kept herself awake with either readjusting the radio station or manually opening the windows every now and then. When at a distance she saw the sign JCt 495 West, she was getting ready to exit to the right lane when she felt the car veer off to the far right. She almost lost control of the car. She panicked, and as she tried to put on her brakes, the car hit something at the side of the road and went into a complete halt. She shut the engine off. The fear of being alone in a deserted place engulfed her almost immediately. Although it was a highway and cars presumably came by, an assault by somebody would be seen by motorists. It was rather dark. She immediately unseated herself ready to investigate. As she hurried to open the car door, the car was sort of hanging. She had to jump down, being short of stature. She walked around and found that the car had hit a mound of dirt. The right front tire had a flat. If the mound of dirt had not been there, the car could have fallen to the deep embankment. Even if she knew how to change the tire, which she did not, positioning the car to be able to comfortably do the job she could not do. She had had the opportunity to watch her father do it in the past. He did it with such ease it seemed not difficult to do.

The best thing was to wait for help. It was the flat tire that had caused the car to veer off the road. Luckily she was on the right lane, ready to take the Route 495 west. If she had been on the middle lane, the car would have probably careened to wherever and possibly hit another car; she would not know how to control it. The weather was not cold, and if she stayed by the car with its headlights on, it would hopefully attract a Good Samaritan sooner or later. But unfortunately, it was also possible that a bad person would try to take advantage of her vulnerability. With that thought, she slowly went back to the car and turned off the headlights and the lights inside the car. She would wait till daylight. She wondered if Andrew and Don had taken a different route. If they took her route, they would definitely see her. There were not too many cars that night.

She thought of her parents, who would be wondering where she was. Mother knew Mr. Petrocelli's number and would most definitely call him. She was very sleepy, but she did not dare close her eyes. She decided to wait quietly, but it seemed like eternity, and she prayed, hoping this would dissipate her fear. Praying for blessings and thanksgiving was a routine on most Fridays in her family. She pictured her father changing a tire and fondly remembered how strong he was. Theoretically she was able to do it too, but admittedly, she was not strong enough to do it. Although it was a nice summer night, the thought of staying in her car all night scared her. Several cars sped past without seeing her. She was glad because she did not believe that people were all that helpful, and so whoever stopped for her would probably not have her well-being in mind. She would not know how to defend herself in the event of an assault. Elderly motorists would be most helpful, but due to changing times, they would choose to close their eyes since they were defenseless.

It was funny how moments like this one tended to cause serious thinking about life. Monalai never had these moments. There wasn't a weapon except the screwdriver in the trunk. Despite her fear of agitating the car, she slowly got out and walked to the trunk to get the screwdriver and looked around her at the same time. She was about to open the trunk when a light shone on her. She turned to face the light, and she stiffened. The car had stopped. She experienced intense fear until she recognized a smiling face from the party. It was the passenger of the car she had parked. She did not take notice of the plate number nor would she remember it even if she looked at it because there was no reason for her to commit it in her mind. As they pulled up at the back of her car, the passenger got off. The driver stayed in the car.

"Trouble? Can we help you?"

They dimmed the headlights and shut the engine off. Although she was happy to see a familiar face, she did not trust them. She had heard of rich boys committing heinous acts, and they got away with it since they had money. The passenger approached her and walked round to survey the car. She was scared and prepared to defend herself in the event of an assault.

"It's a flat tire—let us fix it. The flat on the right side made you veer to the right. Do we have tools and a spare tire?"

"I think so."

She handed him the keys, still unable to talk. She was fearful.

"Kent," he said and simultaneously extended his hand, but she did not respond. She was fearful and unaccustomed to such formality.

While walking to the front of the car, he signaled his companion to come and help. Kent conveniently seated himself halfway on the driver seat and, with his left leg on the ground, maneuvered the car while his friend pushed it at the front, thus dislodging the car from the mound. In no time, they were ready to work on the car. Kent opened the trunk, and as a car owned by a handyman, it was equipped with everything to fix a flat.

"Do not worry, we will get it done."

They rolled up their sleeves and started to work. They looked funny being dressed in expensive clothes fixing a flat of an old car. The funny thing was that the Caucasian had a distinctive accent, almost as strong as her mother's, although his grammar was perfect. He was rather tall (almost six feet), slender, and handsome. She did not mean to be unfriendly or ungrateful but smiling might look like flirting, and will be misconstrued as an invitation. Finally, the driver spoke with a very fluent English accent.

"I am Darren, and your mechanic is my cousin."

Darren had very fine manners, and she mistook him for a snob. They worked as a team, never saying a word but just a quick signal with a forefinger or an eye movement. It was a sight to watch how the two of them, rich as they were, knew how to work with their bare hands.

Kent said, "I used to do this all the time for my father."

Monalai stood still, not knowing what to do. She had nothing to say. She could not believe that a rich stranger was kind enough to help her. She always had the impression that the rich never cared for other people, especially the poor. The rich never understood what poverty meant because they never experienced it. He did it with such ease that he looked like a professional mechanic. She had a crush on him. She stopped looking at him because he might see the glitter in her eyes. In no time, the car was ready for her to drive.

"We will follow you to your place. And by the way, do not be scared . . . we will not harm you. It is very late, and your parents must be worried sick."

It was as if Kent had read her mind.

"Where do you live?" the cousin asked.

Monalai replied, "I live in Hempstead, near the Nassau Clinic."

Darren replied, "We live north of Hempstead."

In no time, Monalai arrived home safely, having had two reliable men as her escort. As expected, her home was well lit, and her parents were worried sick. Mr. Douglas, a handsome black man, stood firmly as he opened the door, wary of the accompanying strangers. He hid his apprehension and met the guys with a controlled smile while Monalai tried to explain who the men were. When he heard it, he changed demeanor and thanked the guys, even inviting them into his humble home as he looked out to see that they were obviously rich, driving an expensive car.

"I thank you very much for helping my daughter," he said while extending his hand.

"Glad to be of help."

"May we invite you for some refreshment?"

"We thank you, it is late."

They exchanged telephone numbers in hopes of getting to know each other if all the boys would accept a later invitation. Monalai's mother stood there quietly and just smiled at the strangers. The cousins paid their respects and left quickly since it was very late. The couple was rid of apprehension and talked about the incident, so very grateful that their only daughter was home and safe. It could have been worse. Monalai was tired and promised to explain the episode in the morning. The bed and her room were warm, and although it was simple and poor, the safety of being home was more that she could ask for at that moment. The fearful experience kept her up for a short while more so because she had met a man she liked a lot. Her mother allowed her to sleep late. It was Sunday and her family went to church without her. Just moments later, she heard the front door open and went downstairs to meet her family as they returned from church. Her mother immediately made breakfast. During the meal, she recounted the events of the night. Her father hardly spoke. Monalai took it as fear of what could have happened to her that night. He did not want Monalai to know. After breakfast, she resumed her nap.

Chapter Two

The drive home to Glen Cove did not take long. There was no traffic. Kent liked Monalai and was hoping the family would really invite him over for dinner.

"Be very careful," Darren warned. "You only have eight weeks here. A serious relationship would be very difficult."

"Who says I'm serious?" Kent asked with a smile. "But I'd like to know her better."

Kent and Darren were cousins. Darren, a nineteen-year-old lad, was the younger brother of twenty-year-old Dahnow. They were both born in the Philippines, and their parents, both doctors, brought them to the United States when they were young. They were well off, financially. Darren's home was a sprawling four-bedroom ranch on a one-acre lot in a cul de sac section of Jove Street in Glen Cove, Long Island, New York, north of Monalai's home. It was an upscale neighborhood lined with large homes, well-manicured lawns, and expensive cars parked in the driveways. The circular driveway in front of Darren's home could easily accommodate eight to ten cars. An oak tree stood on the right side of the home just a few feet from the road, which on a sunny day would cast an uneven shade to the street and part of the driveway. The driveway wrapped around a bed of flowers and edged upon a manicured lawn. A wide descending space led to a two-door garage, which was part of the whole basement where the music room was located and stairs that led to the kitchen area. The front door had a spacious patio as wide as the front of the house supported by two sturdy columns. The wide glass doors opened into a wide space of polished wooden floors so spacious it looked like a dance space for the guests to perform a waltz. The ivory walls enhanced the beauty of the space. A Steinway piano stood by the window on the right side as one enters the room. It was furnished with the best furniture, which coordinated the drapes on the wide glass windows. A white cushioned sofa facing each other with cushions pale green in color accented it. White padded chairs were strategically placed in several corners. Large leafy plants on the window sills and by the entrance enhanced the décor of the place. The dining table room seated eight people situated by a large window to view the yard outside. A swinging glass door separated the dining from the kitchen. The bedrooms were situated all the way to the back where the piano was located away from the inquiring eye.

The den, a space on the hallway, was located a distance from the living room leading to the bedrooms. The family spent most of its time having conversations, listening to music, or watching television in this room. Books lined the walls and the entertainment center in between it, and a wall displayed photographs of the family. The windows were simply draped with white curtains. A large desk stood in the corner. Two large black leather couches faced the television, and various pillows and blankets were sprawled on them. The kitchen almost as big a space as the dining area was painted ivory, and the kitchen windows were draped with white embroidered thin fabric. The wooden kitchen table sits six, and the furnishings were all white. A small working table overlooking the yard sat at the far end of the kitchen, with a manual typewriter and several papers on the side. There was an underground pool in the backyard surrounded by chairs and oversized umbrellas. It was clearly a home only the rich could afford. Although rich, the children were not arrogant. They were brought up to help the poor, when a need arose. Their manners, although very refined and a proof of proper breeding, were never condescending. Darren's dad was an internist and his mother a pediatrician. They had a thriving private practice. When they arrived in the United States, the family first lived in Ozone Park, Queens, New York. They bought a small home and supported themselves with money from property that the family owned in the Philippines. They lived modestly while obtaining the licenses necessary to practice medicine in the United States. When their practice was established, they moved to Glen Cove, but their practice remained in Queens.

Kent Bonedoto was just visiting and intended to stay for eight weeks. He had just finished a liberal arts degree from De La Salle College in the Philippines. He had not decided what career to pursue. His adoptive father was Darren's uncle. Although they had grown up far from each other, they were close. Darren visited the Philippines a while back and incurred a vehicular accident. It was Kent who took care of him when he was recuperating in their home. In fact, when Kent arrived, Darren insisted that they should share a bedroom. The party Darren and Kent had attended the night before in the Hamptons had been at the house of Darren's friend. They knew each other from New York University. Dahnow, Darren's older brother, was in Connecticut studying law. The family belonged to the upper class in the Philippines. All the boys in the Bonedoto family took their elementary schooling at a Jesuit-run school called Ateneo de Manila. Darren and Dahnow were taken care of by family while they were left in the Philippines to finish elementary school. The boys then joined their parents in the United States. While the Bonedoto family from Cebu owned several businesses and buildings in Cebu and Metro Manila, Darren's mother did not have rich parents. The couple met when they both attended medical school. Because their mother did not come from a rich home herself, she did not spoil her boys. Due to the fact that they were sheltered in a private school throughout their childhood and youth, they were shy in nature and formal.

When the cousins pulled up at their house, it was almost three in the morning. The home was dark and quiet except for a night light at the main entrance. They choose to enter through the kitchen area so as not to disturb anyone in the house. The light on top of the stove was on. They settled at the kitchen table, and started a conversation so subdued, almost like a whisper. They had no secrets, but trying to be as quiet as possible, they inadvertently behaved as if they did. Darren took a glass of lemonade from the refrigerator and gave one to Kent.

"I really liked that girl. She is demure and rather pretty," Kent started again.

"Beware of the culture difference is all I can say."

"But she was brought up by an Oriental mother. She'll know how to behave in a proper Filipino way."

Kent paused for a long time and was very quiet. With his left forefinger on his upper lip and such a pensive mood, he was on the verge of tears. He was imagining how he was going to approach the girl he just met to tell her how he felt. Kent was like a brother to Darren. His worries would be his as well. They talked until they could hardly keep their eyes open. So they went to the bedroom and fell asleep almost immediately.

They woke up when Darren's mother knocked on their door at about eight in the morning. It was time to go to Church. It was the anniversary of his maternal grandmother's death. They had to catch the early mass at a church nearby. Darren's father had left at five thirty in the morning to make his early rounds. His mother was not working that day, although her partner could call her for a consult at any time. The parents' schedule was busy. Sometimes his parents would leave in the middle of the night to see a patient. It was a stressful and difficult profession but a rewarding career nonetheless. Darren was considering a career in medicine too. When they came home from church, Kent received a call from Monalai's parents inviting him for dinner. Kent was so delighted.

Chapter Three

Dinner at Monalai's

It was a brisk afternoon in July. Kent was supposed to be there at five. Darren drove Kent and would pick him up two hours later. Monalai's street was lined with cars, being that most of the homes had a one-car driveway. The homes were mostly matchbox type with possibly two bedrooms; some of them a bit rundown with peeling paint and an untended front lawn. Monalai's home seemed larger than the rest, being a four-bedroom dwelling. It was painted in pale gray with black trimmed windows and stood on a quarter acre lot. The front yard was evidently freshly mowed. Flowers of red, yellow, and pink surrounded the sides. Compared to most of the homes, the home was well cared of. The unpaved one-car driveway was empty, presumably reserved for Kent to park. A station wagon was parked at the front of the home. It was a residence of middle-income families who could not beautify their homes to be presentable. The front door was open when Kent arrived, and as he rang the bell, the man of the house met him with a warm welcome. The house was clean, and the aroma of food cooking permeated the home.

"Come in, Kent. Glad you came to honor us with a visit."

"I would not miss it for anything."

He was led into the sitting room, which seemed spacious because it was sparsely furnished; there were only two matching couches of faded brown, with a reclining chair in between and a lamp by the door. The round glass table at the center stood a vase of fresh flowers on a white doily. The television stood by the window, next to it, a fan. There was beige carpeting on the floor, obviously worn thin with time. The rest of the house had the linoleum floors so typical of the time and class. The sitting room was separated from the dining area. The sitting area opened into a dining area and the kitchen, which doubled as the laundry room. A glass table seated eight at the far right corner of the kitchen, and beside it was a glass door that opened into a small yard. Four plastic chairs could be seen on a cemented space right outside the door. At the far right corner near the white fence was a newly planted tree. The green lawn with specks of dry grass was spacious, and there was a vegetable garden by the fence.

Monalai's mother peeked in while wiping her hands on a towel and quickly said hello and introduced herself with a smile and a quick hand gesture. She hurried back to the kitchen and continued with her work. Moni stood around five feet two inches, very lean and well-proportioned and looked taller than her measured height. She had brown skin, a smooth, beautiful face, high cheekbones, and a sincere smile. Her fine-featured face with its high cheekbones was so beautiful, particularly accompanied with a smile. She was oblivious of her looks and wore no makeup. She did not need it. Her long black, brown-streaked hair was shoulder-length. That afternoon, she wore it in a ponytail. Her round hazel-colored eyes smiled often, which emphasized her long lashes. Her features were not of a typical oriental woman. She looked more like an East Indian woman with very fine features. It was hard to determine her origin. She was dressed in a plain white blouse and a black skirt that reached just below the knee. She walked with a straight brisk step. She looked beautiful and elegant, too elegant for this nonelegant home.

Mr. Arthur Douglas was a good-looking black gentleman in his forties. He stood about five feet and nine inches or so, lean and muscular, and he walked with a firm, bowlegged gait. He was fair-skinned for a black man. He was not a college graduate but had some credits in a technical school and was well-spoken and articulate. Judging from his demeanor, he was born from a well-bred family in the South. He was dressed in beige trousers paired with pale yellow polo shirt which looked new, as if it were bought for this occasion. He showed respect to this young man who rescued his daughter and brought her to safety in the middle of the night. Kent was dressed in well-pressed black trousers and a white long-sleeved shirt and yellow polka-dot tie. His loafers were newly polished. He felt overdressed, but it would have been an affront if he had worn his favorite jeans. Like Mr. Douglas, he dressed the way he did as a gesture of respect to this very gentle man, whose manners impressed him the first time they met.

When they were both seated in the living room, they chatted somewhat formally. Kent told him he was on vacation, staying with his uncle. Mr. Douglas told Kent that his wife, Moni, had originated from the Philippines, and they had been married for a good twenty-two years. A few minutes after, Monalai and her younger brother arrived and said hello. They then proceeded to the kitchen to greet their mother then went upstairs to change.

Monalai, barely seventeen, was attired in beige pants and a flower-print black blouse tucked in her pants that revealed her gorgeous stature. She had inherited her mother's good looks although she had darker skin and was probably an inch taller. She had curly black hair that gently touched her shoulders. Monalai excused herself and joined her mother in the kitchen.

Arthur Junior was fourteen years old and was as tall as his father. He was fair-skinned and had inherited his father's looks except the almond-shaped dark-brown eyes he took from Maxi, his maternal grandmother. His dark-brown hair was cut short to his scalp. He sat on one of the seats, looked uncomfortable, and glanced at his father for approval every time he spoke. He nodded often, smiled, and with his hands clasped, leaned slightly forward, listening to the conversation intently. He looked very attentive.

Dinner was called. The table was set beautifully on a lace tablecloth, and at the center was a tall vase that held three delicate white roses surrounded with ferns. The olive-green-colored leaf shape placemats complimented the table. The baked chicken garnished with parsley leaves and mounds of thin sliced carrots sat at each end of the table. Coleslaw, yams, and mixed green salad completed the meal. Kent was very impressed. Although the table was set with inexpensive dinnerware, it reflected the expertise of the lady of the house.

Moni assigned their seats, and Mr. Arthur said grace, noticeably having been brought up religious, as exhibited his manner and delivery of prayers. Formal introduction was done, and Kent introduced himself as an adopted son of one of the members of the Bonedoto family from Cebu. Mr. Douglas mentioned his Jamaican origin and that of his wife as well. Kent was excited about Moni's origin and mostly the dialect that she spoke. Moni did not elaborate her roots. It was almost like she did not want to discuss it. The dinner was delicious, and they all expressed it to Moni. The conversation was lively. Mr. Douglas reiterated how grateful he was to Kent. Kent learned that the couple worked at the Nassau Clinic, him as a maintenance personnel and kitchen staff respectively. Monalai was studying liberal arts at a community college, and Arthur Junior was still in high school.

Kent wanted to talk to Moni, but she hardly spoke to him, did not even look at him. There was nothing to say. She knew, judging from his family name, that he had originated from one of the richest families in the Philippines. She had nothing to say about her background, nor was it interesting enough for him to know. She was insignificant and poor, at least by the standards of someone from the Bonedoto family.

"I am here on here on vacation," Kent explained.

"Mrs. Douglas," Kent continued, "where did you come from in the Philippines?"

"Leyte."

Moni took so many glimpses at this stranger, almost wanting to know who he was, but she kept quiet, although she was never talkative. Moni served the dessert but seemed to avoid the table. When Kent was having coffee, he asked Moni, "Mrs. Douglas, have you visited or stayed in Manila at all?"

"Yes, I worked and took courses in Manila to become a teacher."

Moni excused herself and kept on cleaning. There was no more conversation after dinner that Moni participated in. She kept herself busy cleaning. The rest sat in the living room. Only when it was time for Kent to leave was Moni diplomatic enough to hug him good-bye. This time, she looked at him intensely as if she knew somebody who resembled him. When Kent left, Moni commented that Kent came from a rich family and was obviously condescending to the poor. It was a comment that she wanted everybody to hear. It portrayed Monica's dislike of the young guy. It was almost eight in the evening.

Darren picked him up as arranged and offered to stop at a diner to have some coffee, but Kent refused the invitation. He wanted to head home. Kent was very quiet. Darren stole some quick glances at Kent when he had the chance. It was obvious that Kent's evening had not gone well. Kent was in deep thought. The home was quiet, illuminated with night lights in every room. They entered through the kitchen door at the back. Darren turned the light on, and Kent immediately slumped on one of the chairs, put his hands on his face, and sobbed. Darren immediately sat on the chair beside him, stretched his right arm, and pacified his cousin by rubbing him gently across his back.

"Just when I get to like someone, the family does not like me." He Continued in the dialect," Wa-a ko'y suerte; wa-a pa'y ginikanan, wa-a pa'y gugma. Kalo-oy nako." (He said he likes someone, but the parents do not like him. He has no parents and no love as well.) It was customary in the Philippines that the woman's parents must like the suitor. If the parent did not, the suitor would never be accepted in the home again.

There was nothing Darren could say that was good enough to calm him down. Instead, he stood up and served his cousin lemonade. Kent gulped it down as if to drown his sorrows in alcohol. Darren encouraged his cousin to go to the den. Ken dragged his feet, but eventually, he followed.

"Don't give up as yet," Darren said. "You have another four weeks. Did anything happen?"

"Not really. Monalai's mother just gave me the cold shoulder."

There was a long silence between the two of them. The television was blasting, but they did not hear it. They did not even hear Darren's parents come home until they called. The both stood up together to kiss their hands, as is a customary gesture of respect toward the older generation. Darren's mother asked them how the dinner went and the both shrugged their shoulders. No one wanted to tell the elder Bonedoto what had happened. They thought it unnecessary, even though they really did not agree on what to say to the elder in case they ask.

"Darren, if it was you . . . how would you handle this?" Kent asked.

"I don't think I know how. Honestly, I will probably try to forget about it. Hmm . . . Easier said than done. Sorry I am of no help to you."

"Don't you have an opinion at all?"

"I do, but you would not like to hear it."

They retired early. Darren had nothing to say that could pacify Kent. Trying to avoid conversations that might hurt his cousin.

The following week was concentrated on calling Monalai. A call to Monalai's was almost not entertained if Moni answered the telephone. One afternoon, Monalai told Moni she was going out with Kent. It was a simple get-together to the park and a simple dinner at an Italian restaurant. Darren would bring and pick them up. The get-together went well. Moni was not interested if her daughter talked about Kent. Moni would repeatedly mention the cultural difference of their family and Kent's status in the Philippines. Finally, Kent had to return to the Philippines. He promised Monalai that he would call and would visit again the following year.

Chapter Four
Monica's Origin

Monica was always called Moni for short. She was born in one of the numerous islands that comprise the Philippine archipelago. She grew up in the island of Villalon, Leyte. All the islands in the Philippines are separated by water; therefore, an interisland vessel was needed to navigate the water between the islands. The townspeople often used a small sea vehicle to reach one shoreline to another since it was faster than taking land transportation. Besides, the sea transport was more numerous and inexpensive compared to the land buses. Most of these sea vessels, the *sakayan*, were made by the townspeople with some carpentry experience. They were but a larger modified version of a fishing boat, equipped with a motor for it to sail faster. They were made of hardwood shaped like a kayak with hyperextended bamboo tied together on each side. The purpose of this was to level its weight. A canvass covered the middle area, supported by an angled bamboo roof to shield the passengers from the piercing sun or drizzle. The passengers were seated on a strip of made-up bamboo seats, attached securely on each side of the boat. The narrow middle aisle served as passage for passengers. The *sakayan* accommodated around ten passengers, and each passenger was allowed one or two lightweight pieces of cargo since there was no designated space for it. It was placed at both ends of the vessel. The *sakayan* was not made to sustain fierce winds so no one traveled when the weather was bad. The passengers would stay with a friend or a relative for the night or in church until the weather cleared up.

Other means of transportation was a small bus, but it took longer to get to the destination.

Leyte is geographically located in the southeast, in between the islands of Samar and Cebu. Leyte may be known due to General MacArthur's famous saying, "I shall return." Otherwise, it is an unpopular island, being mostly uncultivated then, and has not produced some significant contribution to the general economic status and popularity of the Philippines. The products were mostly limited to copra and corn. Copra is dried coconut meat, a main ingredient to make cooking oil, shampoo, and sorts. The economic value of corn was limited to home consumption and its residue milled to feed the hogs. Most of the inhabitants in Villalon were poor, aside from the landowners who had tenants working for them to till their land. Although, some families owned some land handed down to them by their ancestors, tilled it, and lived on selling the produce. Moni's family was one of those families.

Moni's town was approximately twenty miles in radius. It had a sprawling shoreline, where people congregated during market days. Vendors sold their wares on portable bamboo tables protected from the piercing sun by ripped umbrellas, or they wore wide straw hats on their heads. They seemed happy despite the heat. The *sakayan* would land on the shore, delivering their passengers from the mainland or from a town nearby. The shoreline was not paved with cement or asphalt, nor were there steps for passengers to step off the boat and onto dry land. Once the boat landed at a spot strategically chosen by the boat owner, barefooted he jumps and stand firmly at the center of the boat with a long piece of bamboo held down deep in the waters as an anchor to stabilize the boat. While extending his right arm if a passenger needed help. In the meantime the assistant helped the passenger pick up their possessions. It was held down by the boat owner deep down in the waters to stabilize the boat. A flat piece of wood wide enough to accommodate the passengers foot was placed at one end of the boat and the other end on the shore used as a platform. The boat owner tried to limit its movement with the long bamboo to the ground while he extended his left arm for the passengers to hold on as they walked down the platform to the shore. All this was particularly tricky during high tide. Many a passenger stepped off the plank with their feet wet.

The shoreline was the most populated area. One-room nipa huts were scattered in close proximity to each other, inhabited mostly by fishermen. Living at the shore enabled them to anchor their fishing boats within their sight. During high tide, the nipa hut grounds became part of the sea. The families were used to these episodes and dealt with it. A census was never done to determine the number of people living in that particular town. Some births were not even recorded. The real paperwork was initiated when a child started school, at around seven. Birth records, if kept at all, were notoriously unreliable. There was only one road up north wide enough to accommodate two cars, buses, and farmers riding on a carabao's back. The road was long and stretched to most of the areas. To go to school or to town, the farmers, Moni included, took a shortcut to the main road via the man-made dusty path lined by various bushes in between neighbors' homes. A backyard of an unfenced small acreage owner easily became a path to somebody's house. The climate was tropical. During the rainy season, which would normally be around September to February, the weather would intermittently be very cloudy with fierce winds and continuous rain. Some of the inhabitants lived on a plateau of land which stretched to the mountainous region where coconuts were grown in large quantities. Few of the families lived on that region, mostly tenants who kept watch on the produce from land grabbers who would move the landmark and claim the few feet of land illegally if unattended. Those who owned small acreage grew coconuts, fruits, and vegetables surrounding their nipa huts. They raise their own poultry and a couple of hogs.

A cottage on a five-acre lot cleared from bushes and unevenly fenced by unnamed trees, *biatilis*, and banana plants was the place for learning. It was provided for by the town. The cottage was divided into large classrooms, one for younger and one for older children, a storage room, and a miscellaneous room by bamboo walls. There was no established curriculum, and the three teachers who handled the task seem responsible and dedicated to teach the children reading, writing, simple arithmetic, and social studies. The school was not furnished with desks or chairs. Each child was required to bring a chair made to fit the child's growth with a piece of wide wood attached at the front, sturdy enough for the child to do work, sit, and write comfortably. Underneath this chair was a platform to accommodate the school paraphernalia. The chairs had to be light enough for the student to carry on top of their heads on the first day of school. The chairs were stored at school during vacation and holidays for as long as the student attended school. The teacher had a large bamboo desk with drawers and a comfortable chair. The children seemed to finish elementary grades on time. There was no reported misconduct or rebellion. If a child misbehaved, the parent and the teacher usually addressed the problem. At recess, a yard was provided for the children to play catch, skip rope, and hide-and-seek, and the bell rang when playtime was over. No one ever tried to follow up on the success of the children who left town and pursued a higher education. As long as they were able to read, write, and do some arithmetic they were fit to face life's challenges. Most of them became fishermen, carpenters, and farmers. The girls got married and had children.

Attached to the cottage was a big room that housed all the mail. It was managed by one person who received, sorted, and organized its distribution. His office looked rather disorganized to a visitor, but he was efficient. An inquiry if a specific mail had arrived was answered by a plain yes or no, as if he remembered all the mail that has arrived. His memory was remarkable. The volunteer workers in charge of distribution were children ages nine to fifteen, assigned to deliver mail within the vicinity of their home. The nipa huts did not have identifying numbers on their homes, but mails were delivered in a timely manner, and none were reported to have been undelivered or stolen. People knew each other. Mail was scarce during Moni's time, possibly due to apparent illiteracy of the inhabitants. Moni was one of those volunteers who worked for the mailman, whose name was Noy Tiquio. Noy Tiquio had finished elementary grades. He was not a conversationalist. His hellos to the town people were limited to a nod and a quick smile. He lived alone in a one-bedroom nipa hut on an acre lot, heired to him by his deceased parents, not far from Moni's home. He was salaried, but the townspeople cared for him so that he was supplied with fresh vegetables, eggs, and occasional cooked food. He accepted this gesture as an act of love.

Another cottage by the main road not too far from the school and the post office was the house of worship. The chapel was fair-sized and could accommodate fifty people or so. The roof was made of nipa. At a distance, it looked like an oversized nipa hut. Walls were made of wood with two wide windows that stretched from the front to the back on both sides. The bamboo-strips-made window kept the inside illuminated on a sunny day. A half-made coconut shell and a wick soaked in coconut oil situated on the sides of the cottage held by a four-legged receptacle kept the church illuminated on rainy days. There were several of these located by the entrance, the windows, and toward the altar. An extended roof outside on both sides kept the parishioners dry on rainy days. There were ten bamboo benches five on each aisle. The altar was also made of bamboo. The entire floor was unpaved, and on rainy days it could be muddy on the aisle. There were no pews to kneel on.

The inhabitants did not have formal teaching about religion. They went to church because a Divine Being existed. Prayers were passed on from generation to generation, often without explanation as to their meaning. The priest was fetched from Naval and brought the necessary items with him. He was attended to by one of the town folks who owned a decent dwelling to entertain him. When the weather was bad, he did not come. It was dangerous to travel by *sakayan*. The people would not prepare for church. It was understood as such.

Most of the inhabitants in this town earned their living by fishing and selling their produce of vegetables, fresh eggs, cacao bits, dried fish, and some crafts such as rattan baskets and *banig* (mat made of straw) ornaments made from the town's raw materials, clothes, slippers, and household needs; at the shoreline every Wednesday and Sunday. Most homes had bananas, fruits, and coconut trees grown in their backyard. The folks from the mountain area traveled from the hills and neighboring towns to purchase their needs for the week, such as soap, laundry detergent, and the sort. It was a place to socialize and talk about current events. Death and birth was a common topic. During bad weather, there was no market. There was no need to announce it. It was understood. On the surface, despite the lack of luxury, life was simple and quiet; the inhabitants were content of what they have. The men stayed in their homes after a hard day's work in the fields. Despite lack of formal entertainment, they seemed to enjoy each other's company in their humble homes.

Chapter Five

Moni was born to Simeon Almadin and Maximina Rotilles. They were natives of Villalon. They were married in their twenties. Simeon's family and Maximina lived approximately a few miles from each other. Most of the marriages at that time were almost betrothed. The families got together, and they encouraged the young ones to intermarry. It seemed good for them if the families knew each other. At least everyone knew that there were no violent tendencies. Maximina came from a decent breed of landowners. Although her father did not own too much land, he was considered rather well-off by that particular barrio's standard. She had four brothers, three of them farmers, owning some acres of land in the vicinity. One brother ventured to Cebu, went to school, and was currently working as a clerk in one of the big companies. Their ethnic origin was never determined. They all looked Spanish, although some of them were dark-skinned with most distinct almond eyes. Maxi was more fair-skinned than the rest of her family. Her overbite spoiled her pretty face.

All the children of the Rotilles family finished elementary grades and were able to read and write in English. English was the official language of instruction in school after the Spaniards occupied the Philippines, but it was not spoken at home. Maxi and her brothers helped each other with whatever needed to be accomplished, no matter whether it was building a house, digging a well, or babysitting. They lived near each other, convenient enough to seek help from each other. On the surface, none of them were rich, but they had food to eat, a comfortable home, and such.

SHADOWS IN THE PANTRY

Moni's father was an only child. He was an illegitimate child of Mariana, a half breed of a Filipino woman and an East Indian man. Mariana, Simeon's mother, was rumored to have had an affair with an American GI stationed in Leyte. She had successfully hidden the pregnancy until Simeon's birth. Simeon took after his father's Caucasian features: he had hazel eyes, reddish-brown hair, and fair skin. Mariana could not deny her son's heritage. He stood out among the townspeople. She never disclosed the father's identity, probably embarrassed to have had a rendezvous with a married man. She never got married but dedicated her time to care for her son. Simeon grew up with his grandparents and his mother in a small nipa hut. Although they owned the parcel of land where the nipa hut stood, they were struggling. His grandfather was a fisherman who owned his fishing boat. Most of the fish he caught were sold in Naval by Mariana. His grandmother stayed home. She made baskets out of straw and bamboo and sold them in the market. When Simeon was around eight years old, he accompanied his grandfather fishing. He finished elementary grades. He would volunteer to build houses without pay until he eventually, due to his industrious nature, became a respected carpenter in his town.

Simeon and Maximina built a small nipa hut where Moni and the two younger brothers were born. After a couple of years, they were able to put an extension, and it became a spacious three-bedroom home made of bamboo on a half-acre land inherited by Moni's mother. Her maternal grandfather owned several acreage of land which he distributed to his children, five of them. The family had been known to be industrious, and the acquisition of such acreage of land was from hard work. Moni's home was built by his father with the help of Maxi's brothers. It had a three-feet elevation from the ground. Several large circular pieces of wood cut up from an acacia tree partly embedded into cement on the ground supported the structure. The wall around was made of split bamboo, which appeared like a whole bamboo was used on the outside. The entire roof of the house was made of nipa. The only cemented roof was over the cooking area. The entire floor was made of wood from an acacia tree, and it was always polished with coconut oil. The property was surrounded by cacao trees, which Maxi had planted when she had acquired the property. It served as a fence so no intruders could get through. Several coconut trees and bamboo plant was at the far end of the land. Several plots of vegetable garden spread by the kitchen area stretched out to the backyard for consumption and to sell at the market. Each room has a wide window spared from the rain by an extended roof around the house. Each window was made of stripped bamboo nailed into squares. You could look out but not open it. Inside, a wide array of sliding bamboo sticks tied with twine were suspended on top with smooth round wood on a wooden track that propelled them from one side to the other. It covered the window during rainy days. It also provided privacy.

The steps to the house were made of hard wood. The veranda (patio) occupied the front of the house. The door led to the sitting room, furnished by two uncushioned wide bamboo couches facing each other. A small square table was at the center. A half-size coconut shell with a wick anchored in an empty tin can was at the center in coconut oil. This contraption was held by a square bamboo platform to keep it stable. Several of these lamps kept the house illuminated when dusk set in. The dining area, a part of the living room, featured a large wooden table with bamboo benches that could comfortably seat eight people. An extended space made of bamboo on the outer wall stored the preboiled drinking water in a clay-made drinking receptacle (*ka ang*) covered with a plate. On top of the plate was a small bucket with a handle to dispense the drinking water from the receptacle. Drinking water was stored in glass jars, and the eating utensils were stored on the space as well.

Separating the dining area from the kitchen was a bamboo wall. The kitchen was a small space that could only accommodate two people. There was a cemented space as high as the waistline with two three-legged clay burners. Underneath the space was a stack of cut-up firewood. Cooking utensils consisted of a bamboo stick attached firmly to a polished half-size coconut shell. Cooking pots were made of clay normally lined with banana leaves to cook rice or corn. Fish was either dried or cooked in vinegar. A rectangular shape made of bamboo loosely nailed a foot deep was the place to wash the kitchen utensils. Underneath it, by the drain, a tube made of whole bamboo was connected to another bamboo cut lengthwise with strategic holes on both sides so the dishwater would seep through to keep the garden moist. The bamboo was situated in the middle of the garden to distribute the water to both sides of the plot. It supported the water needs of the vegetable garden, reflective of the bountiful harvest.

The water well was a few yards from the kitchen area. It was the main supply of water for the household. It was expensive to put up, so it was shared with the neighbors. An enclosed cemented area next to the wood stove was a large water jug, which supplied the cooking and drinking needs and the sort. It was rinsed and cleaned every day and kept covered. Two people filled the large water jug. The person at the well propelled the water bucket hanging on a sturdy rope into the inlet of the cemented enclosure, and that person filled the water jug. The enclosure was the bathing place as well.

This bath's whole structure stood within a foot-deep hole filled with stones to prevent spatter. The enclosure was supported by four cemented posts on each corner. A long bamboo tube attached to a hole in the corner that served as a drain. On rainy days, the surrounding area got flooded.

The home had three large bedrooms, each of them equipped with a spacious three-person bamboo bed. During fair days, the windows were kept open to create a draft and keep the house comfortably cool. Made-up bamboo sticks joined by twine were attached on the sides of the window. There were two panels that met at the center. It was measured appropriately to cover the size of the window. It was equipped with a wooden track and wooden ball that propelled them from one side to the other. On both sides of the window was a string to tie it to the posts located on both sides of the window. These covered the windows on rainy days and were used for privacy when the occupant desired it.

There were no closets, but there was a shelf a foot wide securely nailed to one side of the wall by the door. It stretched from one corner to the other side of the wall. The height could be adjusted according to convenience. It was situated on the left side as one entered the room. The shelf served as a place for folded clothes, grooming needs, school supplies, and the sort. A bamboo storage chest, two feet wide, with the same length of the bed underneath the shelf, accommodated the *banig* (mat), the pillow, and patched-up flannel blankets and a mosquito net. It was placed close to the wall under the shelf. It served as the night table and the lamp. These lamps several of them kept the house illuminated after sundown.

The outhouse was located all the way to the back surrounded by *biatilis*, a wood planted mainly for firewood. The Almadin home was the largest in that town among the common folks. Simeon, a carpenter, had indeed portrayed his knowledge in the building of this home. After he built his house, the rest of the townspeople hired him to build them a house, as expertly done as he did his. Some of them could not afford the fee, so they paid him slaughtered hogs. Moni and her brothers merrily grew up in this town. They had enough food to eat—corn or rice as the main staple, dried fish and fried pork and large amount of steamed vegetables. The family slaughtered a cow once or twice a year and then distributed smoked meat to the family. Sweets consisted of ripe bananas, which could be boiled or fried.

Naval, a bigger town, was located across the shoreline of Villalon. It featured several stores selling various items and a movie theater. Occasionally, Simeon brought the children to watch a movie. If the weather was nice, the vendors from Naval brought their wares to Villalon on Sundays so the townsfolk avoided an expensive trip to Naval. Most of the children wore hand-me-downs; they had one outfit for church and a pair of nice shoes a size larger so they would last a while. They have two sets of outfits for school. Families and neighbors would exchange clothes, and women who knew how to sew would have better-dressed children. Moni's mother was a dressmaker in her own right and earned money making clothes. She did not own a sewing machine but made the clothes with a plain needle and thread. Another source of income were the cacao trees surrounding the property that bore fruit dried by roasting; it was ground and made into cacao bits (*tableya*). It was consumed as hot chocolate for breakfast, but they also sold much of it at the market. Moni had been a vendor at the market as early as eight years old.

The children played occasionally in front of Moni's yard, cleared of grass and bushes. On a moonlight night, the children played *tubig-tubig*, which was comparative to tic-tac-toe. They also played hide-and-seek, *bagol* (with wooden shoes), and *sa-to* (played with a piece of coconut husk placed in hollow ground and hit with a bamboo stick, just like a bat hits a ball in a baseball game). Moni had a playmate named Ernesto, who lived next door. Moni usually asked him to help in filling up the big jug in the washroom since he was bigger and older than Moni. They played all the games a child normally would on that particular side of town. Children started working in the vegetable garden as early as seven years old. They planted, harvested, and packed the vegetables for sale or collected them for dinner. Children fetched water from a nearby well, wearing wooden shoes or were barefoot. If there was an occasion such as a birthday, the family who raised chickens and hogs was able to have a party. Neighbors came to celebrate. An alcoholic drink derived from coconut (*tuba*) would be brought. A person brought his guitar, and there was singing and laughter until the wee hours of the night. This was the only entertainment they knew.

The average townsfolk never socialized with the rich landowners. The rich had their own crowd. The poor worked for the rich as maids, gardeners, and farmers. The servants stayed in separate quarters a cottage apart from the large concrete homes of their employers. Food for the rich was cooked differently and served in polished flatware and expensive dinnerware. The maids ate the leftovers if there was any; otherwise, if there was none, the helpers ate dried fish with corn. They were salaried, and they seemed to be better off than the rest of the townsfolk.

There was no doctor in the village. The rich were transported to Naval if they took ill. There was a small clinic managed by two doctors and a nurse assisted by one help. They did minor surgeries and had had success. They would ask for some amount of money before they rendered any services. Most of the time, money was not there, but the care was rendered. The family later on would bring bananas, live poultry, and sorts. Funding in this small clinic was limited, but they thrived. The government had no participation. This was primarily started by doctors, goodhearted to provide services with little or no profit at all. Although the townsfolk, mainly farmers, rather grateful of the good deed brought them fresh fish, poultry, hogs, and sorts even though their debt have been paid off. So these doctors never have to buy food for their families.

The poor have no means. The *arbularyo* (medicine man) was fetch in case of illness. He, after assessing the client, left and came back after he collected some herbs, which he deemed applicable to the ailment. The herbs boiled, and the sick person drank it for several days. The medicine man was respected. Amazingly, he cured a lot of people. The ones who needed surgery did not survive because poverty prevented them from procuring appropriate medical care. Pregnant women have babies assisted by a *mananabang*. She was usually a middle-aged woman having had many babies and had, in fact, assisted one delivery or more. She was then at that time became an expert in childbirth. She did not have to have education. Those women who have complications of abnormal birth presentations were transported to Naval with funds collected from the generous townsfolk, or they stayed and the mother and child dies. Death was accepted as such; families grieved, and the widower remarried another woman mainly to take over the task of the woman who prematurely died.

Moni's family had some money. They were frugal, innovative, and industrious. Fish was available when Simeon went fishing with his friend. His grandfather's fishing boat was no longer safe to use. Simeon did not own a fishing vessel, but he repaired his friend's boat so he was invited to go fishing, and the catch was shared. His building expertise kept him busy, and the proceeds were acceptable. He finished elementary school. He loved to read, so he was well informed of current events. When he went to Naval to buy carpentry needs, he would also buy a newspaper. He was not friendly and would rather do a project than socialize. Moni's mother, aside from making clothes, would make pastries as well for sale. Moni was a great help to the family. She would pack the cacao bits on a Thursday, ready to sell on Sunday. She even suggested to her mother that they should sell fried bananas at the market. She noticed that there were not too many people who sold snacks. So she did. Her younger brother would log the portable clay stove and some firewood and actually fry the ripe bananas at the market. It was a hard job. She would be full of burns from the hot oil. Besides, she had to go to school the next day. The market did not close until six in the evening, and by the time the stove cooled off, they were not home until nine in the evening. The walk home seemed longer because they were tired. She earned lots of money, it seemed. The only item she had to buy was oil. Bananas and firewood were from the backyard. Moni had a thriving business at a very young age with her younger brother as a main help. Aside from the business, she was the errand person who brought goods to her grandparents.

Chapter Six

As Moni was approaching graduation from elementary grades, she asked her parents if she could continue high school. It was expensive being that she must stay in Cebu. They agreed, so a letter was sent to Uncle Indong, one of Maxi's brothers who lived in Cebu. The reply if sent immediately would take a week to arrive. She needed to know so she could prepare for it. Even though the reply was uncertain, she would put a lot of effort to earn the money, for tuition and anticipated expenses. She never knew how much her mother saved from dressmaking and from the sale of cacao bits. Moni usually gave all the proceeds from the Sunday sale to her mother. As of a month ago, she would know in her head how much she had given her mother. Moni's graduation from elementary school was approaching. After two months, there was no reply from Uncle Indong. Moni was getting worried. If a reply was not received, the answer was no. A telegram would push him. It was best to wait. He was not obliged to accept her. He has two girls to bring up, and another would be difficult.

Finally the long-awaited letter from Uncle Indong came. He apologized for the delay, and the answer was yes. Moni was delighted. They began to plan for her trip. They wanted to save some money, so they searched for someone trustworthy who might travel on or about the date that Moni had to be in Cebu. The search for that someone was not successful. A twelve-year-old girl should not travel alone, and so one of her family members must accompany her. Maxi had not seen her brother for a long time, and it was a good time to renew the old relationship and talk about their childhood. She set up Moni's needs, her medium-sized suitcase made of twine. She planned to bring food items enough for them to carry and to stay in Cebu for a week to get her daughter situated. She had saved enough money. Graduation day finally came. Moni was very happy because her mother bought a sewing machine and made a graduation dress of white lace. She looked beautiful in it. She received several awards. One of them was for being the second-best student. Moni, dark-skinned as she was, with a very beautiful face, stood on that podium for the first time and delivered her short speech. She was very self-assured. It was a grand day. Simeon slaughtered a hog and invited some friends for a party. She had too many things in her mind. She wanted to earn more money to bring with her.

One day in May, they were set to leave. They were prepared with everything to bring. Moni's brothers bade her good luck. Simeon went with them to Naval. They left early to purchase the tickets and spend some time with each other. There were no more items to be bought for Moni. Other needs would have to be bought in Cebu. They had lunch at a cheap eating place. The vessel to Cebu would leave at six in the evening. Simeon went to see his cousin in Naval and gave him some cacao bits. He would stay at his cousin for the night if there were no more *sakayan* trips to the other side. Normally, on a sunny day, there were trips to Villalon until nighttime after the interisland vessel left.

Moni and her mother were the first passengers. There were enough passengers, mostly young people accompanied by a parent and businesspeople. They were average people from Leyte who struggled to earn their living. Two vessels alternately traveled from Leyte to Cebu and neighboring island owned by a family in Cebu. This particular one named after their mother, Senora Lalani, had been the vessel transporting passengers from Leyte and Negros to Cebu. It accommodated one hundred passengers. Both decks were lined with double-deck metal beds with a stripe-covered cushion. They opted to take a space on the top deck because it was quieter, although more expensive. The engine was located underneath the lower deck, and sleeping might be difficult. The passengers brought their own mat made of straw and a flannel blanket. The beds were lined up in rows spaced enough, allowing passengers to get in and out of their beds. The rails of the vessel were all equipped with canvass, rolled and tied to the side in sections, ready to unroll and cover the open window when the boat was to leave the port. As the canvass gets unrolled, it was tied to each corner. The midsection tied to the railing (waist-high) of the vessel kept it from swaying to the beds of the passengers. It inhibited the entrance of gushing winds as the vessel crossed the vast ocean. Despite this, it was very cold at night as the wind nudged through the cracks of the canvass. The passengers who traveled often appropriately attired themselves with thick pants and long-sleeved shirts. Maxi, despite the rarity of her travel experience, remembered those nights, and both of them were dressed appropriately. Their snacks were all set in the event of need, but on these trips, one preferred to be abstinent, since the restrooms were unkempt. As expected, the departure time was delayed. Some of the cargoes were not loaded on time. People never complained. They were used to it.

This vessel owned by C. Graciano Shipping was rather old and required aesthetic repairs. This lack of beauty never bothered the customers because it had most often been there for them and had brought them from one island to the other. It had serviced the public for several years; presumably the engine had been maintained well enough to keep it running. It was kept clean, unpolished floors mopped as the passengers came and went. They both settled. Moni took the upper deck, and Maxi, the lower deck of the bed. Their mats were opened, and their patch-up flannel blankets were ready. Their small suitcase made of twine was wrapped with a pillowcase and utilized as their pillow. The rest of their belongings were placed on their side, cradled to protect them from unwanted hands. Money was securely placed, pinned to the inner clothing. The rest of the baggage was stashed underneath the bed. It was risky to leave belongings unattended. If one traveled alone, one made friends with the next person in hopes that he or she would be honest enough to watch it for you when you needed to leave for a moment. This trip to Cebu was approximately fourteen hours. They were to be at Cebu early morning.

SHADOWS IN THE PANTRY

It was around eight in the evening when it was announced that the vessel was to leave and all nonpassengers had to disembark. Simeon got up to bid his family good-bye. He caressed his daughter, which he had never done in the past. He was aware of the possible length of time that he would not see her. He, at that particular moment, thought of how precious this little girl had been, and for him to realize it now was sad. He had never given her a word of appreciation, nor had he hugged her to convey his love. He bade his wife a warm good-bye. He thought that he must change his ways and try to express his feelings more openly. He looked at her daughter and hurriedly left to hide his feelings. As the vessel slowly left the port, Simeon stood at the pier to have a look at his family, as much as he could visually decipher. Maxi stayed by their bed, and Moni stood by the railing of the boat and waved her father good-bye. As night fell, the canvass was unrolled. It was a good night to travel. The sea wind and the waters were calm. There was nothing to see in the bleak darkness of the sea. The soft sway of the boat as it cut into the wave looked like a crib being rocked to appease the restless beings. There was nothing else to do but rest. The dim light was enough to light the path for the weary-eyed and for those who wished to be up, possibly to watch as the boat drifted into the ocean. Most of the passengers were quiet and settled to rest. Moni, being very young, dozed off immediately. Maxi had a lot of thinking to do. She would miss this child who for all those years had been a help to the family. She hoped that this child would have the luck of happiness in the future. Nevertheless, she was able to rest.

In no time, the night was over, the trip uneventful, and as they awakened, they could see at a distance the port of Cebu. Moni, as young as she was, slowly descended from the top deck, ran to the railing, peeked in between the canvass, and viewed the sight. The pier occupied the whole shoreline, and to Moni it was so lengthy that to walk it, would probably take a whole day. Moni did not know where to look first. This was her first time to see other places, and her excitement overwhelmed her. The vessel sounded its horn, as if to alert the town that they had arrived and they were not seen. In Moni's young but very intelligent mind, she interpreted it as such.

The vessel had shut its engine, for it seemed to be crawling to reach the pier. The small traffic boat was visible to her young eyes, and she was looking down at it intently. Her mother was busy packing their belongings; so were the rest of the passengers. They did not have to watch all that was happening, for they had, on numerous occasions, seen these maneuvers, whereas to Moni, it was a sight to see and to remember. The pier looked cluttered; there were mounds of sacks of corn and rice on elevated wooden platforms, different machineries unknown to Moni. Blue-shirted men lined the pier in anticipation of the vessels' arrival. Vendors sold varieties of food, snacks on rattan-made baskets carried on top of their heads. She thought of herself doing such a thing on weekends to earn a few centavos, such as what she had done way back home.

Several *sakayan* were propelled by small-statured, malnourished children looking up, and passengers threw coins, and before they reached the water, several of those children swam to catch the coins. The waters were very deep to keep the ships afloat, and it was pitiful how these children swam these waters just to catch the handful of coins for them to survive. There were several of them surrounding the vessel. Moni watched all this poverty around her and felt lucky that she had never had to do that. Despite her town's proximity to the sea and though most children, including her, were able to swim, she could not maneuver to catch a coin in these waters. As the vessel draw closer and all maneuvers were done and vessel anchored, the passengers slowly approached the intended disembarking space. It was early in the morning an hour before the anticipated arrival. The ladder had guard railings on both sides for the passengers to hold on, as they made their descent to the pier. She looked back and made certain that her mother was behind her. When the ladder swayed as the waves hit the vessel, she gripped the railing tight with her right hand. A small bag of cacao bits hanging on her elbow and the suitcase in her left hand, she cautiously walked with her new tennis shoes, toes cringing on the horizontal elevated wood spaced to prevent the foot from sliding down as the passengers descended to the surface. That short descent seemed like eternity. She felt her knees were shaking. For a child who normally walked fast, she walked that ladder like an earthworm. The blue-shirted men with name badges met them and inquired if they needed help. They did not. Maxi had planned it as such. Her companion, a skinny little girl of twelve, could only carry lightweight packages. They had to find transport. The walk to the place where the jeepneys were was far. But Maxi and the child were accustomed to long walks in their town where there was no available transport. The immediate pier area did not allow cabs to enter without a permit.

A jeepney is a land transport specifically made by the people of the Philippines. The front looked like a jeep used by soldiers in the war. The driver at the front sat with either two or three passengers, depending on the stature of the passengers. The back was extended, with a padded seat on each side that normally sat four or five depending on its length. The passenger entered at the back provided by a wide sturdy step, enough for the foot, as one hung on the metal guard for one to get in. At the front, on the driver's side, a sign written in bold letters alerted would-be passengers of his route. The passenger signaled the driver to stop. He stopped if he had space. The walk to the particular stop to fetch the jeepney was a distance away. Moni's straw bag was getting heavy. She did not complain. Her mother, a medium-weight woman, was struggling to carry the packages, which became heavy as they walked several feet to the jeepney stop. She endured it. The wait at the corner was not long. It was only six in the morning, and besides, it was Saturday. The jeepney was not full. Maxi had to inquire as to the cost of the fare so she would have enough change. If the route was the same, it should pass the corner street where they will have to stop. Maxi whispered to Monica as to the landmarks to watch. Maxi had not visited her brother for almost a decade. She looked around and noticed that there were not too many changes, but new buildings had been erected. The route was the same—no reroutes, no new roads. They were approaching the Chinese cemetery on the right side of the street, which was the landmark Maxi committed to memory. Heading south on Cebu's main road, Maxi asked the driver to stop. It was Moni's first ride on a jeepney, and she was learning how to alert the driver. Her mom said, "Para, Dong." (Gentleman, please stop here.)

The driver found a space to appropriately locate his vehicle before he stopped so as not to impede others. The walk to reach the corner was a few steps away. The climb to Careta Street, a two-car-wide dusty, pebbled street lined with wooden dilapidated houses, was not pleasant. Clothes were hanging on ropes in front of the second-floor windows, which were still closed. No one was there. Homes built almost directly on the road were mostly stores presumably named after the owner. Most of them were still closed, except a few. They sold household needs such as packages of laundry detergent threaded on a string hanging on the sides, canned goods, and various fruits in a straw basket displayed on the counter.

The road had a slight incline. As Maxi remembered it, her brother's home was an unpainted wooden house, built way back from the road. Maxi was holding her brother's letter where the number of the house was written. The house numbers were not in order. Finally, they reached the place. The home number, 46A, was properly numbered at the main door. Uncle Indong's home was concrete. It stood far back from the street, several steps to the main door. It was a large house divided at the middle; each had a door and a front patio, a small space with a flower garden. Both entrances had a green-painted steel gate. The place looked dark. They waited by the gate, since it was locked. Maxi's letter, which advised him of the date and approximate time of arrival, should have been received. No sooner did they surmise the place then the door sprang open, and there was Indong, who apparently had seen them up from the third floor when he looked down. Indeed, they had chosen the right door by which to wait. He lived on the left side of the property. He was almost running as he opened the gate and, with open arms, hugged his sister with such warmth and sincerity. It was a sight that Moni enjoyed. Indong was the brother five years older than Maxi. Looking at their reaction to each other, they must have been close. They held each other for quite a time. Watching this, she thought of how she and her younger brother Avelino came close to this kind of a bond. Uncle Indong was dressed in loose, shortened, unhemmed trousers and a worn-out sleeveless shirt hanging loosely on his body. His slippers were threadbare on the heels and falling apart on the sides. Despite this careless manner of dressing, indeed he was a handsome man. He stood around five feet seven inches, probably a hair taller, balding but very charming. He had a slight protrusion at the middle, but he stood erect, poised with a capturing, enigmatic smile that was so endearing. His dark almond eyes, fair skin, and face marked a distinctive resemblance to his sister as they stood side by side.

The sitting room was very small. It accommodated one padded couch that seated four, a narrow rectangular bamboo table at the center, and two metal folding chairs. The wooden stairs leading up was on the left as it curved from the ground. The whole floor was tiled recently, clean and shiny. There was a small divider; a counter space with wooden square spaces and figurines on each and unpainted clay pots with green ferns separated it from the dining area. The dining and kitchen area was double in size compared to the sitting room, where a wooden six-person table tightly fit the area. A long stretch of furniture was attached to the wall with a counter space, and shelves underneath it stored the dishes and silverware. It was enclosed in glass, which slid from one side to the other. The counter served as a buffet place and storage of certain items, such as notebooks and books and miscellaneous items. The kitchen had two burner gas stoves facing the wall. A small window by the kitchen door was a small space where an open sewing machine was located. The kitchen exited into an open space where clothes hanged to dry. There in that small space was a bountiful vegetable garden, although not enough to provide the family's needs.

Uncle Indong was the only one who was up. He was introduced to Moni, and as a very warm person, he hugged Moni and welcomed her in to his home. Maxi placed the gifts on the dining table. Uncle Indong expressed concern and thanked them for the trouble. Uncle Indong told Maxi that they would eventually own the whole property, and the other door, which was being rented. He had not paid for the house, which had just built a few years ago, but his salary had been paying for it every month. The interest was minimal since his boss was the one who had taken the loan. He had ten more years to pay it off. It was rather impressive for a man who had started as a laborer and now was a clerk at the firm. He worked as a storekeeper of several *bodegas* (a warehouse made of concrete at the pier that stored bags of corn, rice, and sorts). His boss, Manny Manguerra, owned several of them. Even though he did not earn much, he was grateful to have been able to borrow money to buy the lot and build a duplex on this prime property. It was a few miles' commute to the city. All in all, he was doing well. The rent he received every month and his wife's earnings as a seamstress maintained the rest of the bills.

Delina, Uncle Indong's wife, came down, hearing the commotion downstairs. She appeared very tired, wearing a faded house dress. She seemed tall (stood five feet and four inches or so) and very lean, her straight black hair hanging loose, which looked uncombed. She was fair-skinned, had a black round pair of smiling eyes, and was personable. Maxi had had a chance to meet Delina in the past. After a brief introduction, she started cooking breakfast, at which Maxi stood up right away to help. She placed the gifts in their proper containers. She thanked Maxi for her thoughtfulness. The supply of smoked meat was enough supply for a month. The daughters soon came down and joined them. Pina, the eldest, was fourteen, and Dorothees was eleven. The conversation was lively, and getting to know a close relative they had not seen was most informative and enjoyable. Pina was rather tall for her age. She stood around five feet four inches, was fair-skinned, and took Uncle Indong's features, while Dee (short name) was a little over five feet, rather heavy, and took after her mother's features. Soon it was time to inspect where Moni would settle.

Indong accompanied her sister upstairs. The second floor had two bedrooms. The bigger one situated at the back was the parents', and the smaller one overlooking the street was the girls' room. The bath area was located in between the two rooms. The parents had their own entrance, accessed from the bedroom. The girls could access the bath area from the hallway. The bath area had a nice shower head, but apparently, they still used the big water receptacle with a handheld bucket to rinse. This way, water was never wasted. The toilet even flushed. Moni was amazed. It was such a luxury to her. The stairs leading to the third floor were located on the left side of the wall, visible as one stepped to the second floor. A wall closet could be seen right outside the parents' room. The parents' room seemed larger in space, had a thin-cushioned two-person wooden bed and a small wooden night table with a lampshade. A glass window overlooking the back almost extending from one wall to the other, draped with cheap printed material accented with a green border, illuminated the room. It was plain looking with no significant décor but a wall painting of a vase with flowers. It was hanged at the top of the bed.

The girls' room had a double-deck metal bed and a single-person bed by the window for Moni. Each bed had a cushion covered with patched-up sheets. The wall closet with sliding wooden doors was more than enough to hang their clothes. It was located on the opposite wall from the door. One side of the wall closet was a mirror. Moni was told to take the closet space near the window. Her cousins did not have too many clothes, judging from what was hanged on the other side. Moni had three house dresses and a couple of nice clothes for church; a flannel robe and uniforms would be hanged there. A wooden box at the bottom was provided for books and notebooks and a small one for shoes. It was organized. There was no other furniture to be seen. Maxi was emotionally touched that her brother had prepared for Moni's coming. The warm welcome from Delina was sincere.

The stairs to the third floor were rather steep. The third floor was an empty screened space with polished wooden floors, the area as large as the bedroom's space down below. A glass window at the front overlooked the street below, and a wide sliding glass door at the back exited into a small veranda overlooking the small backyard. A veranda was a skimpy space with an above-waist high guard rail that could comfortably sit four people sitting on metal chairs. It was a place to look out, to think or air the mind, and to have lengthy private conversations away from prying ears. There was nothing to look at except roofs of poor homeowners' clothes hanging on the line attached to each, swinging as the fierce winds caressed it. Moni and her mother would stay on the third floor for a week. The floor was spacious enough for their sleeping mats.

Monday was going to be a busy day. Moni was to enroll at the high school that the cousins went to. The reputation of the school was known as one of the best. It was a government-subsidized school, and the fee was minimal. Maxi went with Moni to the city. Abellana High School was located on a busy street on Jones Avenue. There were three buildings at the front and large grounds at the back for tracks and other sport activities. A grandstand for spectators occupied half of the ground space. Several small structure buildings were scattered around for cafeteria, home economics, and a technical place for boys to learn carpentry, plumbing, mechanical, and electrical things. The back of the buildings had numerous trees, encircled by wooden benches that provided shades for students who might wish to relax in between classes, and a paved walkway for students as they moved from building to building. The middle building housed the library on the second floor, and the ground floor was the administration and classrooms. After the enrollment and fees were paid, they had a stroll on the grounds. Her records were in order, so the process went smoothly. The requirements were listed, and on they went to purchase the necessary items required. Maxi, despite her minimal education, sort of knew what it would entail. To Moni's surprise, there was enough money to spend. She knew how to earn money at a tender age but did not know how easy it was to spend the money, which had taken her long to earn. The money accumulated from the cacao bit sales had been saved for her schooling. Finally, the errands were done. They spent time together and looked around in this big city. They watched a movie and ate out. It was very expensive.

Maxi decided to shorten her stay. Instead of a week, she opted to leave on Thursday. During her stay, she assisted Delina in hemming the clothes that were finished. Moni felt the loneliness when her mother told her she must leave. There were things to be done at home. Moni would not be there to sell the wares at the market. Maxi and her younger son would have to do it. Wednesday night, Moni saw her mother give Uncle Indong an envelope. She also received her money for the daily expenditures. She could only spend fifty centavos a day, which was enough for her fare to and fro the city and some food. It was discussed as such, since Moni never had this liberty to spend money, and she was fearful that she might go beyond her budget. The money was good for six months.

Wednesday night, she clung to her mother and did not want to part from her. They were by themselves on the third floor, in this empty space, with their mat spread out on the floor, when she started to cry. Words were not spoken, but the tears said it all. Maxi tried to pacify this child whom she loved so much and has brought so much pride and joy. Uncle Indong was to take off early from work to accompany Maxi to the pier. He would purchase her ticket, since he was not too far from the ticket office. Thursday morning, Maxi and Moni went to the city to buy items to bring to their town. Maxi needed some fabrics for customers to choose from so they did not have to go to Naval to buy material for a new dress, thereby saving time and fare money. She also purchased miscellaneous items, gifts and sorts. She was given patterns to follow by Delina so she did not have to design clothes. They had an early dinner and enjoyed getting to know more of Delina and the girls. She packed some rice and meat for herself, for the boat ride. They sold drinks at the boat. Maxi had a heavy load of items to bring, and they took a cab to the pier. Uncle Indong met them at the pier to see Maxi off. The boat would leave at six in the evening and would arrive at Naval by Friday early morning. Maxi knew most of the *sakayan* owners at Naval, and she would seek help from them. Moni stood by the pier for a long time as the boat's anchor was disengaged and the maneuvers were done, ready for departure. She stayed at the pier with Uncle Indong until the boat could no longer be seen as it drifted to the deep sea and darkness engulfed it. She could only see a vision of a tiny object that swayed as the wind caressed it. Then she moved to leave. All that time, Uncle Indong stood by her side and said nothing. He understood her feelings; for some time in his youth, he had left his home to venture into the world of uncertainty.

Chapter Seven

The ride to her new abode was quick. She did not talk. Uncle Indong held her hand when they stepped down from the jeepney, as if he knew that this simple gesture would pacify her loneliness and insecurity. The street was full of people. It was half past seven, and it was dark, and the people, consisting of young people, seemed like dark shadows as Moni saw it. The stores were dimly lit, kept open for late customers as they walked past them. The climb up the hill seemed faster than expected, and in no time, they were home. As soon as they arrived, her uncle got ready for bed. He had taken an hour off, and he was expected to be in an hour early. Moni had a week to rest up and mentally prepare for the first day of school. She checked her money pouch and securely placed it underneath, in between the pillow and the pillowcase. Moni was mentally occupied, mainly by the memory of her parents and brothers in that nipa hut. Although she was in a comfortable home with water that was accessible from the faucet (a wonder she needed to know about), the privacy of an outhouse that was inside the house that flushed (which she was very thankful for), she still missed her bedroom, even though it was only illuminated by a coconut-oil lamp. The cushioned bed was also comfortable compared to the noncushioned bamboo bed where she had grown up. Those accommodations were more than what others had in their town. The white window curtains trimmed with varied colored prints kept the glaring shine from the lamplight into her eyes. It was thoughtful of Aunt Delina to have spared her from this uncomfortable predicament. As she glanced at her wristwatch, it was already nine in the evening. Indeed, this graduation gift that she was wearing was very useful, not only at school but at times like this, when she needed to know that she had to sleep. She parted the curtains and pressed her face by the windowpane to look outside. It was quiet, and it was no longer dark, like what she had seen. Her sadness brought that darkness, or was she imagining the world without her parents and grief had momentarily engulfed her? She was teary-eyed and almost sobbed. She held herself, afraid that her cousins might thus awaken from their sleep. She now shared a bedroom and had to be considerate. She recalled her mother's advice: to be always helpful, to be considerate, and to be aware that nobody had invited her and that she was living in the premises for free. She had to return that favor whenever she was able. She planned to wake up early, cook, pack Uncle Indong's food, and wash clothes. She had to prove herself to be a helpful nonpaying guest. She did just that.

Moni was excited to start school. The previous night, she had prepared her three uniforms of white blouses and two maroon pleated skirts. She ironed them. Her black shoes and white socks were ready. Her school supplies were checked according to her list. This, to her, was very organized, having been given a list to follow. She would wake up early like she always did and would set up for breakfast and pack everybody's lunch. To her surprise, Aunt Delina woke up early too. Moni was the assistant cook, and the work was done quickly. There were several lunchboxes to pack. Breakfast was filling, consisting of fresh-cooked rice, eggs, and sausages. Moni had never had it before, and she ate a lot. She realized that she probably ate more than the rest. The rice and fish to each lunchbox was laid out to cool off. The wait for the bath area had caused anxiety to Moni. She would wash up at night so others could take their time in the bath. Despite her fear, everybody was ready on time.

Dressed in crisp uniforms, properly groomed, the young ones walked down that hill. Uncle Indong wore faded beige trousers and a white ironed shirt, whose collar was mended from wear. His shoes were polished. He walked with a firm gait as if he were a drill sergeant. He said hello to almost everyone he met and went without stopping. He had no time. The street was almost crowded, with people hurrying to catch the jeepney at the corner street, dressed for work, and uniformed adolescents like Moni represented the schools that they went to. Younger children with their straw-made school bags were dressed clean, and wooden shoes clattered on the street. Clothes on top windows no longer hanged. The street was full of life. Moni was looking at her uncle and thought, as she had learned from nightly conversation with her mother, that he had left Villalon and earned his high school diploma by going to school at night. He was employed as a servant by a rich family. He then looked for a clerical job but could not find one. He took a job as a laborer at the pier, lifting bags of rice, corn, and sorts on his shoulders and carrying them to the warehouse. He became friendly with the owner of the warehouse. It was when he was hired, originally as the person to oversee delivery of sacks of corn, rice, and sorts. It was his job to do inventory to assure that the amount of bags on paper coincided with the amount inside the bodega. He did not get a break from work since the bodegas were open all day, and he had no relief. He worked six days a week and did not get a vacation. Work was hard to find, and complaining was never a thing to do. His job was sought for, and besides, he had to be grateful to this guy, who had helped him finance his house. In time, he would own his home and be well off, by his standards. She thought of all the hardship he went through while walking this half mile stretch to the main road. A lot of thoughts came to her during the walk.

On their first day of school, they needed not be on time. The wait for the jeepney was long, and to Moni, she would have to be up half an hour early to make it to school on time. The jeepney was almost full. If any one of them would have been a little heavier, they would not have been able to sit and would have to wait for another one. That vehicle could only accommodate five passengers on each side. This time, it had to fit six. Moni was the sixth one. She was seated with a guy that had not seemed to wash up, and she was holding her breath to avoid smelling him; plus she was hanging on to her seat uncomfortably, digging her shoes to the floor to remain seated. She swore that very moment that she would get up at four o'clock to catch the jeepney at six in the morning. That way, she could sit comfortably and might be able to choose a seat apart from somebody who had no consideration to others. The other choice was to walk to school. She might not be allowed, since the vehicles, if she was not careful, would run her over. The place had so many obstructions. Her town had none. Moni did not complain. Luckily, the girls were dropped off first. Dee's school was next to Abellana School. Uncle Indong got off last. His job did not start until eight in the morning. Uncle Indong paid for their fare. Monica saved fifteen centavos. Should she give him the money, or was it customary for the elder to pay? She was not sure. She lived in their household, and she had caused extra expenditure for Uncle Indong.

It was agreed that Pina and Dee would meet her at a specific spot so they could take the jeepney together on the way home. It was a routine they agreed on, but if one took off early for various reasons, they would go home separately. The time was set. As directed, Moni and Pina went directly to the back of the middle building. The information of the section and room number would be posted there. Moni was in section 2 on her first year of high school. She was considered one of the best, judging from the section that she was listed in. Pina was in section 5, on her third year of high school. The lower-section students were those who possibly did not study and, hence, did not have grades to qualify them in sections 1 to 3.

Moni's record revealed a student of high caliber due to her grades. Although when she was asked if she participated in sports, she had none. She was never credited with a written statement when she delivered mail accurately in her hometown. The first day was meeting the teachers in their school room. They were given instructions on what teachers expected and about adherence to rules. Moni knew how to follow those rules. The city folks seemed different. Her classmates comprised of boys and girls who seemed to be older than her and knew a lot. Lunchtime at the cafeteria was an experience. The rest of the students did not bring lunch but bought their rice, two dishes of meat, and vegetables. Pina bought a dish of vegetable and some meat dish, and they shared it. The water fountain was there, and glass cups were provided for. They spent twenty-five centavos between the both of them. To Moni, who was very thrifty, it was too much to spend. Although Uncle Indong had paid for her fare, she was actually within her budget. Come the afternoon break, she was hungry. She had money left, aside from the fare money to head home. She abstained herself from the expenditure. That day, they really did not have school, but the next day would be different. Class would begin, and she could not be hungry. In their hometown, most of the kids, including her, ran home for snacks of fried bananas or boiled yams (*camote*). Money was not spent recklessly. She had knowledge of how difficult it was to earn money. Under that blazing sun, protected by an oversized straw hat, she had sat there, squatting until sundown to sell the goods. She and her younger brother would run home after a long day, before it was dark.

As agreed, the three girls waited for each other to take the jeepney together and reached home safely. Dinner was already cooked, and they had a lot to say to their mother about school. Aunt Delina was pretty well-dressed that day and, admittedly, appeared attractive. She had a new housedress on, and her hair was combed, pulled at the back with a nice ribbon. There was no occasion. She was feeling well, having finished making several dresses for the past week, and she went to market to buy some bulk of canned goods, some fresh fruit, and vegetables. They needed not buy meat and fish for a long time. Moni's family provided for that, and Delina mentioned it at the table. It was important for Moni to bring up her fare that had been paid by Uncle Indong, to which he said that his sister had left him ample sum of money. The girls cleaned the kitchen, soaked the dirty clothes in hot water, and said that they would do them the next day when they came home from school. Aunt Delina was grateful and said she admittedly would relax that day after four nights of work. Relaxation meant reading the daily paper and listening to the radio. The dining table had to be cleared up, since it was a place for them to do homework and study.

That night, Moni did not have anything to study. She was getting ready for the next day. The family sat in the sitting room and listened to the radio. She talked about her mother getting home safely. There was no news of a boat that sank or bad weather that could have drifted the boat, other than its destination, so her mother must have arrived home. What Maxi did was hire a person from the shore to accompany her up north, which was a mile away. That night, Moni took her shower. Despite the shower head, she used the handheld bucket to rinse and conserved water, the way she was accustomed to. She rested early. The next day, she would need only a quick sponge and the washroom would be free for the three of them. Her cousins were still downstairs when she started to doze off. She was in bed a few minutes before nine in the evening and would surely be up early on time to fetch the early jeepney. True enough, she did. She was up before everybody and prepared the lunches and a breakfast of fried rice, pork, and hot cocoa. It was a hearty breakfast. She was ready and sat in the sitting room, to wait for them. Pina woke up late, and they had to wait for her. It was quarter after six, and true enough, they were fifteen minutes early than the previous day. It was a better time. The jeepneys were not full, and the wait was not long. Uncle was impressed. After several weeks, Moni left before the rest. She wanted to be at school an hour early.

School, for Moni, was rather hectic. The teachers seem to talk faster, and they did not repeat what had already been said. She had to catch up. Admittedly, she was slow. She could not cope with the fast pace that the city kids had been accustomed to. Her background, although she was one of the best in her town, had not prepared her for this speed of learning. She would study the assignment and read ahead in hopes that when it was discussed, she would totally understand and retain it. Despite these efforts, she did not do well. She was barely passing. She was embarrassed, being in that section of the smart ones. Moni would study in the library on her break time and stayed up longer at night.

Aunt Delina did most of the marketing early on Saturday mornings. Monica, having noticed this, wanted to help. She asked her if she could go with her. She then realized that the vegetables and sorts that they always had in the garden had been worth an enormous amount. She wrote to her mother that if ever she happened to visit, to bring her brother and bring lots of stuff to alleviate the expense of the household. Moni continued her attitude and did most of the washing with Dee. Being that she normally woke up early, the wash would almost be done by the time Dee got up. It seemed that Pina hardly helped in the household. She noticed that she hardly talked to her mother.

Six months went by, and she was still performing poorly at school. She borrowed books from the library to read. The extra reading might enhance her comprehension. She did not entertain the young boys at school who would attempt to propose to her. For her, they were a hindrance, and she had no time. She was almost considered a snob, which she did not intend. She did not know how to express herself. She would just be quiet. She participated in a sport that was inexpensive to join. She had saved money to buy the outfit. She became a track runner. It occupied her on Saturdays, so she would do the wash on Friday nights. Dee helped her out. This way, Delina did not have to do it. She did not say anything about Pina hardly helping and staying in bed late. A fight would be embarrassing since she was only a relative living in the household for free. She would surely be at fault.

She participated in sports. Being a track runner was a challenge. In her home, she mostly walked to places and, indeed, walked fast to reach her destination right away. Running was harder due to the competition and the goal to run faster than the others. She would be up at night thinking of it, just to discover after thorough thinking that there was no strategy but practice. The mental attitude and physical endurance were factors she must consider. The uniform was inexpensive, and it fit her budget, saving fifteen centavos every day. The school had big grounds, allowing her to practice after school. She became a competitive runner, and she represented her school.

Moni wrote a letter to her mother. Maxi immediately came to visit to see her win the second place. Maxi brought so much food with her. There was good news. The cacao bits business had flourished. They bought the seeds from the neighbors to increase the quantity, roasted it, and in large supply, they sold these cacao bits to a grocery store in Naval every week. Simeon took trips to Naval and bought items from there to sell at the market so Maximina could afford these trips to Cebu and some money for her school needs.

After her first year, her grades were not impressive. The eight weeks' vacation from school was refreshing. She wanted to go home to help out with the business, but her mother wanted her to rest. What she did was help Aunt Delina mend and hem the clothes. She watched while she would cut the fabric, separate the remnants, and save the bits of fine materials to make a pillow. The neighbors came to have dresses made and clothes to be hemmed or altered. Delina was sometimes overwhelmed with the work.

Moni was Delina's assistant. She became a seamstress assistant. She ironed the newly made dresses and hung them, making it presentable for customers to pick up. She did most of the cleaning and the cooking and washed the clothes at night, ready to dry in the morning. Dee and Pina cleaned upstairs and did most of the ironing. The amount to be washed was small, being that they had no school. It was only Uncle Indong's clothes and their house dresses that needed to be washed. With all these tasks that the girls did, Delina made each of them a dress. She even bought Uncle Indong some shirts. There was also some good news. Uncle Indong had a pay raise.

Chapter Eight

Her second year in high school was not as difficult. The extra reading she did in the library had indeed helped her comprehension. She still participated in track, and although she did not receive a medal, she was one of the best athletes. Moni was better in her second year even though she was in section 5. She seemed to adjust to the fast pace of learning. All through high school, she did not involve herself with boys her age. It was almost not normal being a teenager and avoiding trouble. Her dream was to become a teacher dressed up in a skirt and blouse, a distinctive belt, and shiny shoes. She would not attempt to do anything to spoil that dream.

Pina graduated from high school, and they celebrated her graduation at home with restaurant food. Pina also received a wristwatch. Her graduation dress was made of lace. She would enroll at the University of San Carlos for an accounting degree. Moni's third and fourth years were a breeze since she had learned the art of listening and taking short notes which only she could decipher. She felt that this time, she belonged with the smart ones. She was in section 2 for two years. She even made it on the honor roll. She made it as number 9 in her class. Her parents came to attend her graduation and were proud to pin the Medal of Honor. They could afford to come, and Moni was very happy. They brought lots of food, since her father had come along. The celebration was done in her uncle's home. There was roasted chicken and noodles with shrimp bought from the restaurant. Her parents stayed for a few days. Moni took advantage of the opportunity by telling them that she wanted to apply for college. With Uncle Indong at the table, she asked the couple if she could stay another four years to pursue a teaching degree. It was agreed that she could. The teaching school was just across the street from her high school, so she immediately enlisted. Normal school was a two four-story building surrounded by grounds with some trees and benches. It was a school — mostly for students who intended to be teachers. The school only accepted students with high grades and good behavior. Students must keep up with the gratifications-required when a student enters the school. Furthermore, the tuition was reasonable; and a student may pay monthly. If she gets accepted, school and work will be manageable. It was thirty-minute walk to work.

Pina was now enrolled at the university, taking accounting. She was ahead of Moni, but she was not doing well. She kept repeating her classes and costing Uncle Indong more money. College tuition cost much. Moni thought of finding a job to help pay for tuition. In the meantime, she tried to help her aunt. This time, she would go with her to deliver clothes to her new customers. Dresses, at times, needed to be altered because it did not fit, and measurements had to be done. Delina would ask Moni to assist her, and Moni was willing to learn. They would practice at night. Moni would do the measurements at the customer's home with supervision. The rich had their clothes made every week. The trip to the city was fun since Delina treated Moni out to eat. They would have a bowl of steaming hot *arroz caldo* (steamed rice with chicken and cut-up cabbage). After several deliveries accompanied by Aunt Delina to the Bonedotos' home, she was finally sent alone for those errands, and they knew her well enough to be admitted into their home. She became friendly with the help in the household. Moni did the delivery herself and took the measurements if alterations were required. Sometimes there were other guests in the household aside from the family. She was never introduced to them, nor was it necessary to introduce the guests to her. She was there to do work for her aunt, and she had to do it well. She would do her work as accurately as it should be done to avoid return trips to the city, which were expensive. They did not charge extra for these alterations.

Now she could confirm her enrollment at Normal School. In the meantime, her vacation from school was boring because she did not earn money. She had money saved, plus her mother had left her some. She enrolled in three subjects, which were English, psychology, and history. The school did not require the whole tuition paid, and it could be done on a monthly basis. She chose the morning classes. She was lucky to have made the decision early enough to be able to choose the time of her subjects. Classes would be in the morning, and a job in the afternoon would be the plan. She would have to organize her time well to cope with school and work so her grades would be acceptable. While she was in the city, she looked for jobs, any job she could find. She applied at several stores, restaurants, and bakeries. She was told to return and check after a week. She told Uncle Indong and Aunt Delina of her plans.

Finally, she was scheduled for an interview at nine in the morning at the Gold Department Store. A housekeeping job was a good job to start and easy to do. She was there an hour before the set time. It was still closed. When it opened, she was the first to sign in. Moni was dressed with a white blouse and a flowered pleated skirt. Her worn-out black shoes had just been shined. She was clean; her shoulder-length straight hair was shampooed, pulled at the back with a black ribbon. She had a black purse that contained her ballpen and identification from her school. She was presentable. There was nobody but her in that room with unfolded metal chairs as the only furniture. The application form was filled out on a clipboard. The middle-aged lady who was seated at the desk signaled to have her sign in. There was a padded chair in front of her for the applicant to sit after the interview. She was preoccupied with paperwork and fixing folders. Two more women applicants came in, unfolded the chairs, filled out the application forms, and sat quietly. Each of them smiled at each other, almost like they were wishing each other good luck. Soon after that, a beautiful, well-poised, fair, silk-skinned woman came in. Her short black hair was parted on the side and flipped under; it was shiny and almost glistened as she walked past them. She stood tall, five foot four inches, was very thin, and smelled clean as she walked past them. She was dressed in a striped black and white dress to her knees with a wide white belt that revealed her small waistline. Her black and white two-inch-heeled sandals complemented her manicured toenails. Moni admired her feet. She walked in, never looking at anyone. She went directly to the room marked Personnel with a confident walk that a woman with status represented. They sat there in awe, admiring this woman. Moni felt like a pauper sitting on this metal chair, not worth a glimpse. The secretary immediately unseated herself, picked up one of the folders on her desk, and ushered Moni to follow her to the door. Moni entered, and her folder was placed on the table. The secretary immediately left the room. This very good-looking woman of pure-blooded Chinese origin, seated on a wide, shiny desk, did not look at Moni. She was not told to sit on that chair to accommodate a potential employee, but she remained standing in front of her. Moni stood there, maltreated with a cold attitude. To a spectator, it would appear that she was standing in front of the employer being reprimanded. Moni felt she was too poor and ugly for her to look at.

She was accepted as a housekeeping employee after the interviewer looked at the application form. She was told to avoid being seen at the store unless necessary and to concentrate on cleaning and mopping the restrooms as often as she could so they would not smell. She was to report next Monday and not to bring a big purse. A big purse would get her tempted to steal, a ready container to hide the stolen items. All this time she was talking, her head was down; she did not spare a look at the new employee. She talked to the open folder. Monica said to herself, *She must have eyes on her eyebrows, being that she never looks up.* The woman said that most of the things Moni needed to know would be explained by the secretary. She said, "The interview is over."

Moni hurriedly exited the room. She sat in front of the secretary and was told in a very subdued manner about the job. It was almost as if her job was being a detective, as no one should know who she was, or it could be that the job being so menial that she thought Moni might not want anyone to know about it. She speculated that the latter was the reason. She would work three days a week—on Mondays, Tuesdays, and Thursdays—and it stated her pay. She would be provided a name badge and two white aprons signifying her line of work on her first day. Orientation to the job was mostly location of supplies, inventory, and schedule. It was assumed that she knew how to clean. She was told to be prompt and early so the place was all clean when the workers and customers came in. She was to start at eight in the morning, before the store opened, until four in the afternoon. The night guard would let her in. There were several bathrooms to clean, and she would be called in between to mop and dry a floor in the event of need. The pay was meager. She had the option of working ten hours, which she accepted. She had some benefits, which included discount coupons to be able to buy expensive items, which would be unaffordable by an employee such as her. It was good enough for her. The plan was to look for another job before school started because currently, this setup would not allow her to attend school. Fridays off would be the day to look for a job, which she did. The job went well.

After four weeks of working as a cleaning person, she noticed an advertisement on the bulletin board where the employees took their breaks that the store was looking for an errand person. She inquired about the details of the job and applied for it. It would be easy to follow it up, being that she was working there. She had no references, and she was not called. She has given up the idea and was planning to leave few days before school. In the meantime, her mother sent her a money order enough to cover the tuition fee. Her mind was set on school. Her savings were not enough to last for six months.

She was called for an interview one Tuesday morning by the same person at the personnel department. When she reported for the interview, she was told that it was not necessary, being that a letter had been written by the interviewer that she was accepted for the job. A two-week orientation was required before becoming permanent. Moni was grateful, more so because she was spared the trouble of being condescended upon. On the other hand, she thought that woman at the personnel department probably liked her, having remembered in her mind how she looked like. Indeed, she had eyes on her eyebrows. She was given the night shift. It would start at two in the afternoon until closing time, which was around eight in the evening. She had to work six days a week.

She would be off every Friday. It involved expenditure because she had to buy two navy-blue skirts and two white collared blouses. The schedule of the job was just right. She would be at school in the morning and work in the afternoon. The acceptance made her so happy. She informed her guardians.

The Gold Department Store was located in the heart of Cebu City. It was accessible from a nearby church, a college, and a movie house. It sold items such as clothes, shoes, school supplies, ornaments, some appliances, and groceries. If she passed the probation period, she would earn more money than she did with the housekeeping job. School was three times a week in the morning, and her job was six days in the afternoon. Theoretically, it was manageable, being that she was young, but she was doubtful if she could handle the stress. The tuition was paid, and the uniforms were purchased. She had two weeks left in her current job. The timing was right. She would work as an errand girl a week before she actually started school. The store had three floors. The cashiers, two of them, were located on the second floor and one on the first floor. To accommodate the customers, the errand person brought the items to be paid to the cashier, and the customers waited in a special place, properly seated. The most expensive items were displayed on the third floor. The first floor had a wider diameter than the second floor, and it sold most of the items a customer would normally buy because of need. The winding stairs were wide, allowing several people to go up, not impeding on the customers. There were four of them to do the job. It required a lot of walking or running, depending on how busy the store was. The orientation was either a week or two weeks, depending on their performance. It was not difficult. As a young girl, she had used to help out delivering mail in her hometown, so walking sounded easy. Now she was confident that she could afford to stay at school. She had a job to cover her allowance and other needs. It was again a good year. The subjects were not too difficult. She learned to listen to the professor and took notes as accurately as she could. If everything went well, she might take more subjects.

There was a good-looking young man at work who would talk to her during dinner break. He was respectable and quiet. He worked as errand personnel for three years and was not going to school. He said he was partly the breadwinner of his family of five. His father worked as an orderly at a government hospital, and his income was not enough to support them. Moni felt sorry for him. His name was Armando. She expressed her dream to him of becoming a teacher. He wanted to go to school too, anything within his means. At the moment, it was not possible. She denied his advances and told him she did not want headaches. Nevertheless, they were friends. School and work were manageable. She used her store coupons to buy expensive food items, such as cooked ham and fruit cocktail. She continued on helping Aunt Delina deliver finished clothes to her patrons on Fridays. She was well-liked by the Bonedoto family. If they knew she was coming, the help were instructed to pack most of the cooked food that could not be consumed and give it to Moni. She would sometimes have an ample supply of rich people's food for the weekend.

She would walk to work from school, a good five miles, which was easy for her. At work, she even learned to carry lots of items and was able to know which item came from which department. The customers never had to wait long. She was fast, light on her feet, and methodical. After a while, working and going to school proved difficult, but she could not refuse the errands on Fridays. She thought that for the next semester, she would only take two subjects. She noticed financial hardship in Uncle Indong. She then would do the marketing for the week. Pina's tuition was costly, and the electric bill was high. She wrote a letter to her mother and requested her to come and visit her and to bring a large amount of meat. Her mother did not reply but arrived one day in a cab with lots of cooked pork, dried fish, and coco bits. It was a Saturday. Her mother stayed for two days. She went to buy items to bring back to sell at her hometown. Moni was not able to see her off because she was working, but she had grown, and she was able to accept these circumstances. She had time with her mother, short as it was, and she made it memorable. Moni was able to buy an expensive blouse for her mother at half the cost because of the store coupons.

Chapter Nine

It had been several weeks that she had not delivered clothes. Aunt Delina had her rest, but money was scarce. Presumably, the ladies of the house were on vacation or had enough clothes to wear. Neighbors came to have their clothes shortened and have various alterations, so the proceeds of such, although small, helped in the purchase of food. Moni noted the hardship. Being that her tuition was paid and her pay was more than enough to cover for her expenses, she gave her uncle half of her monthly pay. With that, she still had some left over that she saved in the bank, in case she lost her job. She was new at the place, and she would be the first one to go in case the sales would drop. Moni kept on giving money to her uncle. There was enough dried pork and fish to last for another two weeks. Moni had a pay raise of a few centavos an hour, which was very helpful.

One day, Pina did not come home. It was a big worry to the family. Uncle Indong could not take off. He needed his job. Anyone with a college degree would readily grab his job. His dedication and loyalty had kept him working in that place. The police were called. They were not helpful. They suspected that Pina had eloped with a young guy. She was not doing well in college, skipping classes and failing. Aunt Delina kept on crying. She went to church every day, early enough before anybody was up. She thought praying would alleviate their worry. God would watch over her daughter. They had no means to hire a detective. Uncle Indong sometimes stayed out on Fridays after work to look for her, anywhere he could think of. He told his friends at the pier to help. He was exhausted not only from worry but also from occasionally staying out late at night to look for Pina, which was tiring. After a few weeks, a letter was received, addressed to Uncle Indong. It was from Pina stating that she was all right. Indeed, she was with a guy named Ido. He was a native of Danugo. It was a town which was far south from Uncle Indong's home. She stated that she would come to see her parents. They were disappointed and had lost hope in her future, but it was a relief to the couple to hear that she was fine. The couple could not wait to see their daughter.

Several days after the letter was received, she came with a man. They were having dinner. Uncle Indong was seated at the head of the table. Delina was on his left side, seated with Moni and Dee They were halfway through finishing their portion when there was a knock at the door. There appeared Pina with a heavy-set, dirty-looking dark-skinned man in his late twenties. He stood around five foot nine inches tall, was rather stocky with a slight protrusion at the middle, and had a round face with a nervous eye that kept blinking almost every second. He was dressed with a faded denim trousers and a multi-flowered polo shirt. Uncle Indong, at the head of the table, was stunned and surprised to see his daughter. It was a moment that he had prayed for in his heart, yet he did not know how to react to this supposedly happy occasion. Pina looked pale, malnourished, and disheveled. Indong looked up to see who it was; he was expressionless and became angry and rather disgusted. He looked down at his plate, stirred the food with his spoon, and started to cry. His tears flowed with subdued sobs, and he kept wiping his eyes as if embarrassed that a man could cry as much as he did. Nobody stood up to meet them, as if their presence was not a welcome sight. Aunt Delina, seated at Uncle Indong's, left, got up after what seemed to be a long silence, squeezed through the back of her husband's chair, and met and ushered them to sit in the living room. She said hello and led them to sit, but Pina did not. Instead, Pina ushered Ido to the dining room and introduced the guy to everyone, and nobody said a word or gave a nod of recognition. They went back to the living room and sat with Aunt Delina.

Everybody stopped eating. Uncle Indong stood, took a plate from the counter by the dining wall, and covered his plate. He walked to the kitchen door, opened it, and looked outside the small yard as if looking for someone to assist him in this dilemma. His face was sad and in deep thought, with his head down, still teary eyed. He reentered and attempted to resume his seat, when Pina met him and slowly grabbed his right hand and kissed it. It was a gesture of respect and a plea for forgiveness. Her father stood there motionless and, without expression, returned to his chair, uncovered his plate full of food, sat, and resumed eating. The spoonful of rice he was trying to put in his mouth was as if it were a morsel so distasteful that he had to drop the spoon on his plate. He turned his face to the wall, almost like he did not want to take a glimpse at his daughter. Pina grabbed a chair, sat beside him, put her right hand on his right arm, and said nothing. She looked at him, unable to speak, since saying sorry would never pacify him. She sat there, but her father did not say a word, his head looking down at his food. Pina stood up and went to the sitting room and grabbed her friend to bring him to the dining room to pay respect, but her father did not even look at the guy. Pina introduced him formally to her father, and his name was Ido Gianga. He attempted to kiss Indong's hand, but he did not allow him with a hand gesture. He was so distraught; his head remained down, looking at the table. He did not look up to see his face. Delina stood up and led the couple to the sitting room. Dee, still sitting at the dining table, did not know what to say. There was no confrontation. Moni, seated beside Dee, slowly ate the rest of her food and stood up, proceeded to the kitchen sink, and washed her plate. It was quiet at the sitting room and elsewhere. It was as if nobody was there. The man remained at the sitting room with Aunt Delina, but they did not talk. Nobody knew this guy whom Pina chose to elope with. He did not appear liked, being branded as disrespectful for having caused such a worry to the family. Delina sat there, not knowing what to say. Minutes went, and the silence was unbearable. Delina whispered something to Pina, who was sitting beside her, almost like a motherly gesture to pacify her. Ido looked on, sitting on a metal chair. Finally, the discomfort was too much for Pina to take, so she finally stood up, went into the dining room, and kissed her father's right hand. It was limp, almost letting her do it unwillingly. Uncle Indong, with his head down, still teary-eyed, did not move to recognize his daughter. He was controlling his emotions of anger and disappointment of his daughter. Pina was embarrassed, proceeded to the door, kissed her mother, and said good-bye to the rest with a quick wave of her right hand and exited. Ido, his head down, followed Pina. He did not look back. Dee and Moni looked at Pina with pity and worry on their faces. Pina's father did not even look up to see his daughter leave. No one dared ask where she was living or what her future plans were. It was as if everybody was afraid to say anything. The silence that engulfed the room almost seemed a departure of someone never to be seen again. It was a night that reassured the family that she was well but a night of disappointment for the whole family.

The next day went as usual. There was no talk about Pina. The atmosphere was sad. Moni did not understand the family's reaction to Pina. She did not have an opinion. She felt sorry for her cousin who, at a very young age, had gone astray, and wondered if she would be able to recover from this and continue with life smoothly. After that episode, Moni noticed that her uncle would be in deep thought. He was awfully quiet. He seemed not to hear his wife telling him to forgive Pina and to accept the deed of waywardness as a moment of adolescent confusion. The good news was Dee would soon graduate as an honor student from high school. She was number 5 among the graduates and excelled in science. The event pacified the current problem. Aunt Delina's sewing picked up again, and there was money. Dee had a lace graduation dress, and the event went well. Moni could not attend the pinning ceremony. She, however, picked up a nice purse for Dee and contributed some money to buy restaurant food.

Moni was doing well at school. She did not think that she would make it to the top ten of her class. She was proud of her accomplishment. Being a working student was not easy. The first semester went well. Her mother came to visit, and it was a surprise to her. As usual, she brought lots of smoked meat. Apparently, they slaughtered a cow, sold some to the neighbors, and smoked the prime part of the cow. Uncle Indong was very pleased at his sister's thoughtfulness. Maxi stayed for three days and bought items to sell in her hometown. She had become a businesswoman, so much so that if neighbors needed some gift items, they knocked at her door. Moni could not see her mother off. Uncle Indong accompanied her sister to the pier.

Six weeks' vacation from school was rest for Monica. Working six days a week was fine. If a coworker took a day off, she covered it for extra money. She exchanged days off if necessary and made friends at work. She was preparing herself in the event that her mother would come and she wanted to spend time with her. She enrolled for her second semester. She had ample money saved for tuition and then some. She continued giving money to Uncle Indong, but this time, she did not give her half of her pay but only a quarter. She reserved some money for books and other school needs. Dee had no money for tuition, so college was deferred. She wanted to take subjects to pursue nursing, and the cost was enormous. The subjects required laboratory fees, and they could not afford it yet. Moni suggested that Dee might be interested in applying for a housekeeping job. She inquired and took an application form. There was no opening for such, but she was offered a job as substitute in the housekeeping department, which Dee accepted. She would be informed through Moni if an employee took ill or needed a day off.

One Friday, Moni brought Dee, with her mother's permission, to the city and accompanied her to every place they could think of to apply for a job. They went to places that Moni had not even gone when she had started looking for a job. They went to movie theaters, restaurants, and drug stores to file an application. They would have to check on it after a week. They had a good time in the city. They had *arroz caldo* at the place where Aunt Delina had brought Moni when they went to the city. They even went to see a movie. Dee was pleased since she had never been to a movie. They barely made their rent, food, and such, that a movie was a real luxury. In fact, Moni had never gone to a movie, except that time when her mother enrolled her. This was her first time to spend all this money for the longest time that she had stayed in Cebu. She counted every centavo that she spent for the day. Although Dee did not find a job, they spent a memorable day together. Moni admittedly loved this cousin of hers. They did work together, doing the wash and cleaning. Pina had gone, and no one knew if she would be back at all. Aunt Delina did not have work for the week. It meant hardship with money. Monica had to do the Saturday market, and she spent her whole week's pay. Life again was difficult.

    She had been working long hours at the store, since one of the errand personnel took ill. She did not have school, and the extra hours were manageable. They went back to the city to inquire if Dee had a chance for a job at those places they had gone to. There was none. After a week, Moni's co-employee returned to work, and she was on regular time again. All in all, she had twenty-five hours of extra time. There was no overtime money—rather tiring, but it was worth doing. She had money to buy items for the household. One afternoon, she was called in by the personnel department at the store. Moni was asked if Dee could come for an interview. Moni could not wait to get home to tell Dee the good news. Dee was interviewed, and it went well. Moni asked her if the interviewer looked at her. Dee said she did not notice. Moni admired her young cousin's temperament. She was so eager to get a job that a condescending attitude was not an issue. It could be that the interviewer liked Dee better. She would start the Monday after that week and would work for ten hours three times a week and more if there was a need. Dee was excited but anxious. The parents felt sorry for her having to work long hours at the age of sixteen. They had no choice. That Sunday, one of the helpers at the Bonedotos' came, asking Aunt Delina to come. It meant there were dresses to be made. She was scheduled to go on Monday. Meanwhile, Moni planned to accompany Dee to teach her the job. It was actually to allay her fears. Dee liked the job mostly because of the money that would help her family.

    Aunt Delina brought home several materials from the Bonedotos'. It was going to be busy. Since Moni had no school, she helped with the hemming and sorts. She organized her time efficiently to help as much as she could, such as doing most of the laundry and cleaning. Dee talked every night about her work. Uncle Indong was amused to hear how his child was enjoying her job. She was not ashamed of it. When she got paid, she gave it to her mother.

It was most admirable how she would just take enough to pay for her fare and her snacks.

Moni went with Aunt Delina to the Bonedotos' on a Friday to deliver the finished clothes. She made six dresses, one of them a long gown. They had to take a cab. They spent the whole day fitting and doing measurements at the Bonedotos'. They were offered lunch and *merienda*. Three dresses had to be altered, so they had to bring them back. The long gown looked nice on Mrs. Bonedoto and required no alterations. That was a difficult job, since the beads had to be sewn by hand and designed as a leaf on the front. The multiple colored beads blended together well. Aunt Delina had done that herself, mostly at night when it was quiet.

The vacation was almost over for Moni. She was able to take three subjects, and she was able to pick them to adjust to her work schedule. Her mother did not send any money, but she managed to pay for the month's tuition and books. It was again three times a week. The work schedule was the same. She did not have to buy new uniforms but two new blouses and a pair of shoes. Everything was set.

Before school week began, her parents came by surprise. They brought provisions for the household. It was a happy occasion. Monica's mom gave her tuition money, enough for six months. Even though she told her that she had paid for the month, she was trusted to hold the money to be used for that purpose. They even bought restaurant food as a celebration. They talked and went to church together. Moni was able to exchange a day off and spent time with her parents. They all went to the park in the city. They were home late. It was ten thirty in the evening. They got ready to go to bed.

Chapter Ten

Maxi and Simeon were settling, their mats laid up on the third floor, when a constant, almost distant knock at the front door was heard. The couple hurriedly went to the front window to see who was knocking at that late hour. It was dark, and they could not tell. Simeon went down to knock at Indong's door, which was answered immediately. He went down, followed by Delina to the front door. He peeked through the side glass window by the door, and the lamplight shed some light on the caller's face. It was Pina. It had almost been two months that they had not heard from her. Indong immediately opened the door and held her close to him.

Pina was emaciated, shabbily dressed, and with disheveled hair; her left face seemed discolored in that dim light. She was crying. All the adults were at the door when they slowly led her inside. Simeon and Maxi stood by the stairs in a far corner, helpless and dumbfounded. The girls ran downstairs, sat by the steps, and watched the sad scene. Delina immediately asked her daughter if she had eaten as she was led to the sofa. Pina shook her head. Indong, in a controlled state, was pacing the small dining space and sat by the dining table with his fist tight and pounded the wooden table. His face was down and angry; he uttered nothing. He took a glass from the kitchen, had a glass of water. Maxi, watching this, was worried. She slowly went to her brother and placed her hand on his shoulder. She had known him as a peaceful man; he had been a levelheaded person who, in his adolescent years, had not had any physical encounter with anyone. She was fearful that this time, he may in the aftermath silently avenge this violation on his daughter. Delina got up to get a plate of food and brought it to the table and ushered her daughter to eat. She was very hungry and noticeably so, the way she ate.

Apparently she had walked from Danugo since noon, which was a good thirty miles, to her parents' house. She had no fare money. Ido had hit her on the face, evidenced by her swollen face and black eye. Sobbing and crying, she told her story of abuse. She had failed to cook for him since there was nothing to cook, and he was upset. When Ido took a nap, she slipped out of their shack and walked the back streets so she would not be seen. Pina finally got washed, had a change of clothes, and they all went to bed. Indong had to get up early to work; so did Dee. Simeon and Maxi settled upstairs, but Simeon could not sleep. He felt the agony of a father whose child had been trespassed on, and he could not do anything. He stood there by the front window, looking out, burning inside with anger. He held himself together. Simeon was up early that morning, and he and Indong had a man-to-man talk out in the courtyard before Indong left for work.

Pina stayed in bed late. Breakfast was already cooked when Moni woke up. Uncle Indong's lunch was packed. Her mother knew the routine. Delina stayed in bed since Maxi did most of the morning chores. Dee and Indong stepped out of the house together. Simeon went to the city to buy items, mainly carpentry needs and equipment for the farm. Maxi left that afternoon to do her errands as well. Moni enjoyed the company of her parents and the news that the cacao bits business was doing well. Nemesio, her younger brother, was finishing elementary grades and has no interest in school and would rather do construction work. He had a passing grade. He had been a help to the family. Avelino, who was two years younger than the elder brother, had expressed interest in school and might follow Moni's path. The neighbors who lived near them and the rest of the folks that she knew were the topic of conversation. She asked about the young girl who used to accompany her to deliver mail and sorts. Melita harvested the vegetables on Saturdays ready for market on Sunday. Monica used to pay her a few centavos. She was younger and very industrious. For some reason, her parents seem to enjoy the talk. Moni was pleased, but she had to leave for work. She had until

Thursday. She asked her coworker again if she could take off. She was given the Thursday afternoon, which was just right, so Moni and Uncle Indong went to the pier to see them off. This time, Moni took the parting well. The boat did not leave until seven in the evening. They had a memorable time. Moni would call on these moments when she missed her parents.

During the ride home, Uncle Indong expressed his gratitude to Moni. Her parents' thoughtfulness had touched him immensely. When they arrived, Pina was helping Delina hem the clothes. It was a sight that Moni had never seen. She quickly said hello and goodnight. Surprisingly, Uncle Indong kissed his daughter goodnight too and went upstairs with Moni and got ready for bed. Dee was still up when Moni went inside the bedroom. Dee and Moni had some conversation about the incident before Pina came up because she stayed up with her mother helping her hem the clothes.

Monday was a school day for Moni. She left very early. She had three classes three mornings a week, and she was anticipating a hard day. She would be at class until twelve thirty and work at two in the afternoon. She had no time to study as planned. After she had a quick lunch sitting at the bench in the school park, it was time to walk to work and get there on time. The only pacifier was the fact that she did not have to wake up early the next day. She needed to buy some books. Work was the same. That day was busy. Some parents were still buying items for the schoolchildren.

Pina was better. Her facial swelling and discoloration had subsided. She was conversant. She woke up early to cook. Moni was late getting up and had a quick breakfast. She went out to do errands and the school library to study. Three subjects and having to work six days a week proved difficult. Dee was working, participating in household finances. Uncle Indong did not look worried. During her off day, she still did some chores. Moni had not been able to do much, except do her clothes. School and work meant a busy schedule. Uncle Indong was doing some wash on Sundays. Monica admired her uncle's attitude and helpfulness.

Simeon and Maxi arrived at Villalon safely. When Simeon arrived at Villalon, he had a meeting with Maxi's brothers. It was a get-together, and the conversation was subdued. Maxi took it as a business strategy to build a house. Nobody had a drink that night. Everybody seemed to be in deep melancholic thought, almost out of the ordinary, as Maxi had observed. She left it at that.

Pina finally spoke to her mother of the ordeal she had gone through. She had been brought to a dilapidated shack in Danugo. The friend had two brothers, and they all made guns for a living. They were making them there in the shack. She had met him six months or so ago before she disappeared. One afternoon in between class, she was having a snack at the café across the street from the university where she went to school. She occupied a table all to herself, and he asked if he could sit and share the table with her. It became a weekly meeting, rather innocent in the beginning. He would join her while she was having a snack. He would offer food and seemed to have a lot of money. He told her that he was into buying and selling hogs. He bought them from the island of Camotes, a small island, which is a thirty-minute ride to Danugo via a *sakayan*. He was very impressive. She did not intend to elope with him.

One afternoon, he offered to bring her home. He called for a cab, and instead of bringing her home, he took her to Danugo and kept her there as their maid. He was rough and threatened her with a gun if she refused his advances. The shack did not have facilities. Contrary to his story, he did not have ample money. The shack was on a small piece of land surrounded by bushes a few miles from the city. It was not accessible to transportation. They lived together in a small four-bedroom place with his two brothers. The hog business was not true. They were very poor. The brothers were ill-mannered, and they ate like savages, almost having to grab food from each other, since there was never enough. She hardly ate. There were no leftovers. To get by, she would steal a cup of rice as soon as it was cooked and some vegetables. The amount had to be negligible so nobody would notice it. It was a horrible existence. She has been trying to get away and was fearful to get caught until that night when she finally arrived hungry and beaten.

The police came one day while she was resting in the bedroom, and the police questioned him about a killing that had happened.

Pina overheard the whole conversation. Pina suspected Ido to be one of the hired assassins of a government official of Danugo. She was not sure, but after that police visit, Ido was very nervous. He peeked at the window every time a jeepney drove through. He always had that nervous eye, and it became worse after that night. He would only go out at night for business and arrive at dawn, very sweaty. She never knew where he was going and was afraid to ask. Nothing came out of that investigation since the police never came back. Apparently, an activist of poor extraction had complained about the corruption in Danugo. A few weeks after the strike led by Vicente Umpas, he was shot in front of his small hut late at night. He died right there in front of his wife. He left two young children. That was the reason of the police investigation.

Pina intended to file a report at the police station of her plight in the event Ido would pursue her, but she was too weak. She had not left the house since that night she arrived home. She was afraid of being seen and unable to get away from him. If he tried to kidnap her again, the uncles from Leyte would surely get involved. Pina and her mother became very close to each other. She confided in her. It was a big decision for them to make, whether Uncle Indong should know the truth about that day when she disappeared and the events that happened. Delina was trying to spare her husband the grief of what had occurred. Even though Delina was upset, a woman normally has a different reaction toward unwholesome events. A man would normally resort to aggression, and the problem could escalate. In fact, Delina did not agree on a police report. She was scared.

Weeks went by, and Pina was doing well. She wanted to find a job in the city. She wanted to help the family. Delina told her to wait. The family was managing, and if they stayed within the budget, she needed not work. Delina had several dresses to make. As usual, she had the radio on. There was a news break of a massacre that happened in Danugo. Ido and his two brothers had been decapitated, but the wives and two sons were not there. The wives did not come to identify the bodies. The neighbor had to identify them. The mayor of Danugo went to see the sight. He had no comment.

That night, Indong brought the paper. It was a topic of conversation at work. He had no comment. Pina, admittedly, was breathing freely as if her problem was solved. She had nothing to say. She wanted to say "Thank God," but she was embarrassed to say it in front of her parents. They attended church every Sunday, missing it only occasionally, and being happy because someone died would not be proper.

Dinner that night was almost sad. Nobody talked about it. It was as if they had it in their minds but were afraid to mention it. It had been a one-time meeting with a man who had caused them harm, and forgetting the sight of him was not difficult, but erasing him from their memory was not possible. Delina was ashamed of how she felt about the news. It delighted her. She did not express it. In silence, she knelt down and was thankful to God that He, the Supreme Being, had made the decision to spare her daughter from further worry, and she would be grateful all her life.

After that night, it seemed that the family was talking to each other. Pina's plight had hurt the whole family. It was never said, and a burden seemed to have been lifted. Sunday was a celebration. Dee could not attend mass with the rest. She had to work. The sermon that day was "Revenge is not ours." Delina had nothing to say but was grateful that Pina could now move on without fear. Indeed, Pina told her mother that she wanted to look for a job.

The next day, Pina went out as early as she could to look for a job. She thought of the problems she inflicted on her family and would try her very best to change and promised to become acceptable. All the places that she went did not have any vacancy. She was sad to have failed in finding a job. She was very tired. It was a long wait for a jeepney. There was a lot of traffic, and most of the jeepneys were full, and it was getting late. She was hungry. She only had a few centavos enough for fare money and could not afford a snack before heading home. When she arrived, Delina was still up, and she offered her food. Pina looked very pale. She sat to eat, but she had no strength. She forced herself to eat. She had a spoon or two and wanted to go up to rest. She took some hot coco, and off to bed she went. Delina stayed downstairs and kept on with her work. Pina slowly ascended the curved ten-step stairs to the second floor. As soon as she reached to open the door to the bedroom, she lost her strength and inadvertently pushed the door with her falling body, swinging the door, hitting the double-deck metal bed, causing it to shake, where Dee was sound asleep. The force of the door woke Moni, and she saw Pina facedown, slumped on that wooden floor. Moni got up, quickly stood up, and screamed for help. The loud call and the unusual sound brought Delina up the stairs running to investigate. Pina did not respond to the call. Indong was sleeping but woke up hearing the commotion. He immediately turned her over. Pina's face was bruised from the fall and not able to respond. Indong, having been a laborer as a young lad who lifted hundred-pound bags on his back, immediately positioned Pina's body, ready to lift her like a bag of rice. Delina, having never seen such aggression, told him he could not do that. He was no longer able to, due to his age. Immediately they positioned themselves. The elders took hold of both shoulders, and the young ones lifted both legs. Together they lifted her down the stairs. There was no phone to use or a neighbor who owned a vehicle who could transport them. Clad in faded house dresses and Indong in his ripped trousers, they headed down the street synchronically at times, half running down the hill to reach the main road. Although Pina was barely one hundred pounds, she was limp, heavy, and seemed unconscious. The bodily state Pina was in was a sight to the family, who with all their might were trying their very best to save her from impending death. It was late at night, very quiet and dark. No one noticed how late it was. There were no jeepneys. All the stores had been shut, the main road was dimly lit, and the unpaved sidewalk was bumpy. The only sound that they could hear were their agonizing breaths of helplessness and anguish as they ran as fast as they could to reach the hospital. It was quite far from where they were. For all they know, they could be lifting a dead body to be rescued. They could not pause to look nor ask for help but kept on toward the hospital.

    As they reached the junction of the main road and Mango Avenue, an empty cab was slowly cruising. The driver saw the predicament and immediately stopped and unseated himself to help. In an awkward, slow but hurried motion, they lifted and situated Pina's limp body at the back of the cab. Her head was pulled by Delina from the opposite door of the cab as she seated herself, positioning Pina's head on her lap, while Indong did the same, supporting her, bending her legs on his lap on the other side of the cab. The two young ones tightly sat at the front. The cab driver, without a word, accelerated the cab to a speed that none of them knew a cab was able to do. He did not need directions. Red lights were violated, but the cab driver cautiously drove through.

Dee ran out to alert the hospital personnel, who responded right away with a stretcher. When Pina was lifted, a gush of blood came out from her. She had to be rushed to the operating room. Admitting procedures were being done, only to realize that when the admitting officer asked who was responsible to pay the bill, Mr. Rotilles was the one. Moni approached him and whispered to him that she had brought some money. It was a long wait in the waiting room. Moni was the only one who had brought some money, having kept cash in a pouch hidden in between the pillow and the pillowcase. In the event of an emergency, she never had to search for it. They were able to give a downpayment when the cashier requested it. That was when they noticed that the cab driver had left and was not paid. Pina had to undergo surgery. The doctor explained that she had to be cleaned out after a miscarriage. Besides that, she had to receive blood to replace the blood loss. As Moni sat at the waiting room, she thought of how they could have lifted Pina. She could have laid out her flannel blanket and placed her on it, making it easier for them to lift her. Time was of the essence, and thinking moments could have jeopardized her life. She remembered that night when Pina had come with a man to see her father. Uncle Indong, who was upset, could not face his daughter and ignored her. If he could have forgiven her, possibly she could have stayed that night instead of going with that man. Moni could never recall his name, and as her thoughts went back to that night, she thought of how this episode could have been prevented.

The family headed home after Pina's surgery, and she was moved to the floor to get some rest. They walked half way to the main road until they found a cab. There was no talk. They were tired, and there was nothing to discuss. On their way home, Uncle Indong planned to borrow money to pay the hospital. Moni had money in the bank that she would have to give to Uncle Indong. They slept for a couple of hours.

It was a surprise they woke up on time to either go to school or work. Moni could not concentrate at school. At work, she prayed that the store did not have too many customers, and her prayers were answered. She took her break, which she never did. Armando, her friend, did most of the running after she told him of her ordeal. Armando and Moni left the store together. She learned that her father was also sick at the hospital. He was confined in a charity ward at Island Hospital. That night, he would stay with him. Moni could not concentrate on his story and heard just half of it. She was very sleepy. Dee went to work, and being very young and with such a temperament, did the day as usual. However, when she arrived home, she went to bed without hesitation. Delina went to see Pina at the hospital that afternoon after a nap. She found her resting and unable to talk to her. She did not know her mother was there to see her. Indong had a worrisome day. He was not able to ask his boss for money to pay for Pina's hospital stay. Pina had to stay in the hospital for two more days.

That night, they visited Pina. She was supposed to be discharged the next day, which was Saturday. Moni offered her two weeks' pay to help. It was not enough. The Sisters of Charity ran the Succour Hospital. Indong had to request the sister-in-charge if he could pay the balance by installment. He did not know where to get the monthly payments, but he asked her anyway. His job identification was a guarantee, being an employee of a large company that owned half of the storage houses at the pier. The next day, Moni cashed her paycheck at the store and gave three quarters of it to Uncle Indong. There was no agreement as to when she would get reimbursed. Moni regarded it as a help to the family that had taken her in their home for several years without rent.

Pina was finally home. She was weak and nonconversant. She was still uninformed of the events that had occurred and not able to comprehend the worry that her family had gone through. She could hardly walk. Meals were served to her, and she stayed on the couch all day. Delina was very busy with clothes to make for neighbors, mending and alterations, and Pina to take care of. Dee was able to be there three days a week to help out, but sometimes, she stayed late in bed on her days off. Half of Dee's pay went to Pina's hospital bills. Uncle Indong delivered it conscientiously to the hospital. Moni did most of the marketing on Saturdays. It was an event that caused this family to almost fall apart.

Meanwhile, there was some follow-up news about the massacre at Danugo. The detectives suspected that the assassins, judging from the uneven edges of the wound, an unsophisticated instrument used by farmers to do various tasks was the weapon. It was a poor version of a machete. The neighbors did not hear or notice anything that night when it happened. Possibly due to the hatred they had for Ido, they probably heard a commotion but kept it quiet to the authorities. Ido was an outcast from the rest of the family. Nobody came to bury the dead. The wives did not come. The town buried them all at the paupers' graveyard. Ido had stolen from the neighbor's backyard, such as bananas and vegetables from the garden. If seen, he would continue doing it as if it was his. No one dared to tell him, afraid of having an altercation and ending up dead. It was rumored that he worked for the mayor, although nobody knew the kind of work he did. He was the bodyguard of the mayor. It was a scary town to live. One kept their property heired to them by the parents because nobody would buy it. The mayor owned most of the business, a cement factory, and employed several with meager pay. A meager pay was better than no job at all.

Pina was recuperating. She was able to serve herself and was almost independent. Her ability to speak did not return, although she had never been one to elaborate on a topic. Her affect was blank although she could follow some simple instructions. Delina enjoyed Pina's presence because she had never had any moment with her in the past. Despite her affect, she was satisfied that she was there. She tried to make the best of it. Dee never complained about work, and that money that she earned was spent to maintain the household. If she worked an extra day, she would buy special food for Pina. She hardly bought anything for herself. She wanted to save money for college, which was now impossible. It worried her that if she stopped school, she might not be able to cope with studying when she was ready. She was happy that the hospital bills were almost paid off and she had some liberty to buy food that only the rich could afford, such as a pound of grapes.

Chapter Eleven

Since Pina's incident, Armando and Moni became close friends. They would have lengthy conversations on their break time. Nobody knew that his father was sick. He had to be the primary provider while his father was confined. The extra hours that the store offered were taken by Armando. Moni gave some of her discount coupons so he could buy food. Moni offered to meet him at the largest market in Cebu to show him how to plan the menu and be able to buy affordable food. The place, although not presentable, sold everything that one needed in the home. Most vendors sold their items on made-up bamboo tables, rather shabby but the items cheap. One had to know the price range to be able to market effectively. He was very thankful.

Armando's father was not better. Moni felt his pain. He never told anyone except Moni. As much as Armando had feelings toward Moni, he respected her denial to his advances few years ago. He wanted her friendship. The only way to keep it was to remain in love and not say anything. He respected her denial of his advances. Moni kept giving her discount coupons to Armando. Meanwhile, her Uncle Indong's family had been managing.

Thursday afternoon, Armando did not come in. The call was received just an hour before his tour began. His father had passed on, and he would take a few days off. Moni never knew where he lived. She wanted to help to him. She made inquiries at the personnel department and collected some donation from her coworkers to help Armando in this crisis. That Saturday, she asked Uncle Indong to accompany her to his home after he finished work.

It took them two rides to reach the town where Armando lived. They had to ask around and were led to a well-lit crumbling home made of patched-up bamboo strips. It stood in a crowded area, homes so close to each other that only a one-man path separated these homes. The door was wide open, and they climbed up some wooden steps on a house supported by what looked like shaky wooden stilts. The space where the coffin was laid out was tight; acquaintances and friends sat on metal chairs surrounding the coffin in hopes that their presence would comfort the family in their moment of grief. Monica looked around to search for Armando. Uncle Indong and Monica slowly tiptoed with their heads held down to respect the people and said,

"Maayong gabi" (Good evening), answered by a unison greeting as well.

A young lad called for Armando, and he appeared from a squeaky door just beside the spot where Monica was standing. Armando was dressed in his best outfit. He was a good-looking young man, rather tall, five feet eight inches or so, brown-skinned, and with high-cheekboned, chiseled features, who presented himself despite his means. Moni never thought he was this poor. He never showed it nor did he behave or appeared like one. Moni tried to put on a pleasant face. He lived in a very small home occupied by a family of five. The bedroom was probably used as a closet. The wood-burning stove and a small kitchen table could be seen by the door. Armando met them; his demeanor of embarrassment showed. She immediately handed him the packages, containing several loaves of bread, sandwich spread, a jar of instant coffee, canned milk, and the envelope. Armando smiled and said thanks to both of them. It was customary for the host to offer snacks to those who came to offer support to the family in this moment of grief. Some mourners might have been able to offer help, such as Moni, but if most of the mourners were his neighbors, they could not contribute food or money to the grieving family. In fact, some, out of poverty, came to have something to eat.

There were no more seats. A young girl attempted to get up to offer her seat, at which Moni signaled to tell her it was all right. Moni and her uncle approached the wooden coffin and saw a wrinkled, thin-to-the-bone man dressed well in a new white long-sleeved shirt and black pants that were too big for him. His arms folded on his chest, his hands clasping a black rosary; he seemed to be at peace. He had had a hard life and had been unable as a man to provide for his family. He probably never wore clothes like this when he was alive. Armando dressed his father the way he always presented himself at the store. Too bad his father could not enjoy it, nor was he able to say thanks to his eldest son. Armando's father had probably been a handsome man in his prime. Indeed, Armando took after his father's features. As they stood there saying a prayer, Armando approached them with a woman whom he introduced as his mother named Sarah. His mother was engulfed in grief and managed a smile. A frail woman, she stood with drooping shoulders and slowly walked away to sit again. She looked very tired. She was very tiny, five feet tall or so; her printed cotton dress hung loosely with a belt to make it fit better. Her wrinkled face was fair with fine features and depicted deep sorrow. She struggled to smile, which was sincere, despite the deep sorrow. Armando pointed to his two younger brothers, who approached Moni and said hello. Their names were Podong and Seray. They appeared young but worried. The talk was brief. His father had an illness that the doctors could not treat. He had actually died in his sleep.

 It was almost eleven at night. Jeepneys were rare; the place was quite far from their home. Uncle Indong asked Moni as they were walking to the main road, "Imo kadtong trato?"

 "Dili oy, amigo nako sa trabaho."

 Uncle Indong had asked Moni if that was her boyfriend. Moni denied it. She told him Armando was a good friend and always helped her at the store. When she was tired, he would do most of the hard work at the store. They finally reach the main road, and they opted to take a cab, since they would have to take two jeepneys to reach home. Moni pictured Armando's trip to work and possibly the long walk to defray transportation cost. She felt so sorry for him. She recalled her home in Villalon, how spacious it was, owned and erected on a large piece of land while Armando lived in a squatters' area (a term used to name those individuals who occupied a land belonging to someone else). Some arguably paid the landowner some rent, but the majority did not. He lived in a falling-apart shack so small that the family probably slept on the floor where the body was laid. At this time, they probably slept in the small room where Armando emerged. He was very, very poor. Now, having lost his father, he alone would have to provide for his family. As they arrived home, Moni could not sleep. She wanted to help him. His mother was so frail and had no means.

Armando reported to work, clean as usual and with a smile. He thanked everybody, his coworkers, for the help. He did not talk much nor complain. Nobody except Moni knew how miserable he was. Mostly, he was grateful to Moni, whose effort to help was admirable. In silence, he was ashamed that she had discovered how pitiful and poor he was. His love for her had gone deeper, knowing the real person she was. Since that episode, they became good friends.

Chapter Twelve

The semester went by, and Moni finished another phase of her life. Her grades were acceptable. The job was fine, and she received another raise. She was even offered a salesgirl position, which she refused due to the responsibility that it entailed. She intended to continue her studies, and the added responsibility might be too difficult. Delina's business picked up again, and Moni delivered the clothes. Pina had not been able to help except for tasks such as hemming, mending, and some ironing. She was not capable of procuring a job outside the home. Her mental state, such as it was, was not quick enough for her to handle a demanding boss. It was never disclosed that the bleeding event could have affected her mental state. A doctor was not consulted. There was no money to spare.

One Thursday night, Moni asked her coworker to cover for her. The request was granted. She spent the evening with Uncle Indong. She bought restaurant food and made fruit salad. She expressed her gratitude to the family and how she was accepted as if she was their child. She also told her uncle that she requested four weeks' unpaid vacation, allowing her to visit her parents.

Moni's mother was surprised to see her. The home she grew up in was the same, except the portion of the dining that needed some repair. She was gone for almost six years, and her father had been doing construction work elsewhere, unable to fix his home. During the four weeks' stay, it was almost difficult to sleep in her noncushioned bed. It was rather embarrassing to think of it, having been in this bed until age twelve. She kept herself busy and tried to help her mother make clothes. Moni was not good at it. She was limited to hemming and sewing button holes, ironing the finished product. Her mother made several clothes in different sizes. She brought it to Naval, and the store sold it. Moni thought of it as ingenious, and her mother thought of it as amazing. Her mother denied that it was her idea but, rather, the store owners' offer. She started making three clothes of three sizes to start with and went into six garments of each design. She was very busy. The boys were alone doing the coco tidbits, and they delivered the merchandise and the clothes to Naval every two weeks. They could now afford an occasional trip to see a movie. In fact, they did when Moni was there. Moni visited her grandmother often. While she was there they had long talks about Moni's father and his effort to please her. The days went so fast but memorable. She almost did not want to go back to Cebu.

When she arrived at Cebu, Delina had so much to do. She was up most of the night, and it showed. She looked very tired and weary. Moni had to go back to work. While she was gone, Aunt Delina did the delivery of clothes herself. Moni was back, and the Friday afternoon routine to the Bonedotos' resumed, if there was any to deliver. She went to school to enlist the subjects she had to take for the coming semester. The subjects she wanted to take were full. She had to take another math subject and history. As experience taught her, she only took two subjects to be able to cope with school and work.

Friday after school, she hurried home to do Aunt Delina's errands. It was midday, and the trip back to the city might take long. As soon as she arrived, Aunt Delina had the package ready, labeled properly. As predicted, the trip was longer than usual. Jones Avenue, a broad street, was packed with jeepney drivers waywardly overtaking each other to catch the passengers, nannies picking up schoolchildren, university students heading home, and all sorts. Moni stopped at the corner and hurriedly walked to the inside road. It was faster. She prayed that all the clothes would fit right and no alterations would be required. True enough, it was a good day. She received the money. Marcelina, the lady helper, always packed the leftover food and gave it to Moni. They became acquainted with each other although they never had a chance to have a talk. Again, it was a good afternoon with gourmet food from the rich. As Moni was hurrying to leave the house, a beautiful well-dressed woman entering the household accompanied by one of her servants called her attention and wanted to speak to Moni about something. It was rather important. The lady took her address and said she wished to see her by Sunday. She requested her to be home. Moni immediately told her that it must be in the morning, since she worked at two in the afternoon. She did not think about it, since she had a job. The walk to the main road was quick. She could not wait to look at the food she was bringing and, admittedly, wanted to eat it. They had a feast that evening.

True enough, Sunday morning at nine, the lady came. They were all up preparing for the ten o'clock mass, which they normally attended. Uncle Indong opened the door to meet a uniformed man and a white car parked on the street where a lady was waiting inside. When he appeared at the door, the lady stepped out to meet him by the gate. Judging from her demeanor, manner of dressing, and being chauffeured by someone, she was somebody with money. Despite her status, she slightly bowed her head as she entered, a respectful gesture of a young person to an elder. It was not expected because rich people normally would never do such a thing to a person of lower status. Uncle Indong invited her in. She introduced herself as Esther Romualdo. She was asked to sit on the couch, which she readily did without hesitation. Uncle Indong unfolded one of the metal chairs and sat in front of her. She did not look around to investigate the property but sat comfortably speaking to Uncle Indong in a rather respectful way that a younger person would speak to an elder.

Uncle Indong, thankfully, was dressed in church clothes. They introduced each other. She said, "Si Esther Romualdo ako."

He asked, "Manga Romualdo sa Tacloban?"

"Bitaw, gikan sa Tacloban."

"Taga Leyte usab kami . . . sa Villalon."

"Unsa ma'y ato?"

"Ako untang hangyo-on ang imong anak nga si Moni maoy mobantay sa among inahan."

"Oh! Si Moni akong pagumangkon. Nganong ka-ila man ka niya?"

The conversation was that the lady and Uncle Indong had originated from the same province, which was Leyte. They spoke the same dialect.

"I saw her at the Bonedotos' when she delivered clothes. I happen to like her and I am here to offer her a job. Being that she is young, I thought I should meet the parents or guardian out of respect."

She continued, saying that she, Moni, would accompany Esther's elderly mother to the United States to visit her other daughter for two years. Her duties would be as an attendant to her mother. She did not have to cook nor wash. Her compensation was fifty dollars every two weeks, which he as her guardian could collect in Cebu if he wished to do that. Esther would need an answer in two or three weeks. There was a time limit so they could find another one in the event Moni refused the offer. Uncle Indong understood the proposal. She gave her telephone number, and Uncle Indong told her where he worked.

Moni came down eventually and met the lady again. She was surprised to learn of her request, since they must have several helpers in their home who presumably were more familiar to the elders' needs and sorts. She did not say what was in her mind. Logically, the offer was difficult to refuse, because financially, it was a lot of money. If she agreed, she could save fifty dollars a month, and in two years, barring any circumstantial problems, she would have enough tuition money and miscellaneous expenses. She would be a full-time student with the possibility of excellent performance. She would be older.

The lady left with some hope, especially the fact that they came from the same region and that Moni spoke their dialect. They usually walked to the nearby church on Sundays, but that day, they took the jeepney because they would be late. Moni thought of this offer all the way to church, at church, and from church. Theoretically, it was a good offer. Others would grab it in a heartbeat. Dee was not there. She had to work an extra day. After church, they talked about it for a short while because Moni had to leave for work. Her uncle did not encourage her to take the job nor otherwise. It would have to be Moni's decision. Moni never spoke about it at work. It was something she could not talk about because the lady could change her mind. She concentrated on her work and tried not to dwell on it. She was home late due to several customers who came in a few minutes before closing time. The store had to accommodate them. The store did not offer overtime money, nor was a worker compensated for the extra time the employee extended to entertain the customers. Nobody complained, afraid of losing their job.

Uncle Indong stayed up and was reading the Sunday paper. It was obvious he had read it over and over again. It was most kind of him to stay and wait for Moni, mainly to speak to her about the offer. Moni smiled at him, a gesture of thanks for being kind enough to be interested in her welfare. Although he was her guardian, it was never formally stated as such. He advised Moni to write to her parents about the offer and her possible decision and to give them the authority to express their opinion on the matter. He could also write a consent letter for them in the event that it was required immediately.

She wrote a letter to her parents about the offer and to ask for their consent. The job offer was there for the taking, and it was up to her and her parents if they would allow her to accept it. It was theoretically positive but risky as well, since nobody knew how she would be treated in that foreign country. His concern was molestation and her inability to fight, being poor and underrepresented. It was a job that sounded so lucrative, yet her safety was so uncertain. A few weeks went by, and no word was received from Esther Romualdo. Moni had almost forgotten about the offer and concentrated on school and work. Pina had been well and helping Aunt Delina with her sewing. Dee continued working at the store without complaining. Moni did not receive any letter from her parents about the request and was worried that the letter was not received. She sent a telegram instead of writing again.

Tuesday night, Uncle Indong notified Moni that Lady Romualdo had called him at work and inquired about her answer. A decision had to be made since processing the papers took long. Moni said it would be unfair to the lady if she consented to it, just to tell her later that she was not. She might have trouble finding someone to their liking. The troubling news came when a telegram was received that Moni's parents did not consent to it, although they stated that they were coming to address the issue. She confided to her uncle about the decision. He apparently asked the secretary of the company, whom he knew quite well, if she would write a consent letter for him as the guardian of Moni. It was all prepared and ready for her. It would be kept in the drawer, since this letter might offend Moni's parents. They might think of it as overstepping their grounds. This could cause family disunity.

To Moni's surprise, her parents came one Friday morning when she was just leaving for school. It was a temptation to miss school. Moni never missed school unless she was ill. The short hello at the door kept her excited. Her parents came on a day when they could enjoy an evening together. She hurried home from school. The discussion that night would be about her trip abroad. It would be a long talk, and she prayed that her parents would eventually consent to it. She did not want to hurt their feelings, having to defy them. Her parents' concern was understandable. The tone of their voice changed when Uncle Indong told them who offered Moni the job. The Romualdo family had a reputation of treating their workers fairly. Although Moni did not have a definite answer that night, the decision seemed favorable. The parents would talk further that night. The evening went well. Dinner was delicious.

Moni was anxious of the possible outcome. She had no school, but she had to work the next day. She was hoping that the final decision would be good for her future. Morning came, and they were having breakfast. Moni was trying to be polite. She waited until the subject matter came up. It was almost a long wait. Uncle Indong was going to work late and wanted to participate in the discussion at dinnertime, which could have been the reason that they deferred talking about it until Indong came home. Finally Simeon brought it up. They would indeed sign the consent. Uncle Indong pretended to tell them that he would have the papers drawn and it would be ready that afternoon. Simeon and Maxi were not leaving till Monday, and they would have the chance to meet Esther Romualdo. Uncle Indong called Lady Romualdo and asked if she could come to his home to meet Moni's parents. He apologized for the short notice. In fact, she was very accommodating and was delighted to meet the parents.

Sunday was the day. When Lady Esther came at nine in the morning, they were all ready for her. She was on time. Uncle Indong left the parents and Moni in the small sitting room with Lady Esther. She was very pleased to meet Moni's parents. She reiterated to them the terms of employment. The necessary papers must be procured so a visa application could be filed. The suggested time was four to six weeks after the necessary papers were received. Moni's parents were not so happy, but they complied. Moni was able to take off that Sunday. The three of them went to the city.

Moni expressed her gratitude to her parents. She had mixed feelings about the job. She did not understand the reason for choosing her, since the lady did not really know her. She promised to be good and would continue to behave. They talked about her years at Uncle Indong's home and how well she was treated, the ordeal that the family went through when Pina took ill, and the emotional and financial hardship they had to bear. Simeon said that the family of Ido had been massacred by a simple weapon that farmers used to cut bushes. Moni was surprised that her father knew about it. Although, looking back to her childhood, her father had read the papers whenever he could get hold of one. It was news that the family in Leyte celebrated. After all, he had committed heinous acts toward a member of the family.

Maxi would be busy procuring the necessary papers. The town of Naval was rather small, and obtaining the papers should not take long. The boat left that Monday, and Moni took a night off to see them leave. It was agreed that when Moni left for Manila, they would come to see her. The length of time from that moment on was not certain. For all they know, Moni might not be approved to leave. That week, Uncle Indong received a call from Lady Esther that she was mailing some important papers to his home. It was actually to ascertain if somebody would be home to receive it. The big brown envelope was delivered Thursday morning and received by Aunt Delina. It was instructed that Moni was to contact Langyaw Travel Agency for further information. A letter of definite employment stating Moni's name was enclosed. The letter confirmed it all. A check was also addressed to Moni to cover the cost. Moni's fear was her inability to finish the semester, in case it would happen soon

Moni did not count the days. She was eager and worried and wished the days would be longer. It was almost a decision that she regretted since she was content—at school, at her job, and she had parents that were lucky enough to afford her tuition. It disrupted her plan in life. The eagerness to see other places had enticed her to go. Being a daughter of a poor family, this offer to travel fully paid to the United States was an opportunity one would regret to pass up. In her young mind, she never entertained the thought of going to places beyond her means. School and work were the same, and the days went quickly. Aunt Delina had been bringing Pina with her to deliver clothes. In time, Pina would be able to assist her in anticipation of Moni's absence. Moni was happy that Pina might be of help to her mother, although Pina was still slow in her interaction and understanding instructions. Moni, having done those errands for Aunt Delina, doubted her capability and was sad that Aunt Delina would not be able to rely on Pina to do errands for her. In time, perhaps, Pina would return to normal.

The express mail from home with the required papers arrived. She brought it to the travel agency on her way to work. She was informed that it might take four to six weeks for the visa to be approved if everything went well. Then a ticket would be purchased. Moni told Aunt Delina of the possible date of her departure. In the meantime, Lady Esther called Uncle Indong about the possible outcome and the anticipated date of departure. Moni did not want to leave if the semester was not over. It was a question that she did not want to ask even though she thought of this before she decided to go. She was hoping her wishes would be granted, without causing trouble. She was doing well in school. She might get second place in her subjects. Despite being a part-time student, she would be recognized if her grades were excellent. Six weeks went by, and there was no news of the visa being approved. Moni had four weeks to finish the semester. She might still finish, would be credited for the subjects, and be considered for the first year at teaching school. In the meantime, she had another raise at work and was able to save more money. She continued buying food on Saturdays even though Uncle Indong was not financially hard up. Dee would take some subjects that coming semester and possibly work at the same time. Coordinating work and school might be difficult, but the way it looked, she intended to attend school full-time. Dee, after some serious thought, finally left her housekeeping job.

Uncle Indong received a call from Lady Esther that Moni might leave in four weeks. She would finish the semester. She would prepare her clothes for the trip. Aunt Delina was contemplating on making a jacket lined with two flannel fabric to keep her warm for the trip, a crocheted vest made of wool, and a pair of slacks to travel. The small straw suitcase would be sufficient to bring her clothes. They might leave at the end of November, and Lady Romualdo advised her that it was winter in the United States. If her job was to attend to the elder's needs, then fancy clothes were not necessary, and whatever she had would be sufficient. Her one outfit for church was presentable enough according to her standard. If the coolness persisted, she would need another sweater. She had no idea what cold meant, but assuming that they were well off, the main house must be warm for the elder, and she would be warm too. At night, as the days went on, and the date of departure had not been set, she would think of her parents, her bamboo home, and her temporary abode, wondering if she made the right decision or if her ambition to see places and earn an easy buck could cause her failure to enjoy life. That need to excel might result in unhappiness. She had plans to help Dee. She would send her two weeks' pay to Uncle Indong to help him pay for her tuition. Uncle Indong did not know her plans, but if everything went well, she would be able to afford it.

One Friday night, Uncle Indong wanted to have a long talk with Moni. Seated at the dining table and Moni sitting beside him, his palms grasped Moni's left hand lovingly and held them on the table. He expressed his gratitude and appreciated her for being such a behaved young adolescent who had, in fact, been so considerate and generous with herself. He mentioned how Moni at a tender age had participated in the family's affairs and problems. He recalled his daughter's ordeal and how she was so smart to have brought some money, which he, the adult, the head of the family, did not think of. He was smiling, shaking his head, embarrassed of his inadequacy; he had allowed his anxiety to overpower his sense of responsibility. In hardship and crisis, Moni was there to help, not only emotionally but financially. He, as stated, would not be able to pay back the money she had given nor did he make note of how much he owed her. He was sorry for his lack of skill and, admittedly, almost unable to handle such a challenge. Her help was most appreciated, and he hoped he had conveyed his love and gratitude and that she was treated well, living in his humble home comfortably. If she was uncomfortable living in his home and felt maltreated, it was inadvertent, and he apologized for it. Moni shed a tear of happiness that in the years of her stay, she had been recognized, although it was unsaid until that time. A feeling of sadness and happiness engulfed her, being that in a few weeks, she would have to leave this family whom she had learned to care for. As a young girl, she did not know how to respond, nor was she equipped with words to articulate how she felt at that moment. With her head down, she let her tear drop, occasionally wiping it with her hand, and she said in almost a whispering sob, "Salamat," a thank-you that she hoped was heard since a lump in her throat had prevented her to speak. He added that he was concerned about this venture in such a faraway land, so unreachable for a family of no means to rescue her in the event that she would be oppressed and maltreated. If a misfortune should happen, she should not hesitate to write for help and help will be sought for. His boss was the grandson of a senator and might have some connections to address the problem. He understood her ambition to do better and hoped that her dreams would come true. He had ventured in his youth, and the long and thorny path he had struggled to tread has finally cleared. It was a memorable night for her, still trying to absorb and recall Uncle Indong's words. In her bed, she looked out the window on her knees to view the scene outside and, in between, would lie down staring at the ceiling. She did this several times. Pina was asleep; so was Dee. After all the restless moving, she finally dozed off.

It was several weeks, and she had not heard from Lady Romualdo. She would have enrolled already if this offer had not come up. The anxiety of being in limbo and missing school was bothering her. She did not tell anyone. She was almost embarrassed to have accepted the job just to be informed that it did not go through. If, after all, the job was canceled, she would miss a semester of school, and it would devastate her. December was fast approaching. She would put in extra hours at the store if asked. She had no school. She would do most of the chores and the large bulk of the wash with Dee's help on Saturdays. Aunt Delina did not have to do it. Pina was not able to do heavy work but able to iron and mend clothes. She kept on accompanying her mother with errands, hoping that she would learn and eventually do it by herself. Aunt Delina did not ask Moni to do her usual errands. Dee was now a full-time student. She studied every night and was not able to talk, and a short hello was all she would say. Dee was very serious with school. There were occasions when they were doing the wash in a cemented space just outside the kitchen door, squatting, doing the wash by hand. Each of them would have a large basin when Dee would pause to look at the wash as if reading and murmuring something. Moni thought, *Dee must be studying in her mind while doing the wash*. Moni never commented on it nor did she make any faces, rather admiring her for the seriousness she put into her studying to succeed.

Chapter Thirteen

Christmas was fast approaching, and Moni bought gifts for everybody using her discount coupons. She purchased shoes for Uncle Indong's family. She was planning to take a week off to visit home, probably after the Christmas holiday when the store might be not be as busy since gift shopping was over. If the request would be granted, she would buy shoes for her family as well. The request was filed. There was no word from Lady Romualdo. The request for a week off was denied. Moni was sad. There was no reason since nobody was taking off. That second week of December, she purchased shoes for her family. A surprise call was received by Uncle Indong at work from Lady Romualdo. The visa was approved, and the anticipated departure would be the first week of January. Moni sent a telegram to Villalon. Her whole family came a week before Christmas. As usual, they brought an ample supply of smoked meat, which could last for six months if the frugal habit of consumption was kept as such.

Her parents looked well. The clothing business and sales of cacao bits were better, more than expected. Avelino took the responsibility of bringing the goods to Naval and various crafts such as baskets. He would hire the *sakayan* and would have people handle the wares efficiently. He was only fourteen, and he showed business expertise negotiating with storeowners. Her father built a cottage at the back of their home to store a large amount of bamboo for sale. Nemesio maintained the bamboo business as well as process them ready for the customer. Maxi's younger brother, Meliton, had been an assistant to Simeon and watched the business while they were gone. Avelino expressed his desire to go to school in Cebu. Uncle Indong and Delina were happy to hear it, having had a pleasant experience with Monica. The town built a health center near the school. Simeon built it for the town. Everything was good news. The only sad news was Moni's departure.

Moni stayed on the third floor of Uncle Indong's home after work. She spent every waking moment with her family. There was a lot of floor space to fit all of them. Most of all, she wanted to be close to her mother. Her parents felt the loneliness of her leaving and would stay up most nights to talk. Despite her definite departure, Moni had not filed her letter of resignation at work. She was so attached to her job plus there was the fear that her trip might not be true. She took a sick time, and for the first time, she lied that she was sick just to be with her family. Nemesio went to the city almost every day, and Avelino went with Uncle Indong to work. He was introduced to the big boss. Uncle Indong was hoping to get him a job after he finished school. Avelino enjoyed the days with Uncle Indong even though he was not paid. He was a welcome help to his uncle, who for so many years had worked alone without a break.

Maxi helped Delina with her craft. There were many dresses to be made, and they had to be ready for the Christmas Eve mass. It was hectic. Pina could only hem clothes. Her ability to help remained limited. Her parents accepted the fact that she might not be independent and would have to be cared for the rest of her adult life. When Indong and Delina reached their twilight years, help might be necessary to keep things going in the household. Simeon would look at Pina with such pity, and in silence, he felt the agony of her parents. He would never say it. He would recall that night when she had come hungry and hurt. He sometimes had a grin on his face, which he tried to hide.

The family had a get-together Christmas Eve. Moni gave her gifts, and it was a grand occasion. Noodles with shrimp were a delight to all, being it was an expensive dish to cook. Pina kept smiling and never said a word. Moni's family and Uncle Indong all received a pair of shoes. They were amazed that Moni knew their shoe size. Moni had bought them one at a time using her coupons.

They were all stashed underneath her wooden bed. There was lots of laughter that night. There were stories of Uncle Indong's childhood when he would eat most of the pastries up from the coconut tree before selling it. Therefore, the sales money was not as expected, and he would be questioned by his mother. When she learned that he was hungry, his mother would feed him first before he went out. It solved the problem. It was a memorable night. In between, Uncle Indong and Simeon went outside the courtyard and had an intense talk. Everybody went to bed late that night.

Moni slept with her mother and talked about her future. Moni mentioned the chance of saving enough money for school and never having to work in between. There would be enough tuition money. She was looking forward to seeing places that no ordinary person would be able to. Maxi listened to her daughter's plans, and although she never approved of her leaving, she realized the need for children to fly and find their own nest. She assured her that since her new employer spoke the same dialect, she would get along with her. They talked about letters to write and to watch out for her mail. Moni suggested that Avelino could help delivering mail so Moni's mail would be processed readily. Apparently, Noy Tiqiou had a part-time assistant in sorting the mail. He had been hired by the town due to an increase in population. Days went by so quickly, and Moni's family had to leave. They brought all the necessary sale items to bring home. Moni went with them to the pier. The boat had few passengers when they boarded, so they had the first choice. The items bought were all stashed underneath the bed and were all set. It was rather windy and cold that time of the year. Uncle Indong joined them from work and informed them of Moni's departure, which would be in a week. Moni would be brought to Lady Esther's home the night before since they were leaving for Manila at dawn. They were leaving for the United States that same day at ten in the morning. Moni's family listened carefully to have a little knowledge of their daughter's agenda. It sounded complicated—being farmers and unaccustomed to complicated plans in life. Moni stayed until they were ushered to leave. They had nothing to talk about. They looked at each other, feeling the closeness and love they shared.

It was a moment Moni would always remember. Nothing was said. It was not a custom in her family to hug each other, but this time they did. It was awkward. She exited quickly and down the ladder, afraid of her indecision. Going down that ladder, she thought of the length of time she would not see her parents. Moni watched the ship leave the harbor and forbade herself to cry. Moni's parents stood by the railing and waved. Indong and Moni stood by the pier for as long as they could see her parents. Uncle Indong held her hand until the ship was beyond their sight. He knew how she felt, for once upon a time he had also left his hometown to explore. It was a slow walk to the corner, as if Moni were carrying a heavy load and thinking if she made the right decision. The decision had been made. Her pursuit of becoming a teacher was deferred. If her plan would materialize, she would be a teacher in her town and live a respectable life. She would be comfortable. That was the future she was looking forward to. She would miss her parents, Uncle Indong, whom she had learned to love, and her friends. It was late and the jeepneys were not full, so they arrived home in time to get enough rest. Aunt Delina was still up, doing finishing touches on a dress. Uncle Indong was quiet and went to bed. Moni could not sleep. She was kneeling by the window, looking out. No one was there. It was past midnight.

The week went by, and Moni kept recalling the time with her family and kept pacifying herself that two years would go quickly. Moni filed a letter of resignation two weeks before her anticipated departure. She asked Dee if she was interested in taking her job. Dee thought it over and looked at her schedule. At the moment, it seemed impossible. She would, however, think about it and fix her schedule so that she would be off afternoons. The job was available by mid-January, and coordinating school and work might be possible. Dee was intent on finishing school, and working was not in her agenda. She had to compete high marks to be able to be accepted at the Island Hospital School of Nursing. There were many candidates, and Dee had to compete. Dee opted not to take the job.

Meanwhile, Armando had been working many hours. He looked thin and weary-eyed. Monica, having seen his father, was looking at his father without the coffin. He lost his smile and was cranky. Moni, being close to him, commented on his behavior. He readily accepted the criticism and tried to change. The reason, of course, was he was overworked. Moni, during the weeks that she was there, would allow him to take naps while she would not. It was the least she could do for him. He had been good to her at the time when she needed it. She continued giving him the discount coupons and brought him some smoked meat from her home. The news of her resignation was big news at the store. Her coworkers bid her good-bye and wished her the best of luck. She did not tell them the real reason for leaving. She told them she would concentrate on school to become a teacher. Despite her coworkers' lack of means, Moni received farewell gifts such as embroidered handkerchiefs, scarves, and sorts. There was a small get-together after work at a small restaurant, paid for by everyone who was there. She had never known she was well-liked until that moment. Moni had to let Armando swear to secrecy about her future whereabouts. She took his address, which he said to address it to the town. He lived in Labangon, and he had a friend at the town office who would receive his mail. It was arranged that she would write to him. Moni's friend at the Bonedotos' had to be informed, so she wrote a note to Marcelina. There were no clothes to deliver nor was there any chance to go there. A surprise visit by someone of her status would not be proper, so a letter was mailed to her.

She did not want the day to come. It would mean not seeing her family for two long years. Christmas with her family at Uncle Indong's was a treat. Dee talked about her school and how difficult it was to obtain high marks. She was trying her very best but doubted her ability to compete. Moni had left her job. She was given three six-hour days' separation pay, which was a big surprise. Being that she had money in the bank and her parents did not need money, she gave half of the money to Uncle Indong.

Moni was surprised when her parents came to see her for two days. It was memorable. January in this part of the world would be cooler than usual. The winds were so fierce and strong that an underweight, small-statured person would have to brace oneself and stop in between walks to remain standing. A scarf had to be worn and both hands placed on face and eyes to keep away the dust and the piercing wind. Normally, a *sakayan* would not risk transporting passengers from one shore to the other, although taking the bus could be an alternative. Above all, the boat ride was risky and the ride very uncomfortable. The boat could capsize. Despite the difficult trip, her parents came, and they had a get-together. Moni was grateful that her parents came to see her despite the anticipated bad weather. Her parents did not stay long. Two days spent with them was precious. Apparently, they arrived home safely.

Aunt Delina made a thick jacket and two black pants for her. Her straw bag was big enough to accommodate the few belongings she required. She would be staying home to care for an elderly person whom she did not know and wondered if she would be easy to get along with. Moni would have to endure the future. The few days left in her uncle's home were most precious. She spent time with Uncle Indong, Aunt Delina, and her cousins. Being inarticulate, she tried to express her sincere appreciation in the simplest way she could convey it. Aunt Delina cried and embraced her tight and whispered what a behaved child she had been and her gratitude toward Moni. She said, "Daghang salamat sa imong pagtabang," basically thanking Moni for her help in moments of crisis. Pina remained the same. She seemed unaffected by her leaving. Moni sat with her and told her that everything would be fine and that she would write. Pina smiled and said a very subdued thank-you. Thankfully, she was still able to talk and understand simple things, but she was slow.

Dee was eager to tell Moni about her progress and the big possibility of her entrance into the school. Dee asked Moni to write and to keep her informed. Uncle Indong seemed financially comfortable, having to pay less payment since the mortgage would be paid off in a few years. The remaining nights of her stay were fruitful and worth remembering. Moni was glad that she had these few nights with them. She used to work six evenings a week, and she never had the chance to have long talks like these.

Chapter Fourteen
The Romualdo Home

Thursday afternoon, Uncle Indong took off an hour early. Uncle Indong and Moni ate a huge dinner to anticipate the night because Moni might not be served dinner at the Romualdo home. She even brought biscuits to prepare for the night when the kitchen may not be accessible. Dee was at school. Moni kissed Pina and Aunt Delina good-bye. She whispered to Pina how much she cared for her and for her to stay well. Pina sat there unresponsive but shed a tear. She wanted to tell Moni how she felt but was unable to say it. She looked at Moni with such a feeling of love that unfortunately she could not express verbally. Uncle Indong accompanied Moni to the Romualdo home. Aunt Delina and Pina stood by the door to see Moni off. Delina wanted to have a last glimpse at this young girl who since age twelve had resided in their home. She had significantly touched their lives with her love and thoughtfulness. She walked up to the gate and watched them until they descended the hill and she could no longer see them.

That was the evening Moni would stay at the Romualdo home then leave for Manila to the United States in the early morning. She was thinking of her second home, where she was most welcome, never considered a burden to the family. She would always remember her adolescent years in Uncle Indong's home, the first day she had met the family accompanied by her mother. Uncle Indong carried her straw bag, which seemed small for a person traveling to the other part of the world. The both of them strolled slowly down the hill as

Moni looked around the poor neighborhood where she had walked every day. She wanted to capture the scene and the warm memories of her adolescent years.

The wait for the jeepney and the ride to Jones Avenue was quick. There were no passengers waiting at the corner, and the ride was quick. The walk to the inner road to the Romualdo home was rather long. It was intentionally done for them to be able to spend time with each other, almost like their last time to walk side by side. Moni was grateful. She took her time, almost not wanting to get there, because walking fast would shorten her memorable time with this man who with his simple ways had guided her all those years. Although she hardly needed help, he was always there for her and never denied her help. She recalled his kind words; the memory of it made her teary-eyed.

His sadness had slowed down his normal brisk walk. It was almost like he did not want her to leave, to venture to a faraway land. Due to poverty and the search for a better living, one had to leave a native land. He hoped that this decision was right. There was no talk between them, as if talking would disrupt the moment of joy. This simple act of walking together was a stroll that she would cherish. The house enclosed with concrete wall occupied half the block. The number 2 engraved on the concrete wall stood on a large piece of land. The concrete fence was so high that the house could not be seen at the spot they were standing. The steel door was wide, with a small entrance fit for one person. They both looked at the place for a good while, almost afraid to ring the bell for fear that it might be the wrong door. They stood there, not knowing what to do. It was too late for Moni to back out. She sort of entertained the idea, but indeed, it was too late. As they rang the doorbell, a uniformed man appeared from the small entrance, asked for the callers', names, and ushered them in. He was well advised to accept them.

The house was grandiose, with wide glass windows on the first and upper floor. To a poor person, it was a mansion. The home was surrounded by green grass and trees randomly planted. There was a slight uphill walk on a wide asphalted driveway lined with multicolored beautifully landscaped flowers. Two large pillars on each side stood in front as one stepped onto the marble floor and headed to the wide, shiny, sturdy wooden door. There were two cars parked in the driveway, and Moni recognized one of them. As soon as they stepped up and approached the wooden doors, a lady dressed in black with a white apron around her waist opened the door and led them to the sitting room. The white thick-cushioned couches were, to Moni, so large that if she sat on them all the way, she would be lying down. The space of the sitting room was triple the size of Uncle Indong's downstairs space. She looked up at the high ceiling and the white railing of the stairs that led upstairs. There seemed to be several sitting rooms, and understanding the setup was new to Moni. This house was much more complicated than the Bonedotos'. She observed all this while her uncle seemed relaxed. He looked as if he were used to this and sat quietly. Each window was draped with fine flowered material tucked at the sides. Several large vases held green plants, strategically placed. They looked real and enhanced an outdoor look. It smelled nice too, almost a fragrance of freshly harvested flowers. Of course, Monica did not see the fresh flowers in front of her on the lengthy glass table. She was too busy looking around. She did not hide her curiosity and appreciation of the place.

The same lady came smiling with a tray containing minute square sandwiches and a glass of juice for two. They were full, having eaten before they left. Moni, a young girl, was always hungry. When she saw food unknown to her, she immediately grabbed a sandwich. After Moni had had several, Lady Esther appeared elegantly, dressed in a peach pantsuit and beige low-heeled shoes. She looked taller, about five feet and four inches, hair pulled at the back, clear skin, delicate nose with full lips, and big brown eyes that smiled at them. Moni had not really looked at her long enough to appreciate her beauty at their first meeting because they had been in a hurry.

Lady Esther was pleased to see them and immediately extended a warm hand shake to both her guests. It was almost six in the evening, and Moni thought that she would have to say good-bye to Uncle Indong soon. Moni was advised of the evening routine. She was asked to go with the lady server and was led upstairs bringing her straw bag. Her bedroom to sleep in for the night was situated in the rear, overlooking the back street. She left her bag in the room as instructed and went back to join Uncle Indong. Lady Esther was still speaking to Uncle Indong, reassuring him that Moni would be safe with the Romualdos. She admitted to him the reason she was chosen. He was proud to learn the impression his niece had inadvertently imparted to the folks whom she had been in contact with of her humble demeanor. Dinner was to be served in an hour. Moni felt bad for her uncle, who would be home late because of her, although she thought he also might want to get to know the family. Dinner was served in another large room, and there was nobody else but the three of them. They were seated so far apart it seemed that either they were fighting or had a contagious disease and the farther they were to each other, the less chance they had of contracting the illness. The white, gold-rimmed dinnerware and sparkling cutlery that Moni saw in the book used in her home economics class was now in front of her. The placement of several spoons and forks and double plates was on that table for her to admire. She had done well in that class, and she, at one moment in her youth, had dreamt of having to sit at such a table. It came true. There were several dishes to choose from. Moni was hungry again. The lady servers went around. She tasted all the dishes—chicken cooked in some blue sauce, a meat dish, and the vegetables seemed to taste different, arranged in such a colorful manner. The dessert of peach topped with ice cream was almost too much for Moni. She ate it anyway.

    Moni watched how adept her uncle was in using the silverware and this manner of eating. She was more interested in eating rather than listening to Lady Esther. Apparently, her husband had passed on, and her son was at school in Manila. She lived there most of the months in a year. She would accompany Moni to Manila and would stay there for a while. She would go back and forth to Leyte, Manila, and Cebu. She was responsible in taking care of things, business management. She presented to Uncle Indong an envelope that contained Monica's passport and her airline ticket to reassure Uncle Indong, in case he had doubts. The evening went well. Moni asked Lady Esther if Uncle Indong could go up with her to see her room for the night and to have a moment with him outside until she should come in to retire. She consented, and her facial demeanor was very kind, almost knowing how Moni felt.

Uncle Indong saw her room for the night. He inspected the indoor lock to ascertain that she would be safe. He was not interested in how the room looked. Immediately they went out and down the wide stairs to go out. It was getting late. She had to be in by half past ten or earlier. As they reached the sitting room area, one of the ladies handed her a package. She said to bring it home. The leftovers from dinner were packed for them. Moni was delighted that Aunt Delina would have a taste of the food. The lady let them out, and Uncle Indong thanked her for her kindness. They walked slowly down the paved driveway. The gatekeeper let them out and told Moni to knock when she was ready to come in. Moni was impressed of the organization in such a home. They stayed out there in silence. Monica did not want to let her uncle go.

Her uncle said, "Sulati baya ko ha?" (Be sure to write.)

Moni nodded her head and ran to her uncle to caress him. In silence, they held each other. They parted and looked at each other as if they had not seen each other for a long time. Both of them felt the need to remember this short moment, for they may not see each other again. Moni was picturing her mother and her uncle that day she arrived in Cebu as they stood side by side. Her uncle, with his head down, looked up at the dark sky and said nothing. They seemed content standing there, near each other. Uncle Indong felt like a parent whose daughter he would not see for a long time. Finally, as if awakened from a trance, he headed toward the main road and waved a quick good-bye. He walked as if he were counting his footsteps and did not have the strength to pick up his feet. Every other step, he would look back and see Moni still there, by the gate, to possibly recall this moment. Moni stood there as if she were watching her parents on the boat and waited until his image was beyond her sight. She was standing there in the dark, crying, then sat by the curve, composed herself, and reminisced her childhood. She was there until she noticed that she was there very long and finally got up toward the door, stood by the gate for a while, and when she knocked, the gatekeeper let her in immediately. She dragged her feet as she walked up to reach the main door. The same lady opened the door for her and accompanied her to her room.

Her room for the night was painted white. A wide flowered rug occupied most of the wooden floors. The one window overlooking the street was draped with white lace curtains. The thick-cushioned bed was covered with a white bedspread on top and two oversized white lace-covered pillows. Beside it, a round wooden polished table held a medium-sized lamp and a radio clock. The room was larger than the girls' room at Uncle Indong's home. A sliding mirrored wall closet by the door with several bare hangers accommodated her straw bag. She was opening her bag to prepare her night clothes, when she heard a knock at the door. The lady dressed in a robe informed her that her night clothes had been placed underneath the pillow. It was for her to own. She was advised that the alarm would wake her up. She should be ready by quarter to five, then breakfast would be served. She acknowledged this with a quick nod.

She showered that night. The bedroom in this home had its own bathroom, so she really needed not hurry to get washed. She wanted to be sure she had enough time to get dressed. The bathroom was wallpapered with fine flowers of multiple colors. The towels and the shower curtain were white with fine light-blue flowers. She touched every item to ascertain that all of it was real. They had no bucket to contain the water. It took her long to maneuver the shower, adjusting the right temperature. She was not used to this convenience of having hot water. It was a shower that she would always remember. There was a terry robe for her and fragrance everywhere. The light-blue pajama set of silk material fitted her well. It was very thoughtful of Lady Esther to provide her with such an expensive wardrobe. She was up thinking of the difference between how the rich and the poor lived their lives. The fact that she had a taste of it was a comfortable feeling. This was borrowed time.

In the meantime, Indong took his time walking up the hill to reach his home. Delina was waiting for him. They talked about Lady Esther, her home, and the dinner. Dee went down to participate in the conversation. She tasted the leftovers. Pina was asleep. Delina told her husband that Pina seemed to feel Moni's absence and was very quiet. They talked about Moni's years in their home and the goodness she had shown the family. They already missed her and wished her the best of luck.

Meanwhile, Moni would think of her childhood and her sleeping quarters for the night. She dozed off after a warm shower and slept well, awakened by the alarm. It was rather loud, and it kept on ringing. She did not know how to shut it off. She left it ringing while she used the bathroom. She was ready in ten minutes and kept her door ajar to alert the caller that she was up. Breakfast was hearty, and she ate enough.

Chapter Fifteen

It was still dark, and the Lahug airport was not too far from the Romualdo home. The drive to the airport was quick. It was a long walk to the plane, and then the climb up the aluminum steps to the top was rather tiring. Moni thought that the elder would never be able to walk and climb the steps. It was Moni's first time to fly, and noticeably she was a newcomer, judging by her surprised look and awkwardness. There was an empty seat between her and the lady. She was very thankful for that because she did not smell fragrant or dress nice enough to sit directly beside Lady Esther. Lady Esther was attired with a pale-blue suit with a matching beige bag and shoes. She sat with a peculiar status and breeding indicative of having grown up with wealth.

Moni had no experience. Even the seat belt was difficult to fasten. She had to side glimpse at Lady Esther and emulated her. The engine's plane was on, and it had started to turn to wherever it had to go when a lady stewardess stood in front to demonstrate the must-know about the flight. One of them was how to fasten a seat belt and other safety procedures to be adhered to and the process to save oneself in the event of disaster.

She was holding on to the seat belt when the plane took off. Her ears were hurting, and the fear was indescribable. She had nobody to tell it to. But Lady Esther broke the silence, and she was kind enough to tell her that she had felt the same way when she flew for the first time. It was a small airplane accommodating a few passengers. As the plane leveled off, there was a welcome announcement from the pilot introducing himself and his assistant, information about the altitude and the length of time they had to fly. Moni thought the plane and the people in it would never survive a fall. Admittedly, Moni was afraid to die. There was never enough preparedness that would save them but an act of God that would keep them afloat in midair to land safely on flat, cushioned land. This thought was interrupted when a young beautiful stewardess came around to serve the snacks. Both ladies were attired in matching dark-blue blouses and skirts accented with a scarf of red, white, and blue. By the time they were done with coffee and *mamon* (cake), it was announced that they were ready to land in fifteen minutes. The landing was uneventful. This time around, Moni was used to the ear discomfort and the swallowing that had to be done to alleviate it. Lady Esther managed with her small suitcase; so did Moni.

They were met by the chauffeur. The elder was already in the car, and they looked at each other. Lady Esther quickly introduced her to Moni. The elder had no expression. Moni sat with the elder, and the lady sat at the front. They had to drive on to the international airport. It was busy, and several cars, including them, were crawling to their destination. It would have been faster if they had walked it. Lady Ramona Romualdo was poised and well dressed in a deep-blue pantsuit. She was stoic, with an aristocratic intense look. Her hair was properly done, her nails manicured. Moni was, for a moment, fearful that they would not get along. The airport was filled with passengers logging suitcases, porters, and families of travelers who were hurried and stressed-looking. They were lucky to find a spot and stopped where the elder did not have to walk very far to the entrance. She seemed able to handle the cane well with her right hand. She walked with a noticeable limp, but she was careful. Passengers were on line to enter, but when the guard saw the elder, she was signaled to go in first, including her companions. Tickets checked and were met by airline personnel with a wheelchair, and he wheeled the elder to the airline counter as directed by Lady Esther. There was no wait because their tickets were business class. The elderly lady did not have a suitcase. Moni's straw bag was the only item to be checked in, so she did not have a bag to carry except the elder's oversized purse and the jacket. Moni was all dressed with her vest and flannel-lined jacket. Aunt Delina prepared this outfit for her. For the moment, she felt warm in it, but carrying it with all the things she might have to do might be difficult. She did not want to lose it. She did not fully understand the meaning of winter or being cold until that time that she would experience it. Theoretically, she seemed to be prepared for it.

Normally only the passengers could come in, but due to Lady Esther's status, she was allowed to check them in. When it was all settled, Moni wheeled the elder, and she was led to a quiet spot where it was all explained to Moni—the important documents, the airline tickets, and the whole procedure, including the arrival at New York. It was placed in the side pocket of the elder's bag for Moni to hold. They stood there for a few minutes while Lady Esther was spending time with her mother. That was the time Moni understood the reason for her employment. She never knew traveling needed some education. Way back home, one took the *sakayan* paid the collector, and they arrived at the port, disembarked, taking their luggage, which was not marked with any identification. Finally, it was time to bid good-bye. Lady Esther kissed her mother and said, "Pag-ayo ayo didto."(Do take care.)

Lady Esther rubbed Moni's back and whispered "Thank you" and to take care of her mother as they entered the door, where only the ticketed passengers were allowed. It was around nine in the morning. They had an hour to find the gate and sorts. Monica felt appreciated for what Lady Esther did. The extent of the elder's communication skill was a nod and shaking her head. Up to this time she did not talk nor did she hear her voice. Here she was, very worried of how she would talk to her. It was most difficult, and most of all, she was not alerted of this hardship. Moni wished she would have been with her a few days before this trip, to get acquainted with her needs and mannerisms. She had two more windows to go through to pay some fees. It was all prepared for her in a labeled envelope, and she need not count the money. It was made easy for her. After passing the booths, she watched the signs and arrows to their assigned gate, which was actually simple. It needed a lot of focus, although if a mistake was made, they had ample time to find the designated gate. There were a few passengers at the designated gate waiting to board Pacific Airlines going to Hong Kong. As instructed, she brought the elder to the washroom. The door to the washroom was too narrow for the chair to get through, so the elder had to get up and use the cane. Luckily, there was nobody following her, since she was very slow. Moni felt so sorry for her. A blue uniformed lady was standing by, ready to clean any mishaps. She told Moni that the chair would be there for her. Moni stood by the bathroom stall, ready to assist her, but the elder was able to take care of herself. She needed minimal help. Moni felt inadequate, but again, she had been picked because they thought she could do the job. True enough, the wheelchair was there for her. She wheeled her near the counter for her to listen to when they would be called to board. Moni took a seat while the elder remained in the wheelchair. They were supposed to be among the first one to board, as instructed. The elder signaled Moni for her jacket, and she assisted her. The elder moved her limbs pretty well.

The elder refused food, which was available either from the various stores at the airport or the biscuits in her bag. Everything was organized. Money was prepared in an envelope labeled as such for Moni to use. It was a lot of money. It was equivalent to her two weeks' pay at her old job and may be spent at the airport if they had to. She was not hungry, which was unusual. The excitement of the trip occupied her thoughts. They were seated at a location where they would be able to watch the goings-on around them, the wide aisle where people went by hurriedly and the wide glass windows to view the large planes landing and taking off. She would be thinking of home and wished her family could experience this moment and enjoy the view. There were times when she was such in a trance that she immediately would look at the elder to check if she needed anything. She always had to remember that the elder could not speak and had no facial expression, although she was able to tap her arm in case Moni was too preoccupied with watching everything around her.

The uniformed personnel, walking briskly in front of them on that wide aisle, occupied her busy mind. Handsome men in blue suits with hats and name badges paraded in front of her, erect, like soldiers marching. The ladies too, in their well-pressed uniforms were all gorgeous. They walked and marched like her uncle as they went down that hill from his home. She enjoyed the sight of God's creatures, which she had no chance of seeing if she had not taken this job. In no time, the loudspeaker announced their flight, and specified passengers were to board first. Moni wheeled her to the gate, and the airline personnel took over the task. She thought the bridge connecting the airport to the plane a path difficult to maneuver, and she was not trustworthy-looking due to her thin stature. Besides, they had to return the chair that made it convenient. Having seen the plane from that window where they were waiting, it was much larger than the one they had taken in Cebu. The elder, slow as she was, managed to lift her feet awkwardly to the ascending steps when she was dropped off, relinquishing the chair at the airplane's entrance. As soon as they entered the plane, their seats were right there. Possibly, Lady Esther had advised the agent of the elder woman's predicament. Everything was planned. The elder took minute steps, and she could not be hurried due to her handicap. There was a long line of passengers, and they would have to basically crawl if they had had to follow the elder to reach their seats. The seats were wider compared to the airplane from Cebu. The seat could have accommodated two small stature persons comfortably. There were a few of them, around twenty seats. It was a bigger airplane and sat more passengers. It was separated with a curtain, as if the people at the back would tell all about the goings-on, in this section of the plane. Moni did not understand it. As she fastened their seat belts, and the takeoff was eminent, she was ready to swallow and clear her throat. She wanted to tell the elder about the routine, but she noticed that the elder was doing the same. It was obvious that the elder must have flown several times, and she had not forgotten the routine. The acceleration of the plane was faster, it seemed, and it leveled off quicker too. It bothered her because she did not understand how a larger plane could levitate faster. Anyway, she could not imagine the technicality of how it flew. She was no longer as fearful, having had the experience. She was picturing a bird flapping its wings and slowing down on air steady as it did and flaps its wings again to ascend. She realized how much in this modern world she would not understand. She hoped she would be able to study it and learn somehow.

The male steward stood in front to demonstrate the safety routine, the exit locations of the plane and the pilot's announcement. Moni listened to it and tried to concentrate since she had to take care of someone in the event of disaster. Surviving a plane crash was nil, and Moni definitely would not be around to answer the interrogations in the event of such disaster. Food was to be served, and the menu was distributed. The elder was capable of choosing from the menu, dishes with strange names. Moni followed suit since she did not understand any of those dishes. Dinner was served. Food was precut, and surprisingly, the elder was again independent. She handled the utensils well except the hot tea, which Monica had to give. She was not a difficult person to please. In fact, after dinner, the elder patted Moni's hand and nodded her head as a gesture of gratitude. The elder enjoyed the meal; so did Moni. It was supposed to be a three-hour flight as announced, so she had to bring her to the toilet before the anticipated time of arrival. She did just that. The descent and landing was uneventful. They disembarked last, in consideration of others who might be in a hurry to catch another flight. As soon as they stepped down from the plane, an airline personnel met the elder with a wheelchair and wheeled her to the waiting area after inspecting the ticket. Moni followed him and was grateful that she need not ask nor figure out what to do. It would be a three-hour wait at the airport. Moni compared the airport in her country and the need for improvement her homeland had to do to compete with the progress the other countries had achieved.

The facilities in Hong Kong were cleaner and more impressive than the Manila airport. She gave some water to the elder, as had been advised and written by Lady Esther. She learned from her the body's need to replace the water that had inadvertently been lost during these flights. She did not really understand it, but she just followed directions. It was all written for her, and she had no reason to say she forgot about it. Again, she knew the reason of her employment. Somebody had been watching her at the Bonedotos' when she had interacted with the family and her ability to listen and comprehend. Her performance at school and her college credits had earned her this sought-for job, which she had almost refused due to fear.

The elder, Senora Ramona, drank the water as offered. She would be toileted before the flight. She accompanied the elder to take some slow walks on the very wide aisle of the airport. Considering her age and handicap, she actually did well. That was their exercise, and they would do another short walk, one before the flight. It would be a nineteen-hour flight via Pan-Am Airlines to New York. If Lady Esther did not rewrite the information on another paper, labeled each envelope as to their contents, with precise instructions as to when she needed to present them, such as tickets and identifications, to show at each connecting flight; she would be lost. It was written as such and so easy to understand. Moni thought the rich are rich because they plan and think of future situation. It was such a learning experience, and she was grateful to have had this exposure, which she definitely would follow when she was fully grown.

They were all set to board, and the airline personnel wheeled the elder down the ramp. Again, they were accommodated in front, and Moni took the window seat so the elder would be able to access the washroom. Moni knew the routine. She was now accustomed to it, and she felt the ease of doing it. She was no longer awkward in her ways. The airplane was larger, and Moni had relived the questions in her mind of how the plane levitates in air. She had memorized the instructions as demonstrated, but she listened to it again. She had trouble understanding it since it was delivered by a Caucasian lady whose accent she was not familiar with. For a moment, she was fearful of their arrival in New York, when everybody there, would surely speak in that manner. She looked at the instructed exits and wondered how in the world they would exit when the plane was in air. She was being silly, and having nobody to talk to, she would hide a smile. A male voice could be heard, identifying himself as the pilot, a polite welcome with information of the altitude, the route, and the length of the trip. After a while, Moni had already memorized the welcome speech and the tone and emulated in her mind the delivery.

She even entertained the idea that after teaching school, she would surely try working as a stewardess. It would be such an opportunity to see places. The elder had been cooperative and did not refuse the activities she needed to do as instructed. Moni was very happy and was looking forward to the years that she would be her caregiver. As she remembered, she needed not wash her clothes nor cook. She would never be able to cook for her, remembering the fancy dishes that had been served at Lady Esther's home. She could not begin to understand how those dishes were prepared. Certain recipes in her home economics class had not even been tried in their kitchen due to the expense.

She would order food for the elder, but as the menu was presented to her, she pointed it out, and Moni would order the same. The elder, despite her inability to speak, was able to read and understood the menu. Everything was delicious. The elder ate with a hearty appetite; she almost finished her portion. She thought of how she would hurry from the Bonedotos' home, bringing the leftover food for Uncle Indong's family.

Moni was conscious of her job and was afraid to doze off, for fear of not waking up when she was needed. Although, it would be terrible for her not to wake up with a light tap on her arm since she was seated beside her. The elder slept after the workers were done with their work. They both slept a long while. Moni looked at her timepiece and was counting the amount of time they were in the air. If the flight was as long as eighteen hours, they had a long way to go. She thought of those handsome, distinguished-looking blue-uniformed men marching in front of her, one or two of them possibly flying the plane to their destination. The elder looked comfortable and she stood up to stretch. She had a glimpse of the people seated on this section of the plane. They seemed to be all rich or hold a high-ranking position in their field. Moni felt small in front of these people. She would keep her head down, avoiding eye contact with them. Although, as she happened to glance back during a bathroom routine, an elderly lady managed to smile, solely to appease her discomfort. How very kind of her.

There were moments of uneasiness when the plane would suddenly lose its altitude and shake. They would be told to fasten their seat belts. Sometimes it would happen when they were serving food. The carts on the aisle would shake various drinks would spill as the workers tried to stabilize the cart. They seemed calm and handled the episode as expertly as they could. Moni would be discouraged, having thought of the job as glamorous. It was not. Soon it was time to eat again. Every time, it was a hearty meal, and the elder sometimes did not finish it. Moni felt like having it—not because of hunger but because it was such a waste to throw that food away. She was embarrassed to ask. She was told by a blond-haired smiling young stewardess that sandwiches were served in between dinner. She would have to ask for it. Moni thought the lady knew she could eat. She pointed to a call button, which she did not know was there, until it was shown to her. True enough, she was hungry, and she rang the bell. They were very accommodating to a poor young girl from the mountains. She would remember these moments. The sandwiches were even better tasting than the ones served at the Romualdo home. The elder had some to taste, but she did not have much. Moni ate enough. Juice was plentiful, and cut-up fruit was served with a smile. The elder slept in between the necessary disturbances and basically had no discomfort. Too bad they could not talk to each other.

They ate several times on that flight. Finally, it was announced that they were almost there. It was a clear sunny day. The pilot would speak, indicating their geographical location and which side of the plane to see it. She was tempted to get up but was embarrassed to do so. As they were descending, looking down from her window, she could see numerous tall buildings, cars on the roads moving like toys at a distance. Trees looked like sticks lined the roads, patches of large space of land, and gardens, possibly a bed of flowers indiscernible from the sky. The sight was like she was in heaven, looking down to enjoy the creatures, although nobody came back to tell anybody there was heaven. Humans could actually create their own heaven, and this moment was heaven to Moni. The announcement was clear that in fact, they would be landing in half an hour. The airplane kept descending in increments, but that scary feeling was there, fear of falling. The plane touched the ground smoothly, and there was some wait on the ground. As she checked the time, indeed they had been up in flight for the anticipated number of hours.

Chapter Sixteen

It was early Saturday morning. Lady Esther had explained the difference in time, but she did not understand it then. She thought of her geography class in high school and sort of tried to recall the globe in the library and the location of the United States which she should have studied again before taking this trip. They allowed the bulk of the passengers to exit first. As advised, somebody would be there to meet them, and they had to wait for their pickup. As the plane stopped and it was announced that their seat belts may be unfastened, she stood up waiting for the others to go. When everybody left, they started to leave. For some reason, the elder seemed slower this time but managed the descent from the plane. She looked tired. The airline personnel met the elder and assisted her to the wheelchair and wheeled her to the immigration area, which he was very familiar with. When they were on line the personnel signaled Moni to take over. A heavy-set uniformed lady directed them to a quick processing line, having seen the elder's weary-eyed look. There were no questions; papers were in order. She was fearful of not understanding the questions, thereby the delay.

Finding the baggage area was another long walk. They had to wait at the circle, which was called a carousel. Moni did not hear the number but followed the rest of the passengers, whom she recognized as they went by. The carousel was not a bunch of statue horses where children took a ride at a fair but something that propelled the airplane's baggage for the passengers to pick up. This was also discussed by Lady Esther—that she had to be alert and listen to announcements. She was grateful for her gift of listening and absorbing instructions. Moni whispered to the elder her plan to leave her in a corner spot within her sight and approached the carousel to look for her straw bag. She asked her to hold her large purse and situated it on her lap. It was probably the only straw bag in that cargo department and easy to recognize. All the other bags were expensive, sturdy-looking, and large. It was again a long wait. The elder closed her eyes, and her head tipped sideways, dozing off because of fatigue or trying to avoid seeing the goings-on, which could tire her even more. As soon as Moni found her bag, she held it with her left arm and wheeled the chair awkwardly to the exit, where another uniformed guy checked her bag against the ticket. Her bag, despite its rough treatment, withstood the handling and remained intact. Moni paused to look around to spot a familiar face.

She headed to the exit, slowly pushing the chair looking about. She was approached by a short Filipino-looking guy who spoke her dialect and immediately greeted the elder. A well-dressed woman resembling Lady Esther also followed. She smiled at Moni, quickly introduced herself, and kissed the elder's hand. It was her daughter, whom Lady Esther had talked about. The guy took over wheeling the elder until they reached outside and they were assisted to a large car. The outside was bitter cold. The guy brought back the chair inside the airport and hurried out to take the front seat. The other guy started to drive, leaving the airport slowly. It was a comfortable car, very large. It was not like the jeepney way back home. Coats were given to them, the car was heated, and the flow of the heat was blasting off. It was rather warm and comfortable. Blankets were draped on their laps, and a crocheted woolen blanket was placed across the chest. The elder was seated with her daughter and Moni. The daughter introduced herself as Erminda, older daughter of the elder. She did most of the talking, basically asking how the elder endured the trip. Moni did all the answering, being able to talk to her in their dialect. The elder was dozing off, her head leaning back. Moni's feet were cold, although her body was warm because of the woolen vest that Aunt Delina had made for her and the thick coat prepared for her. Moni then knew what cold meant. The workers for the Romualdo household were introduced as Anselmo (the man who met them at the airport) and Ting, the chauffeur. They both spoke the dialect. Moni was busy viewing the sights around her. There were various types of cars on the road going and sweeping past them. Moni thought the people here were in a hurry, being that the streets were wide, having several lanes to swing into. In the Philippines, there was only two lanes—one lane for northbound and a lane for southbound. Often the road became three lanes, and care had to be done when driving. Streets had streets on top overlapping at each other, a sight very difficult to describe. Tall buildings as tall as twenty stories high surrounded with balconies. She wished she had ten pairs of eyes to capture and remember the sights. She would write a letter to her uncle and Armando with descriptions of the view she did not know the proper words to use for them to understand. She thought she would tell them that the movies made in America would best be seen. Some roads were lined with various small and tall trees, barren of leaves. They stood naked. Monica thought of the regeneration of leaves as she remembered it from school. She would describe these sights, but it would not be accurate. In time, she would be able to purchase a camera. She was very comfortable being welcomed with such warmth by the daughter and the uneventful outcome of the trip. She did well, despite her inexperience. If she might say so, her performance was acceptable.

Inconspicuously, Moni would take a glance at Lady Erminda. She was much taller, a good two inches, much leaner, and fair skinned. The sisters had similar features, both pretty and elegant. Moni, in her young mind, would dream that someday she would have that status and elegance, despite her nonelegant background.

Lady Ramona, the elder, stood around five feet or more. She was lean and very pretty. She appeared to be of Spanish origin, with light-brown eyes, a delicate nose, and thin lips. She was fair-skinned, and although in her midseventies, she was not as wrinkled compared to the elderly inhabitants of Leyte where Moni came from. Lady Ramona never stayed out in the sun to till the soil. She was sheltered and was spared from work, coming from a rich family. The Romualdos owned several lands, a hacienda in Leyte, and buildings in Manila. They never had to struggle in earning a living. They have people who tilled the land and several helpers to keep the business in order. Despite their wealth, they were nice to their subordinates, it was rumored, but Moni to believe it, she had to experience it herself. She was a child of one of the early Spanish settlers that occupied the Philippines who were educated equipped with knowledge in land ownership and acquired vast property. Most of the Filipinos in those times did not have the education to process land ownership, so majority of them were poor.

Moni seemed relaxed now, and was able to think, since she did not have to be alert as to her needs. This was her long-awaited break. Moni's thoughts were interrupted because they were entering a tunnel, rather dark, illuminated by dim lights on the sides and headlights keeping the path well-lit. The driver said they were entering the tunnel. It was for Moni to know. It was kind of him. He spared her the anxiety of not knowing where she was. The drive was a little slower. As they emerged from the tunnel, they were entering a city lined with tall buildings. Wide sidewalks occupied by hurried people bundled with thick coats, shivering, scarves half covering their faces, and boots that were knee-high. The people were in a hurry to reach their destination or heading to somewhere or trying to evade the cold and find a nook to keep warm. It would be silly and illogical to be seen waltzing on the sidewalk at this kind of weather. Besides, people in a hurry would be annoyed following someone who is slow. She took note of this, and in time, if she would be allowed to walk outside the residence, she must follow suit. Moni felt her warm thick coat purchased for her by her employer in anticipation of the discomfort of the cold weather. Her vest and jacket alone would not be sufficient. There was no more talk, since the elder was actually sleeping, her head tipped back supported by her daughter's arm almost like it was being caressed. It was a beautiful sight of love between them.

They were driving slowly due to traffic, and she had the chance to view the window display of mannequins with various clothes and accessories. She recalled her job while she was in the Philippines. The displays were not as grand and the window space not as wide, but it was presentable enough and worth looking at for a small country of poor people. The car turned onto a narrower street and entered a wide entrance, which led to the underground parking garage and descended into an enclosed space surrounded by a concrete wall. The guard at the entrance, knowing the occupants, let them in slowly. The cemented floor was marked with white painted lines, visible numbers designating the tenant who was renting it. It was rather dark; dim lights on the ceiling and the rays of the sun illuminated part of the garage. At night, presumably, it might be darker. The space occupied the whole bottom area of the building. There were a few cars at that particular time. As soon as the car was parked, the guys were quick, and soon, Lady Ramona was being wheeled to an elevator heading to the second floor. The elevator opened to a wide carpeted hallway with walls adorned with various floral paintings on both sides. The guy was ready with a key to open the door marked number 4 and held it open for them to enter the spacious space, which was equipped with a deep wall closet where they hung their coats and a screened container for umbrellas and a space for boots. They proceeded to the big sitting room where a large portrait of the family hung on the wall. Looking at it, the daughters were in their early twenties, and the elder was most beautiful, seen smiling in that portrait. It was sad that she no longer could express herself, not even with a frown or a smile. The stroke she suffered two years ago, robbed her from that pleasure, not only to herself but also those around her who having known her all these years must miss that beautiful smile. Lady Ramona's husband was a robust, handsome man with intense brown almond eyes, round face, curly black hair, and white skin. He was dressed in an embroidered Barong Tagalog. He had the features of a Spanish man, but his almond eyes, indicated he had a mixture of Chinese blood. It was a portrait of a family depicting wealth and status. There were very few families with that standing in the Philippines.

On one side of the wall was a smaller framed portrait of Lady Erminda and her spouse. Her husband was brown-skinned with features like someone familiar to her. Moni stared at it for a long time. He looked like somebody she knew, but she could not figure out the resemblance. If she was not aware where she was, she would have thought it was someone she really knew. She had to keep her thoughts to herself. Two large flower paintings ornamented the other white walls. Two wide windows facing the street, appropriately draped, illuminated the room. It was furnished with fine print couches, and several white padded chairs were scattered at corners and around the couches. The wall-to-wall thick beige carpeting was clean. Indeed, it was a home that signified wealth of the owner. Moni had been accustomed to the rich dwellings, having seen the Bonedotos' and Lady Esther's, so this did not surprise her anymore. Moni, rather tired, sat on one of the corner seats and comfortably seated herself placing the straw bag and the elder's purse on the floor. As she sat there, she could not fathom the grandeur that was before her eyes; possibly it was a phantom of her imagination. Momentarily, out of disbelief, she felt her chest, her arms, and her entire body to verify her in that room. She had taken a long ride from her world to perhaps another side of the earth where it seemed so plentiful. The room was triple the size of Uncle Indong's whole house. The whole apartment she was now sitting in was a residence of only three people. She was immersed in joy yet lonely. Her family, so far away, could not possibly imagine this feeling of chaos within her. Should she be happy? Could she enjoy the luck that God has bestowed upon her? That for a moment she had touched the ground the rich had walked on all their lives? Could this feeling, momentary as it was, fill her with happiness? In theory it should have, but she missed her family. She would have wished they were there beside her to have a glimpse at this grandeur. She turned her head around to imagine that they were there, only to realize that they were not.

  Lady Erminda immediately seated her mother on one of the couches and showed Moni around to acquaint her with the place. She immediately picked up the straw bag and the purse and followed Lady Erminda. They entered a wide wooden sliding door to the dining room, a lace-covered table that sat eight and another sitting room overlooking another street. The rooms were all decorated with lamps at every corner. She was led to the bedroom, which she was told would be the elder's room and hers. There was a big bed as one entered the room and a lamp situated on a bedside table; across it was a wide bureau, which contained the elder's clothes. A mirror was attached to the bureau. A small bed, which was probably hers, was situated by the window overlooking the street, which was a few steps to the washroom. There was enough walkway for the elder to go to the washroom. It could have been a one-bedded room, but the small bed was placed to accommodate Moni. Both beds were double-cushioned with matching ivory-colored bedspreads.

Lady Erminda showed her the wide sliding door wall closet on the left side as one entered that stretched from the door to the window. The double doors slid from the side on both ends. Several clothes were hanging, and different colored shoes of hues not known to Moni lined the bottom. Scarves on hangers, blouses, and skirts almost filled the closet. A space was allotted for her by the door. She placed her straw bag on it. The elder did have some clothes in this home. She need not carry a suitcase. Rich people never have to worry about menial things. The convenience that money could offer was beyond imagination. Moni, being of poor extraction, would sit in her quiet moments and ponder the big difference between them. Lady Erminda showed her the bathroom. It was equipped with terry robes for both of them, white towels hung on the towel rack, and various supplies were in a basket underneath the sink. The shower area was tiled with white ceramic and a one-step-up enclosure, which the elder could easily maneuver when a shower was due. The multiple-flowered shower curtains looked new. The aroma of cleanliness was a delight.

They exited the bedroom, and the elder was already seated at the dining table, having breakfast. Moni was ushered to have some and was told to sit anywhere she liked. The two-feet-wide table was against the wall in the dining area. It was a buffet table filled with breakfast treats Moni did not recognize. Eggs cooked several ways, sausages, pancakes, and cut-up fruits were on that table for the taking. Moni tried it all and was not shy. It was a sight to behold. That sight could be appreciated in the books. It was an experience she enjoyed. The ladies came to clean up, and Moni did not have to help. She felt like helping, since she had nothing to do. It seemed that Lady Erminda wanted to do everything for her mother. They stood up and were heading to the bedroom, so Moni followed. As they entered, the big bed was already opened for her to lie down. She was told to take a nap too.

The lady said, "Kapoy kamo sa biahe. Kinahanglan matoog." She was basically saying that they needed to sleep after a long, tedious trip. It was so true. Moni, despite her age, was very, very tired. She was very grateful. Again, the daughter did most of the tasks that she was supposed to do. She set her mother up and covered her. Moni dozed off immediately. That was almost noon, and Moni was still asleep until late afternoon, and she was alone in the room. The elder was not in her bed; the bedspread was rolled to the middle of the bed. She jumped off from her bed and went to the bathroom to check and found it empty. She walked briskly to the door and looked around. She ended up in the kitchen area where the kitchen help was standing by the stove and could not see her. She, as loud as she could, called the lady with a "hello" but got no response. She walked over to her and patted her back. Moni was talking to her, but the lady kept looking at her mouth, raised her right arm, and pointed to the living room outside of the kitchen area where the elder was seated. Moni found the elder sitting on the couch in the smaller sitting area by the dining room, watching television. Moni immediately took a seat on the single padded chair by her side, and the elder, as nice as she was, gently rubbed her left hand before Moni was able to tell her about her negligence. She was trying to comfort her. She was almost saying that it was all right for her to sleep through, that she, the elder, was doing fine. It was nice of her to understand Moni's concern about her inadvertent negligence.

Her daughter came and said, "Maa-yo ang imong katulog. Ayaw kabalaka." (I am glad you rested. Not to worry.)

It was such a relief to Moni to be told that she needed her sleep and not to worry. Furthermore, she was told that Lady Esther had been informed of their trip and their safe arrival. This information would be relayed to Uncle Indong. That night, she was thoroughly oriented to the place, the details of her job, such as the financial aspect and her day off. She was allowed to pick the day, which was every Friday. As had been mentioned in the Philippines, she would be paid every two weeks with cash money of fifty dollars. The anticipated length of employment was two years, and if everything went well, she would return to the Philippines with the elder. It was even said that Lady Erminda wanted to share moments with her mother before the inevitable happens. She worked as an administrator for the Philippine embassy, and her husband, a stockbroker, was currently on a trip. They have no children.

On her Friday off, the deaf-mute lady would cover for her. Moni's main duties were to stay with the elder, to toilet her, assist with her bathing, change her clothes, and perform other miscellaneous duties, which her daughter could not think about for the moment. Moni could keep her passport in the event she needed to go out for identification, and she had to take care of it as if it were a precious commodity. She was asked not to leave for other employment and stay until the verbal contract would be over. Moni was introduced to the employees of the household. Preciosa, who came three times a week for general cleaning, was not there. Emma, the deaf-mute, was an adopted daughter; Na Pansang, the cook; and the two male employees, who were already introduced. They walked around, and she was shown the two other rooms, one of which belonged to the couple, and there was another small room for guests. An extended room was for the servants' quarters located past the kitchen where the cook and the adopted adult daughter slept. She was told that when she was hungry in the middle of the night, she was to help herself. The appliances were tested, and she was showed how to use it. She felt comfortable that she would not destroy any appliance because of ignorance. A large closet, half the size of the elders' room, called the pantry, with shelves that held several canned food and various noodles, was stacked as high as the shelves could fit it. It looked like a grocery store. The pots and pans, some cooking utensils, and various items that the household might need, were there too. The lady was not condescending. Obviously, her sister had advised her on her possible lack of knowledge on certain things, having had none of the gadgets the rich people own. Moni was grateful for the accuracy of the orientation.

Apparently, as she learned from Ma Pansang, Emma was deaf-mute, the reason for her inadvertent lack of attention when Moni called her. The elder had taken her in as an infant when somebody had dropped her off in a box at their gate when the elder's transport was exiting the property. If it had not been daytime, they would have run it over. Nobody claimed the child. A search as to her parentage was not done, nor did she have a thorough medical examination to ascertain the cause of her deafness. She was given the name of Emma Romualdo, an adopted child, almost a daughter to the family. Due to her condition, she could no longer care for the elder, especially when the elder incurred the illness, which incapacitated her means of communication. It was reiterated to Moni that she was free to ask in the event a question came up.

On Fridays, she was free to go out. The curfew, not later than six in the evening, was reiterated. The reason was her safety. She was given a key to the place, a note to present to the front desk, written in longhand appropriately signed by Lady Erminda on an engraved stationary.

Chapter Seventeen

Moni attended to the elder as expected of her. She would be there for her at all times. If the elder was up at night for whatever reason, she had to watch her. She showered every other day or more, and she assured her safety. There were times when Moni had to go in the shower to rub her back, getting wet during the process. The showers took long due to the elders' limited capability to move. Dressing and undressing her was also a task that took time. Considering what she had to do, the uncertain hours of the job; she enjoyed it. The elder despite her wealth was not difficult to take care of. She would look at her and pat Moni's hand. That was a gesture of gratitude that Moni has finally understood. Matching the elder's clothes was a chore for her. She was not accustomed to lots of clothes and as a young girl never had the need to dress up, being that she did not have a respectable job in the past. Her clothes were matched, black pair of pants and white blouse.

Moni would take out several pairs of pants and blouses and scarves to match. The elder would pick it out. It would be on a hanger, ready for the week. That first week, Moni would try to match the clothes and put two outfits on a hanger and presented it to the elder. In the beginning, she did not match it right, but every day she was learning. Emma collected the soiled clothes every Thursday, and she also changed the bed linens. The room was cleaned by Preciosa. That was the routine of the week that concerned her.

Her first Friday off was an adventure, and she ascertained that the necessary identifications and Lady Erminda's letter was with her. She tiptoed out and walked to the hallway, to the elevator down, and she was planning her day when she realized she was not dressed appropriately. She forgot to wear her winter coat and felt the coldness as she entered the hallway leading out. She went up again and realized she had difficulty fitting the key to the door but finally learned to open the main door. As she exited the building, she realized that the very green yonder when she looked out the window in the living room of the Romualdo home was a park called Central Park. She went straight to the street, looking back very often to be able to recall the building to ascertain that she would know how to return. She walked slowly, holding her belongings and the sandwich that Emma prepared for her.

She lived—or her employer lived—in a building at corner Seventy-Second and Central Park west. She had retained it in her mind. She walked downtown to Sixtieth Street, which seemed an eternal walk to nowhere. She walked slowly since she was in no hurry and ascertained that she would not impede others who were in a hurry. She did not have an intended destination. It was not very cold since there was no wind to aggravate it. There were lots to see, and she lingered at every sight to examine and satisfy her questioning mind. Nobody noticed her overstay at the window display. Her coat kept her warm, and she could put on the hood if she wanted to. Her feet were cold. She had regular shoes on. It seemed that the weather was not cold when she started to take that walk, but after a while, it became very chilly. She saw people having their sandwich while walking, and she would do the same. She did not see a bench where she could sit. There were several cafes, but she did not even have the currency with her to be able to purchase anything. She did not go far. It was only ten blocks from her place.

She did not speak to anyone. Theoretically, she should have been able to speak the language, English, which was the medium of instruction in the Philippines. She had had some college credits that prepared her for this job, but the fear of speaking had indeed inhibited her from being able to speak to someone. At that moment, her first day alone was not really the time to speak to someone. She might become a victim of fraud, being seen as awkward in her ways. It was early afternoon when she headed back. It was a nonproductive day, not having sold something or earned anything. It was a pleasurable day she never knew how to enjoy. Way back home, a trip to the city was work. On her return, the documents she carried were indeed necessary because she was slow in responding to the questions that the guard at the front desk asked her. As soon as he read Lady Erminda's note, he smiled and apologized.

When she arrived, Emma tried to talk to her in sign language. She signaled, and Moni tried her very best to comprehend. When she seemed to understand, she would act it out and Emma would nod. Did they communicate? Nobody knows. The elder was napping when she arrived. She took over the job and let Emma sleep, signaling with her two hands on the side of her head together with closing the eyes. Emma smiled and left to her quarters. Most weekends, the two guys came and had their breakfast from the dining room. It was customary for the family to have a buffet. The guys ate in the kitchen. The guys rented a studio apartment uptown, and they were under the Romualdo payroll. Moni did not know the meaning of *a studio apartment.* The male employee drove the family for long trips to upstate New York, New Jersey or elsewhere, and picked up and delivered the supermarket goods when Lady Erminda called for the orders. Nobody went to the supermarket, but a call to the manager was all the lady had to do. Prime meats and fresh fruits and vegetables were delivered twice a week. When they went for these trips, they ate at expensive restaurants, and the guys always stayed in the car. A package of food was always packed for them. The elder would be very sleepy for the next two days after a long trip. Moni would watch television in the den and read magazines while waiting for the elder to wake up. The elder normally slept for two hours. After two weeks, Moni got paid. She wrote to Uncle Indong, her mother, and Armando. She enclosed a fifteen-dollar banknote to both her mother and Uncle Indong. She had ten dollars left. The guys informed her how to send some money to the Philippines. There were items she wanted to buy at the pharmacy department, perfumes and sorts. She held her few dollars for something better. Few more days off— she would find a one-day job since she was more confident with speaking, having read all magazines available to her at the Romualdo home. Lady Erminda had not changed in her treatment toward her. She remained nice and always thanked her every end of the day.

Moni had been spending Fridays exploring downtown and the subways. The information counters would be her place to ask, and finally, she owned a city map. Again, her education had helped her in understanding the map and going into places of interest. She learned about the museums, which she enjoyed very much. After a month, she had learned her whereabouts in the city, she would find herself a one-day-a-week job. She was no longer afraid of getting lost or fear of finding her way home. She walked to the west side, and she saw a sign on one of the hair salon for a shampoo person. She walked past the place several times, trying to figure out what to say. She dared go in after practicing in her mind what to say and approached the lady at the main desk.

"Good morning. I want that job." She pointed at the window sign. She continued on, saying, "I can only work Fridays."

Moni was watching the lady who was shampooing somebody's hair. She had just started, and she watched how the chair was being adjusted, the drape to protect the customer from getting wet and the water temperature adjustment. The lady at the front desk sort of surmised her appearance. Monica looked decent. Dressed in her black pants, white blouse, multicolored vest, and an expensive coat, she did not look like a person that might steal people's belongings.

She finally said, "You want to start now?"

"Yes," she said.

"Ask that girl what to do," the lady said, pointing to the person who was doing somebody's hair.

Eager to start work, she did not even ask for details. It was more of doing that drove her, the exposure, and it must pay something. She looked around, and the young person who was the only person working at that area smiled at her. She was led to a room where the personnel hung their coats and belongings and the restroom. It was a small space, hooks on the walls for coats and purses. Boots lined the bottom and packages of sorts. Several unmatched padded chairs lined one wall. She situated herself. She was very happy and could not wait to write to her mother of this job. She has never gone to a beauty parlor for haircuts and sorts. There was one in Naval, and only the rich and professionals had their hair done. Her mother had always cut theirs unprofessionally, and there was no comment of how the cut should have been done. The salon was located in between establishments of a family-owned delicatessen restaurant and a bank. It had ten stations spaced well. It was unimpressive, and the clientele possibly were residents of the area of moderate means and bank employees. For the moment, it was not busy. It was half past nine in the morning.

    She stepped out of the room and prayed for God's assistance. The young lady possibly as old as her said hello and said, "Hello, have you done this before? I am Alisha, what's your name?"

    "My name is Monica, and I have not done it."

    Alisha kept on talking, but she did not understand what she said but nodded to acknowledge her. She pretended to know it, and being that the next chair was vacant, she tried to adjust it as if someone was there. This way, she would be able to do it as if she knew how. Again she called for God. She did not want to be spoken to, so she left Alisha and looked around as where things were located so she would be prepared when a customer came. She tried to work on the faucet and was learning to adjust the temperature. As she observed, the customers talked, and she was afraid she might not be able to deal with the conversation. The next one went to Alisha, and she watched all the sequence to perform the job. She watched and saw how she got paid. The jar on top of the shelf was the receptacle to contain the dollars. The customer dropped fifty cents to her jar. Moni's mind was turning. Each shampoo station had a jar. She figured if she shampooed ten heads, that would be four dollars for the length of time she would be there. In no time, the customers kept coming. She did her job slow and adjusted the water temperature, asking each customer if it was all right. She did exactly like Alisha did. When it was quiet, she asked Alisha if she could leave to have her lunch. She was alone in the supply room, and she had moments to think. Before the end of the day, she went back to the desk and told the lady she could only work until half past five. She was frowned upon, and Moni thought she probably would be told not to come back. She shampooed sixteen people. The fifty cents added up, and the last one gave her a whole dollar. It was a lot of money for her. At around half past five, she bid her partner good-bye, thinking that she would not see her again. As she was leaving, she approached the lady at the desk and asked her if she wanted her to come back next Friday. Without looking at her, she said to call her first at nine in the morning, and with that, she handed her a card. Despite the attitude, she said thanks. If she had counted the heads right, she had eight dollars in her pocket.

She walked briskly and ran in between to make the six o'clock curfew. She was a good fifteen blocks away, and Gail's Salon was on West Sixty-Second street. The business card was mixed in with her money. It was a deep inside pocket, and she felt the other pocket to ascertain that her identification was there. She learned to put it in an envelope, having had travel experience, emulating Lady Esther's organization technique. She made it there at few minutes before six. The guard at the front door recognized her and he let her in readily.

That night after the elder was settled in bed and sleeping, she went to talk to Emma. The cook named Na Pansang was not there. Her daughter had taken her out for the night. Her bed was empty, and Moni sat on top of the covers. She was trying hard to tell Emma where she was, and she brought the coins and quarters she earned. The servants' room had their own washroom, and Moni went in to demonstrate, and she showed her the money. Emma watched her with concentration, not missing any actions that might be significant to the story Moni was telling. She seemed excited and was laughing. That was the extent of talking Moni was engaged in, in that household. The cook was too busy, and being elderly, she did not engage in silly talk. Emma, in her late thirties, loved to talk despite her handicap.

Emma did most of the cleaning, washing, and ironing. After a while, Moni would help her dust, iron, and help in the kitchen, such as cut up the vegetables. Moni was bored and needed something to do especially when the elder was napping. The cook and Emma appreciated her helpfulness. That Friday, Moni, already dressed to go out, called the lady at the hair salon and inquired about the job. She was told to come back. Ready as she already was, she made her sandwich, put water in a jar, signaled to Emma, and went. She walked with such eagerness as if she was pursuing the best-paying job in the world. She was early. This time, the lady at the desk smiled at her. She felt good. This might mean that she was permanent. She shampooed more than fifteen heads. If she earned eight dollars every week, she would deposit it in the bank. Alisha was becoming friendly and talkative. It was not easy, since she spoke different from the rest. Moni could not be honest enough to comment on it since she did not speak well herself. The rest of the hairdressers were nice, especially when Moni swept the whole place without being told. They gave her a dollar here and there. There was a day that she earned fifteen dollars and she did not know how it came to that much. She just recalled that there were many customers that day. She has learned socialization as greeting everybody with a smile and a plain "Good morning" and "Good afternoon." She would listen to people talking and tried to remember how words were spoken as she read it from the magazines. This was a good place to learn the language. There were a lot of conversations going on, almost like gossip about certain people and certain informative daily activities which was worth knowing. This extra income gave her the chance to send money to Armando, and if she kept working every week earning fifteen dollars, she could send extra five dollars to Uncle Indong, her mother, her cousins, and her friend Ernesto. Mother had not answered her back, but she understood it, being that mail in her hometown was slow. Perhaps Noy Tiquio, being older, could be slower now, unable to cope with the quantity of mail to be sorted.

One night, Lady Erminda presented her with two beautiful sweaters to own. Moni figured she was tired looking at her with the same outfit. Moni would wash her clothes by hand and hanged them every night in the shower area. She would not include it with the rest of the wash. She was too possessive of the handful of clothes she owned, even though Emma would insist on doing it with the rest of the wash. She was instructed that these sweaters were to be given to Emma when they got soiled to send them to the cleaners.

Every weekend, they would take trips to areas, at which Moni would be so amazed. Several weeks went by and Lady Erminda bought her two outfits—a blue and pink pantsuit, similar to the clothes they wore. She also received three scarves to wear, which would match the two outfits. She was not treated as a maid but was almost a younger sister who dressed like one of them. It was a flattery to Moni that she had to write a letter to her mother specifically to tell her this spectacular news. The male employee obtained some stamps, and she did not have to go to the post office, and as long as she had stationery to use, a stamped envelope could be dropped off right there in the building. She wrote letters to her family as often as she felt although she seemed never to receive any. It was very scarce.

She became very friendly with Alisha at the salon who lived in the west side, a few blocks from the salon. She invited Moni to her place, but she could not, since she never had the time. Her job went well, since another person worked three times a week, actually covering the rest of the days that Moni thought Alisha would be doing the work alone. Apparently, nobody wanted to work on Fridays. Moni wanted to work until nine in the evening, and she did not dare ask Lady Erminda for this favor since it had been emphasized at orientation that her safety was the concern. Lately, she would come in a little late like fifteen minutes, and Emma was all right with it. She had forty dollars extra every month, which she deposited in the bank.

Winter season still persists, and she bought herself a pair of boots to wear when it would snow. She has been wearing it to keep her comfortable. One day, it was snowing. It was pouring hard, and the gushing wind almost prevented Moni from going out and walking in that deep snow. Despite the fear, she went to the empty parlor, since nobody was there to have a haircut, possibly due to the bad weather. She stayed for two hours until the lady in charge told her she could leave. That day, she earned a dollar. She did not forget that particular day in March when she struggled to tread that snow only to bring a dollar home. It was snowing that week. Although it was not as thick as that first day, she experienced the meaning of snow and bitter cold. After eight weeks of speaking to people and listening, she was more confident of her ability to communicate and learned so many things about the culture. Had it not been for this job, she would not have had the exposure, and her sojourn to America would have been a waste, remaining ignorant of activities the rest of the world engaged in. She would return home and have no information of how things were done differently in another country. Snow was something she was no longer afraid of.

In four or six weeks, it would be spring, a word she did not understand. She heard from the salon that they were looking forward to it, and the weather would not be as cold. The trees would regenerate, and flowers would start to bloom. She could not wait to see it. In the meantime, they were not going out for a drive due to bad weather because the streets were not safe. The elder did not comment, nor was she able to portray sadness or aggravation from staying home. Moni would not know, the daughter would be able to tell if she intended to do things as she knew her mother well enough to notice a change. The routine was the same, and Moni was comfortable getting to know the people at the building and the male employees at the Romualdo home. Moni learned from conversations that the male employees' rent was subsidized by the boss, and the utilities were paid by them. In fact, when the parlor was slow, Moni went to see the place. It was called a studio apartment, which was an oversized room with necessary facilities. It was equipped with a large couch that opened into a bed and a padded reclining chair with an ottoman. It was comfortable and rather spacious. Both of them got along to be able to share the dwelling peacefully.

They seemed decent and respectful. They were hired help at the hacienda (a large piece of land) in Leyte, and they each had a several-entry visa, being employees of a rich person. They were allowed to stay in the United States as long as they remained employees of the Romualdo family. They seem content even though they were away from their family. They were well compensated, and their families lived in the vicinity of the Romualdo property. They had the privilege of returning home every year if they had enough money to pay the fare. They had been under her employ for ten years, but they only visited twice due to financial problems. If Lady Erminda decided to return to the Philippines, they also had to return. They had talks about home, and after a while, Moni enjoyed their conversation about when they would deliver the groceries. Lady Erminda temporarily settled in New York, having a well-paid stable job. Spring came, and true enough, it was perfect weather. On most days, it was sunny and cool. They went out every weekend and most holidays. They even had a two-day vacation in Washington, DC. The elder enjoyed the cherry blossoms, and the male employee looked happy. They stayed in an inexpensive hotel. It was a grand vacation. Lady Erminda took pictures on these occasions, and she gave Moni copies of it for free. Moni wrote to her uncle of her enjoyable experience. Uncle Indong had been writing to Moni, being able to mail the letters readily. His job was near the post office, and he would ask one of the laborers to mail it for him on their way home. His letters were uplifting with news such as that Dee was accepted at the school of nursing and was thankful for the few dollars Moni sent to help him. Fifty dollars proved to be a large amount, being that it paid most of the tuition fees. Moni sent it every month, although she did not promise to do it every month. Luckily, the job at the salon allowed her to save.

Summer came, and this season was also looked forward to by most. They made so many trips to famous places, which Moni enjoyed most. Presumably the elder had seen them all because she seemed not to get excited. Moni never dared ask. She was lucky to have seen several places such as Atlantic City, the Smithsonian, and more. The homeland where Moni came from did not have any interesting sites, and although the weather was almost sunny nobody noticed it. When summer was almost over, there was a rumor that Lady Erminda would go to Europe. The lady arranged the finances such as two months' rent and some cash money and checks signed for the maintenance fees. It was all explained to Moni. Lady Erminda left to spend time with her husband for six weeks or more. Possibly weekend trips would be deferred, but the doctor's visits for the elder were set. Monica was anxious, having been given the responsibility to manage the household.

Chapter Eighteen

Moni was apprehensive of Lady Erminda's vacation. She was mostly responsible now, and she would wake up in the middle of the night to check on the elder. Her fear was instant death and how she would explain to Lady Erminda in the event it happened. She was no longer comfortable going out to the salon on Fridays. She was fearful of the elder's condition. Emma agreed that Moni would call between one and two in the afternoon. Emma would stay by the phone and feel the phone for some agitation and she will pick it up. She would try to make a sound of "Ah, ah," which will signify that everything was fine. When Moni came home that first Friday that the lady was gone, she was trying to figure out how to speak to Emma and the plan if the elder was not fine. Emma would do a funny sound of distress, which Moni had to demonstrate. It seemed that Emma understood it. True enough the communication was fine.

Every day Moni would test Emma's understanding of the code. Indeed, it worked. Although thinking of it thoroughly, Moni was not satisfied, so she asked one of the male employees to stay at the boss's home on Fridays so Moni would be comfortable at work. They did not have to buy food on their own, thereby cutting down on their cost. Normally, they would only go to the place if there was delivery of food to be done and certain errands. Lady Erminda called every other day, which was a comfort to Moni.

One weekend, she asked the male employees if they could drive around the park for her to see the park, so; they did drive around with the elder. They even spent time sitting on a bench at the park. As simple as it was, the elder had some exercise, and it was a good day. The park situated at the center of Manhattan was a beauty. She was grateful to have this rare privilege of having seen it and enjoyed its grandeur. They would never have such a park in Leyte. To allocate that large land for fun was not affordable for the people to pay. As young as Moni was, she had a say as to the activities of the week. She was the main speaker in the household. She was the only one among them who really could communicate and be able to speak to be understood in the event of need. As young as she was, she was respected. Moni felt elated and felt bad for them who, due to lack of education, were not, for the length of time that they lived in the United States, able to properly speak to be fully understood.

Summertime proved a season so productive. Moni earned lots of money. There were several customers at the salon. She shampooed so many heads she would lose count. Her sandwich would get eaten in ten minutes. Even the hairdressers were overwhelmed yet elated to have that much work. After four weeks, Lady Erminda called to tell them that she would not be home yet. There was a number for Moni to call, in fact, two of them in case of emergency. Moni was given the handle of the money to pay utilities, salary, and supermarket bills. Moni could not believe the amount of expenditures to keep the place maintained. She envied the rich, but she did not envy the thinking it entailed. They did not have utility bills in their hometown. The coconut oil they used to light their home was from the backyard, and water was from the well. To save money, Moni cancelled the calls to the supermarket but went with Ting to look for cheap items according to the cooks' menu. Moni had no accounting skills, and one night, she was up trying to put up a system so all the monies would be accounted for. She was not mentally prepared for this task. She did not have any one to consult with. The only thing she needed to do was to be sure the receipts for every expense was saved and tallied. Lady Erminda told her she was to take thirty dollars as compensation for this extra job. This task kept her up most nights, getting up in the middle of the night from deep sleep to tally the expenses versus the money at hand. She had no time to write to her uncle for the weeks that Lady Erminda was away. She could not wait for her to come back. It had been seven weeks that the lady had been gone. The money allocated to run the household was running low. The food had to be budgeted to certain inexpensive items so the money would last. Moni had to have a meeting with the crew. Being that Lady Erminda was a nice person; unbelievably, everyone was very cooperative. Food was now limited to soups and bread for lunch and chicken for dinner. Most of the stored items in the pantry have been used up. Lady Erminda called Moni that she was having personal problems and to cut down on expenses which Moni has been doing for the past three weeks. Moni was too embarrassed to tell her of the existing problems. Moni has not collected her pay, and she has increased her working days to three at the salon with the cooperation of Emma and Ting being the caller in the event the elder needed quick attention. Her increase of working days at the salon had been a help, so she did not have to collect her pay. It earned her twenty to forty dollars a week. She did not send money to her family. She recalled the event at her uncle's home, having to help them out, but her predicament at the moment involved big money. It was not in pesos. If this goes on, they would be evicted.

Summer went swiftly, and it was autumn. Leaves changed colors from green to orange red, brownish color, and falls to fade away. It was a sight to behold. She would walk to the park and view the scene. The large car was kept on hold from use to conserve expense, such as gas and toll fees. The male employees would have their meals in the boss's house, since they were informed by Moni that if the boss did not appear the coming October, they would not be paid. The rent would be paid for that month. They must limit on the expense. Moni bought most of the food.

It was an effort to survive to keep sheltered and have enough food for all of them. The elder seemed to know the goings-on, having to eat soups and nongourmet food she was not accustomed to. No more lavish breakfasts and varied fruits for the moment. One day, the elder asked Moni for her oversized purse that had not been opened for the longest time since they arrived, and Moni was directed to make a check for a thousand dollars, addressed to Lady Erminda and to be deposited to her account. The elder had an account in New York, able to sign her name, slow but accurate, rather crooked but decipherable. That money kept them afloat. Moni was entrusted to allocate this much money. She was proud to have impressed the elder as to her honesty. Another two weeks went by, and Lady Erminda did not call her. Moni had to let Preciosa go for financial reasons. She continued with her salon job, and she extended her hour to seven in the evening to earn more tips. The extra hour that she stayed earned her extra three or four dollars more. Some customers came after work to have their haircut, making it busier after five in the afternoon. The male employee would stay at the boss's house to watch over things, and as planned, he would be the one to call Moni if a problem arose. The elder has been well. It would have been a problem that Moni would not have been able to handle if the elder took ill.

Another week went by, and buying food was now a problem. The thousand dollars went for maintenance of the apartment. Na Pansang, the cook, understood the problem and took off, spending time with her daughter. She would return when the boss came back. Food consisted of soups and bread. No more abundance of fruits. Moni would buy fruit for the elder from her tip money at the corner store by the salon. She would care for her like she was her grandmother, Mariana. After a while, Moni spent her money from her salon job to buy food for all. She was now part of the family, a very rich family that was experiencing a financial problem.

Again, the elder made a check for a thousand dollars. The elder asked Moni to send a telegram to Lady Esther. Just when the telegram was sent, a call was received to have the male employee meet Lady Erminda at the airport the next day. Moni was so relieved that she was coming. She had not been collecting her pay for a good twelve weeks or so. She had not withdrawn money from her savings account, so she had reserves.

Lady Erminda arrived with her husband. She was tired after a seven-hour flight from abroad. She had lost so much weight and had grown older. Her face was wrinkled, and her sunken eyes revealed a deep problem that almost consumed her. Her husband, who appeared well, was smiling and seemed surprised to see Moni. He indeed looked like Moni's father, just like the picture on the wall. The difference was he was rather overweight and shorter in stature.

He had brown skin like Moni's grandmother. Nevertheless, he was very attractive like her father, but he seemed to have that presence possibly due to his education and achievement. He walked with a bowlegged gait and dressed well. The elder was still sleeping when they came. There was no lavish breakfast to serve, like how Moni had been received that first day she arrived. Lady Erminda was rather sad but managed a smile. Moni hurried to the kitchen and signaled to Emma that the lady had arrived. Emma immediately put the coffee pot on and toasted bread and poached eggs, getting ready to serve it at the dining table. They did not have any sausages or ham to serve. Ting brought the luggage in and had something to eat in the kitchen. They were having rice and sardines. Moni introduced herself to Mr. Onaje and immediately removed herself to the kitchen. Lady Erminda smiled shyly at Moni, almost ashamed, and Moni smiled back. She did not want to tell Lady Erminda of her problems, having seen her look of grief, which she tried to understand. She avoided talking to her but allowed her to settle. When the elder woke up and was dressed, she went unassisted, using her cane, and sat at the dining table to have her tea. Moni alerted her that her daughter had arrived. She nodded. The couple finally appeared from the bedroom and paid respects to the elder. Lady Erminda immediately took a seat beside her and spoke to her, whispering to her ear. The elder listened intently, and as usual, there was no reaction. Nobody could tell if she was sad, upset, or happy. Lady Erminda remained quiet and had coffee and toast beside her mother. Mr. Onaje also did not speak a word. Seated at the head of the table, which apparently was his seat, he took his coffee silently. Moni, having known her for these few months, concluded that she had experienced a terrible shock and was hiding her sorrow in a quiet manner.

That noon, a call from Lady Esther had been received that money had been forwarded to Lady Erminda's account, and the estate would assist her of her crisis. Moni thought that the rich had it made, having some money stashed aside in an emergency. Food was ordered, and they had a wonderful dinner. The male employee ate in the kitchen as usual. It was never discussed at the dinner table, what happened. Moni was asked to join them, and she enjoyed the dinner, which all of them had been deprived of quite a time. The lady did not ask where Na Pansang had gone. Moni and Emma did the cleaning up, assisted by the male employ.

As they were cleaning the dishes, Emma signaled to Moni about her concerns. Emma was worried about Lady Erminda. This time around, Moni could communicate to Emma as if she had also been born deaf-mute. After Moni set the elder to retire, she went to Emma's room, and they talked in their own way. It was early in the evening, and everybody was tired. Moni was thinking that in the morning, Lady Erminda would talk to her. She must know the problems that she handled, and Moni needed to tell her of the money. It was obvious that she probably knew about the goings-on, since she handled the books and knew that the money she left was not enough to last for ten weeks or so that she was gone.

Moni did not see the husband after dinner. He had probably retired early, after a long trip. Either he was tired or he did something wrong that caused his wife to worry, and he did not want to be around to either hear it or tolerate the questioning looks from the elder. Moni was worried that she had done an inaccurate job in handling the money and Lady Erminda could let her go at any moment's notice. The night went as usual, and the elder retired early that night. Moni was sleeping, only to be awakened by a subdued whisper and sobbing sound. She slowly peeked from her covers and saw the lady, from the night illumination, sort of kneeling on the floor at the side of her mother's bed. She was on her mother's left ear telling her something. The elder remained still. Moni motionless under the covers and could not hear nor could she speculate on the content of the conversation. It seemed like a long conversation. Moni did not move, afraid of being suspected to be up, thereby interrupting whatever the lady was telling her mother. Luckily, she did not have to relieve herself, so she could wait until the lady left. Finally, the lady got up and kissed her mother for so long she seemed not to let her loose.

Moni waited for a few minutes—long enough, she thought, that the elder would not suspect that she was up all that time. This time, she needed to go to the washroom. She resumed her sleep and woke up early. There were lots to be done, such as cleaning and the washing. Moni, since the financial hardship, became Emma's assistant. Na Pansang returned, probably called by Ting, assuming that the lady could afford the help. Indeed, she could, since financial help did arrive. The breakfast table was set as usual but less abundantly this time. Ting and Anselmo had breakfast in the kitchen. Lady Erminda and her husband woke up late, almost at lunchtime. The lady looked rested but remained very quiet and had breakfast without her husband. He later joined her, but they did not talk. They did not have a fight, nor was it noticeable that a disagreement was apparent. Moni realized educated people did not fight in public, and whatever problems they had were kept secret. True enough, if it was discussed in front of them, they, the poor help, would be too uninformed to present a solution. This was admirable because Moni had witnessed fights at the market about space when she was young, selling her bananas. Her parents did not have fights, and if they did, she did not witness it.

When things were settled, it seemed, the lady called Moni while the elder was at the television room. They went to the bedroom, and they sat by the elder's bed. She was apprehensive, and she did not know what to do. She hid her account notebook underneath her pillow, and before the lady started to talk, she excused herself and took the notebook with her. The lady looked at Moni, and she was surprised that she had a notebook of accounts. Moni did not tell her about the past events since the lady was too distraught at the moment. The lady hugged Moni so tight and was teary-eyed when she let Moni go. Almost tongue-tied, she stuttered and said thank you several times in their native tongue. Moni, also bewildered, could not look at her due to embarrassment of being hugged by an elegant lady. She did not expect this graciousness from her. Moni proceeded to open the notebook and showed the lady what the money was allocated for. In their native tongue, she said, "Moni, I know there was not enough to pay most of the bills. I am surprised we were not evicted. You do not have to do accounting. I want to pay you for your services and whatever monies you have laid out to feed everybody."

"I have not collected my pay since the end of summer."

"Let me know. I will reimburse you whatever amount was required for the times I was away." And she caressed her again. "Lady Esther did not make a mistake having you as the caregiver for my mother. You are so smart for a young person and, above all, very honest."

Moni, being inarticulate, could not speak. The lady left the room without looking at the book. She would keep this notebook for future reference. She listed all the expenses as accurately as she was capable of. Her income from the salon was not actually listed down. The day went by and Lady Erminda's husband stayed out of sight. There was no talk about him, and nobody asked about his whereabouts. Moni continued with her job at the salon, and there were more customers, hence more tips. She resumed her Fridays, and it was fine with Alisha. The days went on, and finally, after a week home, Lady Erminda returned to work. Mr. Onaje stayed in the bedroom most of the time. He came out for meals when he was called. Gossip was not entertained in the household. Possibly, if Emma had not been deaf-mute, Moni would have some news about the goings-on, which was not really her business. She was most concerned of how she could possibly earn more money. She sent bank notes to Uncle Indong, her mother, and Armando, and the rest was deposited to the bank. Moni was aware of the hardship, and in the event of it happening again, which was very remote, she would be prepared. After a week, Moni was asked to indicate the amount of money Lady Erminda owed, and Moni received the amount as listed. It was inaccurate because the food she bought for everybody had not been accounted for.

The nightly ritual of Lady Erminda visiting her mother became earlier and earlier. Moni could not decide if she would stay out of the room while she was there or pretend that she was sleeping. The elder seemed to understand Moni's predicament and would stay in the television room longer so Moni did not have to go to bed early. Lady Erminda did not talk to her mother outside of her bedroom because she would sit with her mother at the television room and would not tell her anything. Moni would be wondering if she did not mind her knowing about her conversations with her mother. Since she came after ten in the evening, it was understood that she did not want Moni to know. After a while, she would only come twice a week.

Moni never told anyone of these events. They would leave the room unlocked, expecting Lady Erminda to come, and would be left unlocked all night. Moni never locked the room, since it was a very safe place to live, having an armed guard downstairs to watch over them. Emma took care of locking the front door and the entrance to the living room. The elder would normally be in bed by ten in the evening, and if she intended to shower, then they would come in an hour before bedtime. Moni would shower too and clean the bathroom. Preciosa was not rehired, possibly due to financial problems. Moni took over the cleaning of the room, linen changes, and sorting the garments for the elder. It was work that she was not contracted to do, but Moni felt bad for Emma, who would have to do it all. Moni, out of concern for Emma, would vacuum the whole place once a week. She would wait until the husband had his breakfast, and she would tell him she was going to clean his room while he was outside. He was nonconversant and would just nod if he approved the service. There was no need to talk with Moni. She was a hired help and did not have to be spoken to, but the necessary chores she could do for him. If only he knew she had been hired for the elder and he, technically speaking, could not request her to serve him coffee, which he occasionally asked her to do when she was around. Moni did not mind it. Lady Erminda never asked Moni for a cup of tea. The chores were done, and Emma would smile at Moni, appreciating her for her help. That was her way of saying thank you. It was already winter, and the trips were not scheduled because the weather was not pleasant. It would snow, and the roads were icy. The couple stayed home. Moni would pray that the weather on Fridays would be pleasant so the parlor would be full of customers.

Chapter Nineteen

One day Moni asked Lady Erminda if she could go out with Emma one Sunday to the city. There was a lot of thought that went on, but finally, she consented to it, and they were told to come home by not later than four in the afternoon so they could serve dinner. Emma and Moni had fun in the city. Surprisingly, Emma had never been in the city like this—walking, that is. She had had some rides with Ting in the past, but walking and stopping at interesting sceneries was a more interesting experience. They went inside large department stores to look, and not having a large amount of money, or not even enough to buy a simple scarf, was disconcerting. Moni had had a few dollars in her pocket from her Friday job, and after counting it, it was actually just right for Emma's scarf, which she finally purchased for Emma. This lady, who had had a very difficult life, who was so underprivileged at birth and who had a future that depended only on the Romualdos', was so deserving of some gift even as little as a scarf. Moni, a lowly companion, could talk and hold some money and had discretion on what to do. Emma did not have this option. She was not sent to a special school because it was not available. Knowing the kind nature of the family, she would have been given this opportunity. She was not treated as a slave, but she was housed in a room with the maids. Emma was very happy that Moni had bought her a scarf. They even had some money to buy some fruits and some sweets to bring home. They arrived on time to serve dinner.

Lady Erminda noticed the savings and commented on it. So Moni would continue buying food at the supermarket as part of her job, as a help to the family. The episode of hardship had made the lady frugal, and dinners were not as lavish. It was simpler. Moni would be given a list to buy, and Moni would buy some sale items according to her discretion. It seemed that the household was no longer happy but in a state of main survival. Moni thought that the rich, having been used to abundance, felt the hardship more even if the challenge seemed menial. The poor seemed, happy having known of no abundance, and were content at whatever God had provided them. Moni, despite her option to eat at the dining table with the family, preferred to have her meals in the kitchen with Emma.

After a few weeks of staying home on weekends and boredom, Lady Erminda scheduled a trip to Connecticut. Emma came, and she was delighted. Mr. Onaje stayed behind. They stayed in a hotel of moderate means. They had to take a suite and a regular room for the guys. Even that, Moni thought, was too expensive for Lady Erminda. Moni always worried about the finances. She had no idea of how rich the family was and possibly the momentary hardship caused by Mr. Onaje. Recovery from such ordeal was rather quick, she thought, having been poor and never fully understanding where the rich derived their means. The week went well, and there was no scheduled trip. As much as Moni wanted to go out with Emma again, she did not ask, but Moni was allowed to take Emma with her to the supermarket. The outing to the supermarket was a chance to go out. They would have some ice cream before heading to the market. Moni had some cash to afford the treat, and there were no time restrictions because the lady stayed with her mother.

It has been almost a year, and Christmas was approaching. Monica sent banknotes the first week in December for her family to celebrate Christmas. A package of stuff was not practical since she did not have ample money to buy the items plus mailing expense. Being used to gift-giving, Moni purchased inexpensive gift items for Emma, the cook, and the guys. She used her Friday money, she called it. Lady Erminda decorated the tree rather simply and gave each of them a gift. Mr. Onaje spent the evening with them. He was very quiet. New Year was uneventful. Everybody was there, including the guys, to celebrate the midnight greeting. There was lots of food to be had, a ritual hoping that the coming year would be abundant with the main necessities.

Chapter Twenty

For some reason, Lady Erminda stopped visiting her mother at night. Moni never told anyone of the visits. The elder never knew if her daughter was coming or not. The door was always unlocked, and Moni would sleep as soon as the elder was settled. It was very quiet, and Moni, her covers totally covering her, was awakened by a touch to her body. She immediately lifted her covers, and she could see a figure with wide shoulders by the night light illumination. She slid herself down under the covers as quickly as she could and crawled out of the room. She was very fast and went to Emma's room, which was locked. The pantry was next to the room, so she entered it and hid there in the dark. She was afraid to get out since he might still be there. As far as she knew, Mr. Onaje was the only man in the household unless Emma forgot to lock the doors, hence a stranger had invaded the dwelling. Moni was up in that room all night. She exited the pantry at daylight as quietly as she could and tiptoed, as she was barefooted, looking around, afraid that he was there somewhere, looking for her. As she entered the elders' room the elder was up, and she raised her arm, and as Moni was near her, she grabbed her to her side. The elder knew what happened.

The day went on as if nothing happened. Moni could not wait to speak to Emma about last night. It would require lengthy body maneuvers for Emma to understand. Moni had to help Emma serve breakfast. The lady and husband woke up early. Moni did not know how to behave in front of Mr. Onaje stooping. She avoided his looks. She was not sure if it had been him last night since she did not speak with Emma if indeed the front door was locked. The elder ate well and was quiet and expressionless all this time; there was nothing out of the ordinary. The elder was in the television room. After the cleanup, which was almost noon, she had a chance to talk to Emma in her room. Na Pansang was busy in the kitchen setting up for dinner. The lady had left for work, and the husband settled in his bedroom.

As soon as the door was closed, Moni started series of body movements and actions of how she was already sleeping when a man had groped her in the middle of the night. She was trying to tell Emma that she did not know who it was and signaled at the door locking and unlocking it, and Emma was watching her intently, nodding at her when she did the door. That part Moni knew that Emma understood—that the front door had indeed been locked and there was never a chance to leave it unlocked because the door automatically locked when closed. The guys, if and when they had to deliver something, did have a key. She crawled and acted out her wide eyes and the inability to sleep and her fear. Just when Moni was about to finish her story, Emma signaled to her that it had happened to her. That was the reason she had been sleeping with Na Pansang. The lady knew about it. It was a joy on Emma's part when Mr. Onaje decided to leave for Europe to do business there. The household was quiet and peaceful when he was away. It was an hour of storytelling between a hearing and a nonhearing person. It would have to be resumed because lunch was being served, which consisted of sandwiches and vegetable soup. Mr. Onaje did not come out of his room. Nobody called him. Moni joined the elder for lunch.

Moni thought of sleeping in the closet. After lunch, she inspected the closet and tried sitting inside, facing the slightly opened closet. It was spacious enough for a person of small stature. At night, it would not be noticeable if the closet was slightly open just enough to peer through the gap. The closet was actually long enough for her to stretch out. That night, she did just that. At first she would just sit with her knees flexed and wore the terry robe to keep her warm. Equipped with winter leggings, she was dressed warmly. After a while in that sitting position, her legs were numb, and she thought of moving the elder's shoes and piled them slowly and quietly to the other end of the closet so she could stretch her legs. With a rolled bath towel as her pillow, she settled herself on her side with her face on the open gap of the closet to be able to look if a person had entered the room.

The problem was, she would, despite the position she was in, be sound asleep, not able to watch the door if somebody opened it. Even though the hinges of the bedroom door squeaked a little, Moni would not wake up. Apparently, Mr. Onaje kept coming in without her knowing. She would sleep through it. Mr. Onaje never knew that his intrusion was seen by the elder. He was confident that she was unable to speak and could not relay the incident to anyone. He thought that the elder had lost her wits and was altogether unable to comprehend the happenings around her. He would stand by Moni's bed, strip the covers, and look around, almost upset. These episodes were witnessed by the elder, being a light sleeper with keen hearing, and the squeak of the door would wake her up. She was holding her temper, being unable to speak and trying to keep the peace in the family. She was wondering where the young girl has been sleeping.

One night, the elder stayed up to watch where Moni had been sleeping. She watched her moves that night, only to discover that she had been sleeping in the closet. She felt so sorry for her and admired her resourcefulness to keep herself safe from danger. The elder, having imagined Moni's discomfort in that closet, could not sleep that night. Lady Erminda finally stopped visiting her mother at night. Presumably her problem had been resolved. Whatever it was, nobody except the elder knew of the problem. With the elder's silence and her ability to listen, she helped her daughter resolve her problem by the mere gesture of an ear to air her sorrows and never have that fear of her secrets out for the world to know. The fact that Lady Erminda told someone must have been enough to comfort her. Given the elder's condition, she could not possibly give her any advice, although she must have a lot to say if she had been able to.

Only Moni knew about the visits, and her being a person of impeccable character, no one would ever know. Even the elder did not know that Moni was up on those nights when Lady Erminda came in and cried at her mother's side. Moni was wondering if this elder slept at all since she knew every happening there was. Moni wondered if she was a talkative person or if she gave her opinion when she was able to talk. It was a peaceful night for several days. Moni was half asleep most of the time. It was very tiring, being almost a security guard and up during the day as well. She would get up at midnight to lock the door, assuming that Lady Erminda had already slept and would no longer come to see her mother. That was Moni's ritual every night. Sleep was so precious, especially on Thursday night, when she was up on her feet the next day.

After the elder knew where Moni had been sleeping, she invited Moni to sleep with her. As she was very thin-bodied, nobody would ever notice her having the covers on, that someone apart from the elder was in bed with her. Moni, being embarrassed of this gesture, would thoroughly washed up every night so she was clean to lie down in bed with Lady Ramona. One Friday night, Moni and the elder settled in bed early after a warm shower, ready for the next day's trip to New Jersey. Moni could not stay up until midnight to lock the door. She was fast asleep when she was awakened by the elder and signaled to keep quiet. She was startled to see Mr. Onaje stooping down by her small bed, trying to feel the bed if somebody was there, just to find that nobody was there. It happened again. It was the elder who woke up to again witness his bad intentions. They kept quiet, watching him tiptoe and leave the room. Again, they kept it a secret. It would be trouble if Lady Erminda knew. Moni thought of buying an alarm clock to alert her when it was midnight to lock the door. Being that they slept in the bed together, they became very close, almost like how Moni would sleep over at her grandmother's nipa hut. The next day, the trip to New Jersey was deferred. It rained.

The elder did not show anger, although she could not express it. Moni still wondered if she had not been incapacitated, if she would address the problem. The weekend went well. The couple stayed out of sight but appeared when meals were served. Whatever trouble they had must have been resolved since Lady Erminda seemed happy and conversant to her mother.

The pantry was full of canned foods again, so Moni was happy for the family. Every night, Moni was apprehensive. She finally told the elder that she would purchase an alarm clock to alert her that it was time to lock the door. The elder did not shake her head or nod. Moni thought the alarm would wake her up and she might not go back to sleep. It had been the routine to stay up until midnight. She would be able to do it, but sometimes she would sleep through, and being beside the elder all night, she was confident that no one would dare find her in the big bed. Mr. Onaje, despite his character, would not dare do such a horrid thing. In fact, when she was already asleep, she had no idea what went on all night. She never knew if he entered again after midnight. In fact, Mr. Onaje did, and the elder saw him almost every night. The elder must have been aggravated, but could not address the problem due to fear of giving sadness to her daughter.

Chapter Twenty-One

Out of sheer impatience, Moni whispered to the elder her plan to stop the intrusion. As Moni whispered her plan to the elder's ear, the elder nodded her head several times she almost broke her neck. She obviously was very upset about it, and she probably would have done something about it, if she had been physically able. That night, she implemented it. She took a wrapping twine from the pantry and cut two lengthy strings. She wrapped one string around the upper foot of the small bed diagonally and tied it to the foot part of the big bed. The other string was wrapped around the foot part of the small bed and tied across the big bed. Both strings tied like a ribbon at the foot part. It was rather easy to undo. It was a trap, so when he came in again, his leg would get caught as he walked to Moni's bed. Moni did that every night, alerting the elder and warning her to wake her up if she needed to comfort herself. Several nights went by and nothing happened. Mr. Onaje had presumably gotten tired and had given up the idea. The idea made them sleep and comfortable. Moni was tired of doing the trap and also afraid of doing harm to the elder in case she got up in the middle of the night, forgetting that the trap was there. It would surely harm her, especially the midway string, one near the bathroom. That was the last night that Moni was supposed to install the trap.

Moni and the elder were fast asleep when a big thud was heard, waking the both of them. The elder immediately put the bedside lamp on, and with that, Moni slid to the other side of the bed and knew it was him. She knew he was injured. His face slumped on the wooden floor, unable to move. The upper half of his face had hit the wooden floor, and the impact had rendered his whole face bloody. The blood spilled to the sides of his face. The elder, without her cane, managed to walk around the bed to investigate. Moni was dumbfounded, still seated at the edge of the bed, staring at the aftermath of her trap. She looked at the elder, asking her in her most fearful way as to what to do. The elder, having understood Moni, raised her right arm as if directing traffic, directing Moni with her forefinger to fetch Lady Erminda. She quickly slipped out of bed and ran to the lady's bedroom door. She stood there, hesitated, and knocked ever so lightly, not wanting to do it. The lady opened the door abruptly, knowing that at this hour there must be something serious that had happened. The first question was "Is my mother all right?"

Moni did not know if she should nod and said,

"It is Mr. Onaje."

The lady ran past Moni to her mother's room, while Moni followed behind her. As soon as Erminda reached the room, she bent down to turn him over, which she could not. He screamed because of pain. His face was bloody as he lifted his head and turned his face for his wife to see. His front tooth was missing. He tried to speak, but he could not talk. That was the time Moni thought of the string, which was already removed. Moni looked at the elder. She was back in bed in her old spot as if she did not know. The elder did not look at Moni. For a moment, Moni thought of the stroke and the part of her body which was affected and the incapability of this old woman to walk properly, yet she had been able to squat down on that floor to remove the strings, which would have been a questionable sight for Lady Erminda to see. There was nobody who could have removed it but the elder. Moni learned then that the elder was very capable of maneuvering her fingers to have untied the knot in such a short time when she ran to fetch the lady. She did have the agility and the speed to remove the strings out of sight from everybody.

The sight was embarrassing to Lady Erminda, having known the history of her husband. She looked at Moni, rather feeling sorry for this poor young girl who could have been a victim of such abuse. An ambulance was called. He was lifted to the gurney; he had a bloodied face and had apparently injured his right knee as well. The injured knee prevented him from turning. The medical personnel knew the procedure, and despite his cry of pain as they were turning him, it was done causing no added harm to his knee. The proposed story was he had been drinking the night before, became confused, and entered the wrong room and possibly tripped on the edge of the carpet. He would be in the hospital for a number of days. Emma was excited to ask Moni as to what happened. When they had a chance, Moni opted not to tell Emma but shrugged her shoulders and gave the signal that she was sleeping. She lied to Emma, even though Emma did not know the universal sign language and the probability of her relaying the story to someone else seemed impossible; still, one could not be certain. Emma sort of knew what happened. Moni had not expected to cause so much injury to him. From that time on, she would whisper to the elder how sorry she was. The elder would have no reaction. Despite the fact that Mr. Onaje was not around, the elder insisted that she sleep beside her. There was no talk about him. Lady Erminda would come home late every night because she went to visit him at the hospital. Moni would hear her telling her mother while Moni would be sitting with the elder in the television room. She told her mother how he was doing. Apparently a dental surgeon, a nose guy, and a bone guy had been taking care of him. Moni could not understand big words, and what she would hear was simple, and the fact was that she was not interested. Moni continued her work, and her guilt was enormous. She felt so bad for Lady Erminda, and she wanted to say sorry for the injury she had caused. The elder was involved with the cover up. It was a big question whether the elder would tell her daughter about it, if she was able to, but it was almost convenient for the elder to keep quiet since she was not able to speak. With all these, Moni decided on keeping it quiet too. This guilt she would carry with her all her life. Thinking about it thoroughly, Mr. Onaje knew about the string. It did not just get tied there. Someone had placed it there. He knew too that the elder was part of the scheme, since it was obvious that injured as he was, at that particular moment, he must have seen the elder untie the strings from the beds and pull them through, underneath his body.

Winter seemed to pass quickly. There were a few snowy days. Due to the incident, there were no trips. Spring was approaching, and Moni loved her Friday outing. It had been six weeks or more that Mr. Onaje was not home. Moni would be helping in the kitchen and would not be there with the elder when the lady would come home. She did not hear any news. She earned more money at the salon. Each hairdresser would slip her a dollar here and there. Her income at the salon had gone up to almost fifteen dollars every Friday. Several customers had been fond of her, especially a person named Gloria Greene. She was a frequent customer, coming to the salon every two weeks. They would talk while her hair was being washed. She always gave her a dollar tip. Moni kept sending bank notes to Uncle Indong, her mother, and occasionally, to Armando.

Her mother hardly wrote back, possibly having difficulty in writing due to her lack of education; the chores and business kept her occupied. Uncle Indong wrote often, and although she had no news from her, it would have been mentioned in his letter if Mother was not well. Moni kept writing a letter to her mother to keep her informed of her well-being. Armando wrote only once, thanking her for her thoughtfulness. She made some acquaintances, but she was careful not to tell anyone of her affairs. Even Alisha kept inviting her to her place, which she refused since she had a curfew. The salon could not be left without anybody, although they could really leave for a few minutes and the hairdresser could do the job. One Friday, they planned to meet at a corner street an hour early before the salon opened, and Moni saw Alisha's apartment. It was around five blocks from the salon. It was a five-floor walk-up building, rather unkempt, the hallway floors dusty and dark. It was a small one-bedroom apartment. The girl knew how to decorate the small place with inexpensive items, and it looked beautiful.

"Moni, you should stay with me one night, keep me company. I am all alone."

"I have a curfew. I must be in by six in the evening."

"Can't you do it for one night? That's terrible! Moni, I like you a lot. See, I live alone—got two jobs, working nights and the salon, barely making it, but it would be nice if you share the apartment with me."

"That seems impossible, but thank you, I will think about it."

"See, I come from North Carolina. Both my parents are alcoholics. I am pretty ashamed of it . . . had to leave, no future there. School's out of reach for now."

"You will soon . . . keep trying."

"What about you? Parents?"

"Yes, my father and mother live in the Philippines. We are very poor. I am here temporary. Work as a maid. Need to leave when my employer says I go . . . can't say no more."

Moni never told anyone her business. Moni said to Alisha that someday, when her boss consented to it, she might accept the invitation. It was obvious that Alisha did like Moni. Alisha worked at the supermarket as a meat sorter at night. It was almost like Moni's life; only she had it better. She had her family and more. Interacting and talking to Alisha was an experience, more so because it gave her the confidence to talk.

Anselmo went back to the Philippines. His arthritis prevented him from doing his tasks. Ting did most of the chores, errands for the family. Ting, having to go often to the Romualdo home, became close to Moni. It was during the financial crisis that they incurred when Ting learned to admire Moni's mind more so than ever. Being a middle-aged man with a daughter around Moni's age, he was hoping his daughter would grow up and behave as intelligently as her. Ting had to do many errands now; one of them was marketing for food with Moni and driving Lady Erminda to the hospital on weekends. There were no lengthy trips, and the car had been conserved for necessary errands. They always brought a cart to the supermarket and walked a good ten blocks from the store and back. Sundays were busy because the lady had to visit her husband at the hospital. Spring came, and there was no news of Mr. Onaje's discharge from the hospital. Moni thought it seemed like a long hospitalization for a fall. She felt bad for him, but if she did not watch herself with the help of the elder, the catastrophe would have been embarrassing. This way, it was more physical than psychological.

Chapter Twenty-Two

Spring came and went. End of May was rainy. Moni owned a raincoat now. She and Ting continued to do the food marketing, usually when the lady was home. One day, Ting told Moni that the husband would soon be home. Nobody wanted him in this home. Ting finally confided to Moni that for the length of time he worked for the family, which was around fifteen years, the husband was never personable. He was always distant, and if he gave orders, they were brief and unfriendly. He apparently did not originate from a rich family. In fact, he was rumored to be adopted when he was an infant. The adoptive parents were also landowners in Leyte but rumored to have grabbed lands from the poor, who were too illiterate to fight back, thus they accumulated several properties. Moni, having left Leyte as a young girl and very busy with her little business, did not know the details of the family. There were times when her uncles would be around for a get-together and she would hear a passing comment of the family name. Her doubts had been revived by these stories. She could not possibly entertain it now. In fact, Ting had commented that Moni had a distinct resemblance to Mr. Onaje. These comments made her wonder.

Ting was alone in the apartment, and even if the rent was subsidized by the Romualdos', the general upkeep, such as utilities and food, was difficult for him to handle. Moni thought of asking the manager of the supermarket if he had a job for Ting. He would have to work nights, and he would only do substitute work since he worked for the Romualdos'. The application was filled out, and the only person who could recommend him for his credibility, which would bear some weight, would be the Romualdos', but he could not ask. His visa stated against it. Moni, a very young-looking girl who had the confidence to speak and whose status did not have any significance, dared to talk to the manager. The hope of getting the job was nil. The other place he could apply was the corner store near the salon where Moni worked. They went to the corner store that day they had to market. Ting was accepted on the spot. He would clean and do odd jobs such as replenish items on the shelves. He would work every night, which started from midnight until six in the morning. He would start work that night. It was their lucky day. Ting had a supplementary job, and he would be able to keep his apartment. Moni was hoping that there will be no trips requiring long hours of driving at the Romualdos', which he might not have the strength to do. It was very tiring for Ting.

It had been a week since Ting had the midnight job. He was telling Moni that he had to lift heavy boxes and there was no break. He could only do five days, but he would keep on until he could no longer do it. One day, he was called to chauffeur Lady Erminda to pick up the husband. He did not have to do it until four in the afternoon. He was able to sleep for the whole day. Tuesday afternoon, Mr. Onaje came home.

It was almost the end of May. He was wheelchair bound; his face was bandaged across his nose, and his right leg was on a cast. When Moni saw him, he looked pitiful. She was looking at a very handsome man whose face had been ruined because of utter foolishness. He avoided Moni's looks. Moni avoided staring at him except side glances because she did not want to embarrass him. Looking back, what alternative could she have done to stop him from the invasion he did, a total disregard to the elder's status in the family? He thought the elder was so incapacitated or unable to do anything. Sadly enough, it had cost him so much to realize that the elder was able to do things such as untie the strings that caused his injury. In fact, he probably thought that the elder had given those directions to Moni. The elder, as usual, was expressionless when he arrived. Nobody knew how she felt, nor did anyone care. To a spectator, she was not capable of feelings nor was she able to think. Only Moni and

Mr. Onaje knew her capabilities. Everybody was tense since he came. Emma avoided him. The wife stayed home from work and took care of his needs. The few weeks after he was home were uneventful. Ting was busy with driving the lady for medical visits. The elder was almost ignored, and as usual, there was no indication that the elder was upset. Moni loved the elder so much. She wished she had had the chance in the past to know her, which must have been a privilege. Most of the rich were difficult to please, having been brought up in wealth, but she was different.

An employment agency was called to procure help for Mr. Onaje. They sent a rather overweight middle-aged woman to take care of Mr. Onaje. She was to serve his needs during the week. She was unattractive but personable and quick despite her stature. She looked efficient. It was a good decision to hire her. Mr. Onaje would never violate her womanhood. Her name was Opal Ross. She worked for a week and did not come back. There was no reason. Her leaving resulted in the struggle with the household activities with him needing so much attention. Ting was the only male around who could help him with his bath and other physical needs.

The search for someone to care for Mr. Onaje continued. Moni was the main help to Emma and Ting. Lady Erminda was also overwhelmed and unable to cope with the situation. Finally, a young masculine and fair-looking attendant was found. He stood a little over six feet and was brown-skinned and friendly. He was fit for the job, being strong enough to move Mr. Onaje from the bed to the chair and other physical needs. He seemed qualified. Weeks went by, and it was working fine. Mr. Onaje started to walk using crutches. Mr. Jorge Pines seemed to stay beyond his hours, having his dinner with the family. The lady seemed not to be bothered with his presence. Moni was happy that they never had to serve Mr. Onaje. Jorge had an eye on Moni. Moni did not know this. When she was in the kitchen cutting the vegetables, she was surprised when he placed his arms on her shoulders. He smiled at her, and as Moni tried to get away, Lady Erminda entered the kitchen and saw it all. Since that episode, Moni would look over her shoulders to avoid being around him. She would have to stop cutting vegetables or washing the dishes when he entered the kitchen area. There were occasions when Lady Erminda would notice these episodes.

One Saturday morning, Lady Erminda entered her mother's room while Moni was changing the linens. She was asked to sit with her at the edge of the big bed and was told in uncertain terms that she had a week to stay since her services were no longer needed. She would leave the sweaters and the pantsuits that were given to her. Lady Erminda was five sizes bigger, and she would not fit into Moni's clothes nor would Emma fit into it. Moni was afraid she would be told to leave the winter coat, which she needed. She had a paid return ticket and would have to call to book her flight back to the Philippines. Moni was shocked, unable to say anything. The Lady exited the room, as if in a hurry that this poor servant of a peasant upbringing might lay a hand on her out of anger. Moni sat on that bed, unable to move. She did not want to be seen by anyone. She was so embarrassed and worried. Lady Erminda went out that day.

It was the first week of July when this happened. It was abrupt, and she could not say anything. Moni was packing the few clothes she owned and could not tell the elder. It was up to the lady to tell her mother what she had done. She did not know the reason for Lady Erminda's dissatisfaction. She listed down the things she had to tell Ting and to keep her mail, which she would not know when to collect. She did not know what to do. She would be forced to leave the country since she had no place to go. She thought of Alisha and her previous offer. She was hoping it was still open. There was some serious thinking required, and she had nobody to ask advice from. Uncle Indong was not there. If she wrote the letter, a reply would not be received on time for a decision, and besides, her employer has discharged her, and it was final. She had a ticket bound for home. Ting felt devastated that Moni had to leave that soon. Her job was not to be finished until the coming January. He was designated to drive her to the airport.

That night, Moni went to Emma's room to tell her of the news. It was difficult because she was upset and she was not able to think through in silent actions. Emma understood it because she was crying. That week was difficult to bear. She wanted to know why she was discharged because to her knowledge, she had not committed anything offensive. She had to plan the financial matters, such as closing up her bank account. The coming Friday was her salon job, and she would have to do it then. She took advantage in speaking to Alisha about the possibility that she might have to take her offer. Alisha was delighted. Lady Erminda owed her some money, and she was afraid to ask. Her discharge was done diplomatically, so civilized that it was almost like she had not been given some bad news when it was delivered. The rich people had some control of their feelings. Moni admired it and she promised to herself she would do the same sometime in the future. She even admired the demeanor of a person with such control. She could not remember having done a mistake that warranted such anger. She was tempted to ask. She did not. She was afraid to trigger confrontation, and if she was going to be thrown out that night, she would not know where to go.

Most nights before her intended departure, she would visit Emma in her room. Gratefully, Na Pansang was asleep all those nights. Emma and Moni spent time together, and it was almost like a rendezvous of lovers who had to meet in secret. It was memorable for Moni, having a friend. Wednesday night, while Moni was slowly returning to the room, she was grabbed by the elder as she was passing through. She was waiting for her. The elder hugged her so tight and shed a tear. Once again, the elder knew. Moni, having always respected her grandparents, had now sworn that indeed all elders, no matter what category they belonged to, were full of wisdom. Whatever time was left between them was spent hugging each other, and Moni, having been so respectful, could never be physically close to her, mindful of her status as a maid. She had a few days to mentally prepare and kept on with her job and helping Emma.

Friday was the day for her to do banking, withdrawing whatever she had in the bank to anticipate for her departure. Lots of thinking all by herself, of which she was not capable. She was hoping there will be lots of customers at the salon. She sorted and packed her clothes and ensured that the clothes given to her were folded on top of her bed for Lady Erminda to collect. She would ask Ting to save her mail and give him money to send to Leyte. She wrote down all the activities she needed to do, just like Lady Esther had when they traveled to the United States. She would get up at five and ready to go in half an hour. Ting would come to bring her to the airport for the 10:00 AM flight.

As she was leaving the room, all dressed and packed, the elder switched the light on, grabbed her arm, and immediately handed her a sealed envelope. She nodded and signaled to open the envelope downstairs, to get going as she always did with her arm. The meaning was to open it right away. Lady Erminda was not there. She did not come home. Ting was waiting in the den. Emma was up with a sandwich by the door. They hugged for a long time, and they were tearful. Moni was carrying the thick winter coat, not knowing the purpose of it, being that she did not need it. It was summertime. The Lady did not ask for it to be returned, so she thought it was hers. Probably the Lady had forgotten about it, which was thankful for. She would give it to Alisha. She noticed that she did not have a nice winter coat.

They were heading downstairs and reached the first floor when Moni asked Ting for a few minutes for her to open the envelope that the elder had handed her. In the envelope was five hundred dollars with a note written in their native tongue in crooked, almost undecipherable penmanship, telling her not to go home yet. She would be allowed to stay with Ting. Moni showed the letter to Ting and, with his mouth wide open, could not believe what he just read. Nobody knew the elder had a say in this household. She sabotaged Lady Erminda's decision, so she must have some power over her. Possibly she owned the apartment and she had some power nobody ever knew. The garage was dark, and there was a moment of indecision whether to take the car or walk. It was ten blocks away on the west side of town. Ting decided to drive Moni to the apartment. The guard gave Ting a big nod, and they went on their way. Ting delivered Moni at the apartment, and he assisted her to use the payphone located at the small lobby at the entrance of the apartment. Moni never noticed this phone when she first saw Ting's apartment. He parked at a quiet corner street near the garage to let the time pass in case the lady would inquire from the guard as to the time of his return. He just wanted to be sure. He thought of how cruel it was for the lady to have done this to Moni after what Moni did when she was away. He could not understand the reason. Moni too had been searching for the reason of her premature discharge. Ting thought of the elder, who seemed not to know anything and how much she cared for Moni to have written that letter with some cash.

Moni, settled, sitting on the couch, took out her money pouch, counting every cent and dollar bill she had with her. It was her salon money, and what she had just withdrawn from the bank. She had 105 dollars and some cents, not counting the elder's money. Lady Erminda had failed to pay her for the week. She had forgotten about it. She could stay here and buy food for both of them. She would look for a job somewhere else at night so she would not be seen. That was her agenda for the day. She felt like crying and could not cry. This was Uncle Indong's fear. It came true, but it would have been worse if the elder had gone along with it.

The apartment was a poor man's dwelling. She has seen it before this incident happened. The closet, a small one which accommodated a few clothes, was spacious enough to fit her straw bag and Ting's suitcase. The kitchen area had a table that would sit four with three unmatched chairs. The electric stove and the sink area was big enough for one person to prepare the meals. The white-tiled bathroom was rather dirty, and the discolored tub also needed scrubbing. As she looked around the premises, she wondered where she would sleep with Ting's presence. Again, she would have to keep herself awake through the night. It was an unhappy situation for Moni, sharing a one-room apartment with a middle-aged man, a stranger, a predicament she never dreamt of. She had no one to tell. She would keep this information to herself.

Moni settled and cleaned the apartment. She wrote a letter to Uncle Indong that the boss was moving to a new address and she would inform him of the latest development. Telling him the truth would upset him, and his advice might not be applicable, being that the culture in this foreign land was so different.

At the Romualdo apartment, it seemed normal. Na Pansang did not know where Moni went. Ting took his time returning to the apartment. When he arrived, Lady Erminda was not there, presumably at work. The male attendant was already there. Ting pretended to see the elder, who was already seated in the television room, if she needed help, and he told her she was in his apartment. The elder nodded and immediately raised her right arm, telling him to do whatever he was doing. Na Pansang was told where Moni had gone, which was home to the Philippines. Emma did not know that Moni was still in the United States. If she had known, she would not be able to tell anyone. It was only Moni who was patient and tried to converse with her, taking time to do peculiar actions to convey the message. With Moni gone, she had no interaction with anyone. She had added chores since Preciosa was not rehired, plus caring for the elder. The elder had to be checked occasionally, mostly for bathroom needs, since Emma could not hear if the elder called.

A few days after Moni was discharged, the elder stayed in her room most of the time. Moni and the elder used to sit together at the television room most of the day. It was noticeable that she missed Moni's company. On weekends, she avoided her daughter because she went to her room after lunch and stayed there. She would ask for soup and stay in the room, missing dinner. Erminda seem not to know that her mother was not cared for. Emma, having to do lots of chores, would forget the elder. Ting went to the boss's apartment five times a week to help out with various chores. He did the food shopping and tried to follow Moni's methods.

For Ting, working nights and going to the Romualdos' every day was taking a toll on him. Moni was practically alone at night and had the apartment to herself all week, so on weekends, she would stay out, walking aimlessly in the west side area so Ting could sleep. Moni would choose an area where Lady Erminda would never go. She would leave him a note. Moni continued with her salon job. She was hoping to increase her working days, but it was not available. Moni and Ting seemed to get along. Ting had a talk with Moni that he had reduced his working days from the deli and would be home at night to sleep. It was a fatherly talk to a daughter about respect, and Moni was so relieved of her fear. The nights that he would be home, Ting would position the lounge chair facing the window to avoid some discomfort. Despite this, Moni was awake most of the nights

SHADOWS IN THE PANTRY

he was there. She no longer trusted anybody after the incident. The elder was no longer there to watch her.

Contrary to Moni's fears, Ting was gracious and respectable. After several weeks, she was able to sleep. Ting was a decent, reliable man. The elder knew him well, as he had worked for her for a number of years. She remembered the elder's note and the money. Moni cleaned the whole apartment and bought food and sorts as if it were her place. Finally, the salon had her come three times a week and work until the shop closed. She had more tips. Then as she hoped, she was asked by the salon to do four times a week. Tuesday to Friday work was fine. Fridays were busy and the only day that earned her more tips. Fifty to sixty dollars a week was acceptable. She need not touch her savings. Somebody came on weekends permanently. Possibly the weekends were very busy. She would stay until closing time, and Ting tried to pick her up since it would be almost nine in the evening. Sometimes Ting would be so tired and unable to pick her up, so Moni would walk briskly, almost run, and watch everything around her as she walked home. It would be half past nine, and the streets would be quiet. Alisha would also be heading home, but she did not take her route. Ting and Moni shared the cost of maintaining the apartment. Moni was not content with her income. She went to the supermarket and applied for a night job as a meat sorter. She knew the manager from her frequent visits to the place, so she was interviewed. There was no job for her. She was told to come every day to check the status of her application. It had been two weeks, and there was none. Moni was getting worried that she would have to dig into her savings to help Ting.

Moni had inadvertently told her customer Gloria that she was looking for a job and a place to live. She had lost her job since her boss no longer could afford her services. She could not tell her she was sharing a room with a middle-aged man. Nobody would believe she did not have a questionable relationship with him if somebody knew. Alisha reiterated her interest in Moni sharing a space with her. Moni was thinking about it, but if she did, she would be wondering how Ting would manage the maintenance of the apartment. The

Romualdos were still paying half of his rent despite financial hardship, and if she left, he would have to handle the bills alone.

The living arrangement had worked out fine. Moni, being very wise with handling money, had been cooking for both of them. Food was simple, mainly soups made of chicken and beef bones with vegetables. Ting ate everything there was, and the corner store he worked for gave him some cold cuts and some bread for free, which was very helpful. The supermarket did not have an opening for a cleaning job at night when she went to check on her application. She was managing on fifty dollars a week, and she had not touched her cash since she left the Romualdos' home.

One day, Ting brought her mail from home. Dee had finished her first year of nursing internship and was looking forward to a good year. Pina was physically well but had not improved mentally. Nemesio, her younger brother, was to be married to Melit, a young girl Moni knew. The business had been doing well. Her mother had hired a stay-home helper that did most of the heavy work such as wash clothes. The sad news was Mariana's mother had passed on in her sleep. She was ninety years old. Armando also sent her a short note, which indicated that he was fine and taking some subjects to pursue a business degree. Moni asked Ting suggestions on where the mail should go to in the event he would not catch the mail on time and Lady Romualdo might get the mail. He had no idea but promised her that he would watch for her mail. Moni was not too worried since she had written Uncle Indong of her boss moving. Moni did not send money since she had nothing to spare. She entertained the thought of returning home since she had a return ticket that she could use. She thought of it every night. Possibly her parents could afford to support her with their earnings if she could not find a part-time job.

In the meantime, one Saturday morning at the Romualdo home Na Pansang could not make it for the day, Emma cooked breakfast consisting of poached eggs and toast. Mr. Onaje took his time in the dining room, having his coffee while reading the news. Jorge set up his bath and his needs in the bathroom by the hallway. Mr. Onaje, still on crutches, tried to get up slowly and took his chance in walking without the crutches. He walked to his room to surprise his wife of his progress. As he pushed the bedroom door open, he caught his wife fornicating with the young attendant. His wife was naked and almost did not notice that the door was open and her husband was looking at her. Mr. Onaje fell on the floor, bewildered. He was unable to get up. He was not strong enough to hit the young man. He was barely walking. His cast from his right leg had just been removed, and he was not supposed to walk without crutches. The lady was naked in bed, and the door was still open as Emma passed by. Mr. Onaje, being physically handicapped, had slumped on the floor, his body preventing the door from closing. He could not say a thing. The male attendant immediately retrieved his trousers from the floor while Lady Erminda hid by the side of the bed to slip her robe on when Ting passed by. She immediately went to the bathroom. Mr. Onaje was flat on his face on the floor, uninjured. Ting went in and assisted Mr. Onaje with the help of the attendant. The attendant, with his unzipped trousers and disheveled hair, obviously did not belong in that room. They sat Mr. Onaje at the edge of the bed. The attendant, conscious of his appearance, zipped his trousers and quickly left the premises, took the wheelchair from the den, and situated Mr. Onaje in the chair. Lady Erminda dressed up for the day and signaled the attendant to leave. His day was done. The hallway bathroom was the bathroom they used to wash up, and the attendant need not be in Mr. Onaje's bedroom. Ting knew what could have transpired. The elder was in the television room. It could not be kept a secret, although the only person who had partially witnessed the event was Emma as she was passing through, doing her activities.

Emma quickly walked to her room and did not reappear. Lady Erminda was confident that the elder would not know because Emma could not speak. The only person who had taken time in talking to her in silent communication was Moni, and nobody knew. Emma saw the lady in that predicament and said it all. There was quiet chaos. The elder saw the attendant leave before his tour of duty. It seemed that nothing happened. Emma, in her room, needed to talk to someone. Moni was not there to tell it to, and she felt lonely. The lady had not gone out from the room. Emma heated a can of soup and a slice of toast for the elder. The elder suspected something was wrong. This time she had no clue. She was wondering why her daughter had not left her room. That week, lady Erminda took off work and stayed home. She took over the duties of Jorge.

Moni was due her weekly food shopping, and she saw the manager at the store. Apparently a part-time job had just opened. They needed a midnight worker on Thursday and Friday night. Moni accepted it and was told to come on Monday to formally sign the papers of employment. She would earn more money. She could not wait to tell Ting. Moni and Ting were having dinner together, and Ting told Moni of the incident at the Romualdo home. Moni knew why she had been immediately discharged. She had been seen by the lady with the attendant when he was trying to make a pass, even though she did not react to it. The lady was jealous of her. She would not tell Ting of her doubts. She was not sure. The new job at night was hectic. It required lots of lifting. She would do several trips to avoid lifting heavy loads. She has not gained any weight, and lifting heavy objects was difficult. The job paid well. She was given some beef bones to bring home. It was for soup. It saved them a lot of money, and they could now afford to buy fruits. She sent bank notes to her mother, uncle, and Armando. She said she did not want any reply. Both jobs kept her fed, and she was managing. She had no plans to return home. She hoped to save enough money for school.

From then on, Lady Erminda slept in the guest room. Mr. Onaje was ashamed. He was guilty of losing all his money in foolishness. Only his wife knew about it. Lady Erminda's money had been spent. The Romualdo family had been supporting them in that large apartment. The elder living in her household had been ignored, and the lady had gone astray. She obviously was looking for love that her husband could not give her. He was also guilty of so many things, and fighting with his wife was not proper. He was very quiet, and his depression was noticeable. Ting kept Moni informed of the news, at which she was not interested. She was only concerned about saving enough money for school.

Unexpectedly, Gloria Greene told her that her boss might need a cleaning lady to stay in the house and she would not need a place to rent. It paid two hundred a month with free food and lodging. Moni tried to figure out the money, and even though she earned enough, it was not permanent. It was a big decision to make, and she had two weeks to think it over. Gloria would recommend her as to her credibility, and she surely would be accepted.

She thought of the offer and the amount of money she would be paid and how beneficial it was for her. If she stayed in, she would not be able to do her other jobs. Going out at night to the supermarket job and the salon would be difficult to do if she took the live-in job and the fact that it would not be allowed by the employer. She would be inhibited. She figured out the income of the extra two jobs, earning meager, although the potential of earning more was possible. She needed the three jobs. There was no Uncle Indong to consult with. It was up to her to decide. She had not refused Alisha her offer in the event her plan would not work out. The Romualdo home being shaky, Ting might be out of the job soon before he knew it. Ting became the male attendant plus other duties.

Moni went for an interview at the Sloams'. It was a large apartment, much larger than the Romualdos'. She would accept the job if she worked nine in the morning to five in the afternoon with off on Fridays. She would not stay in because she needed to keep her other two jobs. She was accepted. She would start in a week. Therefore, she could reduce the salon job to Friday again and keep her night job. She had it all figured out. If Ting lost his job, she would have no place to stay and would not be able to afford the apartment all by herself despite her three jobs. She would take Alisha's offer if it was still open. She became friendly with her more than she expected. She would be free to go out with her on Fridays or hang out if she wished to. She had not explored the city yet, and she had taken off from the salon for two days before she started the housekeeping job. She would visit the scenic spots of the city. Moni would manage with the three jobs. Ting was a respectable person and treated her like his own daughter. Moni gave him all the respect as he respected her. Moni asked Ting about his schedule so she could coordinate her schedule too and be somewhere so he could get his rest. Moni would stay out until eight or nine in the evening. She found the library, and she learned to take the subway to go places.

Chapter Twenty-Three

The Sloams' apartment occupied half of the fourth floor of a building that stood on Madison Avenue and Seventy-Fourth Street. Apparently, Mr. Sloam owned buildings and some holdings, so Moni was told. Gloria Greene was the nurse taking care of him for the last four years. She serviced him ten hours a day, five days a week. She chose her off days, and a relief nurse covered for her. Gloria never told Moni she was a nurse until that time she recommended her for that job. She stood five eight inches tall and was rather heavy, but she was curvaceous. She walked with an elegant gait and dressed in a crisp uniform and polished shoes, representing the profession. She was brown-skinned, a mixture of American Indian and black descent. She had beautiful deep-set hazel eyes set on a high-cheekboned face, and her lips were thin. Her hair was dark brown, straightened and worn up to her shoulders, properly flipped inward. She was always neat. Her main asset was her inner beauty of utter kindness and goodness to people around her. Her duties were almost like a companion, giving medications and assisting him with his personal care. Most weekends, they went to places and fine restaurants, chauffeured in a large Cadillac. There was no hard work, and she enjoyed it.

Gloria was there when Moni was interviewed. She would not stay in, so her pay was reduced to 150 dollars a month and off on Fridays. She was expected to work from 8:00 AM to 4:00 PM. It was a good deal. Mr. Sloam was a ninety-year-old white man, probably around five feet and four inches tall, a balding, gray-haired gentleman who despite his wealth would always talk about his humble beginnings. He walked with a cane mostly when he was out but preferred the wheelchair when he was home. He was an anxious elderly man, almost always in a hurry to do things and still would try to plan his activities for the week. He lost his wife ten years ago and lived alone in this home with a live-in cook and a cleaning person. The secretary came twice a week, and the chauffeur came every day. The apartment consisted of big rooms, as well-decorated as most rich men's homes. The bathrooms of the five-bedroom apartment were also large and white-tiled; so was the hallway restroom. The large dining room and the ten-seated dining set were polished like new. The kitchen was separated with wooden swinging doors. The cook had a room all the way to the back with her own small bathroom. The hallways were wide, and the supply room, like the pantry, was almost as large as the kitchen, located next to the swinging doors. Moni, having seen the home of the rich, was no longer surprised. It was a large apartment for her to clean, but most of the rooms were not occupied. Theoretically, the rest of the rooms, being unused, possibly did not need so much cleaning. There was no other job she needed to do but clean. The first week was fine. The previous housekeeper had kept it clean, so the follow-up was not difficult. Gloria would talk to her often and would inquire on how she was managing. The month went by, and Moni always took the subway to head home to ascertain that she would not be seen by Lady Romualdo. The lady, as rich as she was, would never take the subway. She was cautious, almost like a thief that was accused of stealing. Mr. Sloam got doctors' visits every month, and when the cook was not there, Moni would be asked to make and serve drinks for a visitor. She would be dressed in a white apron, representing the kind of work she did. She avoided being seen in the sitting room. She needed not be seen and avoided eye contact with the visitors.

In the meantime Ting had reported to Moni the events that happened in the Romualdos' home. Ting took over Mr. Onaje's care, which was not heavy, being that he was almost independent. Apparently, Mr. Onaje was walking with a limp and had a choice whether he preferred to use a cane. His care consisted of setting his clothes aside to bathe and assuring his safety. There were no fights in the home. The couple hardly saw each other. Mrs. Onaje either came home late or did not come home. Ting suspected that she stayed at the male attendant when she did not come home. Mr. Onaje knew but would never confront his wife, having done silly things himself that nobody knew, at least not in the open. Lady Erminda's late visits with her mother after her arrival from Europe were never known, and presumably, Mr. Onaje did not know the elder knew it all. Presumably, Lady Erminda told her mother all her problems. Lady Ramona was ignored by her daughter, although Emma was there to take care of her needs. Lady Erminda was concentrating on the love of her life. The elder, having noticed her predicament, had asked Ting to write Lady Esther, expressing her wishes to return home to the Philippines and to include the information that Moni had been discharged from her job, and the reason was not disclosed. Ting did so with supervision, and the elder signed it with an undecipherable mark.

Moni wanted to visit the elder. If Lady Erminda learned that Moni did not go home, she would have her deported. She had the power to do so. It had been almost five months, and Ting managed to keep it a secret. He did not talk to anyone but the cook, whose conversation with him was limited to the grocery list. Ting had been accommodating to the cook, although he was not good at finding the sales like Moni was. At times, the elder would sit in the living room and face the front door to catch Ting's attention. She would raise her right arm and usher him. She would look at Ting, raise her eyebrows, and nod. Ting would stand there in front of her and would not know what it meant. He would say in a very low voice and speak in their dialect, "Nangutana ka bahin ni Monica?" at the same time turning his head around to be sure nobody was around to hear them. The space was large, and they were in the front room by the window. As he spoke, the elder would nod, and Ting would not elaborate but say, "Maayo man." He was basically telling the elder the young girl was fine. The elder would do her customary gesture of raising her arm and her forefinger, telling him to go and do his business. The lady of the house had been in her own world. She would just pay the bills without looking how much it cost and could not care less.

Mr. Onaje having recovered from his injuries was able to get around. One day, the lady left for the office, and Mr. Onaje also left unnoticed, possibly after his wife left. He did not come out for lunch, and the help wondered where he was. Emma knocked on his door, and there was no answer. Emma called Na Pansang, and both of them went in to investigate. He was not there. His clothes were there in the closet except his heavy coat, and there was no note as to his whereabouts. Na Pansang called the lady's office to inform her that he was not home. The police were called, and he was treated as a missing person, which did not require aggressive search. The truth was Mr. Onaje had dressed in his warmest, most insignificant clothes, without identification, and a few dollars hidden in his shoes and left home to mix with the homeless, where he could never be found. Nobody would look for him there. He did not belong. It was a conscious effort on his part to be unrecognized, and he would possibly die very soon. He had done wrong to the family, and to continue living in a household disrespected was not a life he could continue living. Together with unshaven, rugged men in front of a made-up fire from an empty barrel, he stood there, his ungloved hands spread wide to keep warm. His dirt-painted face was unrecognizable and covered with an oversized hood; he had camouflaged himself as one of them. He did not talk nor hear them talking. His prayer was if one tried to kill him that it would be quick. The crackers hidden underneath his oversized coat had almost been eaten, and although he had money in the old boots, he would not be able to enter a clean store to purchase food with his appearance. The lady seemed not to be concerned that her husband had not been home. The police were not called again to pursue the matter of his disappearance.

Moni was financially doing well with three jobs: housekeeping, the salon, and the supermarket. Her calendar was marked as such. The free beef bones and vegetables from the market were a help because they hardly bought food. Ting still received cold cuts and bread from the delicatessen. They had enough food and were able to save money. They talked about expenses every week to avoid conflict with money. Their expenses were mainly rent, utilities, and washing in the Laundromat. She had saved three quarters of her pay.

The money she had kept in a shoe box had been building up since she had been let go from the Romualdos. In case of unforeseen misunderstanding, she kept her friendship with Alisha so she would have a place to stay.

Ting had been sending money to his wife since his twenty-year-old daughter was at school. She wanted to own a beauty parlor and was taking classes to pursue that goal. He was hoping to keep the job. With the turmoil at the Romualdo home, he was insecure of the job. His plan would be to stay in the country a little longer, and with Moni's help, it was manageable. His rent would no longer be subsidized, although with his extra job, he would have enough money to have his child finish school. It was an eighteen-month course. His wife was never good at managing money, although there was hardly any to conserve. Moni, a young, inexperienced person, had been watchful of expenses. Even the use of laundry detergent and cleaning agents was done conservatively. Moni, being a very helpful person, had managed with her cleaning job very well. The cook at the Sloams' commented on how organized she was with her cleaning, doing it faster than she had ever known. After a while, she would be able to help out in the kitchen since there was nothing to do. There was only one person to cook for, and on weekends, Mr. Sloam would go out for the whole day. Moni would be bored. She felt like going to the salon to do work. She was afraid to get caught. The cook would be resting too. They worked together in the kitchen, preparing dishes.

Two doctors would come to see Mr. Sloam. An elderly doctor came accompanied by a young man. She overheard that the young man would soon take over his case, and the young doctor came with the elder to get them acquainted. There was not much to be done for him but mostly emotional support. When there were guests to serve, Moni helped with the aftercare. She did not want to serve the guests. She was not confident of doing a presentable job. She would stay in the kitchen. Occasionally, if the cook needed help, such as refilling the drinking water, she was there. She avoided eye contact and wore loosely fit black pants paired with a white blouse. Her straight hair was tied at the back with a thin black ribbon. Despite this unattractive attire, she would stand out and be looked at and be admired. The young doctor had a glimpse at Moni, and from that moment on, he would not get her out of his mind. Dr. Robert Schick was an accomplished elderly doctor who also taught medicine at Cornell. He was a gray-haired, slightly overweight man who stood five foot eight inches or so. He had a slight protrusion on his waistline and walked with a straight gait. He was very personable, with a quick smile and a fatherly demeanor. He was well-liked and even-tempered despite his status. He was almost retiring, and the young man he was with was one of those trusted to take over the care of his most endeared clients. The young man, a graduate from Cornell was one of the so-called the brightest not only intellectually but able to practice with quick decisive mind and precise, careful hands despite being new to the trade. He was a very charming lad, light-skinned and fairly handsome, who stood rather tall. He was almost six feet tall and broad-shouldered with a firm, manly gait. He had a smiling face, deep-set brown eyes, and full lips. He did not dress with expensive outfits but looked like he wore hand-me-downs since they did not fit him right. Despite Moni's disinterest in men, admittedly, she did have a quick glimpse at this young man and felt a little twinkle in her heart. She would wish for him to come when she was there. She would be wondering if he would come on a Friday, and she would not get to see him at all. She would pray that he would visit often so she could see him. She would think of him every waking moment and see him in her dreams every night. She wished he was one of her townspeople whom she belonged to. He was not. She would try to forget him, but she enjoyed the feeling, although she knew it was momentary.

Since then, the young doctor's visits became frequent for no reason. He came without the elder. Mr. Sloam welcomed his visits and did not complain. His bill remained at once a month although he could afford frequent visits. He loved having the doctor around. Without Moni's knowledge, the young doctor named Ken Shuman wanted to have a glimpse at Moni as often as he could. He knew she was a maid and probably uneducated. He would know of her name because Mr. Sloam would ask her to do something. Her answer would be limited to yes or no. Most of her duties would be delivering drinks, snacks. It was not her duty, but she was just helping the cook. He was so content looking at her almost like a goddess whom he could look at. Moni never stayed out of the kitchen for a long time for Ken to admire her. He actually would only have a glimpse at this adorable being. He would drink the glass of water so that Moni would appear to refill it. It was only the time she would be seen. He calls her in his mind. He did not care what descent she originated from.

Gloria, the nurse, would be wondering about the frequency of visits, which the young doctor would say he was visiting another client in the building. It was not true. After a while, even if the young doctor tried to be subtle about it, Gloria sort of knew. He was not too old, possibly six or eight years older or so than Moni. They were very different class of people and would never get along in the social standing that he belonged. Gloria did not want to think that way, but her being of black descent knew the reality of it all. She wished that Moni would find love. She was so deserving of it. The limited talks they had at the salon revealed a very pleasant person, sincere and deserving of all the very good wishes. As it was, Gloria sort of saw Moni's nonchalant attitude. Moni showed no emotion, nor did she even give the man a long look when he was there. If Moni only saw her performance, or if a movie director could have seen the kind of acting she did to conceal her love for him, it was spectacular. Gloria could not believe that Moni did not see the endearing look. Moni was trying very hard not to notice his looks since giving it value would make her dream of the impossible. Moni's coldness should have been enough to discourage a man of his stature. He could have any woman he desired. He was not discouraged. He suspected that Moni did not speak enough of the language. When he said thank you, she would bow her head of acknowledgement accompanied by a quick cold smile.

Chapter Twenty-Four

Gloria Greene took a week's vacation, and a relief nurse named Geraldine Keriyas took over. She was charming and seemed intelligent, but she talked a lot. She was not as presentable as Gloria. Mr. Sloam did not like her because she was noisy. She would take over the conversation with the doctor ignoring everybody. She did not act professional. She was temporary, so he tolerated her presence. That weekend, Mr. Sloam stayed home and was taking a nap when Dr. Ken Shuman came. He waited at the sitting room until he woke up. The young doctor saw Moni as she passed by with her bucket of supplies. Moni did not notice him. Moni was very happy with her cleaning job earning a few bucks, a temporary worker in a foreign land. Mr. Sloam treated her well and paid enough for the work that she did.

That weekend, Moni had done all the cleaning and was looking for something to do. She thought of cleaning the pantry, which she had not done since she started working at the Sloams'. The stock room was full of groceries, all varieties of food, almost like a supermarket. All kitchen supplies and linens were stored in this large room. It was half the size of the bedrooms. If there was a shortage of food, Mr. Sloam and his staff could easily survive six months eating it regularly. It was located way back at the kitchen, next to the hallway bathroom. The apartment was so large she would not know who entered the front door if she was way at the back. Equipped with a bucket of cleaning necessities, she arranged the items in the pantry, classifying them accordingly and dusting at the same time. One of the two lightbulbs that were supposed to illuminate the big room was not working, so the room was rather dark. Moni was not there to look for an item, so it was not really necessary to have it changed.

The door was ajar, and when it was opened without Moni's knowledge, the young doctor entered ever so lightly and stood at the back of her, at the same time pushing the door shut with his foot, wherein Moni turned around to face him. She was face to face with this man in that moment of vulnerability. She could not think nor did she have the mind or capability to refuse him. Without words, her knees weakened, and as he grabbed her face gently to kiss her she surrendered to his advances and allowed her feelings to release. It was a long, passionate kiss that Moni did not even know she was capable of. It was a moment, a long caress and closeness with this strange man she adored for in silence. The unlatched door slowly opened revealing shadows outside the pantry of two people that appeared like one. At that particular time, the nurse was passing through to use the hallway bathroom and saw the shadows as she went by. She then tiptoed, passing by to wait by the swinging kitchen door to see who was inside the pantry. Just when she saw the young doctor left the room who was supposed to be waiting in the sitting room where she left him.

Jealousy engulfed her. She, an educated person, was bypassed. Instead, he would fall for a dark-skinned maid, a low-class woman in this household who held no standing, possibly did not even know how to read and write. When spoken to, Moni would hardly answer but would acknowledge with a nod or otherwise. Her opinion did not matter in this space of the world, and besides, her speaking voice was not pleasant to be heard. She did not belong, and if her presence was ignored, it would not matter. She knew her existence.

Mr. Sloam woke up, and the doctor did a quick visit. The young doctor did not know the nurse knew. He quickly left and went back to the hospital. He could not even believe that he did that. It was real, and he really cared for her. His approach was rather disrespectful, but he had no other means. She was evasive. The only thing he was grateful of that she loved him too. His approach was accepted. It would have been such a shame if she screamed, and she ran out of the room and made a commotion. It would be a talk, and his reputation ruined. He had been avoiding advances from women because he was betrothed to someone. He had not flirted with other women until that time. Admittedly, his move was rather aggressive. Moni, squatting on the floor, embarrassed and ashamed, looked around, not wanting to get out of the room. She did not have the energy to continue. Instead, she remained in the pantry, sat on the floor, and looked at the dusty floor she was supposed to clean. She waited to leave when the coast was clear. She tiptoed out of the room, looking around, wondering if she had been seen.

After that rendezvous, Moni was uneasy. She could not believe she had let her feelings go. She was embarrassed to herself yet happy. If he did not startle her, the reaction would have been different, or did she have the emotional control to refuse him? She probably would not yield to her emotions. She dreamt of him every night since she saw him but never pictured them in such a romantic mood. When five o'clock came, she ran ten blocks instead of taking the subway to her humble abode. She had nobody to tell about her new human experience of how weak one could become in moments of love. Those were moments when she did not have control. She prided herself with such control over embarrassing, uncontrollable behavior, but this time around, she did not. Could her mother have felt the same way when she first met her father? Did she also behave like she did, that loss of ultimate control? As she sat on the old, oversized couch and she looked around at the poor people's dwelling, she was imagining the possible outcome of that shameful moment. She kept reliving the moment as if it had not happened. After that incident, whenever the relief nurse came, she would be told to dust and do chores such as give the nurse a glass of water. Moni would follow suit and did not show resentment.

The elder's letter was received by Lady Esther. To allay Lady Esther's concern, she was told that Moni was with Ting and she was all right. Lady Esther did not know what to do. She promised the family that Moni would be safe, and even though a misunderstanding had happened, she was in safe hands. Ting had worked for the Romualdos' since age twenty and was known to be a trustworthy man. There was no hurry to fetch her mother. Her son was graduating from high school, and being the only parent, she had to be present. The Romualdo household was peaceful. Mr. Onaje's absence was not a topic of conversation. The elder was content, and her daughter, who was hardly there, did not bother the elder. Emma tried her best to attend to her needs.

Meanwhile, Mr. Onaje, having been brought up rich, had surprisingly survived in an environment he chose to be in. He enjoyed being carefree. Being an adopted son of a landowner, he was encouraged to marry a woman with status, and at that time, it was a life of luxury and leisure he desired most, being born to abundance. He looked back to his youth of his adoptive mother dying at an early age and being brought up by a nanny. There was no family around, but on holidays and vacation time. He was well-fed, his needs attended to. He was driven to and from school. He wondered why he was almost exiled from the rest of his cousins. He thought of his loneliness, and at the time, he did not entertain it, but being alone at that moment among the homeless, he was not alone anymore. The food he collected from the back alleys of restaurants fed almost everybody, and they were most grateful. He no longer aspired for the fancy clothes and the cars but was content, it seemed, of the life he was in. There under a bridge, he did most of his thinking and his past. Admittedly, he sometimes wanted to go back and retrieve the lost time. He could ask for forgiveness and promise to change. His wife tolerated his misbehavior and kept it a secret, protecting him from embarrassment. On the other hand, his wife, so deprived of love, was seeking for it and found it. He should allow her to be happy. He decided not to return.

He was properly schooled at Ateneo de Manila when he was young, but he did not use it to his advantage. Instead he engaged in womanizing, squandering his money and his wife's belongings. He deserved the treatment and his wife falling out of love.

Chapter Twenty-Five

After Moni's rendezvous with the young doctor, he would wait for her at a corner, and he would follow her, and the relationship began. They would meet at the west side near her apartment. They would go to a small insignificant café to have some snacks. Finally, she invited him in, and there they became intimate. They were two people in love. She would see to it that Ting would never know. She would have a schedule of his work in her purse so she would never make the mistake of inviting him in when Ting was returning home. She would look forward to those days when they could make love and she would be loved.

"Moni, how long can you stay in the country?"

"Not too long."

"Tell me about your origin?"

"Nothing much to tell, but I grew up poor, and my parents, they can read and write, and we struggle on an island called Leyte. You do not know it. It is a poor country, my country."

"It is a tropical place, right? Have to look it up, not too good with geography."

"What about you? You have mother and father?"

"Yes, my mother and father and two brothers . . . nothing to tell."

"I live with my mother in downtown Brooklyn. Have you been around yet? Someday we will go."

"Far from here? Have to check my schedule. One day we go."

Going home to her country was forgotten. Even school was no longer her dream. Gloria noticed Moni's happiness, and she knew.

She would hope that he was not trying to fool her. As Ken Shuman did his doctor's visits, Gloria noticed that he avoided contact with her, mainly because they did not want anybody to know. Gloria would never ask Moni about it at the salon when she probably would tell her the truth. Three months went, and they saw each other as often as they were able to.

One night, Ting had to return to the apartment because the boss had no work for him. As he was approaching the door, he heard a commotion and Moni giggling with her familiar laugh when she was happy. They had no television, and her giggling by herself was unusual. He stood by the door and finally waited downstairs until the visitor would leave. He did not want to embarrass Moni. She was of age to have a boyfriend, and even though he was the responsible person to care for her, it did not include matters of love. Finally, after waiting for an hour, he went up the upper floor by the railing so he could look down unnoticed when somebody exited the apartment. He finally saw him. He looked dignified, the way he carried himself. He did not look like a bad person. Feeling bad about having inadvertently eavesdropped on her, he walked around the block before entering the apartment. He thought of his twenty-year-old daughter, who could be doing the same thing. It was human nature to do it. He hoped nothing happened. Monica had found her love and was enjoying the God-given gift of pleasure. He turned the key several times as if he did not know how to do it, to alert her that he was entering. He told her he was not feeling well. Moni had almost been caught. She tried not to act surprised nor ask questions that would make Ting suspicious. It was his place, and he did not need to explain if he came home. After that incident, Ting would mention it to Moni if there were any changes in his schedule. He would say it as if it were not important.

So Ting knew, but Moni did not know for certain if Ting knew. The affair continued, and the place of her rendezvous was the apartment. Moni would only serve soup and rice, and Ken would eat it too. Conversations were always about Moni and how she happened to be here in this country. She never hid her origin of coming from a poor family, the nipa hut and that sort. Contrary to his thinking about her dumbness, which he was ashamed of it, she was most intelligent and able to carry conversations—in broken English, as she called it—and actually knew of things beyond what Ken thought she knew. If only he knew that Moni had gone to the library every chance she had before she met him. Ken hardly talked about his origin. He was more interested in knowing her past and her family. There was no information that was to be told except her poverty and her quest to become a teacher. Moni did not mention to Ken whom she lived with. She did not know how to explain it, and if she did, it would not be believable. She hoped this was a secret she could keep.

Ken bought Moni blouses and a nice jacket after he noticed that she was always wearing the same outfit every day. Looking around in her apartment, there was a small closet that would only accommodate a few clothes. It was an apartment fit for a humble person with few belongings. That moment in time, Moni was very happy and rather content. She wanted it to last. She wished that he were not a big doctor with such education so high that others would think she wanted him because of his job. She would not go out with him, afraid to be seen. She wanted to hide her newfound love so no one would know. Although one Friday afternoon, she took off from the salon, and they met at the library downtown. She was seen by the relief nurse, Geraldine, outside the library while they were sitting on the steps. They walked all the way uptown to Seventy-Sixth street and Tenth Avenue. The nurse followed them. They did not know.

Ting was staying late at the Romualdo home. He had to drive Lady Erminda somewhere with the elder. Moni had the whole evening with her loved one. Young as they were, lovemaking was all they did when they were together. There were stolen moments, a rendezvous so memorable that both of them did not want it to end. Moni had a feeling it would not last. At times, she would imagine what she would do if he went away. She would prepare herself emotionally if it happened, and she had plans of how to cope with it.

One Saturday, a clear, cold January day, she was given a whole day off. Mr. Sloam and his nurse were going for a drive to Connecticut. They would not be back till sundown. She went out early and started to walk downtown to the theater district. She looked around and really had nowhere to go. It would be an enjoyable stroll since there were no time restrictions. She wore the red blouse that Ken gave her. It would have been a good day to go out with Ken, although she did not want to be seen with him. She never inquired about his schedule. She knew from reading books that a doctor got called any minute. Understandably, no one schedules illness. It just happens. She was content having him to herself and possess him in those private moments when they were together. She really did not know the outcome of this love affair. He was free to think and free to do what he wished. She stopped at every interesting place she felt like. If she had still been in the Romualdo home, she would not have had this freedom, although if Lady Erminda happened to see her, she would surely do something mean.

She looked at some displays and stared at them, thinking of him and his image in front of her. There were several bookstores she went in, mostly of old books, which she wanted to look at, but they were very expensive. She brought money with her, mostly to buy food when the fruit and sandwich she had would no longer be enough. Things were very costly, and aware of her meager income, she would always be watchful. She stopped by a small corner café and treated herself to a cup of coffee and a doughnut. It was getting late, around three o'clock in the afternoon, and she had not seen everything. Memories of these must be recorded. She went to a camera store and looked for an inexpensive used one and film. She then started to take pictures carefully, having only twenty-four shots.

She kept walking on Fifth Avenue and felt like she needed the comfort room. A jewelry shop she was window shopping at was the door she went to. It was a place she did not really browse in since it was a store for the rich. As she was on her way to exit, she saw Ken at the store at a distance with somebody, looking for some jewelry. She almost fell back and simultaneously, out of instinct, evaded the front view, situating herself so she could comfortably see and verify his identity, making sure that she was beyond his peripheral vision. She sort of moved from counter to counter so it was not obvious to the sales clerk that she was only there watching somebody with no intention to buy. She was not dressed rich, although her winter coat was expensive, bought by Lady Erminda. The sight was sad because Moni saw him kissing her on the lips, which revealed that she was no blood relative but a girlfriend. Judging from what she saw, they had known each other for quite a time. Moni decided that she had seen enough and discreetly left the store, assuring that she would not be seen. She crossed at the traffic light and stood across the street and waited to see them leave. It was a good half an hour. They held hands and joyously walked uptown. Moni had to walk home. She did not have money to buy a subway token. She could not concentrate on looking at sceneries around her.

The minute she was in the apartment, she took the shoe box and counted the money she stashed away, the bank book too. From the six months and a half that she had been on her own outside the Romualdo home, she had a thousand dollars in cash and eight hundred in the bank. She had done well. She was devastated. She avoided crying, which was very difficult to do. She did not want Ting to know her problems. He would never ask, but she did not want him to worry. Her happiness had been momentary. It was almost like a dream. Staying in the apartment was lonely. She walked uptown, not seeing anyone, and ended up at the salon. If Alisha was there, she could help out. Her face was red from crying, but the weather was getting cold and windy; she had an alibi that the wind on her face had caused the redness. Although she was brown-skinned, she noticed that at wintertime, the pigment seemed to phase out momentarily and became red when the cold chill hit her face. Thinking about it, Ken probably thought she was white, which she was not. She had told him of her East Indian origin and her family.

When she reached the salon, it was only Alisha that was there. It was such good timing to be able to earn a few cents and keep busy to forget the current problem. Indeed, there were lots of customers. In the few hours until closing, she collected a good six-dollar tip and a few dollars from the hairdressers. She enjoyed the salon because there was lot of interaction, and she learned so much about how to survive living in America. She learned about used furniture, clothing, buying cheap plane tickets, and the sort.

Every waking moment, she would think of the best decision to deal with it. The week went, and Moni did not see Ken. He would normally wait for her at the corner street nearby, her route to head home. Another two weeks went by, and although she missed him, she accepted that she would not see him again. He did not come to see Mr. Sloam, but the elder doctor came instead. She did not overhear any comment, nor was his absence discussed. After four weeks, he was waiting at the corner street, and he accompanied her home. It was still early afternoon, and Ting would not be home till evening. They spent the whole Thursday afternoon, and Moni did not mention the sad event and pretended it was all the same. He was warm, and making love was enjoyable. She decided to enjoy him at that moment to remember him by. He left at around seven in the evening when Ting would return home shortly. Moni was cleaning up the room when Ting came in. The news at the Romualdos' was Lady Esther was coming to bring her mother back to the Philippines. Moni told Ting it was a better idea to tell Lady Esther that she had gone home to the Philippines when she arrived. Ting did not question the decision.

Gloria Greene noticed some change in Moni and thought that she had broken up with him, which she expected. She had not been taking off and stayed on to save money for her trip sometime in the fall. Moni was avoiding Gloria, pretending to be busy. She would clean the bathroom three times a day and would clean the kitchen for the cook. The cook appreciated Moni and, with her German accent, would speak to Moni about it. Moni would not understand it and smile at her to acknowledge what she said, which to her must be praise. Ken was not as frequent at the corner street to wait for her at past five. It was another week, and he appeared at the corner street presenting her a red rose and a beautifully wrapped gift for Valentines' Day. The way it was wrapped was a sight; she had never received a gift in such a way. To her, wrapping it was more expensive, having had experience doing it at the old store she used to work as a young girl. Inside it was a bottle of perfume. He apologized for the delay of the gift because the occasion was a week ago.

It was a good day, it seemed, and Moni was delighted and showed her appreciation. She did not have a flower for him. It was getting more difficult for her to pretend. She was a plaything to be taken advantage of. She treated him as a toy that she totally enjoyed. She was actually teaching herself not to love him anymore. As much as she tried, it was not easy.

Saturday afternoon, she was met downstairs at Mr. Sloam's apartment by two well-dressed men asking for her passport. Immediately they presented their identification saying, "I am James Jamieson, and my partner is George Schultz. We are immigration officers. Is your name Monica Almadin? Your passport?"

Moni was bewildered, and stuttering, she said, "I do not have it with me."

After she left the Romualdo home, she had not been bringing her identification because she did not have to present it to the guard on the first floor. She was escorted to Ting's apartment, where she presented her passport.

She told Gloria about the two gentlemen. Moni brought her identification from that moment on. Gloria inspected her documents and discovered she had the right to stay but said she was not supposed to work elsewhere but at the place who employed her. She was given a few days to leave. Gloria Greene had been working, and gratefully, Moni had somebody to consult with. Gloria was upset that it had happened to Moni and suggested for her to leave the current employ and live with her for the length of time she intended to do. Moni was so surprised to hear the offer. Gloria was trying to think of who could have hated her that much to report a young girl of meager income to the immigration officer. Moni did not tell Ting. She would take Gloria's offer. She finished her work at the Sloams'. Gloria was the one who told Mr. Sloam that Moni would return to her country. Mr. Sloam immediately gave Moni two hundred dollars from his pocket and made out a check for two hundred dollars. He would normally stash money in every jacket, and Moni would find money sprawled on his bed. Moni would call the cook who had been under his employ for quite a time and witness the amount. Moni never knew if this was a trap, but she would not be part of stealing money from an employer.

She stayed at Ting's apartment for another week. Gloria gave her a key to the apartment, and she had a choice of the day she could come. A date was set. That day she intended to leave, she was cleaning the apartment for Ting so it would be clean when she left. She left a note:

> Manoy Ting,
> Daghan salamat sa imong pagtagad. Mo-uli na ako sa ato. Molarga ko ugma. Gibinlan ta ikaw ug usa ka gatos para abang.
> [Basically she said thank you and that she was leaving for home. She enclosed one hundred dollars for rent.]
> Moni

There were enough beef and chicken bones to cook in the small refrigerator for soup. He would struggle in paying the maintenance of the place alone. His night job would probably cover it. He would not be able to send an ample amount of money to his wife. Moni kept counting the money in the shoe box, and she placed her dollars in a pouch. She tied it and knotted the strings carefully into her undergarments. She had a total of two thousand dollars. She kept counting it over and over again, not believing that she had saved that much from her three jobs.

Chapter Twenty-Six

The walk to Gloria's was sad. Her straw bag seemed heavier this time with more clothes in it. She crossed Central Park toward the East End, and she did not view nor enjoy the landscape. She was imagining her time with Ken, so much so that if she happened to meet Ken, she would not know him. She did not know how long it took her to Gloria's. Gloria's place was located in the east side on First Avenue and Eighty-Fourth Street. Judging from the ground floor setup, there were not too many apartments in this six-story building. The mailboxes were few on the wall, and the foyer was small where the elevator was located. As she reached the fourth floor, the hallway was wide, and looking at it, there were only two apartments on every floor. She knocked lightly, presuming Gloria was home, and she did not want to bewilder her in case she might be with someone. They had agreed on the date and approximate time of her arrival. She had a slight trouble fitting the key and was afraid that if somebody happened to pass by, the police might be called that somebody was trying to enter Gloria's apartment. She looked around and was finally able to enter.

Gloria's place was a two-bedroom apartment painted white. The living room was spacious, the kitchen enclosed, and the two-seater table overlooking the river was fit for a single person. It was furnished simply and had a window where there was a small stove with two burners. The sink was very small. As it looked, Gloria hardly cooked since the top of the stove was very clean. The place was decorated to a taste which indicated an interior designer's touch. It looked comfortable. The living room had a couch, which was for two people to sit on. There was enough room to walk around, and it was actually perfect for one person to live in. There was a small round glass table by the couch, and a magazine was on it. The bedroom doors were open, and she kept calling and peeked in to investigate if Gloria was in. As Moni peeked in the rooms, one bedroom was large, equipped with the best of matching furniture. The small bedroom was almost where she placed all her unwanted items, since opened boxes were on top of it. There were large closets in the living room and the bedrooms, so most of her clothes were put away. Moni cleaned the whole apartment. It was not dirty or cluttered. Gloria arrived and was not surprised to see Moni but was amazed how clean her apartment looked.

"I am glad you made it. Be comfortable. Occupy the small bedroom. Just clear it up."

"Thank you for helping me. I do not know what to do."

"You take your time. I'm glad I could be of help. I'll just rest a while, and do whatever you have to do, and thanks for cleaning."

Moni was welcomed with sincerity. She thought of her illicit rendezvous with Ken and how she had almost got caught by Ting. She thought of the same thing, and she would not want to come in and see Gloria with a visitor. She cleared off the bed and settled herself in the small bedroom and was suddenly tired. She too took a nap. When she woke up, Gloria was up too, reading a newspaper in the living room. It was too soon to discuss the arrangement of her living at Gloria's. Moni had a key. There was a telephone that she could call when she was coming, or better yet, she would have a written schedule to alert Gloria. Gloria was appreciative of the written schedule. Definitely, her presence would inconvenience Gloria. The next day, they talked. She did not have to pay rent, but she would be responsible in cleaning and participate with buying food. Moni wanted to give Gloria the two hundred dollars Mr. Sloam gave him, but Gloria refused it.

Moni would leave early in the morning to take the bus cross town to the west for both jobs. She would have to ask the salon again if she could work more days. She still had her Thursday and Friday night job, which was a very convenient job since she was never seen by anyone but her coworkers. She was hoping to work more nights. She got paid twenty dollars a night.

The agreement was generous. Gloria worked long hours, and she practically came home just to sleep. Moni cooked her beef bones with vegetables as usual, which Gloria would have some of too. She was most pleasant, saying that she had come from poor parents herself, had paid her way through college, and she ate everything that was offered. Luckily, the salon asked her to work three days, which was Monday, Tuesday, and Friday. She walked across town to save her fare and stayed in the city to go straight to her midnight job. Moni would be running and keeping her hood in case Ting would be around the area where he would see her. She was very watchful and behaved like a convict. Her stay in the United States was limited, and her overstaying was mainly to earn enough money to continue school. Obviously the immigration department knew she had not left the country yet. Looking back, the immigration officers were not threatening. They were not mean. They were just doing their job.

Moni seem more tired than usual, and despite her enthusiasm to do more, her body did not feel the drive. She rested on her days off and slept more than ever. She kept on with keeping the apartment clean and performing her share as agreed. She would leave when Gloria came home to accommodate her private moments. She would leave a note as to her whereabouts and approximate arrival time.

Gloria took off two days to rest. The relief nurse, Geraldine, called her at home, which was unusual, to ask her specifically where the cleaning person had gone. Gloria was wondering why she had specifically asked for the young one when there was already a replacement. She was most interested in knowing where Moni went. Gloria, then, was suspecting that Geraldine was the one who had called Immigration to have Moni deported.

Moni was all stressed out when she noticed that she did not have her monthly woman's ritual. She had never been regular in her monthly bleeding, but she was worried. When she was younger, she did not have it for six months. A doctor was never consulted. April was approaching, and she did not have it. She was getting worried. She could be pregnant. Ken Shuman had not dared ask Gloria Greene when he came to visit Mr. Sloam where Moni went. Ken's fear of losing her was happening. The reason of his aggressive behavior at the pantry was an act of frustration of not having had the chance to tell someone of his love. Now it was all gone. He would become an accomplished doctor, and he struggled to be, yet his love was not there. He was suspecting that the relief nurse had seen him that day at the pantry with Moni and she had done something to eradicate her from his life. He was engaged to a girl, but when he saw Moni, there was some hesitation of getting married to his betrothed. He did not see Moni. He went to the place of her dwelling and nobody would answer. He would go and wait across the street in hopes of seeing her. His premonition came true.

Gloria would not say anything and pretended she did not know where Moni was when the cook inquired. Ting, having received the note from Moni, was very sad. He missed her company and her efficiency. The apartment was never as clean as when Moni had joined him. He would have a hard time managing with rent, although half of it was paid by the Romualdos'. If it had not been for Moni, he would not have had an extra job, which allowed him to send ample money so his daughter could attend cosmetology school. His daughter had almost finished her schooling, and the tuition was paid when Moni was sharing with the household expenses. Moni's absence was missed. He never realized the thing that she did to make the apartment smell the way it did. Moni cleaned every moment she was home. There was no idle moment. If she was sitting down, she was reading books borrowed from the library.

Ting went to the Romualdo home every day to help with the heavy work in the household. Emma was grateful of his help, which he did out of thoughtfulness. In the meantime, Lady Esther came and still wondered where Moni went. Ting told her she had already left for the Philippines. Ting was ordered by the elder to tell it all to Lady Esther. Indeed, the elder trusted Ting and the things she did not know Ting told her. It would seem that the older sister avoided a confrontation because she avoided lengthy conversations with her younger sister. Lady Esther, having been told the details of the events, needed not talk to her sister, although she did not know the real rea-

SHADOWS IN THE PANTRY

son of his fall in the elder's room. The only people who knew why Mr. Onaje was in that room were the elder and Moni. The elder, unable to speak, could not articulate it, or possibly, she could but choose not to, to avoid gossip between the sisters. She would just say hello to Erminda and very diplomatically leave the premises, giving her sister room to be free with her mother. She shared her mother's bedroom, and if her sister wished to speak with her, she was free to do so.

Lady Esther was getting ready to bring her mother home. She did not confront her sister, understanding the misery she was going through. The thing that troubled her was Moni, who had been discharged without committing an offense. The reason for Moni's discharge, she would never know. Lady Erminda stayed out late most nights, and her alibi was her job was getting heavy to handle. Ting suspected that Lady Erminda stayed in the male attendant's home most evenings. Lady Esther mentioned Mr. Onaje's absence to Lady Erminda, but she ignored the inquiry, so Lady Esther did not pursue it. She assumed her sister and husband had agreed on a separation and no one should pry into it. Lady Esther stayed for four weeks and left with the elder back to the Philippines.

Ting remained as an errand person and a driver for Lady Erminda. Mr. Onaje was never found. There was no dead body found that would indicate that it was him, although a photo was not given to the police, nor was there a follow-up by the family after the initial disappearance had been reported. If a photo had been submitted, then the image of the body found might not have matched with his original photo. Mr. Onaje was not employed in a company. The family possibly had enough means to support him.

Moni kept on working and kept watch so Ting would never see her. The delicatessen where Ting worked was near the salon. He worked there from midnight until six in the morning. If there was a change of schedule, she might be seen. On the nights she worked at the supermarket, she would sit by the subway steps where people would be passing to wait for midnight when she would take the train to the supermarket. The market was almost ten blocks from the salon.

Moni knew she was pregnant. Her black pants were becoming tight on her. She bought two used blouses at a thrift shop to wear over them. She learned where to buy inexpensive clothes at the salon. She would not survive in this country with a baby, and besides, she did not have a visa. She would have to return home. She looked overweight, and in a few weeks, people would notice. She saved another thousand dollars because she did not have to pay rent.

By the end of May, she was ready to go. On her free days, she went to the city to the Battery Park to look at the Statue of Liberty. She could not afford a ferry ride, but even at a distance, she could enjoy the sight and its grandeur and what it represented. She had read about it at the library. The workers at the library were most cooperative in helping young people procure books that interested them. Her time to do this was limited. The places reachable by train or bus were the only places she could go.

The first week in June was her departure date. Friday night at the salon, she told the lady at the desk and Alisha when she was leaving. Her reason was that her visa expired. She told the manager at the supermarket the same. That same night, she told her friend Gloria she was pregnant, to which she said she knew. Gloria, being a nurse, knew, and she even gave her some advice as to care and the date of confinement after she knew the last menstrual date. Gloria, being very respectful, did not pry on her private affairs. She knew Moni was madly in love even though Moni tried with her might to hide it. She did not tell her when she was leaving. She had a week's vacation going places and rested in between. Friday night, she wrote a note to Gloria. She taped it on the bathroom mirror.

> Dear Gloria,
> I did not tell you the date of my departure. I could not handle the miserable feeling. I do not know a better word than a plain *thank you* to express my gratitude. I am not educated enough to express it in better words. I love you.
> My respects,
> Moni

SHADOWS IN THE PANTRY

She wrote a letter to Alisha addressed to the salon.

> Dear Alisha,
> You were my first acquaintance in this country who did not look down at me, at my ignorance and not being able to speak right. I thank you for your friendship. My chance in coming back to this country is almost impossible, so sadly I bid you good-bye.
> Your forever friend,
Moni

These letters were written and rewritten several times to assure its accuracy. Reading the magazines and books in her spare time had taught her a lot. She also wrote a note to Uncle Indong, her mom, and Armando. She indicated that she was well and needed no reply and that she was moving to another address. She needed another suitcase to accommodate some items purchased at the thrift store.

Chapter Twenty-Seven

Early Saturday morning, she took the train with her belongings, heading to the airport. It was a business-class ticket converted to a cheaper seat; she only paid twenty dollars. On the plane, she recalled her trip to the United States, mostly her stay at the Romualdo home, and for a moment, she shared the luxury of the rich. She learned a lot, and it was sad because an incident had happened to have predisposed the aftermath. If she had stayed there for two years, life would have been as planned. Meeting Ken was happiness. It was a moment of pleasure, and although the shame she caused to herself and her family was regrettable, she was carrying the fruit of such love. She was no longer hungry, nor did she listen to instructions. She had enough money to live without working for a year after the baby was born.

It was Sunday noon when she arrived in Manila. She hired some help and took a cab bound for Quiapo. She did not know how to get around in Manila, having been there but once at the airport when she had met the elder two years ago. It was a short glimpse from the domestic airport, being chauffeured from one airport to another. It was not as crowded compared to when she first saw it. She chose the area because it was a busy place and she would get around unrecognized. It was a popular place, being where the Church of San Nazareno was located, a strategic landmark where the faithful followed processions of his image miles long held on his feast day. The cab driver was very conversant, but Moni could not fully understand him since she did not speak Tagalog (the national language of the Philippines) well. She hardly spoke it even though she had learned it at school. She pretended to be preoccupied. There was no need to speak it, not having had anybody to talk to and having lived in Cebu all her life. She only spoke Bisaya, a dialect spoken in southern Philippines, which was her native tongue. She did not want to let the driver know that she was from another island and ignorant, a province girl who knew nothing of the city. He might be tempted to bring her around beyond the route to earn money. The few pesos she had, from since she had left two years ago, should be enough to pay for the fare (although she had prepared a few five dollar bills to add to it). As they were approaching the San Nazareno Church, she spotted a bank nearby where she could have money exchanged to pesos. She separated the big bills, never to be seen. Altogether, she had saved three thousand dollars. She prided herself on having had control from such temptation with all the items to buy in America. She had nothing to show, nor would anyone suspect that she had come from the United States.

She gave the cab driver a large tip, at which he grinned at Moni with a loud thank-you. He even helped her bring her suitcase to the church area. Moni was happy to be able to afford it. The church was quiet; there were few women kneeling on pews, heads covered with a mantilla (*boronda*, as it was called in Cebu, a piece of lace on top of their heads). She had not gone to church since it was not customary with the Romualdos to go to church on Sundays; although, on her own, she had had the chance to see the magnificent St. Patrick's Cathedral in New York City.

She decided to settle in Quiapo. A busy place like NYC. It is the center of business and not too far from other places such as Quezon City, Pasay. Besides a jeepney was accessible and the church was right there. She could afford a cheap place, a hotel, to sleep in until she could find a room to rent. She found a rooming place with a private washroom. It was rather expensive, but it was in Quiapo. She would stay there until she found another room wherein she could comfortably settle until the baby was born. She had money, but she was careful. She treated herself with restaurant food. Her oversized printed blouse where she inserted her money at the seams still fit, and she would be wearing it until her ninth month. She was already around five months on the way. She intended to work so she would keep her money untouched. She walked the Quiapo district where most inexpensive restaurants were located to find a job as a waitress. There were none. She was not anxious. She could live three months in the current place comfortably without worry. She would rest and brought enough food to her room. The place was noisy, and the door locks were strong, but she slept in the bathroom to play it safe. She would rest all night so she would have the energy to look for another room. She went out every day to look for a room and rest for a day from exhaustion. Two weeks went, and she did not find a place to live. She was getting worried that even though she saved enough money, it might not last if she did not find an inexpensive room.

It was early, and the streets were not as crowded. A few blocks from the main road, she entered a street, and a few houses from the corner on a post, there was a sign. It was written on a misshapen piece of cardboard, and it stated "Room for Rent" with an arrow underneath it, and a number was written. She slowly walked the street, and the first house she saw had no number. She kept on, and the next house had number 4 written on it and a sign that read "Na Goria." The ground floor had a wide glass window that stretched from the main door to the end of the two-story wooden home. The swinging screen door was oddly wide too. She entered with hesitation and was met by a heavy middle-aged woman standing by the counter. She was stern-looking. She was almost smiling despite her tired look. Indeed there was a room for rent. The woman was tending to her customers, and she signaled for Moni to wait. The counter was lined with pots filled with hot, steaming food, several of them on cloth trivets and multicolored plates, a wide-mouth glass jar with steaming hot water containing spoons and forks. The handwritten list of food prices was conveniently posted on the wall as one stood to view the food at the counter. The window area was well lit, since the sunlight from the street illuminated it well. The place had two ceiling lights, which probably kept the place illuminated at night. The other wall had two tables and a small window. It was draped with a flowered curtain. The place was pretty clean. The table by the window was not occupied, so she sat there and waited. It was a self-serve place, and looking at the list of food prices at the wall, it was reasonable. Being that she did not have breakfast, she tried the rice with vegetables. She took one of the tables on the other side with a small window overlooking the back of the property. It was a hearty breakfast fit for the moderate-income people in the area. Finally the place quieted down. The woman stepped out of her nook by lifting the flat wood that served as a barrier too. Noticeably she was alone, and she looked disheveled, rather overworked. Her apron was full of stains, and she smelled like a kitchen that needed cleaning. The lady signaled Moni to follow her. The door by the side of the main entrance led to a staircase. Moni followed her upstairs. As they reached the landing, she was led to the room on the left side. The woman fumbled for the key among the several she had with her and opened the door. Finally she spoke. Moni was told that the rent was such, and an arrangement was agreed on. Moni took the room, and the required amount was set. Moni was to occupy the room anytime. The only thing she was adamant about was the rent had to be paid on the first of the month, and if she intended to vacate, she must alert her four weeks in advance.

The room had two small windows overlooking the street just right on top of the main door. It illuminated the room during the day. It was draped with a very thin fabric printed with fine flowers, faded from wear. It was a small room, furnished with a single wooden bed with a thin mattress covered with a worn-out sheet. There was no closet, but there were hooks on the wall to hang clothes. One light bulb hanging on the ceiling with a switch by the entrance was apparent. Moni was led to the only restroom for the three tenants, including her, to use. The restroom was big enough and was not clean. The two rented rooms she never saw. It seemed that the size of them was the same as hers. Her new residence was a two-story wooden house with three bedrooms on the second floor, and the floor area was the eatery and a place for the owner. The outside walls needed repair, but there were no holes that Moni saw. The main door of the house was sturdy enough to keep the occupants safe. It was on a corner lot, and the neighboring houses were concrete. The best thing yet—it was a walking distance to the church. She might go to church often as she planned it. The street only had around ten houses, and the end was an intersection.

She took the room and paid the month's rent. Moni requested to hook up a fan, and she was willing to pay extra for utilities. She could move in as soon as possible. The required amount was paid. Apparently a lady came in every week to collect dirty laundry, which was convenient. Moni booked it for an uncertain period of time. She was given a key and as they headed downstairs the lady said all tenants were women.

She immediately vacated the hotel, took her belongings, and planned her activities of the day. She now had a residence decent enough and affordable. Food was there to be had, and being pregnant, she would never go hungry. The lady was nice enough and too busy to watch anyone. As long as she paid her rent on time, possibly she would have no problem. The place needed sweeping and thorough cleaning. Each tenant did her own cleaning, judging from the dust on the hallway. She would have to do some cleaning herself. She would have to buy the needed cleaning products and sorts. Being pregnant, she needed to use the bathroom frequently, so she had to buy a potty in case the bathroom was occupied. There was one bathroom for the three tenants. It was very inconvenient.

The main door of the restaurant automatically locked at night when one left the premises. Each tenant had a key and was responsible to lock it when one of them had to leave in the middle of the night or might come home late. No visitors were allowed; possibly a woman friend may sleep over for the night. She tested the safety of the place and taped a small sewing thread across the bottom part of the door and went out. When she arrived, the string was detached. It was evident that somebody had entered the room. She inspected her few belongings, and being that they were old, none was missing. She had brought with her the necessary identifications and her money. Presumably, the only person who had access to the rooms was Na Goria. The next day, she purchased the cleaning necessities, a potty, and a padlock.

She cleaned her room fit to sleep and changed the linens with matching pillowcases and bath towels on a hanger on one of the hooks and her robe on the other. It looked marvelous. New curtains replaced the old ones. The owner was so impressed of her cleanliness. The electric fan was not sufficient to cool her off, and for a while, she could not get enough sleep. It was amazing how the body had adapted to the cold weather and had trouble adjusting to this change. It had taken her two weeks to find this place, and looking around for another that might be cooler and bigger was almost impossible. It was a room that fit her needs, and if she could not find work, she had enough money to last her for a year. She had to be frugal. Na Goria and Moni got along, and although the lady hardly spoke, she was actually easy to get along with. Moni noticed she did not talk about her tenants. True enough, she was too busy. Food at the restaurant was cheap, catered to the poor, and there were enough variations. In fact, she needed to work. After a week of doing nothing, she asked the owner if she could work part-time. She could work in the kitchen or serve food. Her application was accepted readily. The pay was meager, and she could work five days. She opted to work three days. The helper, Seniang, was a young girl taking high school courses at night, and Na Goria was left alone to do all the work after five in the afternoon. The help was appreciated, being that the owner needed to rest after the eatery was closed. In fact, she was asked to work five days. She was aware of her condition, and she consented to work four days.

The back room of the counter space where the food was displayed was the kitchen. A door from the kitchen led to Na Goria's room. It was locked by a horizontal lock. Na Goria's room was moderately big to fit a single wooden bed with a thin mattress on the left side as one entered her room from the eatery. A wide open closet was on the other wall, and the space in between was wide enough to get around. Na Goria had few outfits, and two medium suitcases were on the bottom. A few pairs of fairly new pairs of shoes were lined on the bottom as well. The room was sparsely furnished, with a small drawer with a mirror, a small table, and a chair to do her paperwork. It had a comfortable washroom with a shower. A door allowed her to exit to a small backyard where a small tree comfortably afforded shade to a person sitting on a bamboo bench. Right outside the door to the courtyard was an enclosed cemented area to do the wash. A faucet with enough running water and a drain to the underground kept the area dry. A rope from the back of the house was tied to the tree as a clothesline.

The room was safely locked at night from intruders, both to the eatery and the main kitchen. It was a place for her to rest up and relax. The owner lived very poorly in this small establishment without a husband. She was up very early to market and retired by midnight. Moni worked from ten in the morning until eight at night. She was allowed to rest at two in the afternoon when the store was slow. Food was free on work days. They got along well, and even though Moni was off, she was entitled to stay and relax at the backyard, which was cooler than staying in her room. Her income at the eatery was not enough to sustain her, but it was indeed a lot of help.

In the meantime, Lady Esther was troubled by Moni's whereabouts. She was accountable for Moni since she was the one who had hired the young girl and had spoken to the parents that indeed she would be in safe hands. She would give it a lot of thought. She would go to the Bonedotos' and find out if the seamstress had come to deliver clothes. The Bonedoto' were on vacation for an extended length of time, and Lady Esther was puzzling what to do. It was on her mind often. She called the owner of the warehouses if Indong Rotilles still worked at the place, which he did. There was a lot of hesitation on her part to call him for reasons of not knowing what to say. She gave herself time to think things over and decided not to call.

Moni's family had no idea of her whereabouts. She did not want them to worry. Even though her premature discharge from the Romualdos' contributed to her problem, they were not responsible for the predicament she had allowed herself to get into. Moni admitted this and would never blame Lady Esther for what had happened.

Chapter Twenty-Eight

Ken Shuman finished his internship at Cornell University. He would work with Dr. Robert Schick, possibly sharing his practice as an internist/pulmonary doctor. He was engaged to be married, but the wedding was not set. He occasionally went in the vicinity of Moni's place and walked aimlessly across the street, hoping to see Moni. He knew that she shared the apartment with an elder man not related to her. He was looking for a guy that might appear Malaysian-looking. He would literally wait outside the apartment and intended to introduce himself to someone he would not know. He tried to wait on the upper floor to have a look at Moni's door for a few minutes but was afraid of getting caught, apprehended for loitering. He did this several times. It was obvious that Moni did not want him to know. Their love was so short-lived, and he did not remember the specific days when they would normally see each other. The days they met were the days the man was working.

The new office, being recognized as one of the best, was hectic. He focused on his job and needed to prove himself as a worthy partner of a well-respected doctor. Dr. Schick had reduced his working days and was ready to retire. He would be a consultant if a difficult case was to be handled and required his experience. The memory of Moni kept him happy, but he was guilty because he would think of her when he was with Carol Ann, his betrothed. He was now in doubt if he would go through with it. Ken was in love with someone else. It was unfair to Carol Ann. He told her that they would wait because of his new practice.

He volunteered to visit Mr. Sloam in hopes of seeing Moni. He presumed she had gone on an extended vacation somewhere. He never knew the type of entry visa she had held to be able to stay in the country. He had no address to write to, not having the informative details that he probably should have procured. He just knew he was so in love that thinking was not part of the agenda when they were together.

In a café on the corner street near the apartment he would go to look for her. By the glass window, he would stay to view the street and recall the old days. They were so vivid in his mind, and it pacified his loneliness. As he exited the café after a cup of coffee, his limbs were weak, an old man searching for something he would never find. He had made it to the top. His dreams of being a doctor were fulfilled, but being as lost as he was at that moment he never foresaw. He would try to forget those moments, but during times of being alone, they would visit him, and a mixed happiness and loneliness would engulf him. His betrothed, a very pretty lady of education, a psychologist, seemed to understand his problem, having gone through training of taking care of individuals trying to find themselves. She, of course, did not know the real cause of his confusion. Finally, he called her out of respect and met her to have a heart-to-heart talk that he no longer loved her. She accepted it. Ken dated several women and found no one that he wanted to be his lifetime partner. His practice kept him busy and tired.

Ken's mother wondered about his indecision to get married. He never told her. Having a thriving practice guided by an experienced professor who paved the way to his success was an accomplishment she never expected. Ken provided for a well-furnished three-bedroom apartment on the upper east side of Manhattan for his mother. They lived comfortably and afforded comfort to her mother. She needed not worry about anything. Miss Shuman, accustomed to working, took a job at the nearby pharmacy.

They had long conversations of her past, the origins that Ken never knew. He was the illegitimate son of a man his mother hardly knew. Mildred Shuman was a daughter of an impoverished family from Chauncey, Ohio. Her father hardly worked. Her mother was a domestic help, cleaning houses. They occupied a shack with no heating facilities. There was hardly food on the table. She grew up not understanding the reason her father never worked. She endured being mocked by her classmates because she was not dressed well at school. Her clothes were all hand-me-downs from the people where her mother worked as a cleaning lady. She learned then that her father was mentally slow. She finished high school and worked as a waitress at a diner. She had an illicit affair of a man she hardly knew. When he learned of her pregnancy, he told her he was married and stopped parking his truck at the diner. She knew his name, and she was in love. There was nobody to go to for advice.

 She left town leaving a note to her mother that she was fine and she would write, which she did. New York City was a busy town. People minded their own business, and nobody cared. After weeks of being homeless, she landed a job as a store help in an Italian-owned delicatessen. She had no home, and she requested the lady of the house if she could stay and sleep in the storeroom. It was cold in the storeroom. The lady provided her with a portable cot and enough blankets. It was kept a secret from her husband until one night when Mildred inadvertently knocked off items from a shelf, and the noise woke him up. The couple had a big argument. The small room at the top floor used as storage room was re-arranged to accommodate a small cot for Mildred to sleep. Mrs. Punzano begged her husband to let Mildred stay for a few dollars rent a week. Mildred was becoming big, and she could no longer hide that she was pregnant. The lady was sympathetic, and being childless, she automatically took her in and became a loving mother to Mildred. Visitors came, distant relatives they were, and accepted her presence. Lady Punzano's nephew visited frequently and expressed his intentions, but Mildred did not want a relationship. Life was fine. She worked there, paying rent, and Lady Punzano became the loving babysitter. Two years went by, and Mildred was able to save some money and was planning to leave. She was looking for her own place. A tragic event happened when the lady died and the business was sold to someone else. She then moved to a studio apartment in the vicinity predominantly resided by Italians. There was no babysitter she could trust, so she became a welfare recipient until Ken attended elementary grades. When Ken was in high school, she worked part-time and took courses to be a secretary. All this time, she would write to her mother and she never received a response. Traveling to Ohio was too expensive to check on her folks.

Ken grew up in a studio apartment, sharing a bed with his mother until he was twelve or so. A small bed was purchased, also placed in a corner of that studio apartment when young Ken get older. Ken had a loving mother who sat with him to do homework; she spent most of her time with him and brought him to the park and inexpensive places. Mildred concentrated on bringing up her son so he would never be poor like her. Ken would ask about her family, and Mildred would tell him that someday they would go and visit.

When Ken was accepted to medical school through scholarships, Mildred took a trip to Ohio. She did not find her parents. The shack they used to live in was no longer there. Moderate-looking homes stood on paved streets. It was a long time ago, and she did not pursue the search. She went to a nearby cemetery to look, but thinking it through, nobody would have buried them there. She did not know of any family who came by to visit them.

Mildred fulfilled her dream that her son, born out of wedlock, was brought up poor but obtained an education more than she expected. She lived in a place that only the rich could afford. It would have been nice if she had found her parents to enjoy this luxury and let them have a taste of simple abundance such as daily bread. Ken not married had worried her. She longed for some grandchildren, and as years went by, she accepted that she might never have one. She no longer asked for it.

Gloria would see Ken when she worked at various hospitals doing private duty nursing. They pretended not to know each other. Gloria noticed that Ken did not have a wedding ring. Mr. Sloam had since passed on, and she took a permanent job at a nearby hospital. Doctor's Hospital was located near the mayor's mansion. She lived four blocks away. Gloria too found no one among the many who pursued her. She missed Moni, a friend whose company she enjoyed, and was wondering what happened to her. She lived in the same address and wished she would write her a note.

Chapter Twenty-Nine

After several weeks Moni was accustomed to the heat, and after a good wash up at night, sleep was possible. As months went by, the size of her abdomen became visible. Being small in stature, she appeared fat rather than pregnant. The owner did not ask nor did she look at her in such a way to ascertain if indeed she was on the family way. The owner was too busy to know. As long as the rent was paid and nobody was rowdy, she did not have a problem. Moni never talked to anyone about it. She kept to herself, and meeting with the rest of the tenants was limited to a quick smile and a short hello.

Moni planned the day of the baby's birth. She bought thin materials to make shirts, which she made on her off days. The window overlooking the street was most entertaining to Moni, and she would look out, watching people go by, while she was doing her sewing. It was such a comfort to know that she need not worry about money. If she did not work, she had more than enough to last her for a year living in this inexpensive place. The rest of the tenants went on minding their own business. She lived poorly and kept her appearance clean, wearing inexpensive oversized clothes. She was already on her eighth month, and she was avoiding standing on her feet. She has reduced her working hours to twice a week, helping out on Saturdays and Sundays. Being that church was within walking distance, she would attend mass every morning at six. She became the cleaning lady with time to sweep and clean. She considered herself lucky. Despite her mistakes, she was blessed to have the gift of reason, preparing herself for enormous problems, which would have been worse if she did not save some money. She would regret having had an illicit affair, but she had been in love, truly in love, with someone so gorgeous she would have been a subject of jealousy by other women if she had married him. In retrospect, she wondered if he would have proposed marriage if he knew she was pregnant. Or would he disappear from her sight, not wanting any part of her and possibly suggest getting rid of the baby? She would not be able to cope with the outcome in the event it would be true. This way, she had her way, all on her own.

She went to hospitals and planned her move when the time came. She already picked the birthing place. She chose the university hospital. She watched the hurrying personnel, student nurses, some of them with rundown uniforms, presumably ready to graduate, and graduate nurses in a different style of uniforms, which distinguished them from the students.

Gloria Greene computed the approximate date of birth, which was the end of September or the first week of October. In fact, she wrote her a letter, which she did out of respect for her kindness. She did not put a return address; therefore, she could not reply. Moni hoped Gloria received it.

She finally stopped working but helped occasionally, mostly the cleanup at night. Na Goria was most appreciative and gave her free food.

An oversize bag containing a long skirt and money inserted in the seams, some cheap undergarments, soap, a washcloth, a thin towel, toilet paper, a toothbrush, and toothpaste was always brought with her wherever she went. The indigents were not provided with these necessities. The date was approaching, and at any given time, she would have the baby. She would be at a place near the hospital, so an ambulance would not be fetched, nor should she have to search for a cab whose driver might be too nervous to find the place. They might hit traffic, and she might have to deliver in an unwanted place, and the baby's condition might be jeopardized. She would walk to the place. She observed every pain she would feel. Every day, according to the predicted date, she would go out to the place she intended to have it. Gloria warned her that the baby might come either two weeks early or two weeks late from the predicted date. She was nervous, and she had nobody to tell it to. She never had a friend in her childhood, anybody close, but playmates only. At that moment, she wished she had a good friend like Gloria. Gloria was exceptional. She would think of Ken every waking moment. What if she had never met him? Would her life be better? As much as she regretted her mistake, she enjoyed recalling those moments of love. Nobody could take that memory from her.

She would be home before traffic set in, so she took the jeepney. This was her ritual. God had spared her from the hardship of pregnancy, and this time around, she expected to go through the struggle of motherhood. One early morning, she was awakened by a sharp pain on her abdomen. She was always dressed, ready to go for this event. It was a sure sign. She took a cab to her destination. It was only half past four in the morning. When she arrived at the vicinity, she entered a small eatery where students in the university took their breakfast. She took a seat all the way to the back and had some hot cocoa. She sat there for a long while, waiting for another sign. It was almost daylight. She was hungry again, but Gloria had warned her not to eat heavy. She followed suit.

The Saint Thomas University Hospital was located on Dapitan Street and Forbes Avenue in Metro Manila. It was a big establishment that educated students varying from medicine, nursing, engineering, business, teaching, journalism, music, law, pharmacy, and priesthood. A big compound enclosed securely with a surrounding wall. The main entrance facing Espana Street presented a big yard and a sculpture of St. Thomas Aquinas. It was a nice walk to the main building where the registrar and classrooms were located. A wide road separated each building. The university hospital was toward the back, by Dapitan Street. An open gate toward the street allowed entrance for students and people visiting patients.

The university hospital was Moni's choice because they had a charity ward that rendered services to indigents—male and female patients of medical and surgical conditions, children and women having babies. It was managed by the Sisters of Charity, a religious order differentiated by their white floor-length habits and stiff, wide head covering. Several of them could be seen on every floor. Moni would wonder how they supported themselves and who cleaned their attire since it was clean white. Specialists came with medical students to evaluate the cases, and therefore, patients received some attention and expertise from the seasoned doctors. They dressed differently, some rather fancy, and some seemed not to care. The demeanor of confidence distinguished them from the rest. Moni was there to notice all this and was confident that if a problem occurred, she would have the privilege of being attended to by an experienced doctor. She stayed at the restaurant for a good while and entered the gate, heading to the university hospital. The circled cemented seat under the shade of a small tree a few steps from the gate served as her resting place. The abdominal pains had tapered off, and she went to the restaurant to have some soup. Afternoon came, and the pain was gone. She was debating whether she should return to her rented room for the night, but she was fearful of the delivery and having to bother someone to bring her to the hospital in the event it was the day. She was not certain if any of the tenants knew of her condition. She evaded them, and due to the fact that the washroom was always clean, they possibly did not gossip about her. There were no occasions that Moni would have lengthy conversations for them to ascertain her status.

    She decided to sit on that space until late. It was past seven in the evening when she started to exit from the gate to fetch a jeepney heading to Quiapo when a sharp pain was felt again. She hesitated and stood there. She turned around and sat at the bench. The atmosphere seemed cooler on that late September night. Her pains became sharper and more frequent. It surely was the day, and she slowly walked to the back entrance of the university hospital. The indigent patients of various conditions and visitors entered here. The wide space was furnished with metal chairs that lined the wall. It was a dimly lit room with unpainted dirty walls with cracked floors of undetermined color. It was a place where indigent families sat to wait or rest from worries. A place the family discussed financial worry where the sick could not hear. A slightly elevated desk located at the far center of the room was the admitting section. A nurse and a receptionist were there, entertaining a potential patient or a relative being questioned. To the right of this space was the entrance to the male and female ward of medical and surgical patients. Each ward accommodated twenty-five patients. The patient's confinement in these wards was subsidized by the tuition fees paid by the medical and nursing students. The patients had to pay for their medications purchased according to financial availability, hopefully on time for treatment to effect a cure. The entrance to the left was the children's ward, a place for women who were sick and having babies, and the nursery. Moni had inspected these wards before she was visibly pregnant and knew exactly where she was going.

She sat among the people who were waiting for various needs. She was one of the insignificant beings seated in that room. Despite the pain, she did not show it, and no one knew she was ready to have a baby. She was in such discomfort that she finally decided to head to the department where she would appropriately be attended to. She slowly walked to the left, trying not to attract any attention. Moni was passing by the children's ward of crying sick babies so uncomfortable at having to endure the attachments to their extremities, tied down, immobilized out of necessity. Mothers and elderly grandmothers stood by, watching the little ones struggle since the babies were unable to say their pain. It was not pleasant to pass by this part of the hospital. The poverty was more visible, it seemed.

She entered into a wide corridor where several medical personnel were rushing through for various reasons. It was nighttime, and the place was well lit. During the day, light from the wide windows illuminated the hallway. A courtyard could be seen inside the hospital premises, and there was a walkway connecting the area to several departments of the hospital. Personnel and students would sit and relax at the courtyard during break time. Several white painted metal chairs were provided.

Moni was slowly turning to the female ward, and midway when she just passed the nurses' station, the pain was so intense, and she could no longer withstand it. Her knees buckled and she fell while a nurse was passing by and screamed for help while assisting her. A gentleman in white attire came running to rescue her with the help of the nurse. She was flat on the cement floor, and they noted that she was on the verge of delivery, and a stretcher was rushed to get her into it wherein she was all ready to deliver. The baby was out in time when she was on the stretcher. Moni, in pain, was speechless, unable to utter a word out of shame; hence one of the nurses said,

"She cannot talk," and she went along with it. A baby's cry was heard while she was being wheeled to the delivery room. The baby was placed on her chest, and she heard the nurse say,

"Lalaki, pero mukhang puti itong bata na ito." (The nurse said it was a baby boy and he seemed to be white-skinned.) Indeed, this baby was of Caucasian origin. Only if he was born legally, she would have been smiling. She did not smile not because she did not love him but because she felt sorry for him to have been born in such circumstances. She became the Emma Romualdo who was deaf-mute. This way, she would hide her shame and would be anonymous, a person without a name. Moni was transferred to a bed while the baby was cleaned, and the nurse came back and placed the baby in her arm. She had the chance to view the face, cleaned and presentable to a mother's eye. True enough, he was reddish white with light-brown hair. He had none of her features. He was all Ken. Moni continued her demeanor. She did not know how to react. The baby's presence was an embarrassing moment, and truthfully, she did not want to be there. She kept looking at him while the nurse was talking to her, and she pretended not to hear her and kept her expressionless face. After a few minutes, the nurse finally kept quiet. The nurse said to herself, "Ay, talaga palang bingi ire," saying "Gosh, she's really deaf and unable to speak," at which time she left while Moni was still holding him. It was an hour or so when she came back and took the baby without saying anything. The person was deaf, and there was no reason to talk to her. He was placed in the nursery.

Moni was not comfortable in that metal bed, which squeaked when she moved. Despite it, women, tired and weary after having had a baby, were mostly sleeping. It was around nine in the evening. It was a smelly place, full of women who seem not to have washed up due to hurry, or possibly, the linens that covered the mattress had not been properly cleaned. It did smell dirty, and the supposedly white sheets had turned pale gray. Having been a laundry woman, she could not bear the smell of the bedsheet. She took her thin towel and placed it on top of her pillow.

The fifteen-bed-capacity ward was full of women who had babies. Some of them had big abdomens; Moni could not figure out if they were still pregnant or if the pregnancy still bore the remnants of the protruding abdomen. Moni looked around although she had seen this scenario before, having planned her delivery place long before the date. Moni, still wearing her faded housedress and her bag on her side, dozed off to sleep. She was very tired. Being up early and having been anxious of this moment, her mind and body needed a rest.

She was awakened by seemingly numerous people indulging in whispering conversations. It was then she realized that it was around eleven in the evening and the nurses were giving a report. The student nurses, wearing white with white aprons, managed the whole ward. There was a head nurse wearing a different style of uniform and who looked confident, which distinguished her from the student nurses. Moni had seen them from previous visits to this ward, having pretended to visit someone. She enjoyed watching them work, going into their business as they walked briskly through the wide aisle with their crisp uniforms. Moni was debating what to do for the next hour. Indeed it was true that the baby could be born two weeks early. It was September seventeen.

Chapter Thirty

In the meantime, Uncle Indong was wondering why Moni had not written since May, although he had been advised that she would not be able to write because she had to move to another state. He was tempted to call Lady Esther but did not. His family had been well. Dee had been serious with her school work with passing grades, going through the vigorous training of school and work at the hospital. She stayed at the dormitory, which afforded her some restful periods, not having to take transportation from home to school. It cost more money, and the money that Moni used to send was sorely missed. Delina had continued with her sewing, mostly from neighbors. She stayed home, people bringing their materials to be made. Indong kept on with his job, and his loyalty was compensated, having two days off every week instead of none with an increase in pay. The house was almost paid off due to increased payments he had made when Moni had remitted money for Dee's tuition. The family went out on weekends for a stroll, a nonextravagant means of entertainment. Maxi, Moni's mother, visited occasionally, being that Avelino had started high school and was living at Indong's home. As usual, she brought provisions for the family. Avelino, not having a job, did most of the washing for the family. Pina, although physically able, would do some of the light wash, but Avelino did most of the heavy work. Pina did not improve. She was still dependent on her parents on most of her needs, although she had been helping her mother in mending and hemming the clothes. Delina had been grateful with whatever assistance her daughter has been affording her. The main thing was, Pina did not worsen and was still able to help with various chores in the house. She had not mentioned her ordeal and presumably had gotten over the trauma that she had gone through.

So Maxi visited and brought some dried meat and cash money to assist Indong for the maintenance of the household. Maxi's business had been doing well. She hired two more ladies to help her make the ready-made clothes. Maxi talked about Moni and exchanged views of why she had not written. Maxi would read the letters addressed to Indong wherein Moni would always inquire about her parents' welfare. The last one was dated May, and everything seemed fine. Maxi's husband had the same business and was doing well. Nemesio was married to Melit, and she was pregnant with their firstborn. She was a few weeks on the way and having terrible signs of stomach problems. They lived in the same house, which Maxi welcomed.

Chapter Thirty-One

Unexpectedly, Moni gathered her belongings and went to the restroom. The restroom, a five-stall toilet with five washup sinks, was unkempt. The white tiles needed cleaning. The smell from not being cleaned was not acceptable, but those were all the facilities presumably fit for indigents. After getting washed, she slowly walked the wide aisle thoroughfare toward the exit passing the children's ward. It was never quiet on this section and a pitiful sight to walk through. Moni did not listen to the cries since she was not feeling well herself. Slowly she exited the dimly lit room unnoticed. People sitting on the metal chairs, their heads leaning on the wall, were presumably resting. She tiptoed, afraid to wake up any of them. She left the premises carrying with her the oversized bag. Nobody interviewed her, being that she was deaf mute and nobody knew sign language. There were several deliveries that night. Women delivered their babies in stretchers, just like her. They did not have the time or appropriate resources.

She did not plan this move. In fact, she felt like lying down. She suddenly felt very tired. She followed her tracks when she originally came in. This time, it was dark and approaching midnight. The cemented seat under the tree was empty for who would be sitting at that seat this hour of the day. It was a comfort to sit there, and she was wondering how long she could occupy that seat before being found. It was obvious that they were looking for her. She sat there for a few minutes. The gate was still open, although she never knew if it closed at a certain time, so she walked outside the gate and entered the small restaurant, which was still open. She had some vegetable soup and realized that she was very hungry. It satisfied her, and she started to walk toward Quiapo.

The jeepneys were rare, but she was wary to take them. She kept walking very slowly and reached a corner wall where a homeless woman was squatting beside her large rattan bag. Moni was tired and decided to sit beside her, and the woman said nothing. The woman gave her a surprised look and seemed delighted that she had company. Moni took out the thin towel and immediately placed it on top of her head to conceal her young face and spread her flared housedress to cover her extremities. She placed her bag in between the both of them. Amazingly, Moni dozed off sitting in such an uncomfortable position dressed as such beside somebody whom bystanders would not bother looking at because of status. She did not know how long she slept, but she felt rested. She did not have a wristwatch intentionally, since she was going into a charity ward. Her wristwatch, inexpensive as it was, was a gift from her parents when she had graduated from elementary grades. She did not want to lose it. She regretted that she did not purchase one in the United States.

When she woke up, it seemed quieter than usual. It was darker since the storeowner at the corner had shut the lights off. Moni was scared, but frankly, her fears were allayed by the presence of this elderly woman who inadvertently became her security guard. Her smell was the reason that people did not want to bother her. It was obvious that Moni did not mind the odor because she dozed off again, and when she woke up it was dawn. She stood up and patted the elder's arm, sort of saying thank you and bidding good-bye. It was safer to take a cab since it was almost daylight.

The cab was also dirty, and it smelled like fish. The driver was shabbily dressed but very respectful. He was rather young and attentive. The drive to San Nazareno church was quick. Moni went to church asking for God's forgiveness for leaving her son at the hospital. She cried, and as she sat down, she dozed off again. There were a few churchgoers at this time, and there was nobody there to see her. The church just opened for the early mass.

The hotel where she stayed at when she first arrived was not too far off a walk. Luckily, a room was available, and she decided to stay there for several days or two weeks to rest. She had to think of a reason as to the baby's whereabouts. There were few inexpensive restaurants around, and money was no problem. She was prepared. Her rented room was paid for, so her things would be intact, since she had locked it on the outside. She would not call the landlady. She could not really care less what would happen to her. She was too busy.

Meanwhile, the baby in the nursery was well taken care of and doing well. The nurses expected the parent to appear and claim the baby. It was an odd baby, being of a different race among the dark-skinned babies in the nursery. He became the favorite of the nurses, being that he was always there and did not to belong to someone. It was a problem—what to do with the baby in the event nobody came to claim him. The staff doctors covering the nursery had to help fund his stay. Dr. Solam Bonedoto mainly funded his stay. She was the covering doctor and could well afford it. She bought his clothes, toys, and sorts. He received good care. The infant was cute and lovable.

Dr. Solam Bonedoto was a childless forty-year-old head pediatrician covering the nursery. She was well established and respected in her field. She had an office shared by her internist husband and resided in a rich neighborhood, a gated community in Quezon City. It was a town in Metro Manila. Dr. Solam, as the nurses called her, was a graduate of Santo Tomas University, earning the highest honors in her class. She hailed from an average-income family from Nagcarlan, Laguna. Her parents were a civil engineer named Celio Cosiga, who covered the district of Laguna, and her mother was Lida, who taught grade school. They were considered well-off and respected in their community, being well-salaried and morally of acceptable standing. She was sent to Manila to a boarding school (Holy Ghost College) until she finished high school. She had a sheltered life, never knowing what night life was all about that other young girls had experienced. She stood five feet four inches, was fair-skinned, and dressed well. She looked Malaysian, with high cheekbones, black almond eyes, and a full mouth. She was classified as unattractive, but she was personable, rather charming, and walked with such a beautiful, firm gait, accompanied by a very calm, respectable demeanor.

Her husband, also a doctor, hailed from the southern island of Cebu and also graduated from the same school. In fact, they had been in the same class all the four years of medical school. He did not graduate with honors, but he was also in the top section of the then classified "cream of the crop" of the university. He was brought up with money, of grandparents who were landowners during the Spanish occupation of the Philippines. Genetically he looked of Spanish origin, judging from his light-brown eyes and fine features. He did not have the typical Malaysian look but, rather, that of a breed of Caucasians who occupied the Philippines. He stood five feet nine inches and was brown-skinned with a smiling face. He dressed simply and was almost shy and nonconversant. He was not too personable, and his practice, although thriving, had not flourished, possibly due to his very quiet demeanor and almost seemingly uncaring attitude. He grew up with very rich parents, landowners owning several rented buildings in his native Cebu. He had two other brothers, both educated in a prestigious school, Ateneo de Manila, a boys' school only attended by the richest and the brightest. His brothers had attained a standing in the community, being an accountant and a lawyer. His father was a businessman, and his rich mother hailed from the family of the Ayolos, who owned several businesses in Manila. They never had to work for a living, and although his practice did not yield enough, a financial problem did not exist because he received shares from the family's belongings. His life was peaceful, and on the surface, he probably never knew how to struggle, nor did he seek recognition for, indeed, the family was recognized. During the Spanish occupation of the Philippines, the Spaniards had taken ownership of the lands available for licensing since they were educated to process the ownership.

Most Filipinos were not educated. Mostly unable to read and write, they had no knowledge of such; therefore, majority of the natives who were tilling the land would be surprised when a government official appeared at their doorstep and told them they had to vacate it. It was rumored that the Spanish settlers overpowered the natives since they had expertise and education. A few Filipinos who had some education did own some lands, but very few owned as much area as the Spanish settlers. Despite their wealth and education, the Bonedotos were fair to the people that worked for them. They did not abuse the female help nor underpay the subordinates. They did not mingle with people below their category, presumably the reason of Dr. Moises Bonedoto's quiet demeanor and nonpersonable personality, an almost catatonic attitude toward the poor patients that comprised the inhabitants of the Philippines. They tended to marry their rich counterparts, mostly of Spanish origin, educated and with enormous wealth. If they went to restaurants, they reserved a closed room or rented an expensive hall for their parties. They were hardly seen in the public eye, afraid of being known and kidnapped for ransom. Surprisingly, the young ones adhered to the rules of society, possibly as a result of vigorous discipline from the exclusive school ran by the Jesuits. The adherence to the regimen of academic excellence and discipline had been the motto of the school that had kept it so respectable since it had been built. Socialization was supervised, and a hall at the school was provided wherein girls from the nearby school such as the Holy Ghost College and St. Scholastica and other Catholic schools would be invited. These boys were not subjected to the poor class of people below their category.

Dr. Moises and Solam Bonedoto were married after four years of graduation while they were trying to establish a practice. As much as they seem to be the envy of every couple, they had had a share of problems.

Moises was engaged in a longtime affair with his secretary, Juliana Castas, a very pretty forty-year-old unwed woman with three children from three different men. Presumably she needed means to support her three children, and having an affair with a rich man was the way to do it. She had had one year of schooling, and having had some mishaps in her life, she was struggling to pay her bills. When an opportunity came, she grabbed it, and it lasted for as long as he desired it. He was good-looking and rich. Juliana was never ashamed of it. In fact, in the back of her mind, she was hoping the doctor would leave his wife for her. She would satisfy him sexually whenever he wanted it, which his wife of super intelligence was not capable of. They would have a quick rendezvous after office hours in the office where she worked. She would leave for her home and come back to where he would be waiting. It was most discreet. Dr. Moises had a sexual appetite that Juliana was able to satisfy. She was adequately paid for her services and lavishly clothed. She was better dressed with expensive clothes, better than the wife. Dr. Solam never noticed her expensive clothes because she would never look at them. She concentrated on work and on treating the indigent children.

It was a busy day for Dr. Solam, having had several patients at the time who were very sick. She had to go to the office to research an illness, which she rarely did at past seven at night, when she discovered the both of them naked on the couch. Dr. Solam had entered the office unnoticed, and the couple, concentrating on their lovemaking, was unaware that they had a spectator. Dr. Solam witnessed the unwholesome sight. She left the premises immediately before she could say anything because if she did, words might not be enough to release her anger, and some deeds might be committed that she would regret. She inadvertently banged the door and ran down as fast as she could from the second floor and landed on the cement out of balance, sat in her car, and cried. Being both doctors, their hours were never set, and questioning the whereabouts of each was never done. They both assumed that late in the evening they were still working, and doubts were never placed on each other. There were few cars in the parking lot. Moises followed her, but when she saw him coming, she drove off immediately. She had to return to the hospital since she did not have the answers she needed and stayed there, taking an uncomfortable cot to sit for the night. It turned out that the baby she was worried about had finally died, which devastated her more. She was so ashamed that her husband had dared cheat on her and felt so small in front of people. Nobody knew about it, presumably because they were not open about it, having done their business right there in the office when everybody was gone. He kept calling the nursery, and she would answer it, just to hang up the phone as soon as she took it. She did not want the personnel to learn of her private affair, and she had an alibi to stay in the hospital. Dr. Solam was proud of herself, having controlled her temper, and left without a fight.

Her home, a large three-bedroom house in a gated community, was not a place to go. This episode was devastating. She avoided seeing her husband and never answered his questions, afraid of losing herself to human frailty, which was anger. She always tried to control herself in moments of rage when it would be normal to blast somebody if a mistake was committed, which would sometimes cost a baby's life. This moment in her life was a failure, and having spent all her life as a dedicated student, morally adherent, she could hardly accept it. She scrutinized herself, trying to trace her neglect and having had no time to enjoy her life. She would not talk to him and secretly wanted to leave, for she could not forgive him. It was agreed upon that having a baby was something that could wait. They had waited too long until when they thought they were ready, it did not happen.

Her business partner who took over her cases in the event of illness or circumstantial need to be off was briefed on all her cases. It took her a week to do it, being done thoroughly as she always did. She felt comfortable going on vacation, a moment to think. She was reachable if Dr. Linda Lawas needed her. Being classmates at the medical school, they had been buddies since that time and were both dedicated in their profession. Dr. Solam was confident Dr. Linda will cover her cases, which will be difficult since she had her own caseload.

Dr. Solam packed her clothes and quickly left for Nagcarlan, Laguna, to be able to think. She would take four weeks' vacation without telling her husband. She ignored his explanation for there was no need to explain an offense that could have been avoided. It had lasted for years; she never knew how long. Dr. Solam did not want to know. She hired a chauffeur to transport her. When she reached her hometown, which she had not visited for quite a time, she seemed relax thinking of her school days when she would hang out with her contemporaries during vacation time. They went to public schools. They were the low-income folks who could not afford to send their children to private schools. Despite it, they then went to college in metropolitan Manila, becoming teachers, pharmacists, and engineers. They seemed happy in their simple homes and enjoyed the simplicity of life, maintaining a family. They did not live in a gated community, nor did they own things only the rich could afford.

Her mother was surprised to see her home and wondered why she had come home without alerting her. Her mother said she could have requested time off while she was there. Dr. Solam did not tell her mother of her problem. She said she just wanted some time off to herself. The next day, Dr. Bonedoto came to see her. When he came, her mother knew they had a problem, but Dr. Solam did not want to share it.

It was a very quiet meeting, almost like they did not know each other. Dr. Solam had so much to say, but she was aware that she would not deliver it in a calm manner. To avoid confrontation, she kept quiet. He faced her, and he looked at her rather remorsefully, and at dinner, he had a bite to eat, and his words were brief because he was never conversant nor articulate. He was never responded to, almost like he was talking to the wall. This went on for a week, and finally, Dr. Bonedoto returned to Manila. The secretary was let go, and an elderly lady replaced her. Dr. Solam concentrated on reading practically every book she got her hands on, looking up the basic physiology and reviewing the basic knowledge on how humans came about. Her husband would call her every day, and the talk would consist of *hello* and *good-bye*. They did not engage in lengthy conversations. She did not appreciate his calls. She had lost her feelings toward him. She could not accept his betrayal. He had pursued her for four years while she was still at medical school, and to realize that he could hurt her after all these years was beyond understanding. Four weeks went by, and she resented going back. She was obligated to her patients, and it would be unfair if she neglected them because she had a personal problem. If the paramour of her husband did not tell anyone of the affair, and even though she had caught them in the act, it was she who caught them. If they were never seen in public, nobody knew. Admittedly, Dr. Solam was grateful they were discreet about it, which reduced her shame. It would have been so embarrassing if the world knew about it.

Linda had refused accepting more patients beyond her capability to handle. It was a very smart move, which Dr. Solam never did. She would accept everybody, thinking that she could cover them all. She knew she was smart, and she wanted the very poor to have the privilege of her expertise, which sometimes would be unfair to them since she would be very tired, unable to think properly. She would still challenge herself as if she were still at school, having to do it as perfectly as she could. She paid for the medications for those who could not afford. Luckily, she did not need to pay for her home utilities and sorts from her income since her husband was rich. She was thinking seriously now of leaving her husband for his sake. Life was never a bed of roses, although she, all those years had planned her life that she would never be poor. She had fulfilled that dream.

Most of her patients whom she worried about had been stabilized and seemed better. She would plan these vacations more often. She needed the rest, and she had not realized it then. Certain things had to happen for her to look closely at herself and how much harm she had done to her life. After a while, she talked to her husband. She had lost respect for him, and the overwhelming feeling of distrust kept her cold to him. She decided then that a child should not be in the picture to avoid trauma to the child in case of separation, which she thought of every day. As the months progressed after that incident, she seemed to have forgotten it. It was an existence of having to possibly placate her family, in a way, to show them that everything was back to normal. It was not. She busied herself with going to the nursery a lot to fill that need of having to hold a baby. Moni's baby was Dr. Solam's favorite. He seemed not to belong to anybody, being that nobody claimed him. She almost had the right to love him. A parent would somehow, sometime claim him. It was presumed that it would happen. The parent, being poor, had left him in good hands and would claim him when she was ready. It was definite that he was an out-of-wedlock baby, and the mother was probably ashamed of the mishap.

Chapter Thirty-Two

Moni stayed at the more expensive room although she had to go out to buy ready-made food. This was temporary. She rested, but the afterpains of having a baby and the recovery process was difficult. Her breasts were full of milk, and it was painful. She did not know what to tell the landlady in case she asked.

Ten days at the place was too much money. She finally returned to the rented room. She brought some food and various snacks to avoid going down to eat so nobody would pry on her affairs. The rest of the tenants would look at her, inquiring looks that Moni would ignore. Moni was always aloof and had intended to be rather unfriendly when she was pregnant. Nobody would dare asked her since they were not friends. Despite that, she was asked. Her answer was the baby had been stillborn. So it was a gossip in this place that Moni assumed and probably a topic of conversation. Some would have a sympathetic look toward her, and Moni thought she was being pitied or they were thinking that her story was not true. She maintained the cold attitude and the limited contact with others and kept her secret to herself. The landlady did not ask. Na Goria earned enough and probably had more money than people thought. Food was sold, and there were few leftovers, which meant that she was doing well in her business. She expressed missing Moni as her help. Moni was aware that she needed to rest for eight weeks to fully recuperate from the ordeal. She was bored. She would help washing the dishes, mostly sterilizing them before they were put away at night. She rendered her services for free. Again, if there were leftovers, they were given to her.

She wrote to Uncle Indong and her mom that she was in Manila. She did not write in detail. She was fine, and that was all the news they wanted to know. After eight weeks, she took a vacation to Cebu. She paid the room for three months. She could not stay at Uncle Indong to pursue school. She would have to take her education subjects in Manila. Possibly working in that place as a restaurant helper, she might be able to manage financially.

She bought several gifts and brought him money. They were happy to see her. She planned to stay in Cebu for one day to obtain her school transcripts. She avoided lengthy conversations with Uncle Indong to prevent telling him of the sad story. She had been treated well, and that episode which she did not reveal had spoiled it all. Honestly, her trip had gained her some experience and happiness and the chance to see several places, which would not have been possible if she had not taken the offer. Possibly, if she did not, she would have had her teaching degree or close to it. Uncle Indong would have been devastated if he knew it all and would probably blame himself, since he had indirectly facilitated the trip.

Dee was finishing school and would be a graduate nurse in a year. Pina remained the same, dependent on her parents. Delina, being a woman, would look at Moni and felt there was a change in Moni's appearance. Despite Moni's slight change, it was not really noticeable for someone to think that she just had a baby. Moni felt tired after a few exertions, the boat ride and the jeepney ride to places. Her breasts would still pain her, and fullness was apparent. Moni would pad them, and the loose clothes seemed to hide it. Uncle Indong seemed content; he had gained a few pounds, and Aunt Delina remained the same. She looked well rested, probably not having to stay up late at night to make clothes. Avelino had good grades and enjoyed high school. He was in the top section. They had a nice talk about their parents when they went out to eat with Uncle Indong. She stayed three days at her uncle's place. He would follow up on obtaining her transcripts, which should be ready in time when she would pass by Cebu en route to Manila.

The boat ride to Leyte was rough, being that the boat was smaller in size and unable to withstand the rough waves rocking the boat fiercely, making it uncomfortable for some passengers. She happened to occupy the upper deck, so she felt the waves more so than the occupant in the lower deck.

By the time she arrived at Naval, Leyte, she was exhausted. The pier had wider cement steps to descend, convenient for the passengers to board the *sakayan*. The ride to Villalon seemed faster than she used to know, and a portion at the shore was cemented so the passengers did not have to be assisted with a guiding arm and presumably would step on dry land if the tide and the waves were not as high and rough. The man-made paths she used to walk to her home seemed wider, and the bushes on both sides had been eradicated. On rainy days, the path was muddy. The walk was tiresome. In retrospect, she could have rested another two weeks in Manila. This trip could have been deferred until she was physically ready. It was embarrassing to her parents that she, not having seen them for a long time, was rather cold and seemed not eager to see them. She needed rest, and she was inhibited in speaking.

Her parents looked well. They seemed to have grown old, older than expected; possibly the exposure to the sun had enhanced the aging process. Financially they seem fine, with food abundant on the table. They kept the vegetable garden and the bananas, almost occupying a larger area than before. Moni noticed people coming to buy bananas since they could not consume it all. Nobody sold them in the market like Moni used to do. The bamboo business was taken care of by Nemesio. Melit had a nine-month-old baby boy, who was breastfed and was so lovable. Moni held him often, thinking of her baby whom she left at the hospital.

Moni's old room was empty, which was roomy and cool from the south winds. A closet had been added to one part of the wall. The house was made of wood now at the front, and the back was still made of bamboo. Nemesio maintained the house. The kitchen area had been expanded almost to the well, and there was a table made of bamboo as kitchen furniture, where they ate. The dining area had been taken as a working place for fabrics already cut ready for sewing. The living room was the sewing area where three pedal-propelled sewing machines were in place. It was busy. The ladies came almost every day and left before their children came home from school. Her parents did not have time to talk to Moni about things, which was fine, since Moni was hiding something, and talking was not conducive to it. Moni's stay was restful.

At night, before bedtime, she told them about the Romualdos' and how nice they had been to her. She talked about the places she had seen, and she showed them pictures. She did not mention the abuse and the premature discharge. School was a topic, and having money to attend school was mentioned. Moni's mother gave her money for tuition, being a very thoughtful person, and said that the money Moni had sent when she was abroad was used to buy the fabrics, which expanded the business, hence more capital was invested. It was then that the business flourished. Her parents had money to send her to school. Moni was excited hearing it and would surely pursue it.

She enjoyed the fresh vegetables and fruits and the walking. She went to the big town of Villalon to see the Onaje estate and saw a huge land, but the house could not be seen, being surrounded by trees and a huge lawn from the iron gate. Nobody was allowed to go in without an invitation. If indeed Lady Erminda's husband hailed from this family, he had been born to a family untouched by poverty. The days she would spend at her hometown were limited, and to investigate it further was not possible. It was rumored that the Onaje men was abusive to the women under their employ. Fair-looking women avoided being seen by them because they, at their convenience, could kidnap the woman and assault them without repercussions.

Moni went to see Grandmother Mariana every day she was at Villalon. She took over Melit's job temporarily, delivering food. Her great-grandparents had passed on. It had happened when she left the Romualdos' home, and her parents did not have a current address to let her know of their passing. She slept there often. They still talked of the past, mainly Mariana's childhood. Her mental state was intact. Simeon provided her with all necessities.

One Sunday, she went to church with the whole family. The bishop celebrated the mass in the same cottage of worship. As far as Moni could remember, the bishop never came to Villalon. Father

Semana was the priest that normally came on Sundays. The bishop was in his late eighties with a full head of gray hair and was rather tall and lean. His face was reddish white, and admittedly, he was a very handsome Spanish friar. Moni thought he looked like Mr. Onaje, and as she glanced at his father, she wondered why her father too looked like the friar. Mariana, who never attended church, was at the front pew.

The altar seemed bigger and elevated, hence the priest was more visible to those who sat at the back. The worshippers filled the seats, and breakfast was served outside the cottage. Possibly it was a big event, being that the bishop came.

The ten days were over, and she had to head to Manila to enroll if her transcripts were in order; otherwise, she would stay another day or two at Cebu. The good-bye was hurting, but somehow, sometime a child having grown up would have to find her way. Moni, having had travel experience, was used to it, and it became second nature to her.

Her parents went to Naval to see her off. This time, she stood by the boat's open rail to see her parents waving to fill their eyes with memories of their oldest child. As the boat drifted off, she stayed by the railing and sat by the chair to view the ocean. There were many things she recalled of her younger days and her first trip away from home. She cried and thought of the grief and the shame she had caused her family. She spared them from that sorrow.

She bought a larger straw bag because her mother provided her with new clothes. She tied her belongings to the leg of the metal bed. She was able to occupy the bottom of the metal bed so she would not feel the swaying of the boat. She was able to sleep through the ride to Cebu.

It was early when she arrived at Cebu, and the jeepneys were not full. She met Avelino at the corner heading for school and hurriedly told her that he had been able to obtain her transcripts from both schools and papers to enter school should be in order. Moni found Delina sewing this early morning, and Moni presented her with dried meat prepared by her mother as a gift. She cooked breakfast and served her aunt and Pina. Uncle Indong had left for work. Moni had no errands to do except buy her boat ticket to Manila.

Moni thought of going to the city to view any changes and to see Armando at the old store. After two and a half years, there were not too many changes as she walked all over the city. When she entered the Yellow Gold Department store, she did not know anyone. She saw the very pretty niece of the owner from the personnel department, who happened to walk by as she was browsing around. The lady had not gotten old. The lady whose name she never recalled did not see Moni. Moni did not engage in conversation with the salespeople to ask about the names she used to know. She did not want to be recognized. While she was in the city, she bought her boat ticket back to Manila and also bought items that Aunt Delina would not buy due to their cost. It was late afternoon when she returned to Careta. Aunt Delina had five dresses to make, and she did not have time to talk to her. Moni was comfortable doing chores rather than talking. She did not want to slip and inadvertently reveal her mishap.

When Uncle Indong arrived, he was surprised to see her. Uncle Indong was the most conversant person in the family. Moni was careful. He asked her to stay a couple of days because he wanted to bring her to see Dee at the hospital. Moni was in no hurry, so Uncle Indong took off the next day, and they went for a stroll with Aunt Delina and Pina. He was free to take a day off since he was entitled to vacation days, which he did not have in the past. He was now a supervisor, overseeing the ten warehouses that Mr. Manguerra owned. The most experienced guy relieved him when he needed an off day. His loyalty and honesty was rewarded with better pay and security. Some warehouse attendant in the past would cheat by renting a space in the warehouse, earning money on a property that was not theirs. Uncle Indong never did that even when an offer was so tempting.

Dee was surprised to see Moni. She looked fair; she had lost her dark pigment and some weight due to hard work. She looked good in her crisp white uniform. The training was vigorous. She hardly visited her parents, so her parents visited her instead. It was a good day. That day was memorable; eating out and bringing food to Dee for the rest of her classmates was fun. Moni noticed that Uncle Indong was free to spend money. He did not want Moni's money, which she offered freely. He even told Moni that her remittance of fifty dollars every two months helped pay Dee's tuition. Moni was again happy that Uncle Indong appreciated her help. Friday night, Moni sailed for Manila. She was now adept at traveling, but Uncle Indong went to see her off anyway.

Chapter Thirty-Three

The boat ride was uneventful, and being that she had bought a first-class ticket, an enclosed room for some twenty-five passengers, it was almost safe assuming that these passengers would not steal belongings. The food was very tasty as well. A boat named *Super Ferry* was owned by a Spanish aristocrat, and although a little expensive, it was very clean, especially the bathrooms. The accommodations were satisfactory, and most of the passengers in that section were well-mannered. Most of them were quiet and talked in whispers in consideration for others who wanted to sleep. Moni slept well. Disembarking was orderly, unlike the boat rides she used to take when it seemed that everybody was in a hurry, pushing people to be first on line. The pier at Manila was crowded and noisy, but she was able to hail a cab, and in no time, she was there.

When Moni arrived, the landlady was busy setting up lunch, and a quick hello was all she did. Her room was dusty, and she immediately cleaned it. She had a bite to eat. She packed her transcripts and went to FEU, a school that would be a walking distance if she was accepted. Dressed with her newly made clothes, she went and walked as fast as she could, since it was almost lunchtime, and the personnel at the registrar might be off to lunch. Far Eastern University campus was big, and she had to ask around to find the registrar. True enough, everybody at the office was at lunch. It would be an hour's wait. The library would be a place to wait. When she approached the counter to borrow a book, she was not allowed because she did not have proper identification. She was twisting her fingers, wanting to do something. She left the library and walked around the campus, getting acquainted with the place in case she would be accepted. True enough, the hour went by quickly. The lady who interviewed her was rather cold and disinterested. She would have to return the next day because the subjects she would be required to take according to the curriculum might be full. She preferred early morning classes so she could work at the landlady's restaurant at night. Her income at the restaurant would have to pay for her rent. Besides she might have free food again. It was all planned out. She would attend school until two in the afternoon, and she would work five days at night until nine, and she would study after work. She would have two days during the week to research and write compositions. Having had some schooling before she left for abroad, she had some idea of what she would do. The trip abroad afforded her a broad knowledge of the English language, and comprehension was no longer a problem. She was aware that added subjects to the curriculum could prolong her in obtaining the degree.

When she arrived at the eatery, she immediately helped out. Her services were free. To her surprise, there was another woman who was helping Mana Goria. The landlady might not need her services. Three days a week of work might be enough and might be manageable, being that adjustment to the new school might be difficult if she needed more money to get by, she would have to look around for another job. After she helped cleaning up and it was still daylight, she went out and looked for "Help Wanted" signs. She did not see any. It was almost eight in the evening. There were a few people at the eatery, and Moni noticed that the landlady was alone doing all the work. Moni asked Mana Goria about the young girl and was told that she was a niece of the neighbor whom she had hired temporarily and was paid daily. Moni felt sorry for Na Goria, having to clean up until late at night. As she went in, the kitchen sink was full of dirty dishes. She knew the routine.

The landlady looked very tired almost pale from hard work. The eatery was closed early that night instead of ten. The landlady did not have the strength to thank Moni but sat down on the ripped sofa to close her eyes. Moni continued in doing her work, helped herself to the leftovers, and finished up. The landlady slept on that chair and could not move to her bed to settle in. By the time Moni was done, it was eleven in the evening. She left the landlady undisturbed.

Moni was very tired. The washroom was also dirty when she had to use it, and she cleaned it too. She settled in bed immediately because she was anticipating a busy tomorrow. She was up and ready at dawn. She immediately went down to have breakfast, but there was no commotion. The lady was still on that couch. Moni immediately put up the sign "Closed Today" because customers would be coming in soon for breakfast. It was obvious that the lady did not have the energy to go to market; therefore, the eatery would be closed. Waking her up to ask her would be nonsense. Moni left her sleeping. The rest of the tenants left, having their breakfast somewhere else.

She left early. It was not a long wait. She was entertained by an elderly man at the registrar, who was very receptive to her problem. All her subjects were credited, and she enrolled for her second year in teaching. She was ready for school, which was supposed to start in three weeks. She acquainted herself to the area and bought supplies. She had some lunch and went for a stroll, places she wanted to see, since she did not have to hurry. She would have some dinner at a restaurant. Her mother was helping her with school tuition, she had money reserved, and she was comfortable. She enjoyed herself just looking at things comparing prices here and there for the simple quest of knowing. It was rather late, past eight, and she was walking slowly to the place.

When she arrived at Na Goria's, the place was very quiet. She checked on the lady and discovered that she was still sleeping. She thought that she was sleeping too long, and she tried to wake her up. She was difficult to arouse, but she was breathing so loud, almost like a very loud snore. The rest of the tenants were not home, so Moni was by herself to decide what to do. She finally called the nearby hospital. Moni was impressed of the efficiency and precise moves of the ambulance personnel when they saw Na Goria's condition. In a matter of seconds, she was in a gurney, and inhalation on her nose was initiated. Gratefully, it was nighttime, and traffic has died down, so the trip to the hospital was quick.

Far Eastern University hospital was nearby, and Moni walked hurriedly to the hospital. On admission, it was discovered that the lady had a stroke, but they were able to revive her. She was admitted to a ward accommodation of six women. They appeared poor, judging from their looks. They silently watched as Na Goria was being assisted by the personnel, and gadgets were attached to her. The head nurse took the information from Moni, which did not really help since Moni did not know, such as date of birth and history. Moni told them how she found her in such predicament.

The ward was spacious, and the metal beds looked like the beds in the hospital where she had her son. It too had thin mattresses with dirty-looking sheets. It just occurred to Moni that somebody might recognize her, and it was not too long ago that she had her son. She was looking around subtly if somebody would be staring at her. She became conscious and decided not to stay too long, hence a person from another hospital would remember where she was seen. There was nothing Moni could do but leave. She was planning on asking the neighbor if the new help could possibly watch the old lady at the hospital. Moni had money, and she would pay her out of her own pocket because if she received proper attention, it might limit her stay at the hospital. It was almost two in the morning, and she decided to stay at the waiting room downstairs since it might be dangerous to walk home. She sat there, insignificant, and visited Na Goria in between rest. Moni thought of the amount of money required to pay for her stay. She would have to withdraw from her savings, assuming that Na Goria did not have any. There went her teaching degree.

At dawn, Moni went upstairs to check on Na Goria. Na Goria was still sleeping, and she left. When Moni returned to Na Goria's home, and having known where the lady used to keep the daily sales, she took it upon herself to find the box where she had put the sales of the day. She noticed it the first time she ate there. It was on top of the dresser. She found a few thousand pesos to pay part of the hospital expense. Moni took some and placed a note in the tin and put it aside. There was no call from a family, although she never knew if Na Goria had ever received any calls from a relative. Moni had no choice but took the responsibility to take care of her. Her landlady never talked about her family unintentionally, being that she was busy working, and Moni was a mere tenant, who was actually a stranger and need not know her business. The neighbor's niece could not do the job. Moni went to see Na Goria every day, and true enough, the business department did ask for a person responsible for the financial arrangement. After three days of confinement, another payment was required. She took some money from the box again, and a note was placed, which indicated the date of Na Goria's confinement and other information and receipts in case the landlady would revive or a distant family may appear and inquire about the money. Moni was hoping that a family would call to say hello wherein Moni could inform whoever called the events that the family must address. The eatery remained closed, and the sign was put up that it would be closed temporarily. There was no income. The two tenants renting the two rooms had no idea what had happened, so Moni wrote them a note about the event. They had no chance to see each other, but when Moni arrived that night, a note was taped outside her room that their rent was almost due and they would pay it to pay the bills. It was such a beautiful gesture.

    Moni was stressed, but the note was a relief. Despite the money from the tenants, it was not enough, but it possibly might be sufficient for the moment. After a week, she did not hear from a family, possibly saying hello if indeed she had a family. A miracle happened on the eighth day, Na Goria woke up, although she was slow in comprehension. She knew her name and sorts. Her surprise was normal to find herself in a hospital among several women in a six-bed room. Moni visited that afternoon to find her in such state that she almost jumped with joy. The landlady understood her concern, and despite her sluggish communication, she had some recall of where things been hidden. Moni told her approximately the amount of money in the box and the amount she paid taken from the box. They were supposed to pay again, and whatever was left in the box might not be enough. The lady told Moni to get the key to her suitcase, which was hidden and taped underneath the counter area. Indeed, Na Goria had stashed a lot of money, and Moni was trusted to open the suitcase. Moni thought if she was not there, and if somebody else was there, would he or she be honest as she was. Moni admired Na Goria being alone, uneducated and on the surface rather (mentally) slow; but she was not. The bills in her suitcase, organized in denominations labeled as such bundled like a bank. One should not judge the appearance of a person; and she was guilty of such. A discharge was scheduled in two days. Moni was relieved of the problem, which she thought she would have to handle. God was good to her, and she would continue with her plans to resume school. The discharge was uneventful since an ambulance was affordable to bring her home. A list of medications was to be bought and set up for her. A family never called. It was almost disrespectful for Moni to ask her if she had a family. Moni took over the responsibility of her care, being that the eatery was not open yet. It was manageable. Contrary to Moni's concern, the landlady could afford to close the place. The total rent was enough to sustain it, and her savings would support her food and utilities. Moni was glad for her.

Moni took care of Na Goria and would organize her needs before leaving for errands. She then needed to find a job someplace else, which meant she would have to buy her food and would cost her more to live. She went out every day to look for a job before start of school. A store that carried several items such as house needs, a poor version of a department store, needed a person to watch the store from five in the afternoon to ten in the evening. She took it. It was a ten-block walk from the place she rented, and there were some people walking that time of the night. She would try it. She had money saved, and the tuition was paid. Books she would have to buy, and walking to school was possible to save fare money. The semester would be set.

Chapter Thirty-Four

In the meantime, Moni's baby in the nursery was doing well. A favorite among the workers, he would be on someone's lap whenever a nurse had a moment to spare. Even though he was among strangers, he was loved. His stay was still financed by Dr. Solam. It was agreed by the pediatricians that Dr. Solam would be the first on the list to adopt this baby, having been the financier since this baby was born, and her credentials as a pediatrician were an added qualification. Dr. Solam came every day to see the baby. She even came at night before she went home. There were no other babies being cared for except the newborns, so this baby received enough attention from the personnel. Finally, after three months or so, when nobody claimed him, papers were drawn as to adoption proceedings. A special note was written that in the event a parent appeared, and proof of such was evident the adoptive parent must willingly give up the child without a lawsuit, making it difficult for the biological parent to claim him. There would be no financial attachments of the length of time the adoptive parent has financed the child. Dr. Solam gave it a lot of thought and had accepted the fact that if it happened, she would yield to the claimant. Emotionally, she would be devastated, but she would take it as a moment of loving someone who has loved her in return.

The baby was in Dr. Solam's home. The couple named him Clark Kent Moises Bonedoto. He was afforded a well-furnished nursery, enough clothes and toys. Dr. Solam took off for a week to set up the plan and to enjoy the baby. A regimen was written as if the baby were at the nursery. A nurse was there, mostly nurses from the hospital whom on their day off would be paid to give him care. He had nurses around the clock. The baby, accustomed to the nurses, would emotionally bond without problem. Dr. Moises bonded with the baby and treated him as if he were biologically his. The baby did not look so different from him. The similarities were peculiar. He spent time with him, and he carried him when he was home. He stayed home longer, and he talked to his wife often mostly about the baby. On the surface, he enjoyed the baby's presence. Subconsciously, he had probably wanted a baby for a long time. Presumably, Dr. Moises stopped womanizing at that time. Medical students still flirted with him because he was good-looking and rich. There were calls to the husband, which he answered, but conversations were quick. Dr. Solam would ignore it, being that her husband was home more than usual.

His growth and development was monitored closely so an intervention would be initiated immediately if an abnormality was detected. Dr. Solam's family from Laguna came often, and although the baby was not biologically theirs, they cherished the happiness it brought to the family. The event changed the unhappy scenario of the household. He was robust and healthy. Although, despite this happy occasion, Dr. Solam would still worry about the parent who would suddenly appear and take him away. Also, there was the fear of this infant genetically carrying the trait of a deaf-mute mother and might grow up to be such. It was obvious that due to poverty, this baby was nutritionally compromised in utero and would surely affect his mental development. She feared possible problems and the ways to deal with it in the event it surfaced. Ignoring or denying the possibilities was not Dr. Solam's nature. She would try to enjoy him immensely and savor the gift of his presence. She even reduced her working hours to spend more time with him.

Money was no problem. The nurses at the nursery were willing to help out. He had adequate care. A permanent help was sought to care for him as he grew older. Finally, it was set, and his care was assured in this comfortable home.

Chapter Thirty-Five

By the end of November, Moni was to plan Na Goria's care for the length of time she would be at school. It was definite that Na Goria had no family. Food was free for now because she was cooking for her. Moni told her she would start school by the end of November and she would have to find somebody to take care of her. Na Goria was sad, not knowing what to do. She struggled to try to do things for herself, and noticeably, it was very difficult for her. Although Na Goria was able to toilet herself, her gait was unsteady, and there were a few occasions when she was not fast enough to reach the bathroom and a mishap would occur. It was dangerous since a fall from a wet floor would exaggerate the condition if she breaks a bone. Moni had only two days before start of school, and she cooked ahead of time and prepared her medicines to be taken.

Moni thought she would go to the library after school to cope with her studying because if she would not, she would be caught taking care of the landlady, ignoring her prime responsibility, which was school. She would finish, and she would not allow anything to bar her from her dreams. Moni suggested that the neighbor's niece could come to take care of her for hire. Na Goria, still a little slow in understanding, stared at Moni and seemed not to hear her. Moni thought of the elderly Romualdo and feared the events that would seem to ensue. She would have to plan how to handle the situation. She would give her a hearty breakfast, and she would prepare a sandwich. Na Goria was able to get around, and she could easily take the sandwich from the refrigerator.

School was to start on a Monday morning. Moni woke up at five and cooked and fed the lady. She had breakfast with her. Moni would come in between before her evening job to check on Na Goria. She would not be home till late. She would bring with her change of clothes and sorts. Na Goria was alone most of the day, and Moni was concerned. The tenants had their activities, and they were not close to her. The bathroom in Na Goria's small room was a few steps away, but her gait was still unsteady. Moni was worried, but she could not do anything about it. Until that time, Moni did not hear of any relative that could possibly come to assist her with her care. Moni enjoyed school more so than ever. The teachers were more interesting, and there were so many challenges. They would have the chance to speak in front of the class, which at first Moni thought very difficult. She would stay up late to rehearse her motions, preparing the possible subject matter according to subjects assigned for the week. Her first time was imperfect, according to her. The assignments were more than she could handle with working every day. By Saturday, she was exhausted, requiring a whole day of sleep. She continued taking care of the landlady without complaining because apparently she had nobody. The landlady never asked Moni the reason for her late nights. Moni had finally told her that she needed money for things and sorts, and that was the only work she could find. As soon as Na Goria learned of her evening job, Na Goria offered to pay her the amount and more for the care she received.

She had to alert the employer two weeks ahead of time for them to find somebody. The grocery owner actually lived on top of the grocery store and possibly would have to close it early if they could not find anyone. After two weeks, she took the offer. There was no work to be done except serving the lady dinner and setting her up for bed. It was easier, and she was allowed to study in between. She stayed in school and did her studying from noon to three so she would be assured that her studies would be attended to. It was working out, and the landlady offered her free food. The landlady was getting better every day, having followed the regimen of exercises she was told to do, which was more possible to do because Moni was around. Na Goria was almost ready to reopen the eatery and was thinking about it. She offered Moni a partnership of half the net profit even though Moni had no capital. Again Moni was hesitant, afraid of jeopardizing her dream. Moni would do all the marketing, which meant waking up at four in the morning. She suggested starting off with opening the eatery on weekends. Since the eatery was closed for a while, they would start with breakfast and soup for lunch and sandwiches. The dishes had to be simple because Moni was not a good cook. They would have to hire another person since the landlady could not do much but cut up vegetables. Moni figured out and planned the move. She started with offering a job to one of the tenants. She made it attractive by offering free food. She talked to the younger one, a twenty-one-year-old dressmaker working for a small dress shop doing errands, mending, and miscellaneous tasks. She was off on weekends. Her name was Pilar from Cotabato, a place in Mindanao. She spoke the same dialect as Moni.

Moni was very hesitant. She would have to do a lot of thinking, but the landlady, who was experienced, would be there to assist her with the most difficult part, portioning the food for profit. The semester was almost over when they opened on weekends. Moni wrote her mother about the venture. They opened even if Pilar did not respond to her offer. Moni did most of the physical work, and the landlady took the cashier's job. Na Goria recovered the ordeal of her illness with very mild residual side effects. Her mobility was still slow and her gait unsteady, but she was cautious. Mainly, her mental prowess had returned.

The way it looked they just made even. The work was very hard, Moni having to do most of it. They closed early which was half past seven at night. There were hardly any leftovers, being that they did not cook the usual amount as ordered by Na Goria. Moni gave most of the food to the landlady. She ate very little and had some crackers and coffee instead. This went on for a few weekends until people got used to coming, knowing that they had reopened. They had profit then. Pilar saw the progress and asked Moni if the offer was still there, which it was. She would be paid hourly as agreed.

Na Goria had improved, almost back to normal. The motivation to work probably helped her. Her speech was slow as if she had difficulty opening her mouth. She would stare a lot, and Moni would normally speak for her, and Na Goria would nod. During conversations, one would have to wait a considerable amount of time for an answer. She needed help in bathing, but she was able to toilet herself. She was able to make a list of food to shop for the day. The rest of the thinking was done by Moni. She then asked Pilar if she could go to market with her since she did not start work until nine in the morning. She consented. They opened three times a week, one weekday when Moni was off from school and weekends. Sundays was half a day. That was enough for Moni.

She enrolled for the next semester. Her grades were not as acceptable, and she attributed it to being out of school for two years. May was vacation. She was looking forward to the June enrollment, and another three subjects would bring her to her third year (as an irregular/not a full-time student). By June, she would be taking math subjects, which might be more challenging, and overworking might jeopardize her grades. This went on, and she was fine with her math subjects and adjusted to school fairly.

Moni posted a weekly notice to alert the customer of the days they were open. The customers came due to the low cost of food and variations that they provided. Moni had learned to cook with Na Goria's guidance. Even though Pilar was slow; nevertheless, she was a help. She required a lot of guidance and did not see things to be done. The profit was less, and the only benefit was free food and snacks that were available at night when they were hungry. The tenants remained, and rent was uninterrupted, at which Na Goria was elated. The income at the eatery was extra, which served her when she took ill. Pilar still worked at the dress shop during the day and worked at the eatery until closing time. Presumably she liked to make clothes in the future. There were more customers on weekends, and the same people came plus new ones who have learned of the place.

Moni was introduced to a US navy, a fair-skinned black man. He was almost like a white man. The only indication that he was black was his tight curly hair. His appearance was almost Gloria's, the nurse who Moni used to know. He came most weekends to this place, which served cheap food, when he could easily have his breakfast somewhere else. Moni liked him, as he was very respectable. She learned that he was in Manila on vacation, returning to the United States. His tour was done, and he was reassigned to the United States. It was obvious that he liked Moni, having his dinner every Friday at this eatery which catered to the poor class. The eatery offered mostly Filipino dishes, which he was not accustomed to, but he liked it.

Being that they were only open three days a week Moni was open to go out at night during the week if it was all right with Na Goria. Mr. Arthur Douglas asked Moni out after several visits at the eatery. Moni, having had some unwholesome experiences, was very careful this time around. She was alert of his presence and warned him that she would not be taken advantage with, and he was amenable to it. She was impressed because he respected her wishes. Their first outing was fine.

Moni said, "I have to be careful since my parents live on another island. Thank you for being respectful."

Arthur said, "I was brought up as such . . . rather proud of it. Mother was very strict. May I see you again? I'd like to, and we can write to each other. Yes?"

Moni said, "We will see."

They had an understanding to write to each other when he returned to the United States. As promised, he wrote to her very often. Moni received letters rather frequently; she lost count. She would write when she was able to, being very busy with school and work. In the meantime, she would go out with men from her school, and admittedly, she was not interested in getting involved with anyone. It was done because it seemed not normal for a young girl, as pretty as she was, not to have someone. Most men who came for breakfast came to have a look at her. Na Goria was aware that soon after Moni finished with school, she would have to leave. Pilar was not as industrious and helpful. Moni was different.

One Monday, Moni had no school. It was a holiday, and a knock at the front door, and there he was, Arthur Douglas. He had only been gone for four months and said he had asked to be reassigned to the country. Moni did not know how she felt. She was happy but unhappy. She felt bad that he had come back to see her. She was afraid her letters conveyed a message of love, which she did not feel for him. She respected him, and he was worthy of such admiration that any woman who was sensible would accept his proposal. He came to see her every Sunday. Na Goria, being able to serve herself and getting around well, had given her consent to go out with him. Moni had her final exams and was finishing her second semester at school. She was entitled to some free time, and they went out every time he was in Manila. He would buy her simple gifts because she did not need anything that would cost him a lot. They became friends, and Moni learned to like him a lot, although not enough to love him. The difference of culture was a deterrent to the relationship.

    Moni, as confused as she was, was debating if she should tell him about her past. It was a very shameful past, which had been aggravated by her neglect, technically disowning the baby. She observed him carefully for any signs of violent behavior. Pina had had a boyfriend that was abusive, and she did not want to hurry. It was a courtship that she enjoyed. They talked and got to know each other. There was no intimate relationship between the two. Moni loved him for that. She was so afraid of having to make another mistake, which she had once in her life, and she would not allow herself to fall into the trap of utter shame again. Moni wrote to her mother about the courtship. She specifically mentioned the difference in culture and was fearful of the guy since it was difficult enough to marry someone of the same culture, and marrying to another culture would be more difficult. Looking back, she had felt that way about Ken. Then, she was very young and did not think this way. Her mistake had indeed taught her a lot, almost not being human to possibly fall in love again. Moni having lived in America had a little understanding of where Arthur grew up being a maid and had limitations. The fear was there in the beginning, but she was now comfortable and knew that he was a good man. As they went out she learned from conversations that he had a strict upbringing, hopefully he was telling the truth. One thing he ate most of the Filipino dishes at the eatery, and Moni has learned to cook them. Indeed, Arthur was a good man, and as observed, he acted as if he was brought up the way he said he was. If Moni would happen to marry Arthur, she would actually belong. Her past was tainted, a wrong deed driven by her youth and overwhelming love to the man who would always own her heart. If anything, she probably did not deserve Arthur.

Her grades were better, and her mother had been sending her money order for tuition fees. Even though Maxi did not exactly know how much it cost, the amount she sent almost covered it. Her parents were very thoughtful, and luckily, they could afford it. Moni had some money stashed away in the event of need.

Na Goria was physically getting better, and she suggested if they could open the eatery for four days, which Moni refused. She knew she would not be able to cope with the work. Pilar was not a fast worker, and she sometimes had to do things herself because she did it quickly. Admittedly, she wanted to go out with Arthur every time he came to Manila, but her studying prevented her from doing so. Na Goria did not really need the income because she had money saved, and Moni knew there was enough money to pay the bills. She was trusted to pay everything that was required. Her share of the proceeds was more than enough to pay rent and some.

One weekend, she was allowed to go to Clark Air Base with Arthur. It was there that Moni consented to marry Arthur without her parents' consent. It was an impulsive move on her part, mainly due to his persistence, and she was attracted to his goodness. It was certain that he was not married since the navy would have it on their records. When she returned to Manila, she could not tell Na Goria of what happened. It was agreed that she would finish her third year of school. He would come every time he would take off, and they would take a room in the city. Moni mentioned about Arthur's parents and notified them of his marriage. Arthur said that he would tell them soon. It was not mentioned again.

To Moni's surprise, she enjoyed Arthur and almost forgot her memory of Ken. She continued with school, and she took more subjects, having Pilar do more for more money, which she did. Pilar was doing well in her performance faster than she had before. Arthur paid Moni's rent, and she did not need any money. A passport was obtained for her, ready for her to leave with Arthur when the time came. Na Goria suspected that something serious had happened to

Moni. She had a serious talk with her and Pilar. Pilar was given an offer that could actually better her life. Moni gave up her responsibility, and Pilar was supposed to take it over. Pilar would have to leave her job at the fashion place. It was agreed that since Pilar was new, a three-day work week would be enough. Pilar had nobody to go with, to early market so Moni offered to do it with her once a week when the bulk of marketing would be done. A hired help was a necessity, and Moni helped out when she was free. Finally, help was found five times a week, more for cutting vegetables, cleaning, helping with serving, and attending to Na Goria's needs. Her name was Suri.

After the third year of Moni's school, they went to Leyte to visit. Moni's parents were surprised and almost could not accept Moni's decision and her marriage to Arthur. Moni was sad. Maxi was very quiet and cried. The visit was not a happy one. Nemesio also was unhappy. Moni's father took it rather well. It could be because he had never known his biological father, and he also was of a different breed, although he had been brought up in the Philippines, and adjustment to his wife was not an issue. Their return to Manila was sort of unhappy. Moni managed to pacify Arthur from such rejection from her family. Arthur suggested renting an apartment somewhere else. Moni told Arthur that she was safer in the current place, being there were other tenants and she had access to cooked food three days a week. Moni was rested, although she would help Pilar with the work when she was done studying. After a few months, Arthur was moved to Hawaii, and there was a big discussion if she would go with him. The semester was almost over, and she wanted to finish the semester, to which Arthur agreed. Arthur left for Hawaii without Moni. Moni finished the semester and would have another six months to finish teaching school.

Moni wrote to her mother how regretful she was for the impulsive move of getting married without their consent. It was the only way she could pacify her for the mistake she committed. Maxi never answered her letter. Moni could not undo what she did. If she would relocate to the United States, she would go and visit her parents without Arthur. Arthur took the rejection to heart, writing to Moni often of what he could do.

Chapter Thirty-Six

Lady Esther Romualdo tried to forget the incident at her sister's house and Moni. Apparently, Mr. Rotilles never knew what happened to Moni since she had not received a call from him. She was not sure. It happened, and gratefully, Moni possibly had safely returned to the Philippines, as Ting said. She still could not understand the reason for Moni's premature discharge. Erminda said that Moni had been such a help during the crisis. She failed to thank her for her deeds and the care she had rendered to her mother beyond her call of duty. She mailed a check to her uncle's address via special delivery. It was equivalent to her six months' pay at her sister's home, which Moni did not receive. It was owed to her, as verbally agreed upon.

Moni was so surprised to receive it, and responded to Lady Esther and Uncle Indong. She was so flattered that Lady Esther had taken her time writing a letter detailing her kindness to the family and told her to call in the event she needed help. Indeed, Lady Esther was nice and grateful. Moni's reply stated her thanks for such an opportunity to see a foreign land and how she was treated. She did not mention the bad events that occurred that led to her immediate discharge. This way, Lady Esther could have peace of mind. The unwholesome events that happened when her mother stayed in New York had not been anticipated as such.

Erminda stopped writing to her sister in the Philippines. Esther had no idea of the happenings at her sister's home. They had had no conflict in the past, and this cold treatment toward her was beyond her control.

Lady Erminda kept on working, and she would spend several nights out of her home. Ting was given six months' notice and would have to leave the country. The apartment he was staying was subsidized by the lady, and aside from not having a work permit outside of his employers' domain, he would not be able to maintain the apartment by himself. He would try to look for a job elsewhere if he continued to live in the United States. He applied for a job at the supermarket. There was no vacancy. A decision would be made soon. Presumably, Lady Erminda suspected that Ting would stay, being that he would be better off if he stayed in the United States. Ting's income at the delicatessen was not sufficient. Three months went by, and he still did not find any work. A four-week notice was required to inform the landlord of his anticipated departure. A room for rent might be an idea if he could find one. Time was running out, and he asked his boss if he could work seven days. The extra day would be food money.

The cook at Lady Erminda's was kept because the lady needed her. Emma was also there because she cleaned. Ting was going to be discharged because Lady Erminda was able to drive and long-distance outings were possible because the boyfriend was there. Mr. Onaje was never found. Lady Erminda did not miss him, judging from her cold attitude. He had probably committed a horrendous act that when Lady Erminda had a chance to find love, she grabbed it without hesitation. Erminda looked happy, as Ting observed. The boyfriend never appeared in the apartment; possibly, Erminda preferred it that way.

Ting decided to stay a few months after he was discharged, hoping to get a job somewhere in the vicinity. Two months had elapsed since he had left the Romualdo household. The money he received as a bonus from Lady Erminda, a good thousand dollars, was kept for his fare. He would stay another six months until his daughter established her business.

Chapter Thirty-Seven

Moni was scheduled to enroll since she had a few subjects to take to finish her teaching degree. She would be a full-time student since she needed not work. The eatery was open four times a week under Pilar's management. Na Goria continued handling the money. When Moni was bored, she would help out with cleaning, especially sterilizing the eating utensils. Pilar and Moni became friends. Pilar finally asked Moni about her pregnancy and the baby, which was a rumor in the building. Moni never knew she was being talked about until Pilar told her. Moni kept on with the lie that the baby was stillborn. She told Pilar she did not want to be reminded and she would rather not talk about it. She always avoided boredom, for boredom brought her to her past, which she intended to forget. It had been two years, and she wondered what had happened to his son. The memory of the bloody-faced infant on her breast and seeing him again all cleaned up was all she could recall. It would be so vivid in her mind. Cry she did of her regrets and would think of the scenario if she had not left him. She would have had to bring him to Villalon, and the shame that she would have inflicted on her parents would have been horrendous. Would she eventually have finished school and be the head teacher? Would she have been accepted in such an environment? Would she have managed? She was confident that he had been adopted by someone rich and was being cared for adequately.

Moni's mother did not write. She was disappointed. She sent tuition money, still thinking of helping her to pursue her dream. A letter would not be enclosed. It was just a bank note drawn at a bank in Naval. It was signed by Nemesio. She sent her mother thank-you notes and indicated her whereabouts. Her teaching degree was achievable, and she would ask her to be there when she would graduate.

Moni would finish her teaching degree in six months. She was excited to graduate. Her worry was Arthur. He was married to her, and they were so far from each other. He was so patient. When Moni graduated, her family came; so did Arthur. She finished Bachelor of Science in Education. She did not get any honors, but her grades were still commendable. They vacationed to Leyte, and Maxi had adjusted to Arthur. Arthur was a very easy guy to get along with. He, being handy, helped Moni's father with men's work, such as cutting logs for firewood. They worked together well as if Simeon had another son. Two weeks went by quickly, and they had to leave. The parents were comfortable, knowing that Moni had married a good man.

Arthur prepared his wife's papers, and they were ready to leave. Moni finally vacated her room and almost hesitated to leave Na Goria's place. She had learned to love her, and the kindness she had given her during those crucial times was memorable. She did not entertain gossip, and despite her lack of education, she maintained a decent living. She was totally independent, and Moni was happy to have rendered those services when she most needed it. Pilar and Na Goria were sad. They expressed their love to each other.

Moni and Arthur flew to Hawaii to finish his term as a recruiting officer. The place was enjoyable, and beaches were everywhere. A rented home subsidized by the government and a vegetable garden at the back afforded financial comfort. It was simply furnished with used items ready to be rid of in the event they had to move again.

Monalai, their first child, was born in Hawaii, a healthy baby Moni enjoyed so much. She need not work outside of the home. She managed financially by being frugal and making clothes for herself and the baby. Arthur ate her simple menus, which consisted of soups and vegetable dishes. Steak was only once a month. Discounted items from the PX were beneficial, and medical benefits from the government were available. All in all, it was a good life. Arthur was handy with cars, and him being helpful with household chores made

Moni's life easy. Arthur did not hang out with men who drank in bars. He was home doing repairs, making toys, or making furniture. She adored him.

The neighbors lived in unpretentious homes and shared the town harmoniously. They were mostly Malaysian in origin, and Moni's family was recognized as if they had lived there for quite a time. They were invited into their homes, and several neighbors came with food. The hostess hardly cooked because everybody brought their favorite dish. Pretty soon, Moni learned the custom and would also do the same. There was a party they went to every month. It was an inexpensive socialization, and they did not have to dress up with nice clothes. Moni expressed her happiness to Arthur. Moni wished they could establish a home in Hawaii, but living there for another four years was impossible. He wanted to put in more years in the navy. Leaving the government job too soon was not a good plan.

Arthur's family could not visit them due to the expense, and the couple was planning to see them. It did not materialize due to limited finances. Four years had elapsed, and Arthur's request to stay in Hawaii was denied. They had to move.

Chapter Thirty-Eight

Moni's uncle in Cebu paid off his house. Mr. Manguerra had bought more warehouses at the pier. He increased Indong's pay, having to oversee more warehouses. Dee graduated from nursing school and worked in one of the hospitals in Cebu. She continued with her schooling to take her bachelor's degree. She needed not give money to her parents but bought food and paid the utilities. She met one of the oldest sons of Mr. Manguerra, and they were getting to know each other. The young lad was working on his engineering degree.

Avelino was almost finished with high school. He also wanted to pursue a business degree. He was not sure if his parents could afford the tuition and his miscellaneous fees. He asked his uncle if he could get a job working weekends at the warehouse, so an application was filed. His chance of getting a job was probable due to Uncle Indong's record.

Pina had an episode of illness, a high temperature of undetermined origin. The family had to confine her for a week. It was after a bad day when a young man entered the home while she was mending clothes. The young man, unknown to Pina, pushed the unlocked door open and said, "Gipatay ninyo ang akong mga uyu-an" (You killed all my uncles) and started to assault her when Pina, sitting down, holding the scissors with her right hand ready to cut the thread, raised her arm to protect herself, thereby hitting his right eye with the pointed end. He then, out of fear and excruciating pain, exited the vicinity, running toward the corner street. Pina immediately followed him and locked the door, afraid he would come back. Delina was out to buy vegetables, and Pina was alone in the house. Pina was crying and shaky when Delina arrived. Delina embraced her daughter—for how long she did not care. Delina thought of Pina's story, and it was obvious that the young man had entered a wrong house because what he said was not true. She thought of the men related to Ido, who were reported to have died from somebody's sword. It was a puzzle she would be thinking of in her quiet moments.

The young man whose face Pina could not remember was somebody who did not live nearby. His face was not familiar. Pina tried to recall his face and would try to associate his features, the dark skin and the nervous eye. That was all she could remember. Her fear of him coming back would haunt her every night. Gratefully, Dee still lived at home, and their bedroom was still occupied by somebody other than her.

After the incident, Pina took ill. Her high temperature required close monitoring, and the fear was incidence of seizures, having had history of losing a considerable amount of blood in the past. It had been several years ago; this symptom almost unrelated. A threat to her had caused her this illness, and Indong would, after the incident, be doing a lot of thinking.

Moni's father came for a surprise visit. He had to buy items for a project Indong and Simeon had lengthy talks everytime Simeon visits. Delina looked at it as men talking. Pina looked at everybody with an injured eye because the injury she had inflicted on that guy was irreparable. It would have left a big scar on his face, even deforming the eye. She would try not to scrutinize if she saw one with an eye problem and pretended not to look, although she would not know what to do if she saw him. Would she confront him or walk away? It was definite that he knew her, and he would surely look at her, probably intimidate her. Pina would spend time thinking of her days at Ido's household. The people at the house who came to visit could have seen her there, and she was blamed for the death of the men in the household. That was years ago, and she did not remember anyone except the faces of Ido's brothers. She was again living in fear because she had injured someone and she had left him an indelible scar, which could result in a revengeful act toward her in the future.

Ido's remaining relatives, in-laws who were widowed, nephews orphaned after the massacre, had been struggling for food. No relatives would take them if they happened to stop and visit. The family of Ido had been stealing from their neighbors when they were alive, and because Ido worked for a powerful official, nobody would dare report the incident. They would keep their mouth shut because of fear. The neighbor's produce such as bananas, yams, corn, and fruits in the backyard would be taken, and even if the landowner happened to see the act, they would continue cutting the banana that had some fruit as if they owned the land. Their reputation was so bad that everybody hated them in secret. The neighbors were relieved when they all died; although they kept it to themselves. When the parents were attacked, the children of adolescent age were assumed to be there but got away. The wives were not there; nobody knew where they were at the time. Nobody bothered with the family nor did anybody care what happened to them. The wives had gone back to their parents and had possibly stayed there in the mountain where they came from, and the children were presumed to be there too. No one knew who was married and how many wives there were that they could account for. The official of the town buried the dead. Presumably the boys lived with their mother and did some farming on government-owned land. They were all uneducated, could hardly read or write. The neighbors had known them as violent people. The town was peaceful when the shack was torn down. It was almost like heaven had finally set forth in their town. Although the town official had been recruiting uneducated people whom they could hire to threaten anyone who would dare talk against the corruption that went on. He had not found anyone yet to replace what Ido's family did. Ido was the person who was hired to harass a family who might try to comment on the corruption that went on. Land would be confiscated when the mayor desired it. No one dared say anything. This went on. The election that was held was actually not necessary since Mayor Ramon Duray was always reelected. Nobody went to the pools to vote but his cronies. A lot of people, especially the educated ones, left town. They would have been the only probable constituent who would have had the courage to speak up, but most of them preferred to keep quiet to stay alive. Death would have been their outcome if one of them happened to complain. The reign of this tyrant seemed to continue and would go on, and the fate of the townspeople was pitiful. The people who owned lands inherited from their ancestors could not leave. Nobody would buy their property. No one in their right mind would want to live in that town. Most of the big businesses were owned by the mayor, including the cement factory.

Chapter Thirty-Nine

The stay in Hawaii did not last long. They had to move again. As anticipated, Moni did not buy expensive furniture, so some of the furniture was left behind since they were items not worth packing. He was given the choice of having to move to Georgia or New York. It took him a long time to decide hoping that the guy who would be assigned to Hawaii would not come; thereby, he would be staying in Hawaii for another two years. He was a fool. Nobody says no to the place. The only place that was left was New York, and they had to move to New York. Moni did not want New York, but she did not say it. Arthur had to go ahead and find a place. It was again subsidized, and there was a limit of how much rent they could allocate. They were careful, since it was rumored that living in New York was more expensive. Indeed it was. They took an apartment in St. Albans, Queens. It is a town East of Manhattan populated by diverse citizens. They indeed belong and adjustment would not be difficult. Moni was dark-skinned and very flexible, quiet, and if somebody made a comment about anything, she would not confront the person nor have a fight with someone. She would evade from it, run from it if she had to. The move was uneventful.

The three-floor walk-up one-bedroom apartment was rather small. Moni, who was used to large spaces despite her poor upbringing, appreciated the space she now lived in. The baby had room to run around in the living room. The old couch they brought from Hawaii was an appropriate seat for them with a toddler. Moni could not work nor explore the possibilities of work due to the baby. She was content to have a degree, and even if she had not taken advantage of the certificate to earn money, it was fine. Arthur was very trustful, and Moni handled the finances, which she had become an expert at since the time she had to do it for the Romualdos'. Again, Moni was able to save money.

She, having lived in New York, would remember those times. Her innermost secret would bother her. Arthur would leave if he knew. What would she do if Arthur left? The baby's life would be jeopardized. She would leave the United States and bring up her child in the Philippines. It was fine in the country where she grew up. Moni would think of Alisha and Gloria. She wanted to see them, but it would disturb the status quo, and although forgetting was impossible, it would be known that she was here in the United States.

Since Moni was not fair-skinned, except during the wintertime when she seemed to lose her pigment, she was accepted in the community. She would babysit for neighbors, earning money on the side. Moni did not entertain gossip. If a neighbor told her something, she would have no comment, to avoid having that person repeating it, thus causing a fight. Her mother never knew how to gossip. They would work, earn a living, and never watch anybody else in the neighborhood. Luckily, Arthur's assignment was extended another year, so they did not have to move. Moni saved more money doing work at home making potholders out of old, ripped socks and selling them. They went out, taking mass transit, and buying a car was deferred. Arthur listened to Moni's financial expertise, and if they saved enough they would buy an inexpensive home in the suburban area with a backyard. He did not want to move anymore when he would get reassigned to another state. Arthur had put in enough years in the navy, so he would not continue if he was moved to another state. Moni allowed Arthur to make those decisions. If it was up to her, she would not stay in New York. Life was uneventful. Monalai slowly turned two, and she looked like her mother except for the curly hair.

They lived simply, and Moni had saved money to put some down payment for a simple home. Arthur had not left the navy, and the decision to buy a home was a plan that could not be implemented yet. Arthur had no idea of how much money was saved. After thorough deliberation Arthur left the Navy.

He was looking for a job in the vicinity of the town they wanted to move. After a long search he found a job at a nearby hospital in the maintenance department. The search for a home was not difficult, especially when he learned how much Moni had saved in the shoe box.

They bought a modest home in Hempstead. It is a town of moderate income community evidenced by the homes that they saw. It is a town East of the city; and the beaches were also near in Eastern Long Island. They would be able to drive there. Also, it was not too far from Arthur's job. It was a four-bedroom home located in a modest- income neighborhood. The downpayment was satisfied, and although some furniture had to be purchased, they proceeded with such a move. They did not have a lot of furniture to move, but the main things such as the old couch, the bed, and a four-sitter kitchen set. They took their time furnishing the place. Arthur's pay just barely made the payments and the like. The benefits of housing allowance and discounts from the PX was gone. Life was more difficult, and Moni, not having work, had a hard time making ends meet. She had a teaching degree, but when she approached the school district, they required several subjects for her to take to qualify. Most of her subjects from her degree were not credited, having accomplished it from another country. She had to be board-certified. The money to continue school was not available.

She took a job at a nearby convenient store at night and coordinated the time with Arthur's job. She was able to help, and food was provided for. A vegetable garden was a must, and vegetables were the main menu on the family's table. The neighborhood was all right, and they belonged, being a low-income family. It was a big decision if they should have another child. Arthur had adequate medical insurance. Moni had the say for another baby. Monalai had nobody to play with, so the baby was an accepted plan. They had a plan, but they waited for the gift, which did not materialize. Moni had a miscarriage; probably conceiving was difficult because she was overworked. She was up most of the day watching the toddler, and sleeping was not possible. She reduced her night work to three days a week, but she still did not conceive. She gave up hope of having another one and was acceptable of her fate.

Her home was big enough for a family of four and spacious to Moni. The yard was big enough to accommodate play. A baby was an anticipated gift but still did not come. Moni was hopeful, and she was young enough. She kept working at the convenient store, but reduction of working days was hurting their budget. Moni thought of the dried meat they had, an ample supply in her home. Her father would slaughter a cow twice a year, and the family, including her uncles, had a share of the meat. This was difficult for Moni to handle. She would just endure having to eat only vegetables, giving the meat preferably to Arthur and the child. She could not tell anyone nor write to her mother. Her savings left from the downpayment of the house and buying the used car were gone. Arthur had a slight pay raise after probation period, and it did help. The store she worked for was a mile's walk, but it was not possible to walk there because she would be off by two in the morning. Everything was done to cut down costs.

Arthur took a job driving a cab on his off days. She was looking for a night job in a supermarket wherein she could take off at six in the morning so Arthur could make it to work at seven in the morning. There was no vacancy. She continued with her current job. One Monday around two in the morning, when she was getting ready to close the front door, a car was pulling up on the parking lot when Moni felt a scary feeling. She immediately locked the front door and shut all the lights. She hid by the cashier's desk and was ready to press the alarm button. The guys were calling out and shaking the front door because they knew she was still there. She stayed in the dark, not knowing whether she should ring the alarm. She decided to stay until six when it would already be daylight. She slept in the storage room on top of boxes. True enough, at a quarter to six in the morning, there were people heading for work, and she felt safe entering her car. Luckily, Arthur slept through the night and did not notice that she had not come home. Working in a convenience store at night alone was becoming dangerous. She kept the incident to herself and was planning what to do and to follow her instincts to keep her safe.

She placed a large box underneath the cashier's for her to hide, and her foot was on the red button every time a customer came in. She was fearful now, and the job was no longer a place she looked forward to. The fire extinguisher was on her side, and she looked at the switch on. She would practice her move. A few nights went by, and it was peaceful. She would close a little early, and as much as she did not like the job anymore, she had no choice.

It happened again. The same car pulled over by the main door, and Moni recognized it. She was alert to close up before they entered. She did not have the time to shut the lights, and she pretended not to hear them when they called for her. She called the owner since he had to know. He was there in a few minutes, and Moni told him of the previous incident. From then on, her husband and child were allowed to stay with her. A folding cot for two and blankets were provided for. Arthur did it without complaining. Arthur would be up and around the store until eleven at night and pretended he worked there. The presence of a well-built man at the store kept them away. The baby was fine, and slept well in the most uncomfortable bed.

After a few months, the supermarket had a vacancy, and she left the convenience store and started working three nights a week. It paid more, and the hours were longer. She coordinated her hours so she would be home at six A.M. when Arthur had to leave for work. It was a moderately big market catering to the folks in the small town of Hempstead. The place was almost a mile and a half from Moni's home. If a car was not available, she could walk it. There were five or six of them on nights. She was entitled to buy meats and sorts at a discounted rate. She was happy that it was a job where she would not be seen by people. She was afraid Ken would see her. It was a town inhabited by moderate-income families, and it was unlikely that he and his rich wife would step in this area of town. She never wanted to see him again. Her life was settled, and they were managing. Her job was packing produce, cleaning up, and the sort. It was busy, but she was able to take an entitled break, and Monalai would still be sleeping when she arrived home, enabling her to nap. Her home was no longer organized and clean, but food was on the table. She conceived again, and this time, she ascertained that she got enough sleep.

The pregnancy was normal, and the delivery was uneventful. Her husband was so cooperative, and he did most of the chores, letting his wife sleep at odd hours. Moni looked back at her younger days when it seemed that she was not as sleepy as this. She had a beautiful normal baby boy. No one could ask for more. She required lots of sleep, and recuperation seem to take long. She was not paid for the nine weeks she was out of work, but she was assured that her job would be there after nine weeks.

When she returned to work, it was almost unbearable because the toddler and the newborn needed care during the day. She hardly slept. She had to keep on working and fought back the fatigue, having nobody to depend on. She rationalized it as old age and having had multiple pregnancies, which had worn down her strength. She saved some money, and they managed. The family was only eating soup since it was cheap and easy to prepare. Arthur was helpful, allowing her to doze off at six in the evening when most of the work would be done. She would sleep a good three hours, and when Arthur was off, she would have enough sleep. Arthur gave up his job as a cab driver. She admired her husband's temperament. She learned to love him, and living life with a man like Arthur was almost heaven. Moni was content. The children were in perfect health, and admittedly, they were gorgeous. Moni would never say it to anyone. The bills were paid, and they had a home.

Arthur was a very good father. He loved to watch the little boy. He was always fixing things, adding closets in each room, and very busy. Arthur was a husband who was the envy of every woman. Moni was afraid to lose him. In turn, she did her best to deserve his dedication as a husband and a father. They were able to purchase another used car, and she was able to get around by herself. Moni's family traveled and brought the children to places within their budget. No debt was ever incurred.

Communication with her family was scarce. She wrote to them when she remembered. They assumed they were all fine. Her parents were taken care of by her brothers and Melit. The last letter stated that her mother had stopped sewing and the business was totally managed by Melit. No illness was reported.

At Arthur's job, there was a job posted in the dietary department, and she applied for it. She kept on with her supermarket job. She kept taking required subjects at a nearby community college on Saturdays while Arthur watched the children when she was at school.

Arthur's family from North Carolina came to visit. Moni never met them. Possibly Arthur was hesitant because he did not marry a black woman. They were both fair-skinned. During their stay, there were no conversations on anything. Arthur brought them to places, and Moni stayed at home. Noticeably, they seemed to enjoy the children, being that Arthur was an only child, and all that time, they were deprived seeing their grandchildren. Moni did not understand Arthur's theory and neglect. She was also neglectful, and even though her parents did not spend much time with the kids, they were informed of such. Arthur presumably did not care, or she never knew if he was writing to them. They seem to accept Moni coming from another culture. They were Baptist and prayed a lot. Moni followed the religion. They stayed a week, and Arthur took off to entertain them.

Chapter Forty

When the children were ages seven and four, Moni was able to take an expensive trip to the Philippines with the two children. Moni learned of a tragic story that involved her grandmother, Mariana. The visiting Bishop who hardly visited the church at Naval encountered sudden death from a stab wound to his chest. The janitor who was cleaning saw an elderly woman exiting the back of the altar when the incident happened. He described the woman's outfit, which fitted the description of Mariana's. The material fit the description of the dress Maxi had made for Mariana. It was an outfit she wore to Naval when she felt like dressing up.

Due to the fact that the outfit was expensive, the women noticed it when Mariana would wear it. One woman distinctly remembered it and had sworn to the police that it was a dress owned by Mariana. Grandma Mariana denied the allegations, and no one among the *sakayan* owners or passengers recalled Mariana in the vicinity of Naval on the particular date in question. The old woman was known in both towns, having grown up in the town and was a respected inhabitant, having lived there all her life. The dress described as such was never seen again. The evidence could not be produced. The case was never pursued against an elderly woman who, physically—in theory, that is—would be able to inflict a fatal wound to a ninety-year-old man.

The children enjoyed the dialy trips to the sea and swimming all day long. Moni and the kids returned to the United States via Cebu after two weeks. Maxi and Simeon was delighted to see them. Moni stayed at Uncle Indong's for a few days. It was a surprise to the couple, and Moni noticed the comfort the couple were in. Dee generously gave her parents enough money every month, being that she was comfortably married to a civil engineer who at the same time owned storage houses for rent at the pier. It was a nice get-together. Moni met Dee's husband and his family. Dee has married into a rich family and looked comfortable. She had no problem adjusting to the rich. Moni was grateful and very happy at Dee's fortune. Dee's children, both boys, were gorgeous with reddish-white skin. Her husband, of half Spanish blood, was admittedly rather handsome, tall, and very well-mannered.

Moni's return to the United States was uneventful. After several weeks, she was hired as a dietary worker at the hospital where Arthur worked. The pay was better and the benefits as well. Moni would bring her children to a neighbor for care. Time had elapsed, and twenty years went by. The mortgage payments were less because Moni paid more than required, and the cars were running all right since Arthur took care of them. Arthur, the son, would help him.

As a dietary worker, her duty was to deliver food trays to the patient's room. Normally, she would not look at the patients, but one morning, she was asked by a pale, emaciated patient with a scarf covering her head for water. She was not allowed to do those tasks for legal reasons. Moni was able to look at her and, for a moment, it was almost like she knew the woman. She called the nurse in charge to help. It was a long wait since the nurse was busy. Moni ignored the feeling until she was home, and it occurred to her that she looked like the nurse who had relieved Gloria Greene at Mr. Sloam's apartment. It had been many years ago. She remembered the voice and her thin, distinctive lips when she used to condescendingly order her to dust a particular area where she was sitting. She had ordered her around as if Moni was her maid. Thinking of it, she was the nurse who was there when Ken and Moni had had a rendezvous in the pantry. She probably knew what happened, and the event prompted her to call immigration. Moni was not sure.

The next day, even though she was not assigned to the cancer floor, she went to that room pretending to collect dirty trays to affirm her suspicion. It had been a long time ago, and she could be somebody who looked similar. When she went up, the patient was sleeping, and Moni stood at the foot of her bed to ascertain her suspicions. True enough, it was her. The eyes were sunken; the pale, sallow look marred the previously clear skin in her younger days. Moni stood there, feeling sorry for her and the illness she had incurred. She was helpless. She did not even have the strength to pour water from a pitcher. It was a pitiful sight. She stood there and recalled that weekend when this woman's hatred had caused her to leave a job. The misfortune she had experienced had led her to live in fear. Moni had no hatred but tried to understand the reason a well-paid professional had such envy of a low-paid maid. She left the room, her head down, and as she took the stairs down, she sat on one of the steps to recall her past. A person in white uniform took the stairs and asked if she was all right, to which she immediately nodded and stood up.

Chapter Forty-One

The kids were grown, and Moni's life was peaceful. The secret she had kept seemed never to surface until one fateful night when her forgotten son appeared. Meeting Kent in her home and his quest to find his parents had occupied Moni's thoughts. She was sad and was hoping he would never come back. Her suspicion of his infatuation toward Monalai could not be true. A very handsome man who had been brought up rich could not possibly like a daughter of a poor family. The year went quickly, and the call to Monalai that he, Kent, was back was news she did not want to hear. It was obvious that a possible relationship was happening before her eyes. His frequent letters to Monalai when he was in the Philippines indicated his interest. Moni told her, "I believe he comes from one of the richest families in our country, and seeing how we live, he could not be serious. Be very careful because he might just make a fool out of you. I will not say it again."

"Mom, I like him a lot . . . and he is a Filipino like you. No culture adjustment, and we get along."

Kent arrived in the United States and called Monalai. Moni learned that he was staying till June. Moni tried to ignore the calls; not answering it or deny that Monalai was home. After a while she must accept that they liked each other. The fact that Kent came back to the United States meant that he was serious. Moni was worried.

Being that Monalai was attending school, both of them did not see each other as often as they would have wanted. Moni was worried that they were becoming serious and Monalai would do as she did, being in love.

When Kent called the house, she asked him to see him and to take a cab. She did not want his cousin to know. Eisenhower Park had a large area, a family park where Moni used to bring her children to run around. Benches were randomly placed for people to relax. Moni arrived early and walked aimlessly not too far from the entrance. It was a sunny day and it was a weekday, so nobody was there but a few elderly men and women taking their quiet walks. She anticipated his coming and chose a distant place so they would not be seen from the road. As she saw him, she waved a subtle hello, always suspecting that they were being watched, and allowed him to follow her to a bench nestled among the bushes. Kent followed her quietly. He had no idea of the purpose of the meeting.

She was not articulate despite her education, more so when emotionally disturbed. The bench was located at the center of the park not visible from the road, and a motorist slowing down to view the park would not be able to see them. Moni was nervous, not really knowing what to say. Kent was dressed in pale denim pants, a very elegant-mannered young man. He looked eager as to the topic of conversation they should engage in the park on this Friday morning. They sat there, far from each other. Moni sat at the other end, her head down, still thinking. Kent pretended to sit quietly on the other end waiting. It was a long moment of silence. Moni would not stare at this gorgeous son who looked almost exactly like his biological father, but his almond-shaped hazel-colored eyes took after Moni's side. Moni would glance at him and would evade his inquiring looks. Despite the rehearsal of what to say, she did not have the ability to say it. She was trembling inside and felt cold and dizzy. Kent finally moved closer to her when she said, "Salamat, Kent, nga nakigkita ka kanako." (I am glad you came.)

Kent did not hear it because it was spoken like a whisper, almost inaudible.

"Mrs. Douglas, is there anything important for you to tell me, that is why we are here?"

Moni tried to compose herself, still unable to speak, and blurted out, almost upset, which was not her nature . . . her palms were wet and clasped in between her knees to prevent it from shaking. She wanted this meeting to be brief and direct and over with.

"Dili ko gusto nimo . . . biya-i ang akong anak." (I do not like you. Leave my daughter alone.)

"Ngano man?" (Why?)

"Basta lang, kay pobre mi, ug katunga siya itom. Dili na siya madawat sa inyong pamilya." (Because we are poor, and besides, she is half black and unacceptable to your family.)

"Mrs. Douglas, dili na mahimo." (No! That's not all right.)

"Akong hangyo nimo, dong . . . mangaliopo ko." (I beg of you.) This time, she looked at him, almost begging for him to listen, and started to cry. "Ayaw intawon siya hilabti, kon mahimo." (Please do not touch her.)

"Gusto gani ko makigminyo niya." (I want to marry her.)

"Unsa . . . wala pa gani mo mag-ila? Dili gyud mo mahimo nga magminyo . . . kay . . . (No, you cannot . . . because . . . You do not know each other.)

"Ngano man? Kay wala ka kagusto nako?" It was delivered respectfully and mildly spoken. (Why don't you like me?)

Moni, still crying, was impressed of his demeanor of composure and respect. He was not arrogant and angry having been rejected by the mother of the woman he loved. The conversation went on, and in between, Moni would be shaking her head because she had run out of words to convince this young man to leave her daughter. Moni immediately got up and was ill-mannered. She did not say she was going and walked briskly out of the place. As if startled by someone, she stopped and turned around. Kent, both her hands supporting his head, looking down, was not aware that she returned. As he looked up, Moni said, "Igsoon nimo si Monalai," and with that, she hugged him close to her.

Kent leaned back, speechless; did not respond. Moni sat close to him and placed her arm around him. She never had the chance to caress him and longed for this moment for the longest time. The reason for her refusal was he was Moni's son and Monalai was his sister. His quest to find his biological mother had made him happy and sad. He did not know how to react. Moni, too, having kept this a secret, could not believe she had finally disclosed it. This was not her plan. She kissed him as if she were kissing a baby boy that she had not seen. She was crying and she could not control the tears. Both of them sat there, bewildered that this was happening.

She finally had the composure to say she was sorry she left him and denied him of the love he deserved. She continued, saying that she was poor and was so ashamed of her mistake. She disclosed his father's name and that she did not know of his whereabouts. Most importantly, she said that no one should know about the disclosure. Her adoptive mother should not be told as well. Kent agreed to all the requests, and they promised to write to each other. They embraced each other, and they did not have the words to express their feelings.

Kent kept looking at the woman who, for such a long time, he had dreamt to see and know. Moni went home, and although the disclosure was abrupt, she was certain that the secret would be kept between son and mother. Kent remained at the bench and tried to recall the circle of events. He had been left in the nursery and was finally taken in by good people and was brought up in abundance. His mother had planned it well, had deprived herself of love all those years. It was a memorable moment, but she was not prepared to deal with it when the time came. Kent thought this woman had nurtured him in her womb and had taken care of him as well as could be expected. That day was not the time to ask her of the events of his birth. She was noticeably embarrassed of her deeds and he, the son, flesh of her flesh, she was ashamed to face because his category was higher than her. Parting was sorrowful.

Kent stayed in that park all night to think of the "what could have been" if she had kept him. He would have been a stepson of Mr. Douglas, or he would have been a penniless boy growing up in utter poverty. Kent realized the outcome of this information. He would do as requested. He was content to have seen his real mother and proud to have a mother who was decent. He had three more weeks to stay, and he met Monalai again. In fact, he brought her to his uncle's home in Glen Cove. It was a quiet dinner, and he presented Monalai to her uncle. The conversation was restrained. Kent was fearful that he might slip and the information would come out. Darren and his parents must never learn of this fact.

He had another meeting with Moni at the park. The meeting was most pleasant. He did not reiterate his love to Monalai. Monalai noted the cold attitude and knew it was over. However he assured her that he was going to write. In fact, he had another meeting with Monalai. It was sad because he loved her. He did not stay. But he paid a quick visit to Arthur Douglas before he left U.S. He expressed his feelings of love and understood the reason, and he forgave her. They would remain aloof to avoid suspicions and assured each other that love and care would always remain between them.

Kent had another meeting with Monalai, and it was most friendly. He did not stay his anticipated weeks in the United States but left a week early. He was very happy to know his mother. He saw her as very pretty and honorable. He was content, more than he expected.

Monalai was devastated and said to her mother, "You were right, he was not serious." Moni had no comment and was glad that Kent had done as she had asked him to do. A catastrophe was prevented.

Months went by, and Moni wrote a letter to Kent of what happened and her inadvertent decision at the time of his birth to pose as a deaf-mute. She requested Kent that if he ever found his father, to tell him she had passed on.

Chapter Forty-Two

Moni as a dietary worker was content with her job. Moni was again assigned to deliver trays on the cancer floor. Again, she saw the same patient, who at the moment had lost more weight and was almost nonreactive. She was skin and bones, and this time, her color was almost yellow. Her eyes were half closed. She suddenly remembered her name as written on her name plate. Her name was Geraldine Keriyas, RN, pinned on her uniform. There she was standing as she recalled her watching Moni dust an area because she wanted to use it. She left as quickly as she could to avoid the sight, so sorrowful and pitiful.

Moni still had those dreams of becoming a teacher. She kept taking one subject at a time to pursue her dream. As agreed, the letters from her son was sent to her work place. Most of the letters were ripped. One letter was so precious because it stated how grateful he was of taking care of him while he had been inside her and his respect for her decision. She kept this in her small purse containing a bunch of prayers. That purse was always in Moni's car.

Monalai hardly spoke to Moni about Kent but would somehow stay in the kitchen and seem lonely. Moni said, "You can look around and you will find somebody."

Monalai said, "Kent was different. He never took advantage of the moment. There are not too many men like that."

Monalai seemed so desperate that she would go out with different guys and seemed to have neglected school. Moni had difficulty talking to her about it. She was not perfect herself, and telling Monalai to be careful of her womanhood might be resented. Monalai did resent her counseling. Moni did not experience going out with a lot of men. It was not the custom, and if she had not come to the United States she probably would have more control of herself. She would never have had a secret rendezvous in their hometown. She had never experienced such love as she had with Ken. It was a most memorable time in her life. Her relationship with Monalai had been a disappointment to Moni. Here she was trying to qualify to become a teacher and she was confronted with all these problems. Concentrating in school was difficult.

One day, Monalai was driving to school and she used Moni's car. The gas was low, and she was searching for money in the car, and she opened the only purse she saw. There was five dollars, and Monalai saw the letter Kent sent to her mother. As she was pumping gas, she thought of the letter. As she pulled out of the gas station and headed for school, she thought of reading the contents, being that it was open anyway. What would be so important in that letter that her mother did not want anybody to know? She had some time before class, so she read the letter. It was a shock to Monalai to learn the truth. Her mother was telling her to be careful, and here she was, having had a baby and leaving him unidentified. She was ashamed of her mother. She and Kent had kept it from her father.

Monalai could not wait to tell everybody what her mother did. She was not holy as she pretended to be. She actually hated her mother, her being Kent's mother and preventing him to marry her because they were siblings. Monalai could not forgive her mother. Moni had no idea her daughter had learned about the truth.

One Saturday at dinner, Moni prepared her newly discovered dish, which she had perfected: ribs in special sauce. She had all the side dishes, such as squash, fresh salad, and blueberry pie. Moni felt like setting the table up because she had had an unexpected raise and she had passed her preliminary exams with the highest grade in the subject. They had a pleasant dinner. As they were having the pie and everybody was enjoying themselves, Monalai produced the letter, which she had been sitting on, waiting for the right moment, and she gave the letter to her father.

Surprised, he said, "What is this?"

"Read it."

Moni recognized it and immediately left the table, not knowing where to go. Arthur read it, and since it was written in English, he did not have trouble understanding it. He looked at Moni, who was washing a dish in the sink. She could not face Arthur. Arthur was dumbfounded and very angry. His control of temper all his life was gone. He blurted, "Why did you lie to me all this time?"

Arthur Junior was bewildered and had to stop eating. He watched his father go to Moni by the sink, trying hard to control himself. He was holding the letter and showing it to Moni and telling her something. Arthur Junior had never saw his parents fight and wondered what the letter was all about. Moni continued on washing a dish that was already clean. She had to do something. She did not answer. She was silently crying and wiped her face with her wet hands while Arthur stood there too. Monalai, still seated at the table, was very upset. She would glance at her mother with such contempt.

Finally, Moni could not take the embarrassment and went to the bedroom. Arthur followed, and as she sat at the edge of the bed, wanted to embrace him and ask for forgiveness, but she was afraid he would push her away, and her embarrassment would be so overwhelming. He would definitely reject her. Arthur was pacing, still holding the letter.

"Why did you keep this from me? You deceitful woman."

"I . . . I was ashamed to tell you . . . always wanted to tell you, but I did not."

'You are pretentious . . . a dirty person . . . and I loved you, respected you . . . you."

Arthur hurriedly left and drove off. Moni was limp as she went back to the kitchen to clean up. Her children were still there. She did not have the face to look at them. She was a cheat, and her secret, finally divulged, was a shameful moment, but a heavy cross was lifted from her shoulder. She never realized the secret she harbored most of her life was so heavy. She, like a robot, cleaned up the kitchen. No one assisted her. She lost control of her family. She could feel the hatred and the anger. She had nothing to say.

The letter read,

> My dearest mother,
> I consider it a triumph to have found you. I thank Monalai for having brought me to you. I have made several trips to the United States, places I could think of to find my mother. I have dreamt and searched for years to have a look at my mother. A look would have been enough, but having been embraced with such warmth was a gift I did not expect. It was a long hug from my mother who has sacrificed herself, inhibiting herself from the warm embrace of her own child, a life that she had cared for in her womb. I hated you when I learned I had been left at the hospital after I was born. In retrospect, I was left in a safe place where my care was assured, and if adopted, the potential parent surely would have the best qualifications. Indeed, you were right.
> I was adopted by parents who loved me, people of high caliber not only morally but financially, wherein I was brought up with love and abundance. You obviously prayed for me, and your prayers were answered. Meeting you made me realize the goodness in your heart, your unselfish gesture to have sacrificed yourself from keeping me, for if you did, I would have lived in squalor and uncared for.
> Forgive me for hating you all those years and being short minded to have judged you. I have kept this a secret from my adoptive parent, as you have asked me. When I learned of my status, she was willing to give me up in the event my biological parent came to claim me. All these years, she was waiting unwillingly to meet you.

This way, she is rest assured that you were gone, and no one would ever take me away.

I was happy you are married to a pleasant man. You have kept this a secret from him because you loved and respected him and you did not want him to leave. It was a decision you made, which looks as if you intentionally deceived him. You stated your struggle every waking moment, and the deception was something that you were ashamed of, to the point that you have lost respect to your own self. I felt sorry for you. If you would have seen your future, having been married to him, you would have kept me, and on his lap I would have sat. A decision you made, which was right at the moment, being that no one could predict the future. The only thing we could do is look back and assuring oneself that the right decision was made.

It is such a blessing that I was given the chance to see you, and in my solitary moments, I will picture your face and I know that you have loved me, thinking of me more than anyone would ever know. You suppressed that love and longed to provide me of a better life, which you knew you were unable to do.

Yes, if I happen to find my father, I will be discreet in my quest and will keep it from his wife and children as you advised. I will not shame him. I will be content to have known him, knowing my origin. Thank you for the very long letter, a life only you could have endured.

Forever loving you,
Your son, Kent

That night, Arthur came home very late and slept with his street clothes on the couch. Since that incident, he slept outside the bedroom. Moni and Arthur hardly talked. He stayed out after work, and although his pay was given to Moni to maintain the home there was no harmony. Moni would cook, but they did not have dinner together. She would do her duties, pays the bills, cleans and washes. Moni, realizing the gravity of her sin, would plan on what to do since it was obvious that her family could not forgive her. She approached her old boss at the supermarket if she could have a job working at night at the produce department until five thirty in the morning for her to make it at her regular job. At the moment, there was none, and she would have to wait. The convenience store was another option. She was older now and probably wiser and would know what to do in case of an assault. After a month of misery, Moni still endured the cold treatment of her family and stayed in the home, which she helped build. Forgiving was very difficult for her family to do. She accepted it as such. Again, she had to endure this trial, and she would stay until she could no longer bear with it. She need not stay in the United States. Her children were grown and could be on their own. Their behavior toward her was obvious. They wanted her to leave.

She was accepted again at the supermarket twice a week, and she would be called for extra work when the need arose. She was happy. Her income at the supermarket would be enough to save for the moment. She managed with her two jobs. She had no toddlers to care for. She would sleep in the car at the hospital's parking lot if she was tired. It was safe. She started to save some money in case her husband would eventually tell her to leave. Moni was excited because if she could work it through, this pay would surely be saved. She would think of herself now and be selfish. Nobody would care for her, and there were times, that Arthur went out with the kids without her. Then Moni fully realized the situation she was in. She was thinking very hard and planned her next move.

Chapter Forty-Three

She kept on working two jobs and would rest in her car to avoid seeing her family. She would cook stews and soups and leave the pot on top of the stove. She would leave so they would hardly see her. If they were trying to avoid her, she would make it easy for them. She did not want to aggravate them with her presence. She worked and worked. It there was overtime to be done, she did it. She would sometimes sleep in the chapel at the hospital if it was very cold to stay in her car. She managed, having come from a poor family. It was a living hell in her home. Most often Moni would be crying while doing all the chores such as cooking and laundry. It was mixed pity to oneself and regret of her past, the simple life she left in the Philippines for the better. The materialism had brought her to this anguish. Her mother, having had a simple life with bare necessities, did not go through the agony that she was feeling.

Vacation time was not used, so she worked through, using time only when she was very tired. It required lots of planning, which she never thought she would ever have to do in this time in her life when life seemed better. Middle age was approaching faster than anticipated. She would have to enjoy her life before it ended. She befriended the same receptionist that kept her letters and asked her if she keeps saving her mail. She was an elderly woman who had never married, had worked all her life, and had stated she had avoided so much grief in her life because she chose to be alone. Harriet was in her late sixties and of American Indian descent and of mixed Caucasian blood, hence she was almost white. Her high cheekbones revealed her Indian descent. Harriet had an English accent, and

Moni had difficulty understanding her. Moni never inquired why she spoke differently from the rest. She handled the paychecks, and Moni would always be late picking up her check since she had two jobs and she would forget it. Harriet mentioned her difficulty in cleaning her one-bedroom apartment, being advanced in age, and Moni volunteered to do it. Harriet was very grateful for the free service as if she had a dedicated daughter. They had a close relationship. Moni never told her of her predicament since it was an embarrassment, a life she was not proud of. Moni also needed company and somebody to talk to about insignificant things. She never knew her friendship to Harriet unexpectedly was beneficial since she would need somebody to save her vacation checks in the event she had to leave. Harriet would send it to her at a PO box, which she would be informed of at a later date. It was agreed, and being that the old lady handled the checks, she could easily do it for her. The date was not set. Admittedly, she was no longer focused on family affairs. She was behaving like a single woman trying to save for her future. She bought the food and certain necessities, but saving for the family was no longer a goal.

 The town of Hempstead was a train away to the city of Manhattan. She, for the many years that she had lived in the town, never went to the city by herself. They did travel to the Liberty Park, New Jersey, Radio City, and a Broadway show. The family trips were occasional since money was not abundant. This time would have been the time to have some trips because money was no problem.

 One day she left for Manhattan, leaving Arthur a note out of respect, and off she went. She went to the Romualdo address and inquired at the door if they still had an apartment in the building. She was informed that they had vacated the place for a number of years now; the guard did not know when. Moni wanted to see Emma most of all. She walked to the place where Mr. Sloam used to live and the nearby hospital and asked if Ken Shuman was still connected there, which he was not. She walked to the corner street where he used to meet her and reminisced a moment in her youth when she had experienced the happiness that only she could fathom. The café where they used to take their snacks was no longer there, and the place often looked different. Moni kept walking and headed to the old beauty salon. Twenty years was a long time ago, and the change was obvious. The salon where it used to be was a bank. She walked to Eleventh Avenue and the old St. Anthony's Church was still there, and she went in to pay homage to the place she would ask for guidance. This time she wished she would see Ken Shuman and make love to him like they used to. She would let her emotions go and would not even care if he was married to someone. She would readily have an affair with him and would be discreet about it. She was already covered in mud, and she could easily be buried in it. He was a good six years ahead of her in age, and if handsome he was then, handsome he would still be to her eyes. She recalled all those memories in this familiar spot of her youth.

She took a walk to Ting's old apartment, and it was still there but had been renovated, and it was no longer a dilapidated walk-up building. It was twenty years ago, and she crossed the street to look at it as if Ken and her were there to have that memorable rendezvous. She almost did not recognize the place, but she was happy to be able to come to see the place again. Moni did not know that Ken visited the city often, and she never knew he would stay across the street and would also imagine the place and recall their youth. Ken was lonelier, having fooled himself that he had not been in love with that lowly woman; it had been a mere infatuation, he thought.

She took a bus downtown where she saw him on that cold February day with another woman. There was no jewelry store in that spot anymore. Moni stood across the street, and it was so vivid in her mind when he and a very beautiful woman in his arms had waltzed outside and joyously paraded themselves on that wide aisle, which to Moni was an aisle where they were wed. She was looking at them in her mind, envious. It was a moment of grief but an acceptance of the events in her life. She walked downtown as dusk was setting in. She watched while people in the city were hurrying to their destination. She walked it slowly while people passed her by.

There were more people than Moni used to remember. It was rather late when she was heading home. She now dreaded the home she lived in and was contemplating if she should enter. She almost parked the car on the street when she noticed that the lights were still on in the living room. It was ten at night. She sat in her car and stayed there for a good half an hour. She did not want to see her family awake. She could not take the cold treatment. She drove off and took a room in a nearby motel. There in the motel she planned her move not to hurt her family although they had been cruel to her. The past year had been emotionally draining, and she would have to endure it more. She had not saved enough money to sustain her for her current plans. When she went home, it was daytime and everybody was not home. She did her usual duties. She kept on working, and her family kept staying in their clean home, and food was prepared.

Chapter Forty-Four

Another year had lapsed. Moni still endured the cold treatment. Arthur Junior took pity on his mother and managed to talk to her without being seen by his father. He probably was warned to avoid talking to her. He would just say hello and would give her a sympathetic look. Moni was too guilty to leave and to face the fact that if Arthur would not have a change of heart, this would be the end of the marriage and Moni would no longer return. She would give her family a chance and planned the day that she would talk to them. This she would do before purchasing a ticket. It was a Friday afternoon, and she cooked and set the table. They sat and started to eat when Moni said, "I have gathered you here so I can formally tell you that my deceit was because I wanted a family, and I did not mean to hurt you. Yes, it was hurtful, especially to you, Arthur. I am asking for forgiveness."

Arthur Senior did not say anything or even look at Moni. He continued having his dinner as if Moni had not been there talking to him. None of them spoke. Monalai gave her mother a dirty look, very condescending, and stood up immediately and did not finish her dinner. The son continued eating, looking at his plate and taking a glimpse at his father. Moni ate a bit and started to clean up and did not say another word. That night, she attempted to speak to her husband, and she was also ignored. It was obvious that her deceitful act was never forgiven.

From then on, Moni slowly gathered her belongings and made a list. It was a gesture of sorrow because she was again alone and had no one to talk to. She missed Gloria and was searching for her to no avail. Presumably she had gotten married and was of a different name. She mailed her belongings to her mother, packing them secretly without anybody's knowledge. She went to the city again to view for the last time the place where she had begun her journey. Her favorite place was the old apartment where Ting lived where she would recall the memories of Ken and her. His memory and the aftermath of the love affair had caused her so much grief, yet the enjoyment of just looking at the place was worth it. She was looking at herself entering the building as if it was still the same. Inside was clean, and the walk upstairs had been changed. She felt strange going up to the third floor where the old door had already been replaced with a new one. She stood a few steps from it and quickly left. She hoped no one had seen her. She was tempted to go to Alisha's place, but obviously she would no longer be there. She went anyway, and the building was not the same.

It was a big decision to leave. Her passport was in order, and she gave herself ample time to think. If she left, she would live in Manila because people were busy and minded their business. There was no gossip. She was still hoping that her family would forgive her. The wait seemed very long, and it was not happening. She started cooking soups and dated them in containers for them in the meantime. Stews were cooked, and the freezer was full. The free bones and the meat she had at the supermarket was a benefit that she would miss. She was now adept in writing letters, and she started to write farewell letters to each of them.

> Dear Arthur,
> I do not how to begin this since we have not spoken to each other since that fateful night when you learned of my secret. I kept it a secret because I wanted you and did not want to lose you. I tried to forget my past and the embarrassment of my mistake. I did it more for my child, who would have been ashamed of the kind of mother that I am.

I have not blamed you for not forgiving me. You were hurt and disrespected. I was hoping in time you would have forgiven me. The only thing that was wrong was teaching the children to hate me too. I have respect and love for you. You were kind and loving, and I could not ask for a better husband. Your perfection as a man has hindered you from forgiving me. Please note that the reason for my resignation at the place would be personal. No need for you to explain to anyone since I have not disclosed the family problem. You are free to have someone I hope will fit your needs. This is a farewell letter. I will return to my country and live there. If you wish to write, send me a note addressed to my mother's house. I will wait for it and will surely return if you wish me to. Thank you for the good life.

Moni

Dear Monalai,

It was unfortunate that you as an adult cannot forgive me. I could have kept it a secret and would have jeopardized your life. I was compelled to reveal it because I am not selfish. I chose to disrupt the peace for your sake. I did it because you are my beloved daughter, and in the future, when I am gone, you will realize the human imperfection, and by then you will understand. Forgive me for what I have done. It was sad that among the many men you have met, you chose and loved a man who could not be your mate.

I will leave to appease all of you since my presence in that household is a hindrance and has possibly caused so much discomfort on your part. I thought you should know that my past haunted me every day of my life.

I cried every day, and the mishap occupied my mind more so in my solitary moments. Although if you, after some serious thought, could forgive me, I will come back. Farewell, and I hope and pray you will have better luck than I did. I will forever love you.

Your mother,
Moni

My dear son, Arthur Jr.,

What has happened was an event that you could not understand yet. You are young, and I must say you were the only one who talked to me and appeased me by your brief diplomatic hello. I appreciated it. Forgive me for what I did.

This is a farewell letter. I will stay and live in my hometown where I belonged. You were young when you visited my hometown, and I do not expect you to remember it. If you wish to write, my address will be:

C/o Maximina Almadin
Villalon, Leyte, Philippines

I love you.
From your mother, Moni

These letters would be placed on the dining table. Everything was all set, and the ticket had to be purchased. The letter of resignation had to be filed, and the person she entrusted to mail her checks was encouraging her not to leave. The whole truth of her decision was not disclosed. The reason for her leaving was very personal. Moni did not want Arthur to explain to anyone in that place the events of their marriage. Her straw bag was handy, and a small suitcase was ready. Packing was no task since a list had been made. Her old clothes had been disposed of, and some were mailed to her hometown. She did not have too many. She considered herself a traveler and was confident. Finally, after a long thought, the decision was made, and the necessary tasks were done for her to leave.

Chapter Forty-Five

The trip to the Philippines via Pan-Am was uneventful. She arrived at night, and after customs inspection and the sort, it was already midnight. She stayed at the airport, being safe inside the guarded area, and possibly snoozed off on a chair not intended for resting. Moni had tolerated the most uncomfortable situations in the past, and as long as she was safe, it was fine. At dawn, she started out with her straw bag and a small suitcase. The traffic was not bad at half past four in the morning. She opted to stay in a hotel near places she intended to apply for jobs. Manila Hotel was at the center, and although it was very expensive, she treated herself to it, but since it was very early, she could not check in, although she had the option to leave her belongings in a safe place.

She then went out and started her new life at age forty-five. It would be difficult to market oneself at this age, and she would settle for any job that would take her first. The PO box was paid for six months, and the mail was dropped off to her friend at the hospital for her to forward her remaining check. It was written simply, only the important information such as the following:

> Dear Harriet,
>   Please mail it to this box. Thank you for your help. A self-addressed envelope is enclosed:
>
> PO Box 2472
> Manila, Philippines.
>
>   Monica Douglas

She returned to the hotel and formally checked in. She was not tired, so she went out and applied for a job wherever she could think of. She went to Quiapo, to the place she used to live. The front had been remodeled to brick, and the door had been changed; it seemed wider and sturdier. The name was Canteen. The inside seemed bigger, and there were no pots on the counter, and the tables were covered with white tablecloths. The space for the counter person who entertained the incoming customers seemed narrow since the old kitchen situated at the back was now made into a bigger room for the kitchen help who prepared the sandwiches and the sort. A sliding glass window opened for the counter person to slip the order in and receive the orders on a collapsible wooden space to hold it. On the left side of the window was a swinging door for the counter person to go in and out if she needed to. The kitchen area seemed wider, and Moni figured that Na Goria's space at the back must be smaller now. That is, if Na Goria still owned the place.

A person appeared from the swinging door wearing a white blouse and black pants and a white apron with pockets, equipped with a pad and ballpen. There were five tables like it used to be. The tables were set the same, equipped with four chairs. Three tables were overlooking the window, and the rest was set at the inner part of the eatery. Moni sat on one of the chairs facing the glass window. There was a menu to be looked at, and they no longer served the rice and vegetables, but it was cooked when the order was written. There were mostly snacks and soups ready to heat. The wait was longer. She ordered a sandwich and a drink. It was rather expensive. When her order came, she took advantage of asking the young lady if there was a room for rent in the place or if she knew of a room for rent in the vicinity. The room leading to the upstairs was still there, but Moni wondered if it was the same. The answer was all the rooms had been rented, and possibly a couple of blocks ahead, she might find a place. Moni did not see Na Goria or Pilar. It was obvious that the owner was different. She had her lunch.

As Moni stood up ready to exit, an elderly woman who looked like Na Goria was being wheeled in by a young uniformed lad. Moni looked at her closely, and indeed it was Na Goria. Her hair was totally gray, and her face looked drawn and blank, and she had gained more weight. Moni was debating whether she should say hello, for it had been a long time ago. The rest of the customers did not even bother looking. Apparently, the stroke which happened years ago could have exacerbated, and she was no longer able to think. She looked that way. Moni waited until Na Goria entered that same door where she had her bed.

Moni went on to find a cheap place to stay. She walked ten blocks, and she found none. She took a jeepney to wherever she could be dropped off close to the hotel. She walked the rest of the way, stopping at a café for a snack. She was very tired. The trip and the all-day walk consumed her, and even though she paid a lot of money for the accommodations, the place was indeed what they said it was. Sleep she would through the night, and she awakened fresh to find a place and to file more job applications. She would stay for another night in the hotel. She found a sleeping space at Quiapo near Na Goria's place and the Nazareno Church and booked it for several nights. She checked out from the Manila Hotel.

Dressed in her best clothes, she filed applications to be a stewardess and for housekeeping and all sorts. Whatever came first she would take. She had money, but not working would drain it faster than she planned. Her certificate as a teacher benefited her; she was received as an educated person who could handle paperwork. There were no openings, and she had no telephone for them to call. Her search for a job was unsuccessful, and she returned to the hotel. It was a whole week of finding a job and she could not find anything. Moni ate only once a day in hopes of saving money.

One Sunday after church, she went inside the canteen to have a hearty breakfast, which was still available at Na Goria's. Pilar was at the counter, a familiar face. When she approached Pilar, Moni looked at her and hesitated, possibly not knowing if she really knew her. So Moni said, "Pilar?" when Pilar blurted, "Alam mo, parang kilala nga kita . . . hindi ko lang maalala kung sa-an." (I sort of know who you are, but I cannot remember.)

The order was hearty. She was given more than the usual portion, but Pilar had to serve other customers and asked her to wait until she was not busy.

Pilar was eager to talk to her, and they began a conversation. "Sa-an ang punta mo ngayon? Balik, ka ha! Mag- usap tayo."

They were trying to get together, and Moni was asked to come back when the canteen would be closing, which would be around five in the afternoon. When Moni returned, they had a long conversation of the years that had gone by. Moni did not tell Pilar the details of her life. Her marriage to Arthur had not worked out, and they had divorced. No children were involved. She had lived in Leyte and was trying to find a place here. She was bored as a farm girl, being that she had not passed the exams to be a teacher. She needed a place to stay and a job. Pilar offered her a weekend job and to fill in as substitute. Being that there was no room upstairs, Pilar offered her the space at Na Goria's room to sleep. In exchange for these favors, Moni would help take care of Na Goria so Pilar would have a chance to do other things. Moni took the offer and moved in with her belongings. It was a relief, being that she was worried about her finances, although she had plenty.

Na Goria never recognized Moni. Na Goria could not follow instructions or able to ask for anything. The caregiver would get her up, toilet her, and place food in front of her. She was able to feed herself and managed to pick up her drink. She was not able to answer or acknowledge. Her mental ability was no longer there, it seemed, although no one really knew. It could be that she was just tired of her life and she just went along with whatever was there. Luckily, the papers had been drawn to establish guardianship before she became too ill to make such decision. Pilar, a good person, did not take advantage of her incapability. Moni would have enjoyed it if Na Goria were a little conversant.

Moni was given a small portable cot, and it was placed by the door leading to the backyard. It was rather uncomfortable, but she needed a place to sleep and a space to secure her things. Moni had a conversation with Pilar and learned when Moni left with Arthur that Pilar had an agreement with Na Goria that Pilar would be her guardian. Pilar would live in the house rent-free and manage the eatery for half of the profit. It was a very profitable arrangement. Pilar would take care of Na Goria in the event of sickness, and some money was saved for it, including for a burial. Pilar was the only appointed heir, and it was written by an attorney. Everything was legal.

Apparently Pilar had gotten married, and the husband left her for another woman after a year. They occupied the same room upstairs free of rent. Life was not difficult for them, being that they had fewer expenses and no children. Even though their jobs did not pay well, they even had extra money to go see a movie here and there, although Pilar said her husband was rather lazy and hardly helped in cleaning the place. He was not helpful, and Pilar was losing respect for him. The fight started when the husband learned about Na Goria's deal with Pilar. The husband tried to encourage Pilar not to care for Na Goria to hasten her death, so they could have it all sooner. Pilar was upset at his plan. As Pilar and Na Goria became close, Pilar learned of her story; before she lost her cognitive ability. Apparently, Na Goria had no close relatives, and she was an only child of a couple who started the business and acquired the property from the proceeds of the small eatery by installment. Na Goria finished elementary school and could not handle high school. She was the main help of the family and never got married. Pilar learned that Na Goria had liked someone, but she had never entertained him. He came to the place often, and they had an understanding, a very subtle one. It consisted of a smile between them and a short hello. She was very young, and her parents had kept an eye on her so that the friendship did not culminate beyond hello. As Na Goria said, he looked so intelligent and had fine manners. He was lean and tall. She was planning on telling her parents about him, but she was so afraid. Na Goria possibly was of the same age as the young man and possibly would be in college as well, if only she was able to cope with school, which she did not. She would dream of him all the time. He looked as if he were going to school because he had books and notebooks with him every time he entered the eatery. Na Goria would give him more food than usual, and it seemed that he was very hungry. He would have his lunch and occasional dinners at the eatery. She never knew his name because they never talked to each other. The dream ended when he was run over by a jeepney as he was crossing the street—to see her, presumably. Na Goria, a young girl then, saw her love dead on the street, not knowing if he loved her. One thing for sure was that she loved him. The papers revealed his real name as Gabriel Osalan, a first-year engineering student at a nearby university, MAPUA Technical School. Na Goria, having learned this, felt so small, being uneducated. She surmised that he had probably come by to take advantage of the large portions she gave him. He would never fall in love with someone uneducated. Since then, she never looked at any man nor entertained their gaze as admiration. When her parents died, she dedicated herself to maintaining the eatery, which catered to the poor. She had the bedrooms rented upstairs as a definite income in case the eatery did not have a profit.

It had been twenty years, and although there were episodes of illness, money allocated for it had not run out. Pilar took care of Na Goria, keeping the eatery open three times a week. Pilar reduced her working days at the dress shop. She loved making clothes. She worked seven days a week altogether and took care of Na Goria. Pilar hired an aide twice a week or more to give the old woman a bath.

Pilar told Moni about her husband, her disappointment, and she became an ear to ventilate her worries. When he was around, Pilar would be fearful that he would hurt Na Goria. Moni listened to this stories, but she did not reveal her secret. The deal with Pilar worked with Moni's schedule. She would get up early to feed and wash up the old lady; she walked her for half an hour and padded her. Moni would have her breakfast, and off she went to look for a job. The weekend job as a substitute counter person earned her little, but she had no expense except her allowance when she went out. She had to take some money from her savings, but she was careful. Even a janitorial job was not available. The teaching job was full, being that there were new graduates who had better grades than her. Her teaching job was not pursuable, it seemed, and she was so discouraged. Four weeks went by, and the PO box was empty. The three weeks' vacation pay from her job had not arrived. She figured it probably was not mailed yet.

SHADOWS IN THE PANTRY

She would be back as early as two in the afternoon, and Moni would exercise Na Goria because she was not busy. Na Goria would stare at her and possibly recognize her because she would attempt to open her mouth. No one could tell if she did or not. Na Goria, a dark-skinned woman, then in her late forties when Moni had met her, was not pretty but had the charm of a person that was kind. She had been heavy-set then, years ago, but she was a fast worker and handled the chores; she kept the store in working order. She was not talkative but a one-word person who did not repeat what she said. She had gained more weight due to inactivity.

Before Moni came, Pilar padded her during the day, and she would manage to return home to change her pad. Moni admired Pilar for her kindness when she could easily ignore her. There was no family to check up on her. Moni thought how Na Goria had avoided the touch of a man and remained single. It was admirable. Moni thought she wished she did that. Moni envied Na Goria for the kind of woman she was. She was a nun living outside of the convent. Moni sort of despised herself for being the way she was, especially having born a child out of wedlock. Moni wanted to visit her family in Leyte. She then asked Pilar if she could leave for a vacation and be gone for two weeks. Pilar had called the hospital for an aide that could watch Na Goria for the days that Moni was gone. Moni waited until they found somebody. The PO box was empty when Moni checked it.

Chapter Forty-Six

Moni wanted to drop off at Cebu, but she opted not to see Uncle Indong. She did not want to lie to him, mainly to spare him from worry that Moni did not have a good life. Moni was a failure. Luckily, there was a boat leaving for Leyte when she arrived at the Cebu pier and able to purchase a ticket. She left that night instead of having to stay at the hotel to sleep. The boat trip to Leyte was uneventful. Naval seemed busier; more stores were built, and more people. The cemented platform, where the passengers descended to board the *sakayan* was wider, and a rail was placed to hold on to as one goes down. It was a sunny day and the ride to Villalon was pleasant. The shore at Villalon allocated cemented steps for the *sakayan* to anchor their vessel – so passengers would land on dry land. Still, a person was at the bottom steps to guide the passengers from the swaying *sakayan* in case a passenger lost her balance; thereby, he was there to hold her. Moni was amazed at the improvement. There was a convenient store by the shore where the *sakayan* landed. The nipa huts were still scattered on that particular piece of land, and eradicating them would be cruel. They have no place to go. The narrow footpaths seemed wider. The straw bag was not heavy since the gifts were mailed.

She did not send a wire that she was coming so her mother was surprised to see her. This was not planned and her coming home was actually a sad one.

True enough, the package was received and the gifts fit them all. The gift items of simple things like bath towels were most appreciated. Her mother was expectedly older, being in her early sixties. She had reduced her working hours and limited herself to doing the most difficult task, which was cutting the materials. Melit, Nemesio's wife, did most of the directing on how to make them to the seamstress that were present when Moni arrived. Moni's father was not home for the moment. He was at Naval. Apparently Avelino, her youngest sibling, built a small general store at Naval after finishing a business degree. He sold everything he could in that store. He lived on top of the two-story establishment. He had remained single.

There was so much change that Moni did not know. Her conversation with her mother was sad. She told her that she had a misunderstanding with her husband. Moni admitted it was mostly her fault, and the children, being grown, decided to stay with their father. She did not discuss the details of the conflict, and Maxi, due to her lack of experience in family matters, did not pursue it. She was very fearful that a conflict would happen due to cultural differences, but she did not mention it to Moni because it would aggravate the current problem.

Moni spent time with Grandma Mariana, who lived alone in her hut despite Maxi's suggestion that she should live with her. Although she was able to toilet herself, she could no longer cook nor wash herself. Melit's son would bring her food every day and clean her hut. Moni would sleep with her and cook and clean while she was there.

Moni noticed her grandmother's smelly pillow, which she would hold on to so close at night. It smelled like sea water, fishy, and it was stuffed loosely with a looked like a garment. She did not use it as a pillow but almost like a teddy bear that she held and cradled all night long. It was stitched hurriedly, and some of the contents were exposed on the sides. It required restitching before washing it. Moni offered to do both, which Mariana vehemently refused. Moni was tempted to do it, so when Mariana was fast asleep, she picked up the pillow from the floor when the old woman inadvertently dropped it. She tiptoed out and walked briskly to her ten-minute-walk home. Moni presented it to her mother. Moni's mother was dumbfounded when she saw the ripped pillow and its contents from the area to be restitched. Maxi needed not open it all the way. It was the dress she had made for her, the material she had bought from Cebu indeed. Maxi pulled Moni to her bedroom and whispered that it was the dress of the person described by the witness who hurriedly left from the back of the church that could have possibly stabbed the visiting bishop some years ago. The witness had not seen the assassin's face. The person was supposed to be quick on her feet due to the fast getaway, so she was described to be young. The witness added that this woman ran as fast as lightning. The witness was in his seventies with poor eyesight, so nobody believed his statement. They were not sure that their premonition was correct, but they, Maxi and Moni, would only suspect. Maxi did not see all the contents of the pillow. Confronting the aged woman would not be appropriate because some senility had already set in, and possibly, there were incidents in her life that she and she alone would selectively remember and keep as a secret. She was entitled to her secrets, and there was no sense exposing it. Moni offered to stitch the pillow.

    She packed up some sewing paraphernalia and brought it with her and hurriedly returned to her grandma's dwelling. Grandmother was still asleep. She did not know Moni had taken it, and the pillow was taken to be looked at. In the other room, she opened the pillow and saw the dress inside it. She tiptoed back out to check her if she was awake. The contents were the infamous dress, the faded unwashed skirt with the fishy smell (the skirt worn by fish vendors as they squatted in the market to sell the fresh fish), and two infant undergarments that had yellowed from the years it was kept. She immediately stitched it up well enough to keep it sealed for the short years that her grandma would live and enjoy the memory of it. She held and cradled it during sleep because it held the secret of her life. The family had to respect it. The contents of the pillow has significant meaning possibly the unwashed skirt was the one Grandma wore when she was trespassed; the infant undergarment was Moni's father's shirt, and the church dress that originally she wore that day ended the story of her life.

    The event could have happened when Grandma stayed at church during rainy days and the Bishop posed as a regular person possibly a janitor. She hated the man that did it to her. Not like Moni that enjoyed her moments with Ken. If her goal was revenge, she did it single-handed.

That night, Moni slept with her grandmother. Moni could not sleep, remembering the events of her life. As far as Moni could remember, her grandmother never went to church. She just did not, but one day, uninvited, she went to church and occupied the front pew. She went by herself. Moni could still picture the Bishop. He was most handsome—with a reddish-white face, dimples on his cheeks, hazel eyes, and long eyelashes. Moni did not bother asking her mother if Grandma had gone to church again. Simeon never forced his mother to go to church with them that after a while, she was no longer invited. Moni was seated then at the back pew and, at that time, had no concept of her grandmother's change of behavior.

The Bishop, as far as she knew, did not celebrate mass again while she was there. It was a short visit. Maxi had no recollection of who celebrated mass, although she would volunteer to cook breakfast for the visiting priest. Trying to sleep, she was in deep thought; she suddenly sat up and saw in her mind the distinct resemblance between her father and Mr. Onaje.

There was nobody in her hometown or the neighboring barrios that she encountered who resembled her father. Filipinos were mostly Malaysian-looking with dark skin and were short. Moni's father was tall and reddish white. It could not be mere coincidence that her father, Simeon, looked exactly like the bishop. Moni thought of his son, Arthur, and how he almost looked like his father's twin, except the almond eyes he had taken after Maxi. Now, as Moni thought of her family, she cried and recalled the memory of Arthur when she had met him and lived with him for all those years.

Her mind flew to instances in her past. She looked at her grandma, who had born an illegitimate son of foreign extraction and how she managed to hid the identity of the man. She asked herself, Could it be that the bishop fathered the both of them? Moni's father and Mr. Onaje? If so, the bishop could be her grandfather! But how? Could it be that the bishop, who in his younger days was a regular priest, had camouflaged himself as a regular person and lured

Grandmother to have a rendezvous with him? Then he disappeared from sight?

If it was true that Grandma stabbed the bishop, how did she do it? She was not a strong woman. She had probably caught him off guard so he was not able to defend himself. Although, if she did it around that date that Moni came to visit he, he was in his nineties. The dress and the contents of her pillow said it all. She need not be interrogated or confronted. Could it be that she had been raped and she had carried that grudge all her life? And she took revenge by stabbing him the minute she had the chance? It was logically far-fetched. So Mr. Onaje's mother also had a rendezvous with the bishop? How? Moni finally got up and sat by the window, as if she would find the answers if she did that. It was all speculation. Knowing the whole truth was impossible.

Grandma seemed lonely and no longer conversant, the way she had been when Moni was young. Moni and her grandmother used to talk a lot when Moni would sleep over during school days. Moni's grandmother used to tell her of her younger days, which were not fun at all. Grandma would leave Villalon at four in the morning to buy the early fisherman's catch at the shore and sell it at the market. She was only fifteen years old. She would tell Moni of how much profit she had when as a fish vendor in Naval, they would compete as to who sold out their fish first. It would mean a full profit for a fish vendor if she sold all the fresh fish at a high cost. Sometimes the fish had to be sold at half the price before it went bad, so the profit was only half. She would purchase enough to sell. The others would overbuy; hence the fish would have to be sold at half a cost before it went bad. She was not greedy. She would go to church mostly every day to thank the good Lord for her fortune. She would bring crackers, cookies and canned goods to her parents. Moni would listen to it as a young girl because her grandma would tell it with such enthusiasm. At age seven, she too became a small businesswoman like her grandmother. She never had the time to think of it and ponder the good old times. Moni enjoyed moments with her grandmother. She enjoyed recalling the past events and wished she were young again in this simple community of people she knew.

SHADOWS IN THE PANTRY

She would remember that Grandma never once talked about Simeon's father. It was something she did not want to discuss because she would be quiet. After a while, they did not ask. Simeon was respectful.

Moni headed home from Grandmother's home, kicking every pebble on her path; she was recalling almost every aspect of the events that could have led to her speculative conclusions. She sat on the steps of her ancestral home and pondered before she went up. She debated if she should tell her mother of what she was thinking. She decided not to. It would open a can of worms that had remained dormant, which, as it was, had kept the peace for all those years. She had another week to stay, but she had things to do, a quest to discover something. For a while, she forgot about her problems and her family. With her absence, they were happy to get rid of a deceitful person.

The next day, she left early for Naval to catch the bus to Tacloban. Avelino's store was still closed, but she knocked to say hello. They had a quick breakfast together. Moni admired the ambition of her brother and had not had the time to ask how he started this store, which was rather big and carried everything that a household needed. Moni did not stay long but told Avelino she might stay in his place for the night on her return to Naval. Tacloban, Leyte, was a big town, and it was the town where the Romualdos' lived. She wanted to see Emma. It should not be difficult to find a family of such status. The bus ride was bumpy, and picking up passengers along the way on several bus stops made the trip longer. When the bus was full, the drive went fast. No one could estimate the length of time to reach a place because of this routine. Nobody complained.

When Moni reached the bus stop, there was no time to look, to admire the progress and compare from before. She had never taken a trip to Tacloban, so she could not compare it from twenty years ago. It was a half-a-mile radius of stores, eating places, a market, a movie house, and all sorts. Moni had seen grandeur abroad, and to look at the primitive city (as they called it) was no bewilderment to her. Her destination was the outskirts of the city, and a cab had to be hailed to reach the place. There were not too many cabs in the city. They all looked like they were ready to be put away in a junkyard, but they seemed to carry on despite their pitiful appearance. The cab driver needed not be directed. He knew exactly where to go.

The home, seen through a gate situated far back from the road, was indeed grandiose; the elder Romualdo's residence, presumably for the length of time she had been married to a rich man. The home was made of concrete with glass windows on both floors. It was large, built on a big acreage surrounded by grass that was no longer green. Small trees were strategically in place, and each had a bench underneath it. Although it needed a touch of paint, the pillars at the front door and the wide paved walkway to the front was a home of such standing in that neighborhood. It was quite a walk to the front. The front lawn had not been carefully landscaped, but it must have, in that time of the elder's reign, been a sight. There were no other homes around. Presumably the whole area of almost ten acres belonged to the family.

Moni was announced by the guard by pressing a bell. After a few minutes of waiting, Emma hurriedly met Moni at the open gate where Moni was standing, never to enter until she was advised to do so. Despite the years, Emma recognized Moni immediately. Emma had a dress with a faded apron covering her front. Her shoes were worn. She remained agile, judging from the brisk, eager walk to reach the gate with open arms ready to embrace Moni. It was such a welcome that Moni did not expect. She was out of breath. There was no hesitation. Emma, still gasping, commented as to Moni's appearance (how pretty she looked and the sort). Emma had not aged. The freshly combed long hair, which was graying at the temples, was tied at the back. Despite the years of not having had contact with Emma, they still understood each other. After a few minutes of hellos, Moni was invited to the garden, and they sat on a bench underneath the shade. As the silent conversation went on, Moni learned that the elder had passed. Lady Erminda was, at that time, living with her male friend, whom Emma could not describe, and Mr. Onaje was never found. Emma did not invite Moni inside the home. Moni thought that Emma, despite her family name, was never accepted as such but had the status of a maid. Moni always felt bad for Emma. As she was surmising her longtime friend, she saw her as a young-faced, carefree woman who had been sheltered and provided for with the basics of life. She never had to go out to earn a living, or possibly, on the surface, she never experienced stress. Moni wondered if she had ever longed for the companionship of a man. Emma gestured by pointing at the ring finger. (Married?) Moni denied by shaking her head. Gratefully, she had not worn her wedding bond when she left her home. She did not have a need for it. Emma lived freely in this vacation home owned by the Romualdos'. It seemed a nice safe place for a woman in her fifties. The place was properly guarded, and after the elder's passing, some provisions must have been written that she be taken care of until she dies. Moni, at the present time, was in limbo. She would worry about her burial in the event of sudden death, which she did not mind. She was concerned about her parents, who might have to handle the responsibility. Emma, in her own way, kept on with stories of what happened at the old apartment and where everybody went. Emma never knew that she shared Ting's place, and he never disclosed it to anyone. Ting was discussed, and Anselmo being a native of Tacloban. It was a good two hours that Moni spent with Emma, in between which she went in to get her a drink. Emma did not want Moni to go yet. Presumably, she did not have somebody she could relate to in this household. The way she acted and her reaction to Moni showed that she missed her because Moni had always taken time to be with her despite the difficulty in understanding her. There was no one there that would do the same. Moni thanked Emma for her kindness, which was the sole purpose of her visit—that and to see her for the last time. She hurriedly said she would have to leave and did not promise to return. Moni was, at the moment, uncertain of her future, but Emma was not told of her predicament. Emma hugged her so tight, and she almost did not want Moni to leave. Moni could sense her loneliness and worry. Despite her comfort, she was very lonely. Moni had no way of comforting her. She almost asked her to come with her to the city just like they did when they were in New York. Moni hurried to leave, tearful and feeling bad for her friend. Moni had emulated Emma's condition as a deaf-mute unintentionally when she delivered her baby. As she walked swiftly to the main road, she saw Emma still standing by the gate as Moni looked back. She waved a quick good-bye. Moni would never see her again.

It was a long walk, and the unpaved road was dusty. She hailed a cab when she first entered the road, but exiting the area, she saw a large home way back from the road on a large uncared-for plot, which could not be seen when one took a cab. It could only be seen when a person walked the road. It was unfenced, a large wooden home, almost haunted-looking. It seemed that it was not occupied by someone. Moni slowed down trying to observe it, but it was almost half a mile walk to the house if she intended to browse. She refused her instinct to investigate. She finally reached the end of the road; she was sweating and very tired. The main road was wider, and she stood by the intersection.

There were no resting places but small huts where people lived, and a few were congregating, sitting on bamboo benches by the road. She paused and asked if she could rest on one of the benches. They saw her sweaty and tired, and one of the ladies walked up into her small hut and brought a glass of water, which at the time Moni hesitated to drink. She was afraid of hurting her feelings, and she would be judged as an arrogant Filipino who looked thirsty, so she took a sip and held it for a while. The water was cool and quenching, and Moni thought of their *banga*, a clay-made water receptacle, which contained boiled water from the well. Moni's water container had moss outside, and even though it was washed every day, the moss was never removed because it kept the water cold. She had grown up with it, and she was healthy. She hoped that the water she was drinking was boiled.

After a few minutes, she engaged in conversation with the lady, and Moni asked her if she happened to know who owned the big house down the road that was surrounded by bushes, which almost buried the house from view. It seemed unoccupied. She was informed that it was owned by the Onaje family that lived in Villalon. It was one of their houses, and a person had been paid to oversee it. The lady pointed to a small hut three houses from her nipa hut to the back, and she said that if Moni wanted some information about it, she could knock at his door. His name was Anselmo.

Moni hesitated, and the name rang a bell in her mind. She sat at that bench, thinking if she should. Without delay, she said a quick thank-you to the lady. While returning the empty glass, she walked to the back, tracing the narrow footpath, and went up the wooden stairs while saying hello. The nipa hut was bigger in size. The bamboo walls were new, and the nipa roof had just been replaced. It was more presentable-looking, having a wide porch and bamboo seats attached to the wall. It was noontime, and the door was open. They were having lunch as Moni called to say hello, going up the wooden steps to the porch. She hesitated as she reached the top steps out of respect to the homeowner, not wanting to peek in. A woman in her early sixties dressed in a faded skirt and ripped overhanging shirt came out from the doorway and politely asked as to who she wanted, just when a gray-haired man appeared from the main door, inquiring who it was. Moni, not having seen Anselmo for a long time, stared at him, and there was some moment of silence as Moni finally, in her excitement, exclaimed, "Noy Anselmo, ikaw ba?" (Moni had basically verified by asking if it was Anselmo.)

Anselmo quickly approached Moni with his hand stretched to shake Moni's hand, which was readily reciprocated. He invited her in for lunch, and Moni saw that they were having dried fish, rice, and chicken soup. It was not really a poor man's lunch. Moni was happy to see Anselmo. He had left the Romualdos' employ due to some arthritic problem, as Moni remembered it. Moni felt bad for interrupting their lunch, so she gratefully joined the family. Anselmo introduced his wife, Anding, who was friendly and talked about who Moni was and the circumstances of their meeting. Apparently, that house Moni was inquiring about was indeed owned by the Onajes of Villalon, and Anselmo was the one who took charge of its upkeep. He went there every day so nobody would burglarize it. He would cut the bushes, but he and his wife had not been able to do it lately due to the piercing heat. He was hired after his employment from the United States and was grateful because he had a steady income, hence he was no longer capable of farming.

He raised hogs, chicken, and a vegetable garden, hoping there would be enough proceeds to keep them fed. Anselmo knew the whole story of Raul Onaje indeed was an illegitimate child of the bishop. Grace Ann Onaje, the mother is the only daughter of Don Horatio Onaje among the five boys. She was pursuing a medical degree in Manila. After several years in Manila trying to study hard to obtain good grades. She took a vacation.

Her mishap happened in an interisland vessel when he met a handsome man and they had a rendezvous. Being plain looking, although well-mannered and cultured; she did not think the man was serious and did not anticipate the aftermath. She enjoyed the moment.

The moment of pleasure produced a fruit when she noticed it; she wrote to her father. Her father agreed to her suggestion even if he was upset.

When she was ready, she entered Phil General Hospital with the indigents under a fictitious name Edna Cruz. Her father would come and offer subsidy to some girls who bore children out of wedlock and adopted the son of Edna Cruz, a maid that worked for him. The adoption was fast due to his money and ability to negotiate being a rich land owner and business man.

Sadly Grace stopped school and went home to Leyte to take care of her son. Due to depression, she had taken ill and the child was orphaned at a young age.

Due to the infant's appearance, the rumor of Don Heratio being the father was not entertained. Raul a dark skinned infant had fine features.

Don Horatio Onaje is a Malaysian looking dark skinned man who stood around 5 ft. 7 in. with a personality and confidence of a respectable man. He was among the educated Filipinos who had the expertise to own lands plus some inheritance from his ancestors. He owned lots of farmlands in Leyte.

Apparently, Mr. Raul Onaje had grown up in that large house, brought up by a nanny, away from the Onajes until he was an adolescent, when he would be gone for the school year in a boarding school at the Ateneo School for Boys in Manila. His mother, a daughter of the Onajes, had apparently died at a very young age, and he had been housed in that particular dwelling away from the rest of the cousins. It was rumored that he was of Caucasian extraction because he looked so different from his cousins. The poor folks never saw him. He was always driven and brought to places. He attended a private school in Tacloban, a school for the rich. He would spend his vacation there, and all his cousins would be there with him. The land was very spacious for playing ball if cleared, and Moni could picture the field, a private field owned by the family.

Moni avoided telling Anselmo of the events that happened after he left. Anselmo, though, continued telling her that he knew of Mr. Onaje's fall and the broken leg. Apparently, Ting had told him when Ting left the Romualdo household. They saw each other when Anselmo went to the city. Anselmo told Moni of the beauty parlor that Ting's daughter had put up, and it was doing well.

Moni was finishing lunch. She did not tell him she had gotten married and the sort. Indeed, she was hungry. Aware of time, she slowly stood up and said good-bye, reaching for her purse, and gave Anselmo some money. He looked at it and was very grateful. It was still hot, and Anselmo's wife gave her a straw fan, at least to cover her head as she was leaving. As Moni passed by the lady who had been gracious to give her a drink, she discreetly shook her hand with a thank-you, and slipped some money in, which she hesitated to accept. It was honorable of her not to expect something after such a kind gesture. She was surprised and grateful.

Moni always thought how lucky she was despite the disgrace she had brought her family, having had the luck of enough money when she needed it. She felt good sharing her good luck. Gratefully it was windy, so the walk was bearable. Moni was walking fast as she normally would and faster since she was watching the time. She had to catch the bus at Tacloban returning to Naval, and she had no idea if she would make it on time. A cab passed by, going the other way. Moni tried to signal the driver with the intention of asking him if he would pick her up on his way to the city. He did not stop. He did not know her intentions, having seen her walking toward the city. She then continued on a desolate unpaved road with only corn fields and numerous banana plants on both sides of the road. There were no more nipa huts to rest in to shield her body from the sun. She held the straw fan to cover her face from the sun. She could imagine walking on this road at night. It must be very dark. There were no street lamps or houses that would illuminate the area. There were no jeepneys; possibly it was a place with few inhabitants, therefore a waste of resources to look for passengers in this part of town. Possibly the town folks had to walk and start early to reach the city.

Finally, she arrived in the city. Numerous stores lined the wide street, and the sidewalk was clean. There was a small restaurant with four tables, which was screened. She assumed there were no flies inside, and customers would enjoy eating without the disturbance of flies, which were common. They had varied dishes, including a vegetable soup, which was steaming hot, and it satisfied her. The place was almost like Na Goria's eatery, where food was precooked and ready to serve. It was almost three in the afternoon, and she must hurry back to Naval.

She looked for the salon that Ting's daughter owned as Anselmo had told her. Clara's was not difficult to find. It was named after her. It was by the bus stop to board for Naval. In fact, the bus was right there, ready to leave in half an hour. The salon was a small space in the heart of town, strategically located. There were three stations, and it was presentable. She saw a familiar sight, the place to shampoo hair. On the far corner was a space for nails to be done. As Moni entered, she asked the young lady about Ting. She confirmed that in fact, she was Ting's daughter, and Moni told her who she was, at which the daughter got excited. Ting had told her about Moni. There were all kind words about Moni. As the conversation went on, Clara talked about Moni's boyfriend. Moni presumably had never been seen with Ken that she knew of. When Clara said it, Moni then knew that Ting had seen them. He had never mentioned it to her. Moni was embarrassed, and she tried to ignore the comment, almost like she did not hear it.

She did not want to say "Who?" or say that he was gone or "That was nothing." She told Clara to say hello to Ting, who was in another part of Leyte called Maasin. Moni immediately left because her bus was leaving soon. Moni did not want to continue the conversation. As she was seated in the bus, she tried to recall how Ting knew when she had been careful to list down his schedule, which was the only day when Ken would come when he was not there. Moni concluded that one could never keep a secret forever. Moni had no recall. It was a long time ago. She kept thinking about it all through the ride back to Naval, which was four hours or so.

It was nighttime, and there was nobody to send a note to her mother that she could not make it home. Avelino's store was still open. The store fit the description as a sari-sari store (general store). It had everything. It was not organized yet, being that it had just opened four years ago. He had two male employees that normally left by five in the afternoon, but organizing had to be done by him. The male employees were normally busy attending customers. His sign said he was open until such time but more often than he wanted it; it would be open till late. When Moni arrived, which was almost eight at night, he was still filling orders, and Moni had to help him.

The store stood on a corner street, which was not in the heart of the city. It originally was a two-story wooden home; he had converted the downstairs into a store. The upstairs he had made into his living space. It was spacious, sparsely furnished with bare necessities. He did his cooking and cleaning. A person came once a week to do his laundry. He quickly cooked dinner with Moni's help. The fish was good, and the company was enjoyable.

Avelino told Moni that when he was at school in Cebu living at Uncle Indong's, he worked at Uncle Indong's job on weekends to finance his tuition. Their mother provided for miscellaneous fees. After school, he was given a full-time job and actually worked seven days a week. He saved most of his money and decided to do business for himself. It was a difficult decision, being that the job paid well and his boss told him he was a candidate for a supervisory job. Uncle Indong advised him to stay. He opted to start a business. The money he saved was not enough, but Mother Maxi lend him some money, which he was still paying. He was doing well, and Moni witnessed it. Avelino knew how to deal with his customers, and his prices were reasonable. He had not found a girl fit to marry, and he said he would wait. They talked until dawn, and he said if he was too tired, he could close the store the next day. He said that was the fun of being a boss.

They talked about Uncle Indong and how nice he was to have helped their family. He took them in so willingly. Avelino tried to give Uncle Indong gifts, which he did not need because he seemed to be doing well. He wanted to repay his goodness and concern as an uncle, which he added that he would never be able to repay. She was also a recipient of such kindness. Moni learned about Dee's marriage when she was in New York, but after that, she did not write anymore. Dee married a civil engineer, the son of Uncle Indong's boss, Mr. Manguerra. She lived in a grand home in Lahug, Cebu. Dee was so deserving of such luck, being such a good person. Moni mentioned to Avelino how Dee, as a young sixteen-year-old, had endured a low-paying job as a cleaning person at the store where they both worked. She would give all her income to help Uncle Indong. She was never ashamed of the job and never complained. Moni did receive a long letter when Dee graduated, thanking her of her help. Moni kept the letter. Moni told her brother about her inability to adjust to living with someone and her inefficiency as a wife to her husband. She did not tell him of any specifics, and Avelino listened to it intently. In his mind, he could not believe his sister was difficult to get along with. But since Moni told him this, he presumed it was true and he would have to believe it. They had a nice visit and Moni stayed that afternoon, helping him at the store. It was again a busy day. The *sakayan* was not filled with passengers as she sailed and waved good-bye to her brother, who walked her to the pier back to Villalon.

Chapter Forty-Seven

Every time she walked the dusty footpaths for home, she would recall her childhood. Moni thought of her younger days, and she wished she had never ventured far from home. She probably would not be in this predicament. She decided to proceed to another path to see her grandmother, who might need her help. Her stay at Villalon was so short, and she would try to stay with her as long as she could. During the day, the front door would normally be unlocked, so she tiptoed up the wooden steps and slowly pushed the door open. Mariana was sound asleep that afternoon, and Moni saw covered food laid on the bamboo table for her. Melit came to prepare it for her. Moni decided to stay until she woke up. She settled by the window and sat to look out where the front was dusty, bare of grass from inhabitants passing by. The nipa hut was spacious since her father Simeon had extended the house almost to the acreage it was erected on. She kept thinking of her grandmother's struggle and to have kept the secret to herself all this time. Moni's father would not know if Mariana had left for Naval, since her path to the shore was different. That day when she left, allegedly to hurt the bishop, would have been in between lunch and dinner because Melit would have noticed that Grandma was not home. Possibly she could have told Melit that she was going to the local chapel, so Melit would have assumed that she was still at the chapel. The rumor about the attire of the person who could have hurt the bishop was possibly a few days after the incident, and Melit would not remember the specific date that grandma was not home. It was a puzzle, and Moni would not dare ask Melit to recall it. Moni was not aware how long she was sitting by the window, and she finally stood up to check on her. Dusk was setting in, and she decided to leave to tell her mother she was already in Villalon so she would not get worried. She quickly tiptoed out, and just when she was about to leave, her grandmother called out from the bedroom inquiring as to who was there, so Moni went into the bedroom. Mariana got up and was happy to see her. Moni had always been there for Grandma when she was in her teens and even before that, when she was around seven and eight. Moni set her dinner and sat with her while she was eating. Mariana kept looking at her and spoke saying that this might the last time she would see her. Moni sat there, quiet as usual. She never knew what to say ever since. She was not gifted in saying the right things and always preferred to say nothing. Moni shed a tear because what her Lola (Grandma) was saying could be true. The old lady continued, saying that she had not done anything to contribute to the world. Instead, she had brought catastrophe, and she was ashamed of it. Moni thought of her grandmother's child, who happened to be her father, born out of wedlock, a product of assault on her womanhood. Grandmother possibly could have assassinated the person who had done it to her, making her so ashamed of herself and undeserving to have a man all her life. She had revenge in her mind, and having had her revenge, she was ready to leave earth. She kept this a secret. Never did she talk about her life nor share her sorrows to anyone. Mariana paused and seemed to have difficulty saying the words, but for some reason, she would look up in between, it seemed, to ask the Divine Being to help her out.

That gesture signified her belief of the Divine Being even if she did not go to church, except that one time when the bishop celebrated mass. She said she did not want any services when she died. She wanted to be buried immediately, and prayers would not be necessary. She continued, saying that she had committed a grievous sin; God would never forgive her. Moni was now sobbing and could not utter a word. Moni looked at her; she would keep that moment in her memory. She had a few days to stay, and possibly, as Grandma said, she would not be able to see her again. Humans came and went, and her Lola (grandmother) probably had seen her end, which might be soon. Although who was to say she would go first?

Maxi was glad to see her, and Moni apologized for her inability to inform her where she was. Maxi understood it, being a native and having had experienced such predicaments often. Since Avelino lived in Naval, Simeon did not worry too much when Maxi could not make it home, which was very common. Moni gathered her things, food to cook for the next day. She was going to stay with her grandmother for the night and possibly another night. This was her chance to stay with her and possibly talk. She did not have things to do. Melit was happy Moni was there. It gave her a break.

Moni would sit with her on the cushioned bamboo couch. They were there, feeling each other's presence on the cushioned bamboo seat. Moni did not ask her how she felt; rather, she allowed her her quiet moments. After that, Mariana repeated what she said and sort of asked Moni if she understood her request, which Moni confirmed. Moni prepared the warm water and gave her a warm sponge bath. The night went well, and Mariana settled in her bamboo bed, and Moni took the other bed in the same room. Mariana talked about when Moni's father was born and how gorgeous he looked. Moni was waiting if Mariana would reveal to her the whole truth. It had been her hardship, caring for an infant in poverty. Mariana could not go out to earn money, so Mariana's mother had to do it, and she felt so bad for her. Moni's great Lola apparently never reprimanded her of her mistake. It was a burden financially because the *mananabang* (local midwife) who assisted the delivery had to be paid in installment. Simeon, as an infant, slept in a box in Mariana's room and stayed there for the whole time until he was a year old. He did not have diapers, but the shorts he wore would be wet, and his urine would seep through the bamboo floors. His shirts as well as his shorts were made from faded skirts sewn by hand. Mariana slept with Simeon all the time in her room.

When he was two years old, Mariana started to work again and resumed her previous routine. Simeon, growing up, did not have many clothes but two sets, which was washed and hanged dry as quickly as they got soiled. He wore wooden slippers, but mostly he was barefoot. When he started attending school, he had a few notebooks and was able to listen intently judging from his good grades. Sadly enough, he could not continue beyond elementary grades. The town did not have a school beyond elementary grades. At age eight, Simeon helped his grandfather fetch water from the nearby water well, having to balance two pails of water attached to a bamboo on his shoulders. He did this before and after school. He had no friends, nor did he have the chance to play but very rarely due to the chores he had to do. He started working as an errand boy for a carpenter on weekends for a meager pay at the age of twelve. After elementary grades, he was doing work almost like that of a big man with a hammer and screwdrivers on his waist. Due to his foreign extraction, he was taller than the rest of the boys his age. He was most handsome growing up. He did not inherit any of his mother's features. He did not go through mischievous periods of childhood such as fistfights and various activities that growing boys got involved in. Moni thought Simeon's father was indeed the bishop because the resemblance was remarkable. In fact, Moni took her father's looks. Simeon, at age sixteen, was a full-time carpenter. He was a quick learner with skillful hands and was good at measurements. Having had limited education, he did not mix with the educated ones, being unable to join the conversation intellectually. He compensated by buying newspapers and reading everything he had access to. He was very quiet, almost shy, but he was very intelligent. Moni had absorbed these stories, which she never had a chance to know. It was a very memorable moment. Mariana finally slept, and Moni did too.

Chapter Forty-Eight

Moni took care of her grandmother the weeks that she was there. She helped Maxi with setting up the patterns, ironing the materials, and doing inventory on necessary items to purchase. Avelino's store carried most of the items for Maxi's business. If there were items to be bought from Cebu, Avelino purchased them when he did his bulk shopping. It was a good arrangement. Despite Maxi's age, as the head seamstress, Melit was learning the trade and seemed capable to undertake the tasks. The proceeds of the business were sufficient to provide the family with its needs. Moni's father had reduced his carpentry work but continued with the bamboo business, which was mostly Nemesio's responsibility. The vegetables from the garden had been bountiful, and occasionally, Melit's two grown children sold them to the convenient store by the shore. The coco bits were still being sold at Avelino's store. Moni's family was far from poor, and although one did not see a flashy home, there was food available and some cash flow.

Her stay at her ancestral home was memorable. The night before her departure, Maxi and Simeon had a farewell party. Avelino came, and they had a feast. Simeon roasted a hog on charcoal, which was delicious. Most of the fat had been eradicated, and the herbs stuffed in the hog's abdomen of garlic and leafy onions made it so appetizing. There was no formality, but everyone just cut into it. Moni's uncles and cousins were all there. Moni could not remember all the names of her cousins, seven of them.

In Moni's room, a low-watt bulb on the bamboo ceiling was on. The coconut oil lamp was still at the bedside table and ready to use in the event of a storm. The bed was now cushioned, and the straw mat covered the cushion. The mosquito net was placed, and it was a comfortable night to sleep with the windows open. She was dozing when her mother entered and wanted to spend time with her alone. They spoke of the old times, and she asked Moni of her problem. Moni made it clear to her mother that it was not her husband's inadequacy that caused the separation but Moni. Maxi, looking back at Moni's childhood, could not find fault that she, her daughter, could possibly have caused the breakup. Moni was very thoughtful, easy to get along with, helpful, and never encountered any problems when she was growing up. It bothered her that her daughter was unhappy and the turmoil could affect her mental status. She suspected that there was more to it than she admitted. Maxi did not extort the information, and she allowed her to keep it as she so desired. Maxi mentioned that the cultural difference could have accounted for the lack of adjustment. Moni denied it, and reiterated Arthur's goodness and respectability. She did not mention Ken Shuman.

Moni took the advantage of telling her mother as to grandmother's wishes to be buried immediately without the ritual of a holy mass and forty days of prayer. They would ask her again and follow it as she desired. Also, Moni gave her mother a pouch containing money to keep in the event Maxi had to bury her. Maxi was tearful and could not say a word. She told her mother that she would stay in Manila for a while, and she provided her with her post-office box number. Maxi hardly wrote so she did not expect a letter. She told her that she would not pass at Uncle Indong's home. She told her mother the reason. Uncle Indong would worry if Moni was not doing well, and Moni's unhappiness made him unhappy.

The next day, Moni woke up early to cook breakfast. His father, wrinkled from the sun with a body fit for a farmer, sat with her at the table. Moni looked intensely at her father, and his remarkable resemblance to the bishop. If only her father knew that he was a son of a Spanish friar. She wondered how many women the friar had fooled. As far as Moni knew, Mr. Onaje was definitely one of his children. They did not look Filipino at all. Moni was dark-skinned, making her look like a Filipino, but if she had reddish white skin, she would not be considered as Malaysian. Her father had a reddish white complexion. Her father was very quiet because his daughter was leaving. He was sad, but his sorrow he always kept to himself. The home where he grew up did not have much conversation just like Moni's. Moni touched his arm to impress on him her love and how grateful she was of being her daughter. He did his job. He provided a nice home and erected it with his bare hands, assisted by the family, and struggled to maintain a business beyond his educational background and did it well. He was not a neglectful father.

Moni felt so undeserving and felt that she had not made him proud. She could have been the head teacher in her town. It did not happen. Human frailty got the best of her. She packed some coco bits and dried meat in case she would have to stop at Uncle Indong's for circumstantial reasons. They also packed the wares for sale at Avelino's store and the merchandise for the clothing store, which Maxi had originally started with the clothing business. Moni noticed this and the planning that went with it. She was proud of him. He was calm and methodical. Nemesio and their father walked them to the shore and sat on one of the benches of the convenience store near the shore where one could see from afar if a *sakayan* was approaching. There were no passengers to board, except the two of them, so Avelino, being that they had a lot of cargo, asked the owner if they could rent it to themselves for a fee equivalent to ten people. They went back home and brought with them all the raw bananas from the house and took advantage of the moment. The owner was accommodating. The weather was fine, and the ride to Naval was uneventful. A hired transport was procured at the port.

An interisland vessel to Cebu was scheduled to leave that night. Being that she was already packed, Moni assisted her brother at the store. Some of the bananas were given to the helpers because it might not be sold on time, and it would just go bad. The male helpers were already there, and they were cleaning the store. Avelino was thankful to Moni. At dinner, Avelino asked Moni if she needed help and not to hesitate to share his place if her plans in reuniting with her family failed. He gave her some cash, which she willingly took. Moni tried to control herself not to be emotional when they talked. She was pretending to have accepted her fate. In reality, she missed her family. She had worked hard to establish a home, and it was all gone.

Chapter Forty-Nine

She was early boarding the boat to obtain the best cot. She was prepared with food in case she would be hungry. The straw bag contained her clothes, which were not too many, which she could carry to the washroom if she had to. Her brother Avelino went with her aboard the ship to bid her good-bye. They had nothing much to say. Avelino expressed his thanks for the intermittent money sent to help him when he was at school. As far back as Moni remembered, she did not send him anything. It was sent to her mother. Avelino explained that the money she sent made their mother's business running, and in turn, Avelino benefited from it. Her brother was most grateful. If anything, Moni felt recognized, and it pacified her grief. Her immediate family had not been grateful to her, ignoring her struggle for years. Avelino waited till the announcement was made for the nonpassengers to leave. It was a long embrace between the two of them, parting, probably never to see each other again. They took advantage of the moment of friendship and understanding for they might not see each other again.

The boat was clean; floors were newly polished. The cots were spaced wide enough so that passengers did not have trouble getting through. It was actually the same ship that she had always taken when she was young, possibly maintained well to still sail efficiently. Avelino waited by the pier to see her while Moni stood by the railing as the boat was leaving.

It was past seven in the evening, and it was not dark. The sea was calm, and Moni had chosen a cot not too far from the railing to be able to look out at the sea, which was beautiful. The boat drifted to the middle of the sea, and it was time to settle in her cot. The canvass was unrolled, and it was a signal that passengers should rest. Nobody was forced to, but it was the best thing to do. She placed her straw bag beside her by the wall, and on her side facing the wall, she extended her arm, cradled her belongings. It was an overnight ride to Cebu. She should be in the port by early Saturday morning. Moni slept but was awakened by a sharp noise possibly caused by the engine's motor. Everyone was up but sat quietly on their cot. Moni sat up immediately because it seemed that she was the only who had slept through the commotion. Her eye was searching for the life jacket to get one as soon as it was advised. She was ready to get one and was embarrassed, afraid of being judged as nervous. However, she viewed it and had figured how to disengage it from the hooks in the event of need. She could easily reach it. She wished there was enough for all of them. The lady near her had said there was engine trouble and there was no worry since the waters was calm. The engineers were working on it. It was an hour and Moni stopped counting because there was no sense doing it. The employees were busy helping out if there was anything that they could do. It was already daylight, and there they were in the middle of the sea standing still. The boat did not have enough food for sale since normally nobody would buy it. Everybody was having some snacks. Moni was not hungry but went for a drink. There was enough of it, and even if they were stagnant for another day, a drink was available. True enough, they were there for a good twelve hours. The boat personnel conveyed the news on land because as soon as the boat landed at Cebu, sandwiches were handed out free of charge. It was a consolation for the inconvenience, but they could have had some encounters caused by nature's fury, which would have been worse. They arrived at Cebu in the afternoon instead of in the morning. Moni hurried to purchase a ticket to Manila. A boat was leaving that night owned by the same shipping company she used to take, reputable and clean. If able to get a ticket, she would wait by the pier until it was ready for the passengers to board. It seemed that there were not too many passengers, so even if the office was closing up, she was allowed to purchase a ticket. The wait at the pier would be long, so she went to the city and visited the old department store she used to work in. As she entered the store, she looked around and looked for someone she knew. She did not see a familiar face. The place had been renovated. She did not know anyone. She left the place and went to have a snack nearby. She walked around the movie houses that were still there. She remembered the movie house where she had watched a movie with Dee. It was almost seven in the evening, and she headed to the pier. She passed by the warehouse which Uncle Indong used to work, and it was closed. She was not sure if her uncle had already retired, and her younger brother was not sure. She felt bad that she did not go to the warehouse instead of going to the city. Unintentionally, she did not want to see him because of embarrassment. The gifts for him, she would just bring them with her.

She boarded the boat, taking the first-class accommodations. It was an enclosed compartment specifically for the passengers paying an expensive fare for some privacy. The passengers in this area belonged there, and possibly, no outsiders could enter because the ticket was randomly checked before one entered the compartment. There were four double-deck spaces in each compartment, and no one was there yet that occupied any of the space. The boat would not leave till ten at night, and it was assumed there were more passengers who had not boarded yet. Despite the accommodations, a locked closet was not provided for the passengers' belongings. Moni lay down to rest. She had had a rough night. The only reason for one to leave a space would be something of dire necessity. The announcement was made that the boat was leaving the port and nobody came to share her cubicle. She had the space all to herself. It looked comfortable, and she anticipated a fair, restful trip. She would normally starve herself except a drink of juice on those rides to limit her bathroom trips, but these accommodations had washrooms within the enclosure. It was surrounded by glass windows for passengers to view the ocean if one chooses to do so. A curtain was provided for privacy so the people at the outer deck could not peek in. There were only a few passengers of fifty spaces, and most of the windows were open to view the sea.

She planned her activities when she would reach Manila. She thought of Na Goria and the eatery. If Pilar kept on working at the dress shop, the eatery would have to be closed. She planned on opening the eatery for four days, and the rest of the days, she would keep on looking for a job. She thought of the kitchen help, who obviously had to find a job while the eatery was closed. It was early morning, and the Manila pier was not as busy.

Disembarking was quick since she did not have any belongings she needed help to carry. She took a cab, and when she arrived at Na Goria's place, it was dark and quiet. She expected it.

The wooden door at Na Goria's room was missing. Na Goria was not there, and the door was disengaged, leaving the hinges and part of the rugged wood hanging on it. The wooden door was sprawled by the exit door to the backyard as if it had been dropped there in a hurry. The room was in total disarray. Moni looked around, so if she had interrupted an ongoing robbery, she would be able to do the appropriate move to hide or to get away and exit the premises so she would not get hurt.

The bathroom was open, and no one was there. She stepped over the wooden door and inspected the door to the backyard, and it was locked. She looked at the open closet and moved the clothes that were hanging, trying to find someone possibly hiding in between the clothes, and no one was there. Her things were still there.

Moni was not prepared on what to do if someone was hiding in this room. He or she would startle her, and defending herself in that tight space would have been impossible. Na Goria's bed had been stripped of its sheets, and the bed was skewed; possibly she was to be lifted to somewhere using the bed linens. It was an emergency move; possibly her condition had gone bad. Moni went up and knocked at Pilar's door, whom she thought at the moment would not be home. There was no answer. She knew it. It would only be Pilar who would bring her to the hospital.

She started cleaning the place so when Pilar arrived, it would already be presentable for Na Goria to return. When Pilar came, she looked weary and teary-eyed. As soon as she saw Moni, she immediately hugged her, unable to speak. Moni knew that Na Goria had not made it. Apparently, Na Goria had been brought to the hospital with difficulty of breathing and had hurriedly been lifted off, the reason the door had been disengaged by some men, unable to maneuver her from the tight-spaced bedroom. It happened that Pilar had woken up to relieve herself at around past midnight, and she went downstairs to check on Na Goria when she saw her gasping for breath. Pilar then did not know what to do but called the nearby hospital for help, which came almost right away. Pilar could not get help from the tenants and had to bear the anguish by herself. Na Goria did not suffer but actually stopped breathing in the ambulance. She was currently being transported to a funeral parlor. Pilar was beside herself. She has learned to love Na Goria, being the kind person that she was. They hugged each other, then being the persons who had been recipients of such kindness. There were no relatives to wait for to view the body. The person in her will was Pilar. She and she alone could make the decision. So Pilar consulted Moni on what to do. They decided on immediate burial. As expected, there was nobody who came at the funeral parlor since Na Goria, while still alive, has conveyed that there was nobody to call when her time came. She was buried after a day at the parlor. They both opened the old lady's suitcase, which Pilar had a key. There was enough money to pay for everything.

    Moni had utter respect for Pilar, who had total access to this bag of money and could have taken it all to spend on whatever she wished for. She did not. They were relieved. There was extra money to reopen the eatery for them to go on living comfortably in that home. The week was spent planning certain activities involved when a loved one passes on. The door could not be fixed yet, so a curtain was placed to provide privacy. Moni stayed at Na Goria's room and could not sleep, it being open, without a lock. So she placed the folding cot, which tightly fit the narrow space, in the kitchen and planned to sleep in that room. The doors both at the front counter and to Na Goria's room had a horizontal lock, which would be dislodged in the event of a forced entry, but Moni felt safe in that room. She would hear the commotion. She bought herself a small fan for comfort. The small window overlooking the backyard was open, which afforded some wind to enter. At Na Goria's room, she would place bottles of water and a pail of water by the unlocked door to alert her if an intruder came in. Moni would be accordingly dressed with worn-out pants and blouse to sleep, ready to do whatever she would think of in moments of crisis. She told Pilar of her moves so if Pilar would enter, she would know it was there and she would not slip and fall.

The kitchen help could not be reached, and opening the eatery would have to be deferred. A sign that help was wanted was posted by the window so it would be visible for passers-by to inquire. Moni took advantage in going out to find a night job. A job as a kitchen help at the hospital, a hospital worker, or a hotel maid would have been fine. A teaching job was not feasible. She had not given up on it, but for the moment, it was out of reach. It was a week that a kitchen help could not be found. Moni, although not paying rent, had to buy and cook food, and out of respect and consideration, she invited Pilar to join her. She had money but admittedly did not want to spend it. She would rather open the restaurant and eat with pay as well. Two weeks went by, and they could not find anyone. Moni was worried. She continued on staying at the kitchen space, which she was already accustomed to and wherein sleep was possible.

She checked her PO box and found a note from Harriet that she had taken ill and she was not able to mail her check so it had been mailed to her home address at Hempstead. Presumably it had been cashed by Arthur, being that her name was still on their joint account. As much as she thought she had planned it well, it did not materialize. Harriet, despite hesitation, reported that Arthur has been seen with one of the nurses. It was upsetting, but Moni expected it. Arthur, her husband, could lure any woman just by his manners and looks. Moni was jealous, but she told herself to accept it. Her family was gone. They did not want her, and it was reasonable. She had forgiven them for their anger, and life meant being alone.

One day she went to see her son's (Clark Kent's) home, looking on how well his life had been and to rest assured that at least there was one thing she had done right in her life. True enough, it was a gated space with high walls, and the homes could not be viewed from the outside. Moni did not ask the guard as to the specific house owned by the Bonedotos for fear of being seen and it be reported that a strange woman had passed by to inquire about them. She did not want the adoptive mother to worry, nor did she want her son to know. It was a quick glance of the area, and Moni was satisfied. She would not return.

One night, while she was fast asleep, she heard the empty bottles at Na Goria's door rolling as if they were high-pitched bowling balls being struck by a professional bowler. As she unlocked her door, she saw a person immobile on the floor. The ray of light from the back door was not enough to determine the person's identity. She folded her cot immediately and placed it against the window and crawled out to remove the pail and the bottles. Her knees were wet, and in the dimly lit room, she would be seen by the man if he was alert, which Moni did not check, and possibly, he would be able to identify her. Moni prayed that he would not be able to do that and immediately exited the premises. She did not want the police to come and be seen and possibly be on the news. She ran out and did not know where she would stand or sit because it was dark outside. She crossed the street and was trying to find a shadowed nook where she would not be noticed and be able to see at a reasonable distance of the goings-on at Na Goria's. She did not have a wristwatch on her; possibly she had left it in the bathroom when she washed up for the night. She had no idea what time it was. She remembered retiring early, by around nine in the evening. She felt bad for the guy who was on that floor and had possibly incurred a head injury. But who could that be? He did have a key because the front glass windows were not broken. But who had a key except her, Pilar, and the tenants? Could one of the tenants' friends have a key too? Could the kitchen help have a key too? Moni was thinking through and watching intently if an ambulance would pull up to take the guy from there. Obviously no one knew what was happening downstairs since there was no commotion nor had someone put the light on. The guy was still on that floor unattended.

Moni was getting conscious of her prolonged stay at the sidewalk of an establishment and if noticed by someone, she might become a subject of suspicion. She started walking at the sidewalk toward the opposite of Na Goria's place and back, passing it. She was getting tired from all the walking that she finally walked to the church and sat there on the elevated cement. The place was not within her sight to view. It seemed like a safe place, being by the church. She could not see the house from where she was but would be able to notice if an ambulance exited the street. She was getting sleepy and possibly dozed off when the ambulance went and left. Finally, it was dawn; the sun was starting to streak its rays, and the street was becoming busy. As she was sitting by the church she had not seen any ambulance enter the street nor come out of it. She had been watching, but there was a moment or moments when she could have dozed off, lost her wits. She opted to wait. Pilar would soon be up to go to work. Moni's fear was Pilar would leave the vicinity and never go to the room, hence there was no reason for her to go in. But the person would surely be visible as the tenants passed to head out, although she would be wondering why there was no breakfast for her. She sat there, not knowing what to do. By that time, after several hours, the water on the floor that caused him to fall must have been dry. There was no evidence of the bottles since Moni had quickly removed them before she left. They were not intended to hurt the intruder, but the noise of them falling were to alert Moni. It was getting sunny, and she headed back. As she fitted her key to the door, she noticed that it was not locked. As she hurried out, she did not close the door. Pilar did not notice that the automatic lock was not on. Moni had forgotten it. If she was interrogated, she would have a reason. She had left the vicinity before the intruder came in. If asked, she would say she was up early to go to church, and presumably, the intruder came after she left for church? Somebody would question the reason for his fall.

The place seemed very quiet. The space where the person had fallen was empty. Pilar had left for work. There was no commotion upstairs. True enough, her wristwatch was on the bathroom sink. She cooked breakfast for herself and stayed in the kitchen space and locked both doors, opened the cot, and started to doze off. It was a cool early morning plus the comfort of the fan and she fell asleep. She was awakened by the persistent ringing of the phone located at the counter. She sluggishly got up just to answer it and it stopped ringing. She returned to her cot, and as she glanced at her wristwatch, she noticed that it was already past two in the afternoon. She did not care. It had been four weeks or so, and they had not found a kitchen help since she arrived from Leyte. She was worried of the current situation, of taking money from her savings. She would remain frugal. She fell asleep again.

There was a knock at the door, and it was Pilar. Pilar asked her where she had been, and she told her that she had gone to church early. She continued, telling Moni that there had been an intruder who intended to rob the place, but he had apparently fallen and could not move. Pilar apparently was looking for Moni and had discovered the intruder on the floor. The devastating news was the guy was Pilar's husband. Pilar had failed to take the key from him, and as he learned of Na Goria's demise, he came to take the suitcase containing the money. He was discovered around five thirty that morning when Pilar was getting ready to work and the police were called. Moni cooked dinner for both of them. Pilar enjoyed it. They spent the evening sitting by the bamboo bench at the backyard. Moni, for the first time in her life, enjoyed lazy moments, which she never did. The phone rang, and it was somebody applying for kitchen help. The telephone had actually kept on ringing during the day, but nobody had been there to answer it. Gratefully, the persistent caller tried reaching them in the afternoon, so a meeting was set to meet the applicant.

Due to the incident of a burglar, it was apparent that Moni's sleeping quarters were not safe. So Pilar invited Moni to share her bedroom space, which she had occupied since Moni met her. Moni had never entered her room, and amazingly, it was two and a half times bigger compared to her previously rented room. There were two medium-sized cushioned beds, and Pilar, being a seamstress, had adorned the room meticulously with tailored curtains and matching bed covers. It was pretty clean, and there was only one closet along the wall which was full of clothes. Moni had a few garments, and Pilar accommodated her a small space to hang her clothes. The dresser was full of cosmetics, and Moni was free to share it. Moni hardly wore makeup. She did not need it. Her skin was clear and her face so pretty that she often hid her face and always stood at the back, not to be seen. Her relationship with Pilar was pleasant. Finally, the door at Na Goria's was fixed, and Moni moved downstairs, still using the cot. She would lock the both doors from the kitchen and to the eatery. It was safe.

The caller was interviewed, and she was finally hired as kitchen help. Tanciang was her name and she proved to be such a help because she had some ideas that might be applicable for the eatery to succeed. To add to it was she was willing to come as early as four in the morning to go with Moni to market. The requested compensation was reasonable, and there was money to restart the business. Pilar needed assistance with paperwork, talking to a lawyer to transfer the property to Pilar's name. Moni, being a college graduate, had a better understanding of the process because Pilar did not have enough education to understand it. Opening the eatery was deferred.

A sign outside the eatery window was placed that it was open for business. It was decided that they would open four days a week. Moni would be free to do errands on Mondays, Tuesdays, and Wednesdays. They started with ready-made soups and sandwiches and various dishes to cook as the order came in. The first day was slow, but the soup was sold out. Moni cooked the bones all night, and it tasted good. They closed late, and the orders of noodles seem to be a favorite. Moni was not lucky enough to find a job. She settled with the eatery, only earning half of the proceeds as agreed. She did not have to pay rent, and food was free. After four weeks, the sales picked up. The female help was industrious and cleaned the area even though she was not expected to. Moni compensated her with free food to bring home. She had two teenage boys. She lived by Dapitan Street. It was almost dangerous for her to be riding the jeepney that early in the morning, so Moni suggested that they market three times a week and she would meet her at the market instead at a certain spot. Pilar was pleased and helped Moni on weekends if she was not working at the dress shop. Moni suggested that either they would purchase a small cabinet or a carpenter would fix the place underneath the counter to display the ready-made blouses and skirts Pilar made. The blouses of different sizes were displayed, and Pilar bought a sewing machine and stationed it in Na Goria's room. They rearranged it that the old medium-sized bed was placed by the wall and there was room for a table to cut the materials.

Some of the display was sold, but most of the customers had limited income and could not afford embroidered blouses. The female help became the laundrywoman of the house for extra income. She was allowed to wash the clothes at the corner cement enclosure where the faucet was located. She would come early on Tuesday morning, and the tenants were pleased. The extra money and the convenience of doing it right there were a help to Tanciang. Moni finally increased her pay, plus more food for her to bring home. Moni kept expecting a call for another job even though the money from the eatery was fine. She was fearful that in the event of illness, she did not have enough savings to pay for hospitalization, although she did get by and did not have to take out any money from her savings.

Chapter Fifty

One Friday morning, a well-dressed guy came and ordered a hearty breakfast. Nobody entered in this eatery dressed like that. He stood out by appearance alone. He was of almost purebreed Chinese and appeared rich. He stood tall, lean, and muscular. He paid for his bill and slipped a card to Moni, saying that if she needed a part-time job to be free to call the number. Moni did not get to say thank-you because he immediately left without expecting a reply. The day went on, and Moni did not dwell on it. She left the card in the round tin with the cash sales of the day. It was a profitable day, selling mostly the cheap vegetable soup, which they increased the amount as the days went on. Moni has settled of being the manager of the small eatery, being that she made most of the decision. She would consult Pilar infrequently, since Pilar concentrated on the dress shop.

One night, as Moni was cleaning up, she saw the business card (Kim Lim Son/travel agent) in the tin can and relocated it inside her wallet. It did not interest her to call because she was settled. She would prefer a job at the hospital as an aide or a housekeeper. Weeks went by, and the guy returned and gave her another one. It was obvious that he had been interested in hiring her since he came back. That Monday, she called the number and she was told to leave her number and availability. She did not have to be interviewed. To Moni, it sounded fishy, and she promised to herself that she would not attempt to try it. She had had mishaps in her past, although she no longer had a family to set an example to and she was no longer watching her behavior. She called the number out of curiosity, and she did what she was told. There was no call back for a week. She forgot about it until one Sunday night she was called for a job, an address to go to and instructions on what to wear. Her cab would be paid for as soon as she reached her destination.

It was Web Hotel, room 282, at Cubao, Quezon City. It was a four-story building on a busy intersection, and Moni was very nervous going up the elevator. The cab driver was met by a personnel, and true enough, her fare was paid. As she knocked at the door of 282, she was met by a middle-age woman who was wearing a white apron. It looked safe and she was ushered inside, introduced to an elderly man who needed a companion for the night since the regular companion took ill. She would do the job for two nights. It was convenient since the eatery was closed. The envelope containing the money was all prepared. The money was all hers. Mr. Kim did not call for commission. Moni did not ask. The week went by, and she was not available. Mr. Kim called that he would like to meet her at a certain place. She told him she was working and she would not be able to meet him. Moni planned that if he will insist, she would not divulge where she lived nor would she say where she originated from. She would say she lived at Dapitan Street.

It had been few weeks, and she did not call because she was not available. The money she earned was extra, and she had put it away. One morning, Mr. Kim came for breakfast again. He left another card with a note stating,

"Tatawag ako" (I'll call).

True enough, that night, around eight in the evening, there was a call, but she did not answer it. If she did, it would reveal that she lived there. If he would call in the afternoon, she would entertain it, assuming she was still there, finishing the work at the eatery. She was going to send Tanciang home at four in the afternoon. She also told her that if there was a call for her to say she had left for home and she did not live there. She took Tanciang's address and wrote it in her small notebook. She was expecting another call sometime, and she would be ready what to say. If he required commission from the money she earned, she would give it without question. Moni was hoping it would not be too much. The phone rang on the days that the eatery was closed, and she did not answer it. She told Pilar about her predicament, and she understood it. Moni was upset that she had allowed herself to get into this situation. It kept her up most of the night. She would leave very early for errands so she would not be seen by someone, presumably Mr. Kim's employee.

The call came Thursday morning as the eatery opened. Moni was given an address for a job. He did not elaborate on the job, and she could not question him. Moni called back the number on the card and left a message that she could not do the job. He called back around noon when it was busy. He was rather upset that she had refused the job. She did not reason out but remained silent listening to him. He hung up on her. Moni was happy he did not talk too much because she could not linger on the phone at that moment. It was a busy day.

One morning, Moni took a stroll at Quiapo and was window shopping when she felt a tap on her shoulder. It was Mr. Kim. Quiapo was a very busy two-mile-radius area of buildings occupying several blocks that housed various stores selling clothing, appliances, grocery stores, restaurants, and snack bars. Two-story structures were rather convenient since it had a walkway wide enough for people to walk protected from rain and the blazing sun. There was a snack bar nearby, and he slowly led her, and they took a table. Moni did not know what to do and allowed him to lead her since it was a busy place and he could not inflict hurt because people would prevent him from doing so. The place had several small square tables for two, although four persons with small orders could fit. They were all glass tables, rather clean. Moni, being a restaurant worker, was becoming aware of these places, always looking for ideas, trying to improve her working place. Mr. Kim was dressed elegant as usual and, admittedly, had fine manners. He pulled her chair to sit as a gentleman would do. Moni was aware that people were looking, and she was fearful that Mr. Kim knew lots of people possibly knew his reputation and being seen with him might jeopardize her status. Thinking through, she had no status in this place where shoppers were to look for bargains and could not care less who she was. Moni, with her head down, did not look at Mr. Kim. The waitress dressed in a fit red skirt paired with a white collared blouse came, and Mr. Kim ordered some lemon drinks without consulting Moni. His gestures, although polished, were rather controlling, and Moni was aware that behind those manners he could be a dangerous man. She could not run nor evade him now. He expected her to initiate the conversation, which she did not. She remained quiet, not wanting to utter a word, afraid of any mistakes. She did not want him to know who she really was, her origin and the sort.

He finally started talking as they both sipped the lemonade. It seemed that he was trying to be nice to Moni because he was interested in keeping her as an employee. He said, "Tumawag ako, kasi may mga customer ako na kailangan ang servicio mo. Nagustuhan ka kasi nang matanda kaya ilagay kita na empleyado." (He was telling her that he would like her to be a permanent employee.)

"Alam ko ang pangalan mo at hind ko kailangang alamin ang apelyedo mo. Ang pera na natanggap mo ay iyo lahat at wala akong paki-alam niyan." (I know your name, and I need not know your last name. The money you received was yours to keep.)

Moni was still quiet. Inadvertently, she pretended to be dumb. She nodded her head and said, "I-isipin ko." (I will think it over.)

The chicken sandwiches came, and they both ate. It was an hour of conversation, mostly with Mr. Kim talking. He was convincing her of the benefits of being employed under him and to tell him as soon as she decided to be permanent. He asked Moni how much she earned, which Moni said he was not entitled to know. Mr. Kim was condescending and did not like the answer coming from a poor person. As they ended the meeting, he again stood up and chivalrously guided her out. Moni kept walking along the several stores that lined the street. The buildings kept the shoppers from sun and rain as they hurriedly rushed by and she could be in the vicinity as long as she wished without being noticed. Moni had nowhere to go, and her intentions were to look around. She was not really looking at the items, but as she browsed around, she was actually thinking of what to do about this new job.

SHADOWS IN THE PANTRY

It was late afternoon when she arrived at Na Goria's home. She was full from the chicken sandwich she had and she did not want to prepare dinner. She sat outside the back bench and did some thinking. A teaching job was her dream even if it was far-fetched. The phone rang, and as she stood and hurried to answer it, she thought of Mr. Kim, and reaching the phone, she hesitated and stood by it until it stopped ringing. She did not want him to know she lived there. She must be alert of the time not to answer the phone after 5 PM. The phone did not ring again that night.

Pilar came late, and Moni stayed up to talk to her. Moni told Pilar about Mr. Kim and reiterated to Pilar that she did not want him to know she lived at Na Goria's. They had an agreement that indeed they would take care of each other. Pilar told Moni that her ex-husband was still in jail for the offense he has committed, and at the moment, they were both safe.

A letter was received by Moni from Harriet:

> Dear Moni,
> I hope you are doing well. I have fully recovered from my ordeal. I have filed my resignation and would be staying home to do nothing. To keep me busy, I will do volunteer work at the same place I used to work.
> Please write and keep me abreast of your whereabouts. I missed you. I live in the same apartment, and the phone number is the same.
> Harriet

There was no news about Arthur. Moni thought Harriet intended to skip it to keep her from worry. One Saturday morning, Mr. Kim called again. She was called for a job to service the old man at the same hotel and the same room. She was to work on Monday and Tuesday. True enough, the job was the same. The old man needed somebody to accompany him. Moni relieved the permanent companion when she was off. It worked out all right because it compensated well. It seemed profitable. The old man named Mr. Lasco seemed rich enough to stay in that hotel, and Moni never knew the business he was engaged in to be able to afford such a fee for a companion with no special skills. After a while, Mr. Kim seemed legitimate as an employer. Moni thought it would be best for Tanciang to apply for the job. Thinking through, Mr. Kim would have given Tanciang a card if he fancied her.

One afternoon, she received a call and she was instructed to the same room at the Web Hotel. She was to go there at 10 A.M in the morning. So she prepared everything so there will be cooked dishes for the day. She reached the hotel and she knocked, and no one opened the door. She turned the doorknob, and it was unlocked. She cautiously entered, looked around, and at the same time called, saying,

"Ta-o po!" (Is somebody here?)

The room was dark, but the rays of the sun that gleamed through the curtains illuminated part of the room. As she set foot inside, the door was shut behind her, and from nowhere, a muscular man held her from the back and clamped her mouth shut with his palm from behind and she could not scream. A cloth was immediately placed on her mouth, and it was in between her teeth, tied tightly to the back of her head. She tried to turn her head to look who it was, but her head was held straight. She was pushed to sit on a chair, then her wrists were bound with a rough twine at the back of the chair and another twine to tie her to the chair. She was then blindfolded, unable to see her captors. Moni kept on praying that God would protect her and to enlighten her captors not to do more harm to her. She squirmed, trying to fight back, and was held tight by strong, muscular arms. She stopped and thought that there was no use but saved her strength for the anticipated fight she would have to go through. She was not an athlete, her body and arms never strong to endure a fight. Her ability was limited to her legs; kick, being a track and field athlete when she was young. That was long ago and arguably lost the skill due to age. She did not hear the door open, and presumably, the captors were still in the room, and no one else entered. The phone rang, and it stopped ringing. It seemed obvious that the captor had answered the phone but no voice was heard. Possibly, Moni thought, he was being given instructions on what to do. There was complete silence.

Sitting there, Moni tried to move, maneuvering the ties off her wrists. A strong hand held her hands so she stopped. Possibly there were two persons, one who answered the phone and one who was watching her closely. She was again in a predicament that she had caused herself. She was trying to picture the room and her location. She had worked for the old man a couple of times, and being blindfolded, she was trying to imagine how she would exit in the event she had a chance. She was not sure where they had taken the chair she was sitting on since there was none in the living room. Possibly they had prepared it there for her, taking the chair from the bedroom. Moni wanted to cry, but she could not. She moved her wrists again to feel the twine that was digging into her. An arm immediately held her, and obviously she was guarded. It must have been an hour that she was there, and the hotel door opened. A person possibly entered, but no one was talking. Moni could not tell how many persons there were in the room.

After a few minutes, somebody untied her from the chair; she was eased up and was pushed to the bedroom. Her fear exacerbated, and she tried to resent physically, but she wanted to save her strength for something that she was fearful of. She was eased down to a sitting position at the edge of the bed, which she was familiar with. The space in between the foot part of the bed and the set of drawers in front had a mirror.

The only problem was she did not know how many people there were. If there were three, she would not be able to handle the struggle. As she thought of it, she was forced down at the edge of the bed, and she was on her back, her legs dangling down the floor. Her both wrists still tied underneath; she was helpless. Her medium-heeled black shoes she still had on, and she would try to kick her captors, which she was planning to do. Before she could act, the guy unzipped her black pants and jolted them down to her thigh. She moved her head up and down, hoping to loosen the blindfolds. It was loose, but not enough to come off. She tried to get up, and a firm hand held her right shoulder down. A guy was beside the bed and another at the foot part. Moni was now certain there were two of them. There was a moment of silence and inactivity.

Then a loud bell rang several times. It was a fire alarm, and possibly the guy or guys had exited quickly, leaving her trapped and possibly to die. She was not sure. There was a lot of commotion that she could hear but being that she was not able to scream, it made her more apprehensive. Thinking that they were gone she immediately slid down the bed and stood up, pulling her pants from the back, and jumped like a kangaroo, quickly toward the door. She turned her body, her back toward the door, and she, on her knees, held the door with her free hand and dislodged her blindfolds by shaking her head up and down on the doorknob. It seemed like eternity while the bells kept ringing and the noise outside the door was apparent. Finally, she dislodged the blindfold, and she had eyes. She ran to the door, holding her pants from the back, and turned around to open the door. Her wrist still bound, she held her pants from the back, and the blindfold hanging on her neck, she ran together with the others, not really knowing where she was going. She just followed everybody to the stairs at the end of the hallway. Luckily, she was on the second floor of a four-story building, and the run downstairs might not be too difficult. Due to her instability, she was almost knocked over twice when she was running toward the stairs, which was to the end of the hallway. Smoke was bellowing outside as she saw it, and it was almost as if she would never reach it because her ability to run was limited. The exit was a long way, and people passed her, not noticing her face with handkerchief on her mouth and bound wrists. The stairs were wide but not wide enough to accommodate the people. Presumably the hotel was fully occupied, judging from the number of people trying to evacuate.

Everybody was trying to escape from the catastrophe of being burned, and it was almost a stampede of who gets to exit first. Moni held on to her unzipped pants, running down the stairs, staying by the wall since she had no balance and being pushed by people to save their life. As she was struggling down the stairs, an elderly man was kind enough to stop, hold her arms, and untie her wrists. Despite his incapability, he took his time, jeopardizing his life for Moni, a girl he did not know. There was no time for formality of saying thank-you, nor did she look at the kind Samaritan who did it to her. She was running with the rest, trying to zip her pants and untying the handkerchief from her face, staying by the wall to reach the main exit. As they reached the front door, people were fighting over as to who could squeeze through the door first to leave the building. Moni had no trouble threading through the crowd, being thin-bodied, running and looking back to quickly view the blaze. The fire engine had not arrived, and the process of firefighting had not begun. The fire would ultimately consume the establishment. Moni was getting away not only from the blaze but from the people who had assaulted her, who were possibly looking at her at that very moment.

The fire was on the third floor, almost right above where she was held captive. She felt her small wallet in her right pocket and ran as far as she could to hail a cab. She was heading to a direction away from the fire, not really knowing where to go. She was afraid of being watched despite the chaos. She would have side glimpses and looked back for a face that she would recognize. In between, she was grateful to the Lord in Heaven, who had protected her in that predicament. Walking aimlessly, her destination was Tanciang's home whose address she did not remember even though she had written it down on a pad some time ago. Sadly enough, the mind did not cooperate during the crisis. She was hoping that as she was in that cab, she would recall it. The purpose of this was to confuse the person who would be following her. There was no empty cab. She kept walking, and it was getting dark. Being a person who had not lived in Manila, she had not explored enough to know the places nor was she able to recognize certain landmarks. She was hoping that she was not too far from Tanciang's home. She recalled reaching for her wallet, she had a few pesos, probably not enough to pay the cab driver the correct amount.

As she hopped in the cab, she told the driver, "Dapitan po, malapit sa UST" (she was saying the street and the landmark of University of Saint Tomas as her destination). The cab was clean, freshly swept, and the seat was wrapped in thick white material. The cab driver was dressed in a mended-off white collared shirt and faded jeans ripped on the knees. Despite his pitiful attire, he was clean. He looked like a typical Filipino of Malaysian descent, lean and dark-skinned, with high cheekbones and almond eyes. He was not talkative; he merely acknowledged that he heard the instructions. Moni was tempted to ask if the place was very far or where they were in relation to their destination. She was fearful of not only the money it would cost because he would be tempted to cruise her around the city far from her destination, or worse yet, the ordeal of the afternoon may occur again.

As they drove on, Moni saw a familiar sight the back door of the university. A quick recall of an event in her life has reappeared. She was trying to remember the conversations with Tanciang as to the location of her home. A few blocks past the university, she glanced at the meter reading and told the driver she arrived at the spot. The meter indicated the amount of money she had in her wallet. True enough, she had enough and more. She walked to an inner street as Tanciang had told her. Moni walked slowly and looked at the numbers of the dilapidated houses she was passing by. A woman dressed up, possibly to go to work, was leaving her home, and Moni respectfully asked if she happened to know a woman named Tanciang with two young boys. She was directed to a house across the street and to ask from that house. As she was walking to the house as she was directed, she thought Tanciang would not be there. It was half past 4 PM and she must be at the eatery. Closing time was 5:30 PM.

Despite this she kept on. If Tanciang would not be there, she would wait at the reception area.

The middle-aged lady opened the door and said that Tanciang was renting a room in that house. It was a rather large wooden house on a property, which would have rooms for rent. Tanciang was called by the helper, and as she descended the wide wooden stairs, her eyes widened, looking at Moni's appearance. Moni, never conscious of her looks, wondered why Tanciang was looking at her with such a bewildered look as if she had seen a ghost. Tanciang, dressed in a faded housedress, led her upstairs immediately. As soon as they reached the floor upstairs, Tanciang exclaimed the emotions she had kept when she first saw her,

SHADOWS IN THE PANTRY

"Anong nangyari sa iyo?" (What happened to you?)

As they went in, she was led to a chair at the small dining table and was given a small mirror, and Moni saw her mouth bruised and across her face. It was ugly, her face swollen and her wrists were bruised as well from the twine. Surprisingly, she did not feel the pain that usually accompanied the bruise nor did she inspect it when she was at the cab. She was engrossed in getting away. Moni had no answers because she did not want to tell Tanciang. Tanciang said Pilar sent her home at 3 PM. All the cooked dishes been sold, and they had to close early. She finally said, "Gusto ko sanang magpahinga. Sabihin ko na lang sa iyo ang nangyari mamaya." (I would like to rest for now. I will tell you the story later.)

With that, Tanciang led her to a single wooden bed at the far corner of the room. Tanciang's rented space was a large room, bigger than Ting's in New York. It had its own washroom—small though it was, they had privacy. The single portable electric burner was placed on top of a wooden table, and beside it was a big basin to wash their kitchenware. They had no kitchen sink. A small square table with chairs was the receiving place by the kitchen area. There was a medium-sized wooden bed with a mat and a small one beside it to sleep in located on one corner of the room. Moni was very tired and asked Tanciang if she could sleep. Immediately, Tanciang accommodated her, was led to a smaller bed, and a wood partition was moved to shield Moni. Presumably it was Tanciang's bed. Moni was comfortable being at a safe place.

When Moni woke up, Tanciang was sleeping in the other bed with the boys. Moni felt bad having to take their bed, but after she comforted herself, she went back to the bed. Tanciang kept the place clean. Moni could not return to Na Goria's place until early morning. Moni was happy that she extended kindness to Tanciang for indeed, in times of crisis, she was willing and kind to help her.

Moni was up early but was afraid to leave before Tanciang woke up. When she was heading to the washroom, Tanciang was up, and Moni told her she would leave as soon as she was done. Tanciang had to accompany her downstairs and let her out. Moni hurriedly walked to the corner and reached the small eatery that she used to stay when she had her firstborn. It was fixed up and cleaned, and she had a hearty breakfast. She had enough for the jeepney fare to Quiapo.

Na Goria's place was quiet. She sat by the bench outside and relaxed. She was debating if she would tell Tanciang the truth. When Tanciang arrived, she did not forget and asked Moni what happened. Moni told her that she was visiting a friend at the nearby place where the hotel fire had occurred, and she was bumped all over the place with people trying to get away from the flame. It was a true enough story but not the whole truth. She would not reveal to anyone her predicament.

That Thursday, the restaurant opened, and Mr. Kim came in, made his order, and saw the bruise on her face. He did not speak to her. He was actually checking her if she was all right. The fact that he came that day meant that he possibly knew. Moni pretended that nothing happened. She covered her bruise with makeup, but it was visible. Moni never knew her captors, and even if she suspected Mr. Kim, she could not confront or ask him. Moni did not notice a different reaction, nor was there any change to his behavior. She thought Mr. Kim was involved as to her predicament at the hotel because he came and assessed her. It was very suspicious. He did not asked her how she incurred the bruises. It is almost like he expected it and possibly reported to that man who assaulted her that Moni was alive. That night, Moni could not sleep, thinking of what to do, and wrote the ordeal on a piece of paper in her native tongue. She intentionally misspelled and coded the words into numbers to confuse the reader if somebody happened to read it. She folded it lengthwise an inch wide and inserted and sewed it in one of the wide seams of her housedress. It was almost like a ribbon was inside the seams. The week went by, and Moni treated the bruise with cold lime juice compress every night. The eatery was doing well, and even though they increased the amount of soup to be sold, there were times that at three in the afternoon, it was gone. It was tempting to close up early, but the notice outside the eatery had to be adhered to. The customers might not come back. Marketing was done according to the demands, and the proceeds had been better. Tanciang remained a loyal and industrious help.

Moni opened a bank account nearby and deposited most of her cash. She was allowed to have a deposit box in the bank for valuables for a cost. She took one. Due to the large amount of proceeds from the restaurant, she gave extra money to Tanciang out of her own pocket. She did not have any expense and could well afford it. She asked Tanciang if she could take her in, in her home on Sunday nights. She said she had to do some work for someone near her address. Tanciang accommodated her. Moni was actually trying to fool that somebody who would be following her. She resented the abuse she received and was still planning to find out who did it to her. A week went by, and there was no call. She was happy but wondered if she would ever know who did it. She did not know what to do if Mr. Kim called again.

Chapter Fifty-One

The week was uneventful. The eatery attracted more customers, and business was doing well. Pilar could not believe the amount of the net profit after several weeks of accounting. Pilar admired Moni's honesty and conservatism with use of supplies. Nothing was wasted, and with Tanciang's help, it was possible. Moni, instinctively, on a Monday, went to the place of her son's birth in hopes to have a glance of the woman who took care of her son when she neglected him. Dressed in a faded skirt and worn-out blouse with cheap slippers, she went to view the place again. The floors were shiny and clean. The space where she had the baby seemed bigger, although she never took much notice since she was in pain and left after a few hours. It was a very short confinement. It was a whole day affair of going to the waiting room at the back of the hospital and going to the nursery to view the newborns. It was almost lunchtime, and it was her proposed last walk to possibly see Dr. Solam Bonedoto. It was a moment of happiness to Moni when she saw the gentle woman who had taken her son in her care. Dr. Solam was dressed appropriately with a skirt and blouse with a white overcoat, her name embroidered on it, was charming, and had a ready smile to her staff, who followed her from crib to crib. Moni did not linger, afraid of being noticed, and a staff who stayed on the job for twenty years might have recalled her features as such, despite her apparent age. Her story must have prevailed even years after it happened. If Moni was one of the workers on that night, she would not forget the event, and an inquiring mind would still look for that familiar face that was cruel enough to leave her newborn baby. Certain events in life, despite the lapse of time, could linger in one's mind, and that moment might be ingrained in someone's mind, thus Moni quickly exited the premises. She would peripherally watch if somebody was watching her leave. Although what would someone do if at all he or she recognized her? She had not been registered with a name. With that thought, she slowed down and reached the dimly lit waiting room heading to the outside. She saw the bench and sat on that same bench where she had been waiting for the warning signs of her son's birth. The bench made of stone had been kept for all the years, and the small tree that kept it shaded was still thriving. Moni sat there, recalling that moment as if it was yesterday. She had no feelings of either sorrow or happiness; she was just remembering a phase in her life.

It was already afternoon when Moni was waiting for a jeepney, but instead, she headed to see Tanciang. Tanciang was not home, but the landlady accommodated her, and she was allowed to wait at the living room. Moni waited for an hour, and she left. At least if someone was following her, it would confuse him as to her address. It was not too late when she arrived at Na Goria's, so she prepared the menu for the week, and a list was made for the next day's market. She cooked, and by the time she was done, Pilar arrived, and they had dinner together. They talked about renovations and future plans. Moni took advantage of her stay at the place by planning how to set up and do something to Na Goria's place. She did not have anything besides this place, which earned her comfort. Moni reiterated to Pilar her gratitude in having a space for free and volunteered to pay some money for utilities. Pilar hesitated, almost negating the idea, but Moni insisted. It was rather fair. She would continue with sharing the restaurant's profit.

That night, Moni counted her savings at hand. She could actually live well in that place without touching her savings. Moni was content, although she missed Arthur and her grown children. She called Harriet that night. There was no news about her family, or possibly, she did not want to share with Moni the sad news.

They had money to change the floor tiles of the eatery to white with a design of pale yellow streaks, which rendered the place looking clean. The curtains were replaced into white as well. The menu had added dishes of more expensive choice. Moni's face had finally healed, but she still entertained the idea of getting back to the person who had done it to her. One night, after they closed, there was a knock at the eatery. Moni hesitated opening it. The tenants and Pilar had their own key. She peeked through the glass window to view the caller, and looking through on the far-side window, Moni recognized the fancy clothes. She was almost certain who it was. The caller looked through the window and almost met Moni's eyes. The eatery was dark, and from the inside, she could see the outside while the caller could not. It was indeed Mr. Kim.

Moni was apprehensive all night. To keep her busy, she cleaned Na Goria's closet. There were papers that had to be thrown out. They were piled recklessly on the bottom; they seemed of no importance to anyone. Moni discovered from reading through the papers that Na Goria had a different family name than what she had claimed to be. She, at the time of her death, had taken the parents' name. In reality, she was the daughter of a mentally ill person at Mandaluyong Asylum. There were the papers that proved her biological mother's name. Na Goria's birth certificate stated the mother's name, who was only sixteen, but the father's name was unknown. There were no accompanying papers that proved her adoption. It was a big decision for Moni if she would reveal this discovery to Pilar. Moni took the papers and put it in her suitcase, so Pilar would not see it. Pilar need not to know this fact. It seemed not necessary to tell Pilar of Na Goria's secret since she had already died. It seemed not necessary, since Pilar had been the heir to Na Goria's estate, and legally, nobody could contest it. Moni analyzed the reason for Na Goria's aloof attitude and insecurity. Either she wanted to hide her past or she did not know. She was a very kind person altogether, and there was no reason to expose her past.

When they got together, Moni told Pilar about Mr. Kim. Pilar had something to tell her too. Pilar's ex-husband had been released from jail, and although he could not independently walk to possibly harm her, in time, he could, and Pilar was fearful. Both of them had a dilemma.

One afternoon, Mr. Kim came again and gave Moni another card to call him. Moni took the card and planned to ignore it. They did not talk. Before the eatery closed up, she called the number and was informed of a job. She refused the offer. She wanted to get rid of the problem, and refusing the job was a good idea. She had enough money, and spend she did not.

Monday night, there was a late call, and instinctively, she almost picked up the phone. She did not answer it. She finally unhooked the phone at midnight. Tuesday morning, they were closed. There was a knock, and Moni investigated who the caller was from the far corner of the glass window before opening it. Again, a well-dressed gentleman whose face Moni could not see was at the door. He stayed by that door for a good while, and Moni was watching him until he left. Tanciang was late that day to wash clothes for the tenants. Moni was afraid that the guy might be watching and would enter with Tanciang. When Tanciang came, she looked by the window first and slowly opened the door cautiously so she would not be seen.

Chapter Fifty-Two

Revisit to Arthur

It has been a few months, and finally, Harriet wrote her a letter. Arthur, her husband, had been seen with a nurse at the hospital canteen often enough to cause suspicion. Harriet saw him when she volunteered at the hospital. Moni cried all night. She believed it because Harriet was a good friend and would not lie to her. She counted her money at hand and the dollars she still had and was planning her next move. Wednesday afternoon, she mailed her important belongings to her mother for safekeeping. In it was the faded housedress where she inserted her mini diary of what happened one afternoon. She stitched the seams again, and only Moni would know it was there. However, a seamstress would wonder at the thickness of the seams and would be tempted to open it. Her plan was set.

She told Pilar she was going to take a three-week vacation to Cebu, so a notice two weeks before her departure was placed to alert the customers. A sign that stated such and renovations were the reason. Tanciang was worried of the lack of income until Moni assured her that she would be paid her regular salary. It would be a paid vacation that Tanciang deserved for her service and to assure that help was there if the eatery would reopen. It was mid-November, and a telegram was sent to Harriet that she was coming to visit. Moni could well afford the trip. Her dollars had not been spent, and the pesos she had saved were used for her airfare. She did not expect any results from the trip. The reason was to ascertain that her future decision of her life would be certain.

SHADOWS IN THE PANTRY

She arrived at Kennedy airport early morning via Pan-Am Airlines. It was a chilly winter day, and she was clothed appropriately. A multiple passenger bus was there, and the wait to collect more passengers was not too long. Harriet was expecting her and warmly accepted her into her small one-bedroom apartment. Harriet, in her seventies, had not aged much since Moni had seen her. Her retirement, premature as it was, did her good. Moni cooked breakfast and took a long nap.

At dinner, they had a long talk about happenings at the hospital. The talk about her family was almost avoided because Harriet seemed regretful for having written the sad letter. Moni pacified Harriet and told her how grateful she was to be told about the truth. Knowing it, she could decide about the future and would go on with her life instead of hoping for something that was impossible. Moni had never told Harriet of the real reason for fear that Harriet might divulge it to other people. Although she trusted her, she would not tell anyone about it and hoped too that Arthur would not tell his new girlfriend about her.

The next day, after she had rested, she telephoned Arthur, and an unfamiliar voice answered. It was obvious Arthur had already taken in a concubine. Moni did not blame him, but her instant reaction was anger, jealousy, and more. She tried to calm herself because she was aware that the current situation had been caused by her deceit. She was ready for this. Gratefully, he agreed on meeting her at a restaurant nearby. The restaurant situated in a space among several stores was simple, and Italian food was the main menu, although side dishes were available. Arthur sat midway inside by the wall of the restaurant, possibly if they were to have a fight, it might not be noticeable. It was early, and it was almost empty. It was a quiet moment, and Moni hoped to have control of her emotions. She was engulfed in grief, and that meeting would be the deciding factor of what lay ahead. She was hoping it was favorable. Moni walked slowly, almost tiptoeing to where Arthur sat. He was looking at her as soon as she entered and surmised her with an investigative look. Moni wanted to think he still loved her and possibly missed her. Moni was dressed simply with a black skirt and a printed striped black and white sweater. She had not changed in appearance but was just worried. Arthur, handsome as ever, seemed darker but looked gorgeous dressed in a plain blue turtleneck sweater. He was wearing the same leather jacket Moni had bought him that previous year when Kent, her son, came. Moni wanted to hug him and apologize for her faults. She missed him terribly but was unable to express it. At her quick glance at him, she reminisced the first time they had been intimate at Clark Air Base in the Philippines. Moni tried to look at him to fill her eyes with her memory of him since she sort of knew that this was the last time she would get to look at him. Moni would only glimpse at him, ashamed of herself. Strangely enough, they could not look at each other lovingly as they once did, but they were total strangers. Moni, a quiet person, wanted to start the conversation, but she could not. It was obvious that he had loved someone else; hopefully as truthful as he was, he would want his mate to be so. It seemed to a spectator that it was the couple's first meeting or a blind date and they were trying to get to know each other. Silence prevailed—as to how long Moni did not know.

Finally, Arthur said, "What brings you here?"

"I wanted to talk to you about us. If you could forgive me, I would make it up to you . . . and start again."

Arthur, looking down, as if reading something from the table, did not say anything and was about to say something when the waitress came by to ask if they were ready to order.

"Moni, what do you want to eat?"

"A chicken salad sandwich on toasted rye and water to drink."

"A ham sandwich with lots of tomatoes for me and iced tea." Arthur remained silent after the waitress left. He was in deep thought and said, "Moni, it would not work. I am sorry."

Although Moni knew the answer, she was hoping he would change his mind. She was teary-eyed when she heard it. There were no words to say, and the lump in her throat prevented her from talking. The order came, and she tried to eat, but she could not. She bit into her sandwich and drank lots of water to clear her throat. She added by saying, "I missed all of you," and stuttering, she said, "I-I want to come back."

"I cannot take you back. I have someone now."

Moni was holding her emotions. She wanted to scream. Instead, she covered her face. She was very embarrassed to be rejected. She wanted to be civil and said, "You look good."

He replied, "I am fine, and work is all right. The kids are fine. Monalai is now a legal secretary and works in a big firm. She is independent and planning to move out from the house. Junior will finish high school and will work as an orderly at the hospital. He wants to be a chemical engineer and will take chemistry subjects to determine if he can tackle the choice."

"I am glad they are fine."

There was not much to say. As Moni wrapped up her barely touched food, she said he could file the divorce papers and would not claim anything from the possessions. She told him, "Arthur, I have loved you, and I respected you. I will not make your life miserable. I admit that the breakup of our marriage was my fault."

With that, she stood up and said, "Thank you for lunch. Send the papers to my mother's address. Good-bye." Moni did not look back and exited the place as briskly as she could. She was so embarrassed. The customers were coming in, and she held her tears, but her face revealed sorrow. With her head down, she walked to a far corner far from his sight and looked for a cab. She walked toward the hospital and did not know what to do. She kept on walking to the street where Harriet lived. She reached the place, and as Harriet opened the door, Moni started sobbing endlessly. Harriet, being a single woman who presumably never had to undergo such emotions that Moni was feeling, sat there feeling helpless. She was quiet, and she did not have the words to pacify this friend. Moni wanted to take a nap after an emotional day. She intended to clean when she woke up. Harriet's bedroom was full of boxes that lined one side of the bed. Although clean, it needed some rearranging, which Moni used to do for her. After the chores she cooked dinner, and they stayed to watch television. Moni avoided lots of talk, not wanting to reveal her secret. She told Harriet she was leaving Arthur and she did not tell her the reason. Harriet did not ask. It was very polite of her.

She never knew any of Harriet's friends. She suspected she did not have too many since there was nobody helping her in her old age. Moni never asked Harriet about her relatives and assumed she had some but they hardly visited.

There was no place to go, but she wanted to see her children; even just a glimpse would be fine. Before she left she told Harriet she might not be home. She rented a small car to drive around town. It was early dawn, and as she passed by, she noticed that the home she took care of had been uncared for. The paint was peeling, and it was unkempt. Possibly Arthur had taken another job, unable to focus on the house upkeep. She parked two houses away, and a scarf had hidden her face. She waited until past six in the morning, and she saw her daughter leave in her new car parked at the front. She looked elegant and rather pretty in her dark-blue suit. She waited another hour and left afraid of being reported to the police. Despite the neighborhood's flexibility in parking rules and the one-car garage in each house, which meant that a car must be parked in front, her stay on that same spot might become suspicious. She did not get to see Arthur Junior, and she was settled on not seeing him at all. She proceeded to a nearby mall and parked there to think. Harriet's place was not a place to ponder because the old lady was worried about her. She was kind to have her stay for free, and Moni would not stay there for another week, which was her scheduled time to stay at the United States.

It was a big decision for her to either stay, being that she had a US visa, and she could decide to resettle in the United States. The parking lot was not as full, being a weekday. The rented car was not due to be returned until the next day, and she could afford to rent it for another day. She did think and cried in between. Her past again haunted her, but she regretted she did not meet Ken, whose memory she would always treasure. She, alone in the car, was staring at the windshield, viewing the events of her past. Despite the loss of her family, she selectively recalled the events that amused her. She remembered the children's faces, mischievous deeds and happy moments when the family was together. Those memories would occupy her and pacified the grief she was feeling at the moment.

Moni admittedly learned to love and respect Arthur. He was gentle and never sexually demanding. She missed him terribly. Depression she could dwell on, but she did not. Moni was not aware of the time she stayed there. It was a beautiful idle moment—it seemed wasted time, but she realized she needed this time to ponder. There was no one that could analyze her life but her, and the secret she had kept had finally been revealed. She planned to bring Harriet for a drive to either New Jersey or upstate New York. She was getting out when two men were walking toward her direction, which caught her attention. She opted to sit and watch. They had packages, and they were parked two cars in front of her. It was Arthur and her son. She was about to meet him with open arms, and some feeling occurred to her, which made her stop. She remained in her seat instead. She was not ready to be embarrassed again from rejection. Moni had a good look at her son, who had grown, and he was at a distance, looking very fair, his skin had taken after Uncle Indong. His fine curly hair was cut so short to his scalp. He had denim jeans paired with a worn-out shirt. Moni could imagine that Arthur, not having to handle money, could not afford to buy him a nice shirt. She pacified herself by thinking that he need not dress up to go to the store. They drove off. Moni was content, having seen her son, which would have understood her if he was given a chance. He was too young to comprehend the problem. Moni was wondering if he missed her and if he would dare ask his father about her. Moni finally stepped out and bought items for Harriet. She inquired for a job at the store, which she did impulsively. Walking down to her car, she thought of staying in the United States if she could find a job, that is, if Harriet would allow her to share her apartment temporarily.

Harriet had already cooked dinner, and they talked about her proposition. Harriet agreed to share her apartment for a year, the time necessary for Moni to save to be on her own. It was set. Moni intended to stay for two weeks or more to find a job. They went for a drive to places where Moni used to go when she was at the Romualdos'. The trip had gone well, and the weather cooperated. Harriet talked about herself having an older brother who had passed on. Her father was half Dutch and German, and her mother was of American Indian blood. No nephews or nieces that lived nearby. Moni never talked with Harriet this long. Their friendship started when she helped Harriet clean and sorts. It was not as often as she needed it. It was done when Moni had the chance, not realizing that sometime in the future, Moni would need this help. Moni was hopeful she would find a job. The time she intended to stay was almost over, and there were no prospects. She was getting worried, so she called Pilar that she would stay another week in Cebu, which had been agreed upon, and Tanciang's salary would be paid by Moni when she returned.

    She went to supermarkets west and further away from her family in hopes that she would find a job. If a job was available, it would be in a poor neighborhood where Ken would never visit. Living at Harriet's place was more embarrassing as the days went. Although Moni had enough dollars to help out with food and utilities; to Moni, she was becoming a nuisance. She was tempted in calling Arthur again to have another talk, but the more she thought about it, the more she did not want it. She did not want to beg. She even thought of finding and looking for Ken and did call several hospitals in New York City, wanting to talk to him. Moni was not prepared what to say if she talked to Ken. She would probably hang up and was again afraid of rejection. She was desperate and seemed to be wanting of a companionship with someone. All the hospitals that she called in the city did not have the name registered on their list. She would sit up all night thinking and dreamt that if she was able to reach him, she would live with him if he was not with someone. Harriet conveniently allowed her to sleep on the couch. As it turned out, Harriet proved to be a true friend, which Moni did not expect. The weeks went quickly, and she could not decide to whether she would stay or leave. She was confident that she had a place to stay in the Philippines, and she was geared to return home. Her stay with Harriet was becoming uncomfortable, not because she was being maltreated, but she was also unhappy, being geographically a stone's throw away from her family yet unable to see them at all. It was not necessary for her to stay in the United States. She took the train to Manhattan and stayed there for the day. She walked her way to the path where her youth had been spent, and the sweet memories she could recall. She left money for Harriet before she left for Manila and promised each other to write. Harriet expressed her happiness and how grateful she was of her visit. It was the end of November, and the trip back home was uneventful.

Chapter Fifty-Three

The eatery was very clean. It was obvious that Tanciang did some work at the eatery being that she was paid. Moni owed her some money. Moni immediately put up a sign that it would be open. The hallway upstairs was clean, as well as Moni's room. The refrigerator was almost empty, and plans for food shopping had to be listed. She would be unable to reach Tanciang so Moni would market by herself. She opened on Wednesday, and Tanciang came. She said she came to prepare the place for Moni's return.

Moni checked her post office box, and she received three letters from Avelino. The first letter, as postdated, was the day after she left for the United States, which stated the death of her grandmother, and they would wait for her until Moni would wire them back. The second letter was three days ago, stating that Grandmother had been buried and her wishes had been adhered to as requested. The third letter was Arthur Junior's, enclosed in Maxi's letter. Moni trembled with excitement in opening it. It was a short letter written hurriedly in a stationery from work. The address was inscribed. Moni was crying, and conscious of her surroundings, she took a seat on one of the benches inside the post office.

> Dear Mother,
> I missed you. I am working as an orderly, a substitute at this nursing home. I use Dad's car, and I earn pretty good to pay for my gas and other expenses. You must be wondering how we

are doing. Dad has a lady friend who stays over occasionally.

Food has been scarce, missing your stews. Monalai has a good job, I think. She buys stuff. Just you know, I have forgiven you.

Please write to me in this address. Use your maiden name.

I love you,
Arthur Junior

Moni cried that she was too ashamed to have a meeting with Arthur Junior. She had missed hugging her son. The walk to the place was fast, passing by the stationery store to respond to those letters. She immediately wrote to them, including Harriet. The eatery was slow. People thought they were still closed. Two weeks went by, and then it picked up again. It seemed quiet, and Mr. Kim came again. Another card was given to Moni. It seemed that the previous cards had been thrown away, or he wanted to be discreet about it, and giving a card was subtler than him talking to Moni. He was smart, and also presumably, he was trying to protect Moni's reputation. Someone might know him, and the kind of business he was in. Moni never actually knew his business. There was again a big suspicion, what his intentions were. He was an agent hiring people for odd jobs, choosing only the good-looking workers. She did not call him. He smelled trouble. She made a note detailing Mr. Kim's looks. She wrote this not knowing what to do. She inserted it inside the seam of her faded skirt and stitched it closed.

One morning, there was a call saying to Moni,

"Call Mr. Kim."

The lady did not elaborate on it. Moni did not call back. That afternoon, as they were closing the place Mr. Kim called and said the old man had requested her again. This time, she consented to it. It was a different hotel. Rosan Hotel was a bigger place in Quezon City in a secluded place. Web Hotel was burned to the ground. It was not renovated yet. Moni was ready with her open safety pin to inflict pain on someone who would harm her. She was a midget warrior with the intention to get even. A woman opened the door, and the anticipated threat to her did not happen. The night was uneventful, and the old man paid her well. Moni was now thinking that the event that had happened to her in the past was not Mr. Kim's doing. Still, she watched the people who came in to see Mr. Lasco. Late at night, a guy came to see the old man, and Moni was scared. He had such a muscular built, not too tall, a few inches taller than her with a noticeable scar on his right upper lid, had both eyes kept blinking as if he was nervous. Moni still remembered that day, and the guy that held her at the back was not very tall, and his arms were very strong. He did not look at her, and when he spoke, he was soft-spoken. Although Moni never heard a voice when she was assaulted, and at the moment, he was not near enough to her for Moni to possibly smell him. If there was anything that she would recall, it was his smell—a distinctive men's cologne that she would be able to identify. It would not be fair to accuse someone from the smell of his cologne. Moni finished the job but kept remembering his face. He did not even look at her, as if trying to evade her.

A week went and there was no call. Moni was at peace. The income at the eatery was more than enough. It was clean money, and she had no expenses. Most of the money was saved. There was another call on a Thursday, and Moni went. It was not an old man waiting but a gorgeous man in his fifties who was gentle and did not want sex but just talk. It was unbelievable. He was not ugly to look at, and admittedly, Moni wanted to have a rendezvous with him. She was cautious and did not give him a phone number. She gave him her mailing address, which was the post office box. She told him her name was Goria. Every day, Moni would check her post office box. Since, this was the only address she gave she renewed it for another year. There were letters from Avelino and none from Arthur Junior. Finally, one Friday morning, as she checked her box, there was a note from the guy. It indicated, Dewy hotel, a date (which was a good seven days from the post marked *date*), "alas cinco sa hapon" (5:00 PM). No room was indicated. Instructions were to stay in the lobby and follow him to the floor of the hotel, but she would stop on the floor next to his stop. She would take the stairs down, and he would sit by the small sitting room and get up to go to the room as soon as she got off the elevator, and she would sit and note down which room then enter that room when the coast was clear. It would be unlocked.

Dewy hotel was located in Quezon City a street off the main road. It was a walk to the interior passing three unimpressive buildings. It was a two-story building enclosure, a wide wooden door to the building. The grounds had several parking spaces, and it was not well illuminated. Surprisingly, the interior was clean, the couches were white, and the lobby was large for a small hotel. Two elevators were located almost too far from the counter. She was having an affair with a man whom she was so attracted to named Guy. The rendezvous was set on various hotels, and instructions were indicated in her mailbox. She would receive it, and the date of the rendezvous would be the week after the written date. He was most gentle, never in a hurry, although Moni as a paid whore must be ready and no foreplay was necessary. Moni was ready for him. She enjoyed him immensely, and there was no talk. He did not ask who she was or ask any information about her. Moni had clean, smooth skin, and she was not talkative. It was enjoyable sex, which no whore probably ever experienced. He was clean, and his skin was gorgeous. His age was not easy to guess. Although graying on his temples, he was wrinkle-free. He sexually performed as a young man and satisfied a woman. It was a temporary affair and they were never seen with each other. He paid very well. An envelope was left for her, full of cash, and he left after they had sex. Admittedly, Moni wanted more, and she would be embarrassed to want some more. She was hoping this would last for a long time. The money she earned in two weeks as a waitress, she earned it in one night. Moni had piles of money working as a whore, who was actually enjoying herself as well. There were no suspicions since she was not dressed to attract but wearing a loose black pants and a white blouse. She was ordinary-looking with a pretty face. She would leave the hotel early morning and arrive at Na Goria's place when everybody was still sleeping. She was enjoying her life and living it. She had nobody she could call her own boyfriend, but she was taken care of with lots of money, but more so, her emotional and physical needs were met. She was aware that she could not claim him nor did he say such, and it was so temporary that it could end at any given moment. She was paid for services rendered. Moni was not in competition with his wife or girlfriend, and she was not hurting anyone. Moni did not cook or clean house, and she no longer wanted to be a wife to someone who possibly treated her as a maid and had obligations to do. She planned to continue this trend as long as he needed it. Mr. Kim had not called her. Presumably, he was paid by Guy on the side.

One Monday morning, she went out. She thought she needed to buy a new blouse, so she went to Escolta, a prestigious place, to buy items only the rich could afford. She strolled along slowly, looking at every store she fancied, and did not buy anything. It was too expensive, and although she could afford it, she knew that the money she had should not be spent recklessly. This moment of abundance was short lived, and the chance to be able to count a large amount of money was indeed a pleasure. She went into several stores and did not see anything that she fancied. Finally, she ended up in a big department store named KLS. It was glass-enclosed, and the items were spaced so well that one could not help but buy since a customer could linger and inspect the items as thoroughly as she needed to. It carried men and women's apparel, jewelry, shoes, makeup, and sorts. She picked an embroidered white blouse, rather elegant for a whore. It was close-necked, fit to wear in church. Since she became a whore, she has not entered church out of embarrassment since God knew it all. She was approaching the register when the man at the register looked at her intently and whispered, "Monica?"

Moni, startled, was hesitant to answer and took a long look at this very handsome man. She said, "Armando?" Gratefully, it was a quiet day, and it would have been embarrassing because Moni, with a high-pitched voice, said, "Armando, ikaw pala?"

He took the merchandise and said, "Ako na ang mobayad ani."

"Ayaw lang oy." (He offered to pay for it, which she refused.)

They both recognized each other, and Armando was an old friend from the past. When the transaction was done, he asked her to wait for him in the vicinity so they could have lunch. The lunch place, a plush corner of Escolta, served fancy dishes that Moni's place did not. It was a short conversation, but Armando wanted to talk some more and invited her for dinner after work. Armando, dressed in a fancy Barong Tagalog indicative of status, looked handsome and poised. Looking at him, no one would ever think he was once poor and lived in a squatter's area. He spoke well; apparently he had mingled with the affluent and learned their ways. He had finished a business degree and, apparently, was offered a job by the niece of the store where they used to work when they were young. That was the same woman who had interviewed potential employees. She had married a man named Mr. Kim, who owned the store. He had moved to Manila and took this high-paying job as the general manager. KLS was owned by Mr. Kim Lim Sun; it was a big company that carried expensive clothing mostly tailored from Hongkong. Moni listened carefully and tried not to react. She had him repeat the name to be certain she had heard it right. Armando mentioned Moni's thoughtfulness at having sent some money, which he had used as tuition money so he was able to finish school. Armando asked her to stay in the vicinity; she went with him to see his place. He had not gotten married and had attempted twice just to break it up because he was not sure. His frail mother, as she pictured her, had passed on a number of years ago. He lived alone.

Armando's place: a four-story building in Quezon City. It was a big property enclosed with a cemented wall. Small growing trees strategically planted on each corner, the parking lot which can occupy several cars partitioned with enclosed grass with trees, to possibly shield the cars from the sun.

A driveway circled the building for cabs and carts to drop off customers, occupants. The lobby is spacious, and two couches in place. It was glass windowed and large vases with green plants on corners. Two elevators were there that was spacious enough for ten people.

Armando's apartment was on the third floor. The apartment he lived in was rather big, much larger than the nipa hut he grew up in. It was furnished with expensive furniture but simple. Despite his status, Armando has remained humble. He owned a car, but he had not used it to work. Moni did not have much to say. She mentioned her failed marriage and visiting Manila for a few weeks. They had a light snack and enjoyed talks of their past. Armando was looking at Moni, wanting to reiterate his admiration, but he could not. Moni, having had a sad experience, possibly needed time to heal. His advances may have been interpreted as pity. Moni had other intentions. She wanted to know about Mr. Kim. That was not the time to ask Armando. He might get suspicious.

Moni took a cab back to Na Goria's place. It was past eight at night, and Pilar was not home. She settled and tried to rest. When Pilar arrived, she knocked and needed to speak with Moni to alert her that her estranged husband had been released from jail and had recovered. He might want to enter the place, and the rest of the renters should know. A plan to change the locks was in order. It was scheduled and done.

The notes in Moni's mailbox was less. She did not get to see Guy every Wednesday night. Either his schedule did not allow it or he had run out of money. Moni did not know where to reach him. She missed him and the physical contentment she enjoyed with him. She would meet him for free. Moni was ashamed of feeling that way and thought of her blood origin; she had possibly inherited the friar's sexual needs even though nobody could confirm it. Moni was almost certain he was her grandfather. It just did not happen that her father resembled the friar's features. Moni prayed that she would be able to control her physical needs. She was rather upset that when she was married, she did not have this need. Possibly Arthur was not as physically attractive as Guy or Moni currently had an emotional problem of being rejected that made her sexually needy. Definitely she was lonely, and this physical need stemmed from her emotional needs. She was afraid to call God. She was ashamed and could not even mention nor think of God. It was almost a month that she had not seen Guy. Moni stayed in the eatery most of the time although she checked the PO box every day.

She went to see Armando. He invited her again for dinner at his apartment. They sat and talked for a long time, and the talk ended in having a rendezvous with him. The bedroom was furnished with taste and by an occupant who have money. The large, thick-cushioned bed was covered with a bedspread of fine printed squares with multiple colors which matched the curtains. The chest and the drawers matched, and the night tables did as well. It was equipped with a washroom. The chest held a large lamp that switched on by the door as one entered. Moni intended to stay all night to enjoy a man's touch. Indeed, she was good at it and no longer embarrassed of the God-given gift of enjoying her body. They were relaxing after an enjoyable moment when Armando, being very tired, did not notice that the front door opened with someone who had a key. The person freely opened the unlocked bedroom, switched the light on, and Moni was seen naked by a beautiful woman, whom Moni recognized to be Mr. Kim's wife. There was a commotion, and Moni, caught in the act, tried to cover herself with a sheet and hurriedly picked up her clothes while the couple were fighting and got dressed to get out of such a predicament. She avoided the confrontation and being recognized as she slipped away. The woman was attacking Armando with her light punches while Moni managed to get out. She was gasping and found herself standing at the far corner waiting for a cab. It was early dawn, and the corner was dark. There were no cabs. She was walking as far as she could from the building. The woman would not remember Moni having been interviewed by her many years ago when Moni was very young. As far as Moni could remember, that woman did not even look at her then. Moni did so much thinking in that dark corner until early dawn, when cabs were racing by in numerous numbers.

Nobody was up at Na Goria's home. Again, Moni escaped a situation when a police would have been ushered if the fight aggravated to be a threesome. Moni hoped Armando did not say anything, or if he did, he would say Moni was a rented whore, which she was. Moni accepted herself as a cheap whore and a woman who had become a sex maniac looking for a man to have a rendezvous with. She had learned to shrug off her embarrassment and followed the wishes of her body. The next day, the PO box was empty. Moni planned to tell him if he called again that he did not have to pay and would tell him frankly she enjoyed him to the fullest.

Weeks passed, and there was no note. Moni was anxious. She did not know where to find him, and looking for him was impossible. The restaurant was busy, and she kept it open until past six or longer. This way, she was tired and did not have time to think of herself. After thorough cleaning of the place, it would almost be past eleven. She went out early morning to inspect the post office box. A week was too long for her not to receive a note from Guy. She wanted to forget about it, and she skipped a few days of inspecting the box.

Chapter Fifty-Four

Saturday morning, she saw two notes from Guy. It was posted three days ago and it was the Hotel Lagoon (5:00 PM, date). It was quite far from her place. A cab would cost a lot. She left rather early and took the jeepney halfway and took the cab the rest of the way. She would always drop off from a corner and walk the rest of the way. It was a two-story hotel, rather cheap-looking. When she arrived at the lobby, nobody was there. Moni pretended to look for the washroom and stayed there for a while. It was already half past five in the afternoon. She then left the washroom and intended to leave, heading to the main door when she saw him entering the lobby. It was a small hotel, and the lobby had few padded chairs and a leather couch. Guy was at the counter speaking to someone, possibly booking a room. He apparently did not see Moni while she was getting a seat. Guy finally turned around and saw her as he peripherally viewed the room. He had a small bag with him. It was not a medical bag that doctors bring to their patients. He never brought a bag from the few times she sees him. He proceeded to the elevator, and after a few minutes, Moni went to the washroom again to confuse whoever was watching, and after that, she went to take the stairs to the second floor. There was no lobby, and Moni did not know what to do. She walked around, and one of the rooms opened, wherein she saw Guy as she was passing by, toward the end of the hallway. She looked around quickly and entered the room. Guy seemed to be in a hurry, and there was no talk. Moni was surprised that he had taken time to shower, and she anticipated and was getting ready. The rendezvous was quick, and he was satisfied, but Moni wanted more, but he did not reciprocate. She remained in bed, hoping that he would know that she needed him again, but he was getting ready to go. She was embarrassed to ask. She was only a whore, and he was paying her. He took the envelope from his bag, placed it on top of the drawer, and with a quick wave, he headed for the door. Moni was devastated. The room was booked for the whole night, and she stayed until dawn. She did not rest. The streets were busy when she headed home. As she settled, she opened the envelope to count the money. It had an insignia belonging to the Bonedoto Clinic. There was a note as to when he would like to see her again.

The eatery was to open at seven, and Moni must get ready. A few minutes after she arrived, Tanciang came and so did the customers. It was a busy day, and Moni did not have time to think about it. The week went quickly, and that following Monday, she went out early and found the Bonedoto Clinic, and indeed, she discovered that the person she had an affair with was the spouse of the lady who had adopted her son. Moni felt ashamed that she was again an instrument of deceit. She concentrated on work.

Wednesday afternoon, she went in the vicinity of the small hotel and waited for Guy to go in. She was across the street in a snack bar and entered the hotel and waited for him to find her. True enough, after a couple of hours, he went down looking for her and pretended to use the restroom for Moni to see him. Moni followed him to the second floor, and they had a quick rendezvous. It was reiterated that he would always check in as Mister Guy.

It had been two weeks, and Moni did not check her PO box. She did not want to be a whore anymore. She checked her box and found two messages. The last one she could still respond to. She called the hotel the day she was supposed to meet him that his wife wanted to meet him at the office instead. Presumably, the desk would think that he was meeting his wife. Moni was hoping nobody had seen her at dawn when she left. Nobody could be certain.

That afternoon, Guy hurried to the office and was ready to explain to his wife of his whereabouts. He found no one. Dr. Moises lingered at the office. It was obvious to him that she had learned who he was. He could not recall how he had inadvertently revealed himself. He was fearful that Solam had again learned of his philandering. He was going home to face his wife.

Solam was comfortably sitting at the kitchen table when Moises arrived. He did not sense anger as he surmised her. She warmly greeted him and offered him food. She was getting up when he said he was getting it himself. Moises never served himself, but that time he did. He did not know why. He was afraid that Solam was holding her temper, and if she stood up, she might do something against her will. Dr. Moises admired the whore, whose real name he did not know, to be so decent to leave such a message. It appeared that he was meeting his wife at the hotel and not an ill-reputed woman. The evening went well. Moises made love with his wife and enjoyed her more than ever. Solam reciprocated his love and finally learned to enjoy her husband.

Moni had some thinking to do. She counted the money she had saved all the months that she had worked as a whore. She had more than enough pesos and dollars to do whatever she wanted. She decided to ignore all the mail from Guy in case he decided to send her a note. She did not check her mailbox but every three days. The eatery earned a lot, and Tanciang had kept her loyalty to the place. Moni would have to leave soon as soon as she could figure out what to do. She had some letters to write, and she had to be certain about the plan of her life. As much as she did not want to accept it, her family had not remembered her, and she was totally forgotten. She would have to do the same. A note was received from her mother that everything was fine. Noy Tiqiou had died at a late age of seventy-eight. He continued on working until he died. He was found dead and possibly died of natural causes. Nemesio, Moni's brother, was offered to take the post office job, which he accepted. He used to help out at the office, so he knew what to do. There was a note from Guy, and she noted it down to respond like she did last time. This way, he would not spend the money to book the room, and she would not come. She would do this until he stopped. She cared for him and wanted the enjoyment of the moment, but she could not continue out of respect to his wife who had taken her son and cared for him all those years. Every night, Moni would be thinking. She was contemplating on opening the store five days a week. She needed extra money for her plans. The eatery was opened Tuesday to Sunday. Tanciang was happy of the extra income and the food she brought home.

Chapter Fifty-Five

Ken's mother had passed on, and Ken had never committed himself to a woman. His dates were fewer, having aged. He moved to a 2-bedroom apartment in mid-Manhattan. He was a walking distance away to the hospital he was connected to. He normally walked or took the subway. He took on two young doctors: and reduced his workdays. Dr. Robert Schick his mentor also passed on. Often he would go to the place where he and Moni went to have a rendezvous hoping to see her again and linger at the thought of her and amuse himself. He regret not being married to her when he had the chance. He was looking for a girl; simple; and not demanding.

Lady Erminda returned to Manila and lived in a modest apartment. Her beau had left her for someone else since he was fifteen years her junior, and she had left her job at the embassy. They had renewed their friendship—she and her sister, Lady Esther. Lady Esther had never confronted her sister about Moni. Mr. Onaje was never found. Mana Pansang had lived with her daughter.

Chapter Fifty-Six

One Monday, when the eatery was closed, Moni packed up the necessary items, especially the faded skirt where she had sewn in the bulk of the money and the written episode of her assault and the truth of her life. She mailed the package to Avelino with a note that he should keep it in a safe place. She would wait for the reply. Two weeks went by, and there was no reply. Mr. Guy wrote a note, and Moni called the hotel with the same reason. She was hoping he would stop. Moni kept the eatery in order, and the net share she saved conscientiously.

As she was going to the post office waiting for the traffic light to turn green, her attention was caught on the news stand at the corner of a very bruised woman, face disfigured, on the front page of the bulletin. She bought a newspaper since she was familiar with the address where the woman had been found. The PO box had Avelino's letter as well. She was hurrying home, almost running, to read the letter and the newspaper. Avelino had received the package. It was intact. The article in the newspaper revealed a story of a woman who was found bludgeoned in an apartment owned by someone else. She was naked, beaten by an undetermined object, which rendered her face bloody, disfigured and unrecognizable. She was unconscious and bleeding from her wounds. There were no clothes nor footwear or identification. She was brought to a nearby Cubao Clinic and was currently in comatose condition. The apartment was registered under the name Armando Guzma. It was assumed that she was a whore rendering service to the occupant.

Moni knew and almost certain who it was. The eatery was already set up as to cooked dishes. She immediately left and headed to the hospital where that woman was confined. The woman was still in the emergency room. Moni introduced herself as a maid and would like to check the victim if she was her employer. Indeed, she was allowed to see her since there was no family who came to claim her. Moni looked at the injured woman, and she was certain it was Mr. Kim's wife. She then denied to the nurses that she did know her for fear of being implicated to the crime. Moni was suspecting that Mr. Kim had learned of her affair and followed her there.

Moni's question was Armando's whereabouts. If the bludgeoned woman was identified as Mrs. Kim's wife, Armando definitely had an affair with her. He will be out of the job. To ascertain the story she headed to see Armando at his job. As she entered a uniformed gentleman was talking to Armando. Moni held the door before being seen. She was surprised to see him there. She did not speak to him and exited the store without being seen. The few nights she closed early after dinner, she posted a sign that the eatery would only be open until half past six in the evening.

She went back to the hospital to have a peek at the injured woman. The injured woman was transferred to a female ward, almost the same setup as Na Goria's space when the old lady had taken ill. It was pitiful. They did not screen who entered the ward so Moni was able to look at her sort of just passing by. The face was still bandaged up, and she was still unconscious. Although Moni was almost certain who she was, she still had doubts of her identity. If Moni could have a look at her feet, she would be certain. She would not be able to do that. She remembered her beautiful feet and her toes wearing those sandals. Moni envied the look of her feet. They were a rich lady's feet that had never wandered barefoot on sand or farm, harvesting corn and the sort.

She would have to see Armando again. Whether she would be able to ask him was the question. Her plans of visiting the injured and seeing Armando were deferred due to the hectic days at the eatery. The marketing was almost done every day, and getting up at dawn was tiresome. Moni's wish to earn money materialized. Moni asked Pilar to work with Tanciang on a Sunday. Her plan was to visit the injured woman and to see Armando.

When Moni went to the clinic, heading to the same room, assuming she was still there, the bed was empty. As much as she hesitated to ask somebody, she approached a nurse assistant instead. The nurse assistant did not know, so she went to ask the head nurse, whose face was not familiar. It was obvious that this head nurse was either off or had taken a break when Moni first came to see the injured woman. Moni was not afraid to ask, confident that the head nurse would not remember her. She looked at a book and was told that the woman had died the day before and was still at the morgue. Nobody had claimed her yet. Moni did not pursue her quest. She was fearful of being connected to the crime.

The trip to see Armando at the store he worked in was unsuccessful. He was not there. Moni intended to wait a little, thinking that Armando had taken a break and would be back soon. Finally, she asked one of the salespeople and was told that he had taken ill. Apparently, he was still employed with the company. Moni took a cab to Armando's place and rang his bell. She did not know his telephone number and could not alert him that she was coming. Moni did not really want to see Armando anymore because she was actually embarrassed to have succumbed to her physical desires. Her curiosity had overwhelmed her. She waited for a good few minutes and left the front door, walking away from the vicinity. As she was turning to another street, she felt a tap on her shoulder. As she turned, it was Armando, who looked so tired, as if he had not slept at all. He begged Moni to talk to him of some urgency. They walked a few blocks to find a nook to sit and have something to eat. As they settled, Moni ordered some soup and vegetables. It was a very small place, accommodating six tables, almost the size of Moni's eatery. Food was more expensive because it was on a front street, and it was fixed nicely with expensive plates and silverware. Armando was hungry and ate it so fast he almost forgot Moni was watching him. After he finished his soup, they started to talk. He was telling Moni that he was afraid that Mr. Kim had learned about the five-year-or-so affair with his wife and a hired assassin had done the job. That night in question,

Armando had left to buy some snacks for the lady and was supposed to have been gone for only a few minutes, but he could not find the food she was asking for on a particular restaurant. He looked around and was not able to buy it. He arrived with no food and found her in such a state, gathered his work clothes and her clothes, and immediately left the place, not knowing what to do. He left the door wide open so that a passerby or his neighbor next door would investigate. True enough, a neighbor went in and called on Armando, and the neighbor discovered the scene early morning. The injured victim had been left in that bed all night. He went to work that day. He was guilty to have left her there bleeding because his instinct told him to do so. He then got a hotel near his work place, so he could work the next day.

Armando revealed his longtime secret. He did not get married because he was a male prostitute. He had been servicing a few rich women who had either been widowed or were lonely in their homes, and he could not stop. They would come for love. He was paid well and was enjoying his carefree life. The injured victim was the wife of Mr. Kim, who in fact was subsidizing the rent of his expensive apartment. She would come twice a week and would call if she needed him. That week, she came every night was the week that Mr. Kim was away on a trip. Mrs. Kim would always be naked in bed. They could not figure out the weapon used to hurt Mrs. Kim. It looked like a horse whip, signified by the numerous lengthy marks on her face and arms. Moni listened to all this without saying anything. It was sad that the both of them ended up with such complicated lives, and although able to have a taste of good living, the good living, it seemed, have led them astray. Moni, a listener, was teary-eyed, sort of sorry for both of them. Armando had not returned to his apartment but staying at a cheap hotel full of roaches. He was out of cash, and he was very happy to see Moni. Moni paid for their food and gave Armando some cash. She would not be able to accommodate him. Her secret was hers to keep, and keep she would until it would be discovered. He told her where he was staying, and she would call him there. There were so many things in her mind, and with Armando's problem, Moni was beside herself.

The room was inexpensive, and on sight, it was big enough, but it was roach-infested. She even bought him pajamas and miscellaneous needs, such as cleaning agents, to get rid of roaches, food, and sorts, and promised him that she would check on him the next day. Armando might have to stay there for a few days to do some thinking. His temporary disappearance he had to explain. It was clear that they had been intimate because she was found naked.

When Moni arrived at Na Goria's, the place was quiet. It was all cleaned, and the tin box was on the table in Na Goria's room, where the sales money was kept, with a note from Pilar that Tanciang had borrowed some money. The money was already counted and noted as such. An early marketing was planned, and Moni went to bed early. Moni was busy with earning money to be able to fulfill her plans, but her plan would have to be deferred due to Armando. He needed help.

She kept buying the daily bulletin for updates on the case. Apparently, the dead woman could not be identified because her face was disfigured and unrecognizable, and they could not find any identification. Even her clothes, purse, and shoes were taken by the killer. Nobody claimed her body, so it remained in the morgue. Moni kept waking up early to see Armando at the hotel. Moni was paying for his room. Tanciang picked up items from the market if there was a need. Actually, the police had been looking for him to ask him who that woman was who was in his apartment.

The rumor at the store was Mrs. Kim had bought a ticket to Hongkong the day after Mr. Kim left for mainland China to plan on a factory for some goods to be produced. The trip was anticipated to be lengthy. There was no mode of communication established wherein Mr. Kim would be able to call his family. Mrs. Kim knew this predicament. The governess had said Mrs. Kim had left, and she had been properly advised as such. The list of passengers who had left via Pacific Air had verified it. In fact, that whole week after Mr. Kim had left, Mrs. Kim came every day to have a rendezvous with Armando. The police interrogated him and he revealed he is a male prostitute. The name of the lady in his apartment was Sowani. She comes and Armando renders the service. Several women of fictitious names comes for the service. That night in question, he left for work early, and did not know what happened after he left. Armando did not know Mrs. Kim was supposed to be in Hongkong. Armando could not be implicated as he feared. He was already known as a male whore but could not be investigated as the killer. The weapon used could not be found, and if Armando was a suspect, he could not possibly own a whip because he did not own a horse, although Mr. Kim, without anybody knowing, owned a stable with several horses in Bulacan.

The employees at the KLS store were questioned if Armando was certainly employed at the store. It was verified by the personnel, but the owner was not there. The general manager was Armando. Mrs. Kim left for Hongkong, verified by the police to have left the next day Mr. Kim left for China. As far as everybody knew, Mrs. Kim was alive and in Hongkong. There was no suspicion that the dead woman was Mrs. Kim.

Mr. Kim had not returned and had no idea his wife was in Hongkong. When he arrived after six weeks, he was surprised to learn that his wife was not there although there was a letter to him from his wife that she was still in Hongkong and would return soon. She signed it with her pet name that only she and her husband knew. If there was any suspicion that the dead woman was Mrs. Kim, it was eradicated because of the note that was received. The note revealed that Mrs. Kim was in Hongkong. So who was the woman who was found beaten to death?

Finally, Armando returned to his apartment. When Moni went to see him at the hotel, he had already checked out. She did not go and see him at his apartment. Somebody could be watching. The next day, Moni asked Tanciang to bring her boys to the store to help out so she could slip out to see Armando at the store he worked in. She went in plainly dressed and pretended that she needed help with an item, and subtly, they had a short talk facing the stack of skirts. She told him to see her at Na Goria's. Moni would have to figure out if she would tell him her whole story. She was gone for two hours. The place was quiet because it was after five, and the customers who had some snacks were all gone. The sign at the canteen stated seven in the evening as closing time, so she kept it open until seven.

When Armando arrived, Moni served him leftover vegetable soup and rice. They had a long talk about needy women who hired him for sex. He was not involved with the family since he knew them under fictitious names. It served him well, being a man needing a woman, and getting married with children was not favorable due to lack of finances. He reiterated his growing up poor and that he could not live the way they did. When the opportunity came to have a better life, he grabbed it. Mrs. Kim was indeed his frequent customer and was the one who paid him well besides subsidizing his rent. She was very pretty and was a good lover. Armando was rather embarrassed telling Moni most of his secrets. They were good friends, and honestly, if Moni so agreed, he would marry her in an instant. Having had a rendezvous with her was a moment he enjoyed so much.

Moni did not tell Armando she lived in the establishment. She told him she managed the eatery and she had some cleaning to do and would soon be heading home. She told him she was renting a room at Dapitan Street. Armando invited Moni to his place which she refused. She did not want to be seen with Armando and be suspected as a needy woman that was renting Armando for sex. Although she was also a whore, nobody knew she was, at least to her knowledge. She thought of the guy who had assaulted her and possibly the same guy she saw at the old man's room. Somehow she suspected that the guy was connected to Mr. Kim.

Moni had to pursue her plans. The money she had hoped to save was not enough. She did not want to ask Armando to pay for his debt since he had problems, and he might lose his job, being that he was on the news and his identity had been divulged. He could actually continue prostituting, but how long he could go on since other women he serviced might be fearful after the happening? Also, he was hitting fifty if Moni remembered it right and would not be able to sexually perform as expected. It would be a full-time job, and maintaining an expensive place could be extravagant. These women, being rich, would want acceptable accommodations to do the act, and he would be forced to keep the place. Moni looked back at the old good days when both of them struggled to live, and here they were ending up in the same predicament. They could help each other. It was a decision if Pilar should know. She decided to tell Pilar half of the story. She omitted the fact that they both knew who the person was at the apartment. She asked Pilar that her friend from younger days might need a place to stay if he lost his job and to assist him if it was acceptable to her. It would be safer to have a male tenant in the house. Moni was preparing Pilar in the event she would have to leave.

The *Bulletin* reported that the victim, named Sowani, was still at the morgue, and nobody went to see her nor claimed her body. Mr. Kim was confident that his wife was still in Hongkong and would return soon. The body at the morgue was buried at the common grave for the unknown and the poor.

After a week, Moni went to see Armando at the KLS store. Monday was supposed to be a busy day, and he was not there. Moni's fear was he was let go. She browsed around for a good half an hour, and Armando finally appeared. Moni asked him if he could pass by the eatery for a chat after work. It was done in such a way that Moni pretended to ask him for an item and Armando said they did not have it. As Moni was exiting the store, Mr. Kim was entering the store. He looked at her intensely as if wanting to catch her attention but Moni saw him first and pretended not to see him. Moni was afraid he would suspect that Armando knew her.

That night, after seven, Armando came. Moni was surprised he had brought some cash and paid her for the hotel bill. It was thoughtful of him. They had another long talk, and Armando confided that he had saved some money stashed away. He was prepared for the inevitable, knowing that the good life would not last. Apparently, he did not get a notice yet. He anticipated it, and he was suspecting that Mr. Kim was looking for a replacement. Moni still did not tell him she lived in the establishment but that she was renting a room somewhere else.

The evening went well after Moni served a simple dish of eggplant and rice. Armando had not changed and ate whatever food was served. He was catered to by rich women who needed his service, and despite the rich food that he had learned to get accustomed to, he still behaved like a simple person of poor upbringing. She gave him the eatery's phone number and told him to call her at specific hours to ascertain that she was in.

Armando was interviewed by the police again. He admitted he had been there, but he had to go to work and left the woman sleeping. He could not remember the clothes she was wearing for obvious reasons he did not want to discuss. Sowani had called, and she came. There was no schedule.

Moni continued planning her next move. She wrote notes of current happenings, almost like a diary on a skimpy piece of paper, and placed them inside the seam of her old skirt.

That week, Mr. Kim came again. Another card was slipped to her as he paid for his breakfast. It was very early, and there was nobody in the eatery but him. He looked worried and had lost weight. He was dressed in his usual manner, but he did not look crisp. She had made a decision to cut off ties with him, so she did not return to call the number as requested.

After a week, he called one early morning when the eatery just opened. It was Mr. Kim. Apparently, he had confronted Armando, and he was seen entering the eatery one night after closing time. It was surmised that they knew each other. Moni denied the allegations. Moni did not want to be implicated with the death of the woman, which nobody had identified. Mr. Kim was suspecting that Armando and his wife had relations, and while Mr. Kim was talking, Moni kept quiet all the time. After a while, he finally hung up. Moni could not reach Armando to tell him of the latest development. She did not have his phone number.

Mr. Kim, despite the situation, did not report that his wife was missing. He had received another note, so he was confident that she was alive. He would eventually hire a detective in Hongkong to find her and the reason for her stay in that place.

Moni was guilty about everything. If only she knew who had done it to her. She still had suspicions of the guy she had seen visiting Mr. Lasco. She wondered if he was Mr. Kim's confidant and knew

Mrs. Kim was having an affair with Armando. How did he enter the place? Was Armando supposed to be killed? Or did he wait outside and wait for Armando to leave? What if Armando stayed and did not go for an errand? Did the killer intend to disfigure her, or had the injury been inflicted inadvertently with no purpose? If Mrs. Kim had gone to Hongkong as presumed, who had posed as her in the plane and in the hotel she had presumably stayed for the days that she was there? Had her signature been identified as such? What would Mr. Kim do if his wife would not surface? Moni knew that Mrs. Kim might have had a secret she was hiding because she never talked to anyone nor looked at anyone, almost like she was embarrassed to face someone, afraid that her eye could be a window that someone could see through. For the years that Moni had worked at the store in Cebu, she had never known someone to have had talks with Mrs. Kim, then called Susu Yan.

Chapter Fifty-Seven

Mr. Kim stopped coming to Na Goria's place. Moni was happy she had resolved the problem. She was preparing her next move when Armando called that he had lost his job and obviously had to give up his expensive apartment. He had no place to go and was asking Moni to help him find a place. Moni recommended the cheap hotel, a place not too far from Na Goria. He had to get rid of his furniture, which was too large to accommodate in Na Goria's room. He still did not know she lived at Na Goria's, and Moni, having seen Tanciang's room, thought of taking the bedroom set, which was oversized but would fit the space in Tanciang's room. There was a lot of coordinating to do, so Armando would not lose it all. He had a month to dispose of the expensive things he owned, having lived in that apartment for a good ten years. He confided in Moni that most of his things had been bought for him by Mrs. Kim, and true, Mrs. Kim had been seeing him for ten years. Although he had other customers, she was the frequent one. Mrs. Kim allowed him to leave early from work and they either would meet at a cheap hotel or mostly in his apartment. She avoided having contact with him, so nobody possibly suspected they had a thing going between them. It was such a mystery as to who knew because they were never seen together. Armando said to Moni that he had money to pay rent for the whole year, but he had no job, and save that money he must, for the time would come he might not have an income.

The PO box had three cards from Guy, but she had not inspected her box for a week and did not get to reply his notes. It was then that possibly he would conclude that she was gone. The news about the murdered person at Armando's place had phased out.

At Mr. Kim's household, the quest to find Mrs. Kim continued. Being that he was in China when it happened, he had heard no news nor cared if, on the news, a person had been injured and died who could have been his wife. It was still a mystery that he would ponder. Six months had elapsed, and there was no news of Mrs. Kim.

Armando was discharged from his job as anticipated. Armando gave up his apartment. He was a male prostitute, and the news coverage might hurt the store. He had to give up his apartment, and the clients that he serviced had no telephone number to call or a place to do business. Tanciang and her sons helped vacate the apartment, and they took the large bed and mattress, which tightly fit the bedroom space in their rented room. Some furniture that would fit Na Goria's room was stored there in hopes to sell it in the near future. It was difficult for Moni to get around in a tight space to begin with, which at the moment, had become a storage room. Moni had Na Goria's bed to rest her body, and there was just enough space to get to the washroom. Tanciang's space to iron was tight. Moni finally told Armando she lived there, renting a room. Pilar, being so cooperative, made this possible.

Armando was oriented as a waiter. He would take all the tips. Armando still occupied a room in the nearby hotel, which for the moment he could afford. Moni could not afford another salaried person. He was hired as a help and shared the tips if there were any. He did not argue. He would keep on looking for a job and was free to go when he needed to. It worked out fine. If Moni's proceeds were more than she needed, she shared some with Armando. Armando took over the marketing with Tanciang, which afforded Moni some time to sleep. He was helpful. They understood each other, and in retrospect, Moni thought of their younger days and Armando's interest in her, which she could have reciprocated. Armando did not dare renew his interest in Moni. He kept it to himself, afraid to destroy the kindness that Moni so lavishly gave him. Moni's plans were deferred for the moment. It was not set due to Armando's problems.

After four weeks, Armando had not found a job. His tips were meager, being in an inexpensive eatery, but the customers kept coming, and the proceeds were larger. Pilar was amazed at the money coming in and said to Armando that if a room would be vacated, she would save the room for him. There was hope for Armando. The money he got from tips and Moni was almost enough to pay for his hotel. Food was free at the eatery. A lot of women customers kept coming, and it was obvious that the women liked Armando. Armando, hitting fifty, looked very young for his age and, indeed, was looking for a girlfriend although he was fearful and inhibited, thinking that some women might remember him on the news some months ago. He avoided conversations and evaded closeness nor friendship. A room was not available for him at Na Goria's, but he was managing. He looked around for a room for rent, but it was either too far or the tenants were unwholesome and he would not take a risk. Some of his furniture was sold. He had no more plans on living high nor did he dream of finding a managerial job. He had not received any severance pay, which he expected, but he did not ask for it. He had worked in that company for a good fifteen years, and although he thought he was deserving of something, he did not complain thinking of the ten years he enjoyed Mr. Kim's wife. It was a moment of pure physical enjoyment accompanied by financial abundance of living well, which he would not have had, had he not indulged in such acts. He could not ask for more. He was a cheat and deserved to be fired. The only consolation was it was not divulged, although it was obvious that the person who did it, the murderer, knew it all. He was not free. He could reappear, but he probably would not because he definitely would be implicated in the crime. He had to remain as such—lowly, still afraid of being discovered. Moni and Armando kept this a secret. Moni taught Armando the ropes of the business. In time, he would be able to take it over. They would sit after hours and figure out the menu and cost of running the place. She reiterated the safety of the place and the event of an intruder that had almost hurt Moni. The anticipated bottles with water had saved her from disaster. Moni was preparing Armando for the job.

SHADOWS IN THE PANTRY

She had not told Pilar of her ultimate plan. Moni would pretend to go out and take a stroll usually after lunch time, so Armando and Tanciang would be on their own managing the work. She was watching cautiously, seeing that Pilar would not be cheated of what would be due to her. Moni never cheated Pilar. The accounting of receipts was done honestly, as close to having a receipt, which normally they would not, being that the marketing was on cash exchange. The money envelope to market was marked as such, and change was recorded to keep abreast of expenses. Moni could have been an accountant in a big firm and the firm would be most credible because honesty was her motto. Pilar secretly admired her and was hoping that she would be with her forever. She knew that this good luck would not last. She had proceeds from the eatery and hardly knew what was going on. Moni knew this but never took advantage of her lack of knowledge. Pilar never found a guy whom she could trust, and up to that time, she was content of being alone financially well off. The rent from the place, the eatery, and her job has kept her content. Her ex-husband has not come around to bother her. She was always fearful because he was mean.

Most of Moni's belongings was packed and mailed to Villalon. It was done in small packages, which nobody knew. Her share from the restaurant was all saved. The straw bag was half full of money. She was now almost certain that Armando could handle the job. She was still watching if he was honest enough. Tanciang's salary was increased, and as usual, some of the food left was sent home. The way it looked, she was content and reasonably compensated. The eatery was open seven days a week. If they needed rest, a note was placed at the front door four weeks ahead to alert the community of the plan. Armando had implemented new recipes, which were rather expensive, but the small amount he would cook would be sold. Moni was waiting for the proper time to speak to Pilar. The notes from Guy stopped. The letters from Avelino came that the packages had arrived in order and the family were fine. His business was doing well, and the store was expanding.

Chapter Fifty-Eight

One night, Moni and Pilar had a heart-to-heart talk. She was going away for six weeks to visit the family, and Moni would either write her a note or call as to the date of her return before the six weeks of being away. In the meantime, she had prepared Armando and Tanciang to take over. She confided to Pilar that she should watch the money from the marketing and to count the proceeds every night. This way, they would know Pilar was watching and knew what was going on. She should not be blind. The eatery was a fine business, and customers were accustomed to having their food at the eatery. Pilar was very sad. Moni had a week to stay, and she asked Pilar to take off a few days to watch over the store. Armando, having a job, was paid reasonably as a temporary manager plus tips; he was surviving, leaving his savings untouched. Moni closed the post office box, and there was a note from Guy. She did not respond.

The trip from Manila to Cebu then to Villalon, Leyte, was scheduled. She did not drop off at Uncle Indong's when the boat landed at Cebu in the morning. She took a stroll in the city and boarded a ship to Leyte that night. She did not have a pleasant story to tell him. She wanted to spare him from worry. Moni had not succeeded because her one mistake of falling in love had devastated her longtime dream of becoming a teacher. Her trip was uneventful, and her light straw bag was the only one she had. Most of the gifts to her family had been received. It was nice seeing everybody. Her parents, although older, had kept themselves healthy. Nemesio had been taking care of them, and proceeds from the small business had been fair, which kept them financially stable. Simeon's grandparents and mother were all deceased. The house they lived in is now rented.

The two weeks that Moni stayed at her hometown were most pleasant. Her mother did not ask too many questions and enjoyed Moni's presence, it seemed. Moni's father kept fixing whatever he thought needed fixing, so the home was maintained well. Moni's niece and nephew had grown and helped out with the gardening and packing the vegetables to sell wherever they could. The tradition of working had been handed down and taught, and no one was lazy. Moni kept busy and assisted Melit with organizing the materials and designed one of the blouses. Her plans were set, and off she left Villalon after the two weeks. Moni told her parents she would return to Manila and she would write. She had no specific plans.

The arrival and staying at Cebu was a big decision. She booked the room for two days. She had a lot of thinking to do, despite the fact that she had given her plan a lot of thought. If she would not succeed, she was prepared to return to Manila, and she would resume what she had been doing and would probably live her life as Na Goria did to hers. She accepted her failure. She opened a post office box and rented it for a year. The inexpensive hotel near the church was her choice so she could see the Virgin Mary to ask for guidance and forgiveness for her past deeds. It was also near cheap eating places she could afford and jeepneys.

After some days of thinking and going to church, she went her way with her straw bag. Dressed in plain clothes and a scarf to cover her head, she walked briskly. It was a mile and a half walk from the main road, and it was a cool, sunny morning. She chose to walk to do some more thinking.

It takes two jeepneys to get to the place. The road to the convent was off the main artery. It was desolate; a few jeepneys and private cars treaded by. The convent was enclosed in high walls of cement that obscured the monastery from the outside. It occupied a large property surrounded by green grass, and various flowers lined the outside wall of the convent. The steel gate was locked. She rang the bell and waited for a while before a person came to inquire who she was. He looked like a gardener, identified because of his outfit.

Moni had no appointment. He went back in and returned to tell Moni she could return the next day to see Mother Superior. She was disappointed. She had given up that room thinking that this was the day she would get in. She was worried the hotel room had been rented and looking for space to sleep might be difficult. The big hotels, although she could afford them, would be too expensive. True enough, she had to wait because a person had not vacated the room yet. The tenant did not leave on time, but she had a room for the night. She booked it for three days. That night she did more thinking and planning. She would leave her belongings at the hotel in case she would be denied, and if not accepted, she would return to Manila or she might go back to the United States. Her visa and passport were in order. That was the alternative.

She left earlier than usual to miss traffic. She did not bring her straw bag in case her trip was unsuccessful. She waited outside the convent and was hoping her plans would materialize. It was again a long wait after she rang the bell and the gardener remembered her and ushered her in without any questions. As expected, the area was large; the big chapel on the right side of the grounds was huge, and the left side was the convent. The paved walkway to the convent was lined with various flowers landscaped beautifully. The convent was a medium size brick building, with several windows on the top floor. Presumably this building had been there for a number of years. The main door was wide and heavy. She entered a dimly lit sitting room with padded couches, facing the office. A young nun wearing all white smiled at Moni, recognizing her presence. She was seated in an enclosed room, almost like a receptionist. The wall was bare except for a crucifix midway to the end of the hall. A large clay pot with a green plant stood by the counter. There were also some pots all the way to the end of the hall. The hallway to the end was dark, but at the end of the hallway was a wide window that occupied the whole space, allowing the rays of the sun to beam through.

Moni was busy with her thoughts. She was wondering how the nuns derived their means to buy food and sorts. The place was not lit well, possibly to reduce cost. She was curious and walked to the end of the hallway as she looked at the window she could see greens, a vegetable garden. She quickly returned to her seat. She sat facing the young nun to see the goings-on in the office. After a while, the young nun signaled her to approach the counter; she entered the door beside the counter and was led to a room which was also dimly lit. She sat across the big desk; on top of it was a movable sign signifying whose table it was: Mother Superior. It was another wait. Finally, a heavy-set elderly nun came smiling to see her. She was most accommodating, which made Moni happy and allayed her fear of this event in her life.

Moni had planned her story; she had written it on a piece of paper and rehearsed it over and over again. This would be her last lie to commit. Her tale was she had been born to parents from Leyte, who died at a very early age, and she was adopted by a maid who took employment in a household of a teacher. This teacher worked in a remote area and taught her to read and write. She was then moved to another household and taken in as a maid after the teacher died. The woman recently died, and she was told to seek refuge in a convent where she would be safe. A certain amount of money was given, saved to be given to the nuns. Moni presented some cash to the nun. She stated that she would clean, take care of the garden, and do whatever the nuns asked her to do. She could do errands since even though her education was limited, she was able to read and write. She need not be compensated for her work. She was content in having a room to sleep in and food to eat and, more so, a decent burial. She had no identification to present, being that she never knew where they were nor was she in a school that would have required a birth certificate. She would be willing to be on probation and would be let go if she was not trustworthy to live in the convent. Mother Superior listened carefully, and she told Moni to return in a week.

Chapter Fifty-Nine

A conference would have to be held, and the congregation had to agree before she was admitted. She had delivered her plea quite well.

The walk to the main road was long, but it was in walking when she did most of her thinking. Moni had to return to the hotel. She had money to stay at the place, being a frugal person that she was, but she was rather worried. She thought of Uncle Indong, and certainly, he had room in his home. If she decided to see her uncle, she would have to have another lie set up. It was not easy to remember another lie. She had run out of stories to tell. It was a walk to church, and she sat there, thinking, and for guidance. She would not be forgiven, but she tried to ask for it. That night she slept well. A week with nothing to do was boring to her. She attended mass every day. The plan was to go to the city, see the old places she used to frequent as a young girl.

One day, as she was exiting the church from the side door, she happened to glance at the front door, and she saw Mr. Guy with another woman, and definitely, she was not his wife. They were engaged in intense conversation, so he was not aware of his surroundings. It was very early, and he thought no one was there. The woman was rather pretty, in her late fifties. Moni reentered the church and sat nearby to be able to view them from a distance. Then she slowly went to the fruit stand to buy some items. Mr. Guy (Dr. Bonedoto) drove off. Moni's back was all he could see if he was to notice her. The woman remained and stood by the entrance of the church and, after a few minutes, walked to the main road. Mr. Guy was still fooling around. He had not stopped.

SHADOWS IN THE PANTRY

Moni went back to the hotel and, dressed in a long flared skirt, went to the pier to have a glance at her uncle in the warehouse. He was of age, like her mother, but carried the poise of a credible man. She walked pass it several times and enjoyed herself watching him as if it had been yesterday when they would walk down the hill from his humble home to fetch the jeepney. It was a memorable moment, and she would not see him again and headed to the city passing the old school, the church nearby, and the old place of work. It was a vacation she had not planned.

After a week, she went back, leaving her belongings at the hotel in case she would not be accepted. She would have to return to Manila and get old at Na Goria's place. Teaching was no longer a dream. She had planned it well, but there were times that fate would not allow it. When Moni returned to the convent, she was received by the same gardener and ushered to the entrance. The same nun was at the counter, who was smiling at her with such a grin. Moni sort of knew she had been accepted. Mother Superior was available at once; possibly she had marked it in her calendar. Mother Superior came to see her almost immediately. She did not have a long wait. She was looking at Moni with such an inquiring look and knew in the back of her mind that this very pretty-looking woman in her late forties had some uncertain childhood and just needed a safe place to stay. She seemed to be physically able to do work, as she said she could, and seemed credible. This was a risk she took, but the rest of the nuns had approved of the decision to take her in. The Mother Superior finally said she would be given a probation period of one month, and she did not take the money. She was asked where she was living, to which Moni was fast in saying a rented room, and furthermore, she was asked, if she would not be accepted, where she would go. Moni replied that she really did not know. She would have to find other employment, and she would spend the money she had to keep her fed until it runs out.

Moni understood the Mother Superior's indecisive attitude. Moni had no character references, and trusting a stranger of a questionable past could cause danger to the convent. The convent comprising of mostly elderly were vulnerable to violence could not on the surface able to physically defend themselves. She had another night to stay at the hotel. It was paid for, and she had plenty of money. The next day, she vacated the hotel and eagerly went to her new home, hopefully to stay.

    When she arrived at the convent, she was welcomed by the same young nun at the desk. She was led to the stairs to the second floor. The wing consisted of small rooms overlooking the big chapel. Her room was located all the way to the back. It accommodated a single wooden bed with a mat and a pillow. The small window afforded some light and a small light bulb on the ceiling. A small closet right at the entrance of the room had a few hangers. The young nun has subtly mentioned it was one of the postulant's rooms. The wing illuminated by windows at the end of the hallway was clean, and the walls were bare except a medium-size crucifix midway to the washroom. It was very clean. She was shown the closet for cleaning supplies, which meant each user cleaned after its use. Moni noticed around fifteen rooms presumably the size like hers. The wing was separated from the other wing that housed the regular nuns. No one was to trespass and go to the other side. One was accompanied to the other side or not go there at all. After the short orientation to her room, she was allowed to organize her few belongings and returned to the first floor. There she waited for Mother Superior to tell her of her assignment and the area she would only be expected to be. Moni, despite the hard work she anticipated to do, was rather excited that indeed she would have a place to stay and a sure piece of land where she would be respectfully buried among the holy.

Chapter Sixty

The tour with Mother Superior and the introduction to the congregation was a moment for Moni to remember. The nuns seemed to welcome her as if she was among them. The written definition of her duties was precise, and she was given an off day of every Thursday. The door beyond the Mother Superior's room was a hallway, and there were series of receiving rooms for relatives who visited. Each room had larger windows and, obviously, well illuminated. The couches were all white, upholstered insignificantly, and served the purpose for which the room was set up. There were several of them, it seemed, and beyond that was no entry. Specifications were said, and she noted it down in her mind, for mistakes on her part would be catastrophic. They had a small chapel aside from the main big chapel by the main entrance of the convent. The kitchen was all the way to the back, and a swinging door allowed entrance to the big dining room. The dining table seated twenty. It was for back then when there were many nuns, but the empty seat signified those that had passed on. There were no more postulants that year, and she was told there were only twelve nuns and mostly elderly, who might need her care. It was a whole hour or so, the tour of the place, and back to her room she went. Dressed in a midcalf skirt, she would start working that afternoon. She stayed in her room, not knowing what to do. As a person who could not sit still, she went to the washroom and started to clean the three stalls. It was not dirty, having been kept and maintained by every single person who used it. It did not take her long. She walked back to her room and looked out the window, viewing the vast space of her new abode. Soon there was a knock at her door, and the same young nun who had fetched her told her that it was time to serve lunch. She followed her to the large dining room with an adjoining kitchen and helped serve food, which consisted of some fish and vegetables, which to Moni was too little for adults. The nuns actually lived in poverty. The majority of them looked so pale and looked more so due to the black habit except the white material underneath the veil. They looked like ghosts. There was not much cooking to do, and everybody sort of helped put the dishes away. It was all a concerted effort, and it was rather admirable to watch that they adhered to their promises supposedly before they committed themselves to be in this prison. Then the help ate, which was the same portion as the nuns. There was the cook and her. No wonder she was needed. Preparation for dinner was immediately started after lunch since there was a delivery of whole chickens from somebody. It seemed that it was a big event when it arrived because the nuns immediately grouped together to say thank you.

Moni began her working schedule, which was mostly cleaning the hallways, the kitchen, and the various visiting rooms on the first floor. One thing she was excited about was she was assigned to do the errands, which allowed her to go out and possibly buy stuff for the nuns. The money she had reserved for them was not accepted. Being a fast and organized worker, Moni was done with her inside work, and she went to the back to weed the vegetables and looked as to what she could do to keep it bountiful. It was not on her agenda as listed. The church was clean, and her daily dusting and sweeping as often as Moni had time kept it clean. Sunday mass was full, and Moni was happy that most churchgoers gave donations, which apparently kept the congregation alive. Some parishioners brought fruits and food items such as whole chicken and cut-up beef. Life was peaceful, as Moni had dreamt it to be.

The probation was over, and she waited for the Mother Superior to tell her that she had not passed it. Several weeks went by and there was no word. Moni assumed she was there to stay. The errand was every week to the city, she sent a letter to Pilar that her stay at Cebu would have to be extended. She bought some food for the congregation and would claim a person had donated it.

SHADOWS IN THE PANTRY

A letter was received, and Pilar stated the she was satisfied with Armando's services. In fact, Pilar was thinking of having him occupy Na Goria's room. Moni was flattered to be consulted about the plan even if she did not own the place. Indeed, Pilar respected and appreciated Moni with all the help she did to keep the eatery afloat. Moni gave it a lot of thought and took time writing her back. Although she was situated, and she planned this move, she was not sure if she was set. Moni could actually return home to Leyte and settle there if the nuns would let her go. The nuns were kind to her, and the way it looked, nobody questioned the stuff she brought to the kitchen. The nuns were now well fed. They had protein in every meal. The vegetables were abundant from the garden because of Moni's expertise by returning to the soil its remnants. When Moni had a day off, she wrote to Pilar and Armando.

Chapter Sixty-One

Mr. Kim was still looking for his wife. He has been taking advantage of the women under his employ to satisfy his physical needs. His children had adjusted to the fact that their mother was not found. In the meantime, an employee of Mr. Kim, a person Armando never knew came to the eatery and left a note for him as he was paying his bill, stating that he knew all about the night in question. The guy wanted to extort money from him. Armando kept quiet, pretending that he knew nothing. He played dumb. He was coming to the restaurant to threaten him, and Armando wrote Moni about it. He knew that aside from the both of them, someone else knew—the killer himself. Moni replied to Pilar of the decision that she might not go back. Armando then was offered the back room for rent, but he did not move because he did not want Pilar to get involved if the person ever decided to harm him. The person would surely attack him in his residence, and having had a history of such, he wanted to keep the eatery's reputation intact. It was Pilar that he was protecting. Armando was fearful for his life. The pay as the manager and the tips was more than enough to maintain his rent. It was a big decision to accept the offer, which was more advantageous to him. It was agreed that Armando would sleep at the back room with Pilar's consent when Tanciang and he had to do early market. He was thinking of doing it three times a week. He followed Moni's advice to keep an accurate record for Pilar to inspect. Armando wanted to keep this job. It was profitable, and he needed not dress up, but being clean was all it required. Pilar did not mind him staying for the night at Na Goria's room when he had to.

SHADOWS IN THE PANTRY

The person who knew Armando kept coming. He would not say anything but stare at Armando while he was eating. He would smile and stare at him and, at times, would not pay. Tanciang noticed it and asked Armando who he was. He would say to her that he was an old friend and he would take care of it. It would seem that Armando did not make an issue of a meager amount, afraid of having to reveal his secret. The person took advantage of it and kept on coming. Moni wrote to Armando whenever she had an errand to do for the nuns. She suggested to him to keep his room at the hotel. He would try to confuse him by going to a cheap movie and entering it, staying by the curtain door and leaving the premises when he would see him enter. He would sleep in the bathroom of his hotel room and placed several pickle jars filled with water by the door every night. He would bring with him a spray of bleach as a weapon in case he would sleep through the commotion and he entered the bathroom door. He would attempt to spray his eyes to incapacitate him temporarily.

Moni kept inquiring about the person's appearance, build, and whatever Armando noticed so she could try to remember the man who could have been her assailant at the hotel. The incident was so vivid to her, and so was the appearance of the man who had visited Mr. Lasco. As Armando described him, he was shorter than him, with a very muscular, chiseled face and a scar somewhere on one eye that blinked nervously. He was not sure which eye. Armando had never seen him before, nor had he seen him at the store where he used to work. Armando followed the advice since he was not trained in any manly confrontations. Admittedly he was ashamed that he would be incapable of protecting himself with his bare fist. All he did was work at the store and attended college for the longest time he almost gave it up. He then could only take two or three subjects due to work and money constraints. Moni used to send him a few bucks, and he spent it for tuition. His brothers, both teachers, finished ahead of him because he concentrated on sending them first, although they both worked as assistant bakers in a bakery to get by. They had free bread, and sometimes, bread bought at half a price was a help to the family.

His brothers did not know of his activities in Manila. They thought he was doing well, being the manager of a large store at the prestigious Escolta in Manila. It was a surprise to the brothers when it was featured on the newspaper that a woman was found naked and injured in his apartment. Armando did not really have to prostitute himself if he took an inexpensive apartment. The temptation was there, and he used his good looks to earn money. He made several women happy, and he enjoyed himself. He was paid for it. He knew it would not last long, so he did save enough money. This fear that he was feeling now was something he had not anticipated. He had not harmed anyone. The women wanted his services, and he gave them. He thought of his frail mother, who had lived poor and died almost after a few years when his father passed on, although she had witnessed his brother's accomplishment and she had some happiness watching her children obtain a degree. Armando's younger brother had finished his teaching degree, immediately took a job in a private school, and had a chance to buy a two-bedroom home in a subdivision, wherein his mother moved in with him. His mother had a few years at a house where she did not squat on someone's land. Armando had remained at the dilapidated home until he finished his business degree. He was promoted immediately at the Yellow Gold Department Store and took a job as a finance manager. Susu Yan then liked him. He noticed it and ignored the idea, being that she was a rich Chinese woman of a high category. He would be called to see her at the personnel office for no reason. She would ask him how the financing of the store was going. She would touch his hand, and he would get scared, thinking that the door would open and someone would see him being touched by this pretty woman. When Susu Yan married Mr. Kim and he put up a store at a prestigious place in Escolta, Manila, he was offered a job and took it. They started having an affair a year after he took the job. It was done discreetly, the meeting at various hotels where he would book it and she would come for a rendezvous. She gave him money to find an apartment, actually to suit her taste, and he went along with it. The only time they did not see each other was when she was pregnant. Armando then had other customers, ladies married to older rich men who would not be able to satisfy them sexually. Money was abundant. Despite this, Armando was smart and saved money for the rainy days. He was now encountering the rainy days that he had sort of known would happen. Moni was always there for him, and he wished she had married him. If Moni had married him, he would have avoided sexual encounters with lonely women. It was her he really cared for.

He was certain the person had followed him and knew where he lived. The hotel routine kept him secure that he would hear the noise, and despite the hard floor on his back, he would sleep and be ready to work the next day. He would wake up at 5 a.m. and walk to work. Nothing happened, and he was confident that the anticipated intruder had finally decided to leave him alone. In the meantime, he wrote Moni of his description as best he could. He was around five six inches in height, of muscular build, dark skin, a round face, wide mouth, and a crew cut. The injury to the eye was significant. He enclosed a letter addressed to the editor of the *Bulletin* to be mailed in the event of his demise. When Moni read it, she was concerned, although the letter pacified her that he was fine. He would indeed move to Na Goria's room, and he was to pay a minimal rent, very affordable to him. A long four weeks elapsed, and there was no reply from Armando. Moni took it as him very busy adding recipes and the restaurant flourishing.

Moni wrote to Avelino that she was fine. She did not know what to tell him but said she was looking for a job in Cebu. She kept it short. Armando had not written to Moni. She presumed he was fine. Moni bought the *Bulletin* every time she had an errand to do. Sometimes two weeks would pass by and she had no errand to do. She was worried that she would miss the news and she would not mail the letter to the *Bulletin*. Moni had great suspicions that the guy who went to see Armando was the same guy who had assaulted her. He had no name but some description that would represent most facial features of a Filipino whose bloodline was of Malaysian extraction. If Mr. Lasco was still alive, he would be able to tell who it was. Moni wrote another letter to Armando and told him of what she knew. Definitely the guy was Mr. Kim's employee. That night Mrs. Kim was bludgeoned was the night that he had also intended to kill Armando. Armando had gone to find a particular food SuSu Yan wanted, and he had gone all over Manila to find it, which he did not; if he had, it would have been evidence of who was there at the apartment. It would have been traced to SuSu Yan who orders it most of the time. It was an expensive fish dish only the rich could afford, and it was to be especially ordered.

Chapter Sixty-Two

Uncle Indong seemed fair, retired with enough money for them to get by. Pina stayed at home, dependent on her parents. The person who had attempted to assault her in their home has not returned. Pina did not go out as often except food shopping. She had a large vegetable garden, which almost occupied the whole space at the back. Dee was doing well. She need not work as a nurse being well off, and the Manguerra family had acquired more warehouses. Dee would allocate some money for her parents every month without fail. She was an efficient help to her husband, who was a district civil engineer and seem to be a dedicated husband. Aunt Delina had stopped making clothes for a fee but continued with her sewing to keep her busy. Avelino had informed Uncle Indong that Moni was indeed in Cebu, which disappointed him, being that Moni had not paid him a visit. He suspected that Moni was in trouble, and she did not want him to worry. He thought of her all the time, hoping that she would come. She never came.

Moni intended to stay in the convent as a maid and an errand person. She wrote a farewell note to Mother Superior and made several requests specified in the letter. She did not forget to mention her respect and gratitude to the congregation for providing her a safe place to live and to assure that she would have a decent burial. The monies would be left in the envelopes with specification on each as to whom it belonged. She placed all the letters to be mailed in a large envelope addressed to Mother Superior. The letter to the *Bulletin* from Armando was also included.

She separated money for some marketing as she anticipated, possibly for the length of time she would possibly live. She was approaching fifty and did not expect to live long. She wrote the farewell letters to everyone she could think of. She made a skirt flared enough so she could fit all the monies into the very wide seam. She was tired, thinking of her misdeeds, and if heaven and hell existed she was ready to go there anytime. It was such a comfort to be with the nuns and having the certainty that her dead body would surely be handled in a holy manner, although she was undeserving of such.

Armando had not written for a long time, it seemed, and Moni missed the news of the person who tried to extort money from him. Moni continued with her duties—keeping busy with the early morning setup for the nun's breakfast, assisting the cook, serving them their dinners, and in between, gardening, cleaning the church and the yard, and tending the flowers outside the convent wall. She helped everywhere, except when she went for errands, when she would spend the whole morning and late afternoon in the city. It was the jeepney ride from one place to the other that took long. Although when she checked her post office box, she would take time at the place to write a reply, being prepared with a stationery. As the months went by, Moni was enjoying the peaceful life.

One errand day, she received a note from Armando that he had moved to Na Goria's room. His furniture at Na Goria's room was sold, and there was some he kept. There was some news that the last night he was at the hotel he had left the place because he was hungry and he had some things to do, so he had gone to Na Goria's to eat and intended to return to the hotel but did not. The precautionary pickle jars filled with water were lined in a circular manner a foot and a half from the door. As the intruder entered, he would surely slip and the noise would surely wake him up.

That night, an intruder went in and slipped on the pickle jars, but he was carrying a knife ready to stab the person who was in bed, and the intruder went off balance and inadvertently stabbed himself on the chest. The door was shut as he fell, and nobody discovered him until the next day when the maid came in to change the linens. There was no sign at the door not to disturb the occupant, so the maid went in. The intruder bled to death. The intruder did not have identification with him. Armando returned to the hotel to check out when he was told of the occurrence and to call the police. He was being investigated because he had rented that room. The police did not know where to find him. The whole day, he worked at the eatery and did not know about it until that evening when he had finished counting the proceeds and miscellaneous tasks to be done. The police investigation was long, and it was at another precinct different from the first one, and nobody remembered him. He was asked if he knew of somebody that would attempt to kill him. He denied knowing someone who might want to hurt him. It had been a few months when he had been featured in the news, and gratefully, he was not questioned about the occurrence at his apartment. Apparently after thorough investigation it was confirmed that Armando was not at the hotel room. There was no signature at the front desk signifying that he entered the hotel. He could not have been involved because the knife was not his. The position of the body did not indicate the dead man had a fight with someone and the position of the body confirmed that he inflicted the wound to himself. The letter was long, and Moni replied to it right away and expressed her happiness that presumably the enemy had been put away. She was not sure if that was the guy that had assaulted her, but she was almost positive that it was him. Armando had been freed, but his conscience was there to haunt him. He knew it all.

Chapter Sixty-Three

One night, the Mother Superior ushered Moni to her office and requested her to arise early to clean the chapel thoroughly. A wedding was scheduled at half past nine in the morning. It was supposed to be a big wedding, especially because the family had been frequent donors to the congregation. Moni settled in bed early to be able to wake up earlier than usual. The church bells usually rang around five in the morning, but she needed to wake up at four. She was up by three. She was equipped with keys to every room she needed to clean. The cemented semicircular stairs to the basement were normally dark except for the light from the glass window located on the top part of the chapel wall. All her cleaning supplies were there in a closet. A switch light on the wall midway down the stairs kept it well-lit as one descended the steps. A faucet was provided to fill her water needs. On top of the stairs was a washroom. The chapel was also dimly lit, and she started to clean the whole chapel. As it was cleaned every day, it was not difficult. She was done by half past five. She swiped her fingers at random on areas to test if she had done a good job.

When she was done, she went back to her room to nap. After her nap, she would help in the kitchen. It was an early day for the congregation due to the wedding arrangement to be held at the chapel. As rumored, the bride was a niece of the Mother Superior. Moni wanted to see the ceremony. She had never had a church wedding because they could not afford it then. The curtains on both sides of the altar enclosing the back allowed the spectator to peek through behind it. As she parted the curtains with one eye, she was able to watch the ceremony. She was just in time to see the bride walking the middle aisle of the church lined with white thick linen. The bride looked pretty walking with her parents to the altar and the organ playing with several nuns subtly chanting the "Here Comes the Bride" hymn. The entourage of bridesmaids escorted by very handsome young lads all dressed in expensive Barong Tagalong was a sight. The groom was waiting by the altar, facing the bride with his elders. Moni could not see the groom from where she was standing. As they turned around to face the altar, Moni was surprised that it was her son Clark Kent who was to marry the bride. Moni's heart was pounding with mixed feelings, especially seeing Dr. Moises and his wife. Moni was aware that somebody could be there watching her because she started to sob because of mixed emotions. Her tears rolled down her cheeks so heavily her vision was blurred, and she kept wiping her tears with the edge of her wide below-the-knee skirt. Her son looked handsome in his Barong Tagalog; so did his parents, who were dressed in expensive customary Filipino garments. They were happy. They settled in their seats and the ceremony went on. The guests were the rich of Cebu, all dressed so elegantly in their long gowns escorted by their partners. Moni looked on and could not get enough satisfaction from mere looking. She thought this could be the last time that she would ever take a good look at her son. She had to avoid being seen and be recognized. Her wide ripped straw hat, which she wore when doing gardening work, which kept her from the burns resulting from the piercing sun, would be the head wear to shield her face from recognition.

When the event was almost over, Moni ran down the cemented steps and took the straw hat and a gardening tool. She would situate herself outside by the flower garden, which nobody would care to look at. The big chapel had wide doors on the side, so she waited until the ceremony was almost finished. As the entourage walked toward the exit, Moni slowly walked toward the gate exit and, dressed in a flare skirt and a wide straw hat, pretended to weed the garden by the convent wall. She glanced sideways and did some cutting. This was the last time she would ever see her son, and look she did within the time she was able to.

She saw Lady Esther with a younger lad and a young lady. The rest of the guests she did not recognize. Most of the guests had left, and the nuns were still there watching them leave. As she looked around, she noticed somebody very familiar in Filipino attire who stood far from everybody, almost like a mere spectator. He was watching it with intensity and stood aside from the group as the crowd thinned out, embarking into their cars. In between, Moni would dig the garden so no one would suspect she was looking. The man remained standing like he was not part of the group. He was wearing a Barong Tagalong. He looked so familiar. He looked handsome as ever, with his wide shoulders, and still had the presence of an attractive man in his fifties. The crowd had cleared, and Moni, her heart pounding, had to remove herself from the place or she would get recognized. Although her attire of a wide faded skirt, a long-sleeved shirt, and a straw hat would not in theory catch attention, she was careful. She slowly stood up, but the straw hat fell when a fierce wind drifted it, and Moni was not fast enough to retrieve it to replace it on her head. Her face exposed, she ran to the small entrance to the convent. The spectator had a glimpse at Moni, and although unsure of what he saw, he noticed that the fast run of the person he almost recognized was an indication that this person had possibly something to hide. He was quick and chased her to the backside of the chapel, not thinking of the repercussions while the nun was still there to have watched the episode. Moni quickly entered the side door of the church and headed down the basement and slipped as she stepped on her wide skirt. She lost her balance and hit her head on the last step of the cemented stairs to the basement. She lay there, helpless, face down. Ken followed her down and rolled her over and totally recognized this poor dark-skinned woman as Moni.

He whispered to her and said, "Moni, at last I found you."

At the same time, he lifted her up the stairs while Moni was limp and unconscious with an open wound on her head, bleeding. The ascent on the steps was difficult for him, being aged, and he carried her in his arms and exited the gate, looking for transportation. All the guests have left. Transportation was scarce in that area, and the nun who saw him did not know what to do. Ken, carrying Moni's thin stature, was running as fast as he could to find transportation. As he was halfway through, a jeepney approached, and Ken stood in the middle of the road to catch his attention, and the driver had to stop. Kent begged the driver and the three passengers to bring them to the nearest hospital, which nobody argued. The jeepney was not an ambulance, so despite its hurry, it had to yield to traffic. Moni was laid on the seat since the passengers emptied it to accommodate the sick woman and Ken on the floor, holding her in that skimpy space.

As they reached the hospital, there were many patients to be attended to, and a skillful nurse took note of the situation and immediately took care of her. Ken introduced himself as a doctor and tried to explain what had happened and suggested several recommendations. He took his wallet, and luckily, he had his identifications. An intravenous was placed, and radiographic films were taken. Indeed, Moni had intracranial bleeding, and immediate surgery had to be done. In the meantime, Moni surprisingly woke up from unconsciousness, and with a blurred vision, she spoke Ken's name, "Ken, you are here." She slipped into a coma. The call to the convent so Moni could be operated on proved useless because there was no written agreement that the Mother Superior was the guardian. Moni Almadin, as she was listed, had no history of a family, and as they scanned the telephone book for the same family name, there was none. The time elapsed was too long, and surgery was not performed. Moni finally died and was buried among her favorite people.

Chapter Sixty-Four

Moni was buried in the back of the convent with the nuns where she wished to be with. Mother Superior opened her straw bag and a written note in Moni's handwriting as legible as a teacher would write the words in the blackboard stated as such:

> Dear Mother Superior,
> My name is Moni Almadin. I am a liar and was compelled to lie to be able to have the time to repent for the many sins I have committed. Contrary to my story, I originally came from Leyte, a daughter of a farmer. I went to teaching school and obtained a teaching degree eventually from Far Eastern University in Manila. I was married, separated from my husband after he learned of my illegitimate child whom I hid from him for twenty years. Forgive he could not, so I left. My dream of a teaching job did not materialize, so I became a highly paid prostitute, and finally, after some serious self-examination, I decided to work for you in this holy, safe place and be assured of a decent burial. My dead body entombed with the holy. That was my last request.
> I am most grateful to you for taking me in and that I was given the chance to pray and ask forgiveness for my sins. Thank you for mailing the letters to my loved ones. A faded skirt with

wide seams I will give to the congregation. The seams were made wide enough, and in it, there is some amount of money that I have saved for this occasion. Again I thank you for the kindness and acceptance to stay under the care of the congregation. I hope I have serviced your congregation. Good-bye.

Moni

The letter to her parents basically stated the event of her life that she concealed from them. Presumably Maxi would relay to Uncle Indong the contents of her letter according to her discretion. The letters to Harriet, Armando, and Pilar were short, mostly thanking them for their friendship. Arthur Junior's letter was lengthy, stating forgiveness and love to her son. It was addressed to his workplace.

Ken read his letter, which was addressed to Arthur Junior to mail, and he was overwhelmed with grief. It was most detailed, especially when Moni had seen him at the jewelry store. Ken stayed in Cebu for a week, and having seen the address of Moni when the Mother Superior opened her straw bag, he took a trip to Leyte and met the family of Moni. It was an occasion that should have happened forty years ago, and Moni could have been spared the loneliness and lifelong grief being married to Ken. Maxi and family received Ken with such delight, not really knowing how and why Moni did not marry Ken.

Armando and Pilar got married, which Moni never knew about, and they lived at Na Goria's place. Armando's letter to the *Manila Bulletin* was not mailed since there was an advisory note to send it to Armando in the event of Moni's death. The person who had assaulted Moni at the hotel was under the employ of Mr. Lasco, an elderly man who, with Mr. Kim, had recruited young pretty girls for men who wanted companionship. It was most discreet because Mr. Lasco owned several businesses and stores. He would be the last person who would do it since he was wealthy. Moni had been on the verge of becoming a true lady companion. The hotel fire had saved her of such predicament. The person's name was Bortong Gianga, a native from Danugo, Cebu. He was buried in the pauper's grave just like his uncles. He had killed Susu Yan and would have inflicted the same to Armando if he had been there after several instances when she went to see Armando for a rendezvous. Bortong never revealed to Mr. Kim the philandering his wife had been doing. He and Armando knew it. He was not certain that Moni knew the whole story. Susu Yan was never identified as such, and Mr. Kim assumed that his wife was still alive, living in Hongkong. Mr. Kim kept receiving letters from his wife, and the address was never known. There were more letters pre-written by Susu Yan. She had been most unhappy when she was living with her husband amidst the wealth. He was mean to her; this was the reason for her looking for the gentle touch of a kind man.

The look alike Susu Yan who was paid to fly as Susu Yan still lived in Hongkong, afraid to return. Her passport indicated that she was Susu Yan, and she was trained to portray that role for a year. She was left plenty of cash to sustain her for several years if she was frugal. She was renting rooms in a poor neighborhood and moved often to prove she was only visiting. The money sustained her living in a room among strangers. She had taken that job for money and never thought of the future. She had no idea that her boss died. She did not speak the language, and to be able to afford staying there was uncertain. So she would have to learn the language, which she already had, and she would have to find a job to acclimatize. She could not return to the Philippines.

The End

About the Author

The author has three grown children and four grandchildren. She lives with her husband in Long Island, New York.